EVENT/HORIZON

Eamonn Vincent

ARBUTHNOT BOOKS

This edition published by Arbuthnot Books
https://www.arbuthnot-books.com

ISBN:978-1-9164813-4-3

Cover illustration: Christina Koning

For the Beaconsfield Terrace gang: Chrissie, Andy, Bill, Henry, Jane, John.

L'amour supplée aux longs souvenirs, par une sorte de magie. Toutes les autres affections ont besoin du passé: l'amour crée, comme par enchantement, un passé dont il nous entoure. Il nous donne pour ainsi dire, la conscience d'avoir vécu, durant des années, avec un être qui naguère nous était presque étranger. L'amour n'est qu'un point lumineux, et néanmoins il semble s'emparer du temps. Il y a peu de jours qu'il n'existait pas, bientôt il n'existera plus; mais, tant qu'il existe, il répand sa clarté sur l'époque qui l'a précédé, comme sur celle qui doit le suivre.

(... love has a sort of magic which makes up for long-standing memories. All other human affections need a history, but love, like an enchantment, can create a past to surround us with. It gives us, so to speak, the feeling of having lived for years with a person who until recently was almost a stranger. Love is only a single speck of light, yet it seems to illumine the whole of time.)

Adolphe, Benjamin Constant

CONTENTS

Reality Checkpoint

CLEAR SPOT

STEVE PERCIVAL PROPPED HIS bike against the railings of the Co-operative Dairy just off Sleaford Street and went inside. He glanced at his watch and saw with relief that he was a few minutes early. On the way to the dairy he had been giving some thought to what the cardinal traits of a milkman might be, and had come to no satisfactory conclusion. He was, however, pretty certain that punctuality was a core competence for any interview, whatever the post.

He looked around to get his bearings. To his left was a loading bay, beside which a milk tanker was parked. Standing over a hose, which snaked from the tanker, a thick-set man in overalls nonchalantly rolled a cigarette from a tin of Old Holborn while watching a gauge at the rear of the vehicle. Otherwise the depot was remarkably devoid of activity. No doubt most of the roundsmen were still out on the road or had finished for the day. Steve approached the tanker driver and asked where the foreman's office was. Without taking his eyes off the gauge, the tanker driver nodded in the direction of a dirty prefabricated building, not much bigger than a shed or cabin.

Steve crossed the yard, knocked on the door and pushed it open. Through the fug of cigarette smoke he saw a middle-aged man sitting behind a cheap wooden desk closely studying a copy of *The Sun*. Steve coughed nervously to announce his presence. *The Sun* reader tilted his head in enquiry.

'I've come for an interview for the roundsman vacancy.'

'You Steve?' asked the foreman.

Steve nodded.

'I'm Sid, but round here I'm known as the gaffer. You a student at the Tech?'

Steve thought his application for the job might be marginally more credible if he seemed to be a Tech student rather than a University undergraduate. Taking a leaf from the gaffer's laconic style, Steve nodded and responded with a scarcely enunciated 'Yeah.'

'Live nearby?'

Once again, Steve grunted something that could be taken for assent and turned his head briefly in the implied direction in which he lived.

'Clean driving licence?'

This one he could answer in good faith, but confined himself to an imperceptible nod of the head.

'Right, let's see what your driving's like.'

The gaffer unhooked a set of vehicle keys from a peg behind his desk and tossed them to Steve, who managed to catch them with unaccustomed aplomb. The gaffer pushed his chair back and headed out of the door of the cabin towards a series of parking bays. Steve felt a rising sense of anxiety. It hadn't occurred to him that he might be required to pass a driving test and while he was a reasonably experienced driver, he had never driven a milk float. As it turned out though, it was not a milk float that they were walking towards, but a small flatbed truck. The gaffer climbed in on the passenger side and indicated to Steve to get in on the driver's side. Once they were both inside, he said, 'You okay with a crash gear box?'

Steve wasn't sure that his policy of confirming the gaffer's assumptions was entirely advisable when it came to driving on the public highway, but it seemed too late to change tactics now and he nodded with what he hoped was an air of insouciance, even though he had no idea what a crash gear box was. He studied the dashboard in the hope that it might provide some hint, but there was a notable paucity of dials and switchgear. At least this made it relatively easy to identify the slot for the ignition key. He found the right key and pushed it in. He then gave the gear stick an exploratory waggle. The gear stick was so loose and so close to the calliper style handbrake, that he wasn't at all sure whether it was in neutral or not. He pushed the pedals to get an idea of the amount of travel on each, dismayed at how heavy the clutch was.

With mounting apprehension, he realised that the first manoeuvre he was going to have to execute was to reverse the truck. As if in answer to his unvoiced question, the gaffer said 'Reverse gear, across to the right, press and pull back.' Steve depressed the clutch and searched for reverse. After a brief struggle he found the slot and then returned the gear stick to what he hoped was neutral. The gaffer sighed heavily, 'Well, come on then, get on with it. We haven't got all day.'

Steve gulped, pressed the clutch in again to be on the safe side and fired up the engine. He repeated the sequence for putting the gear in reverse and was relieved to get it to stick in position. He slowly let the clutch out and simultaneously pushed down gingerly on the accelerator. 'Handbrake,' growled the gaffer. Steve hurriedly squeezed the calliper handle and felt the truck jerk backwards. He checked the wing mirrors and then swung on the huge steering wheel. He gave the engine some more revs, grateful that he had plenty of room in which to execute the reverse leg of the three-point turn. Once he'd got the truck pointing in the right direction, he tried to engage first gear, but the gear stick didn't seem to want to engage. In desperation he banged it in. The truck lurched forward and they kangarooed across the yard. When they got to the gates, the gaffer indicated that they should turn left and proceeded to guide Steve around the narrow streets he had just cycled through.

He had only been driving for a few minutes, but Steve was already clammy with sweat. The truck was by some way the largest vehicle he had driven on a public highway. The truck was by some way the largest vehicle he had driven on a public highway. It didn't help that these backstreets were very narrow and he hadn't yet got a good feel for the width of the vehicle. Fortunately there was little traffic about. More worryingly he had still not got the hang of the gearbox. Each gear change brought forth howls of complaint from the gearbox, but so far he had managed not to stall the engine.

They came to Coldham's Lane, despite its name a considerably wider road. His gear changing was still not any smoother, but at least did not need to change gear so frequently now. The only problem was that he knew from earlier forays into these parts that he was eventually going to have to deal with a roundabout. He was only slightly consoled by the thought that other vehicles seemed to be giving the dirty old truck he was driving a wide berth.

At the roundabout the gaffer indicated that they should go all the way around and head back the way they had come. Emboldened by the fact that there were no other vehicles on the roundabout, Steve misjudged his approach speed and swung around it rather more enthusiastically than he had intended. The gaffer sighed deeply again, but said nothing. Soon they re-entered the network of narrow streets near the dairy and the gaffer guided Steve back to the yard and nodded at the parking bay. Steve, relieved that he had not been asked to back into it, brought the vehicle to a halt, pushed the gear stick into neutral, engaged the handbrake, switched off the engine and only then took his foot of the clutch.

The gaffer turned to Steve and shook his head slowly, 'Fucking awful.' He then climbed out of the cab and stomped over to the cabin. Steve cursed under his breath, his plan to pay off his college bill before graduation already crumbling in ruins. He sat in the driver's seat for a few moments, trying to collect himself before climbing out and taking a deep breath of the sour air. The gaffer's judgement had been unequivocal. Steve wanted to get away from the dairy as quickly as possible. He had little desire to subject himself to a frank assessment of the inadequacies of his driving skills. But an atavistic politeness forced him to thank the gaffer for his time. He pushed open the door of the cabin and stepped inside.

'Er, thanks . . .'

'Fucking awful. I've had some bad drivers in here, but that takes the biscuit.'

Steve shrugged. What could he say? Best to exit as gracefully as he could. He turned to leave and said over his shoulder, 'Well, thank you anyway.'

A brief grin flashed across the gaffer's face. 'Not so fast, matey. I need a few details.'

Steve turned back. 'What details? If I haven't got the job.'

'Who said you hadn't got the job?'

'But I thought you said I'd failed the driving test.'

'I said it was the worst bit of driving I've ever seen. But you didn't fail. The fact that you started in second gear most of the time, but didn't stall and that you managed to change gear without double declutching once suggests that you have hidden talents. I'm blowed if I know what they are though. At least you're resourceful. Anyway an electric float is nowhere near as tricky to drive as that old jalopy. It wasn't really a driving test. We get plenty of students turning up here. I need some way of weeding our the wankers.'

'You mean I've got the job?' Steve said in disbelief.

The gaffer nodded and started filling in a form.

He asked Steve a few questions, outlined the pay and conditions and then said, 'Right, we'll see you here five-thirty Monday morning. And don't be late. You'll have to be up early, seeing as you live in Victoria Road. Thought you said you lived around here?'

Steve realised that in his dazed state he had given his real address. But what other address could he have given? Giving the college address wouldn't have been any better. But the gaffer was on to *that* too.

'And you don't go to the Tech neither, do you?'

Steve shamefacedly admitted that was the case. By way of explanation he said, 'But I really need the job.'

And then after a pause, recognising that the gaffer was a wily old bird, 'I need to put together a bit of money quickly.'

The gaffer grunted dispassionately. Clearly that was a motivation he had no problem accepting.

'But let's get one thing clear. I don't want you giving me some eyewash about how far away you live when you're late.'

Steve gulped and nodded.

'As you will be,' he added.

Steve already understood that it was better not to protest. This guy had heard and seen it all.

'Right, back to business. I'm going to put you with Ron for the first week. You learn his round, then you run it on your own for the rest of the summer, while Ron covers people who are on holiday. Ron knows all the rounds. He's our top man and a bit of a stickler. Ex-squaddie. So there'll be no slacking when you're with him. Upside is you'll be finished early, downside you'll be absolutely knackered. When you're on your own, I won't be expecting you to get the round done as quickly as Ron. But that doesn't mean you can roll back after lunch.'

Steve was already feeling apprehensive about his first encounter with Ron, but decided to put it out of his mind.

He walked back to his bike and pedalled slowly down Mill Road wondering what he had let himself in for. Uppermost in his mind was the job's ungodly start time. And, until he found accommodation closer to the dairy, he was going to have to build in enough time to traverse Cambridge. Fortunately the tenancy of the house in Victoria

Road was coming to an end. A friend had told him about a postgraduate student called Beth Rawsthorne who wanted to sublet a small house off Mill Road for the summer. He had dropped a note off at Newnham for Beth a couple of days previously and was now waiting for a reply.

When Steve got to the bottom of Mill Road, he crossed over onto the path that led diagonally across Parker's Piece. At the magnificent lamp post in the middle of the green, he dismounted and admired once again the beautiful new paint job that had mysteriously appeared the previous autumn. He was pleased to see that the words *Reality Checkpoint*, which had previously been inscribed with a marker pen, were now properly painted. He'd always considered the inscription to be a joke on those stoned undergraduates making their way across the expanse of Parker's Piece in the fenland fogs that frequently engulfed the city, but now he saw it as symbolising the transition from life as a spaced-out student to one full of crash gearboxes and canny gaffers.

Back at the shared house he let himself in by the back door, made a cup of tea in the kitchen and went up to the room he shared with Angie.

Angie was writing at the little table in the bay window of their room. She looked up. 'Wow! You've been a long time. How did it go?'

'Got the job. I start Monday,' Steve said, with a sheepish note of pride, as he threw himself on the bed.

'Amazing. They must be desperate.'

'What? You mean to take on an incompetent like me?'

'No I didn't mean it like that. For them to want you to start on Monday.'

'Yeah, well, they need to organise holiday cover and so on. And I'll have you know that the driving test was a bit of a bugger.'

Steve then proceeded to give Angie a somewhat exaggerated account of driving the flatbed truck around the narrow streets off Gwydir Street. Angie realised that Steve was probably embellishing the account. He always did that. But she could also see that he was looking drained. She came over, climbed on the bed, gave him a sympathetic hug.

'Were you expecting a driving test?'

'Well, I thought they might show me the controls on a milk float or ask me to drive one around the yard. I didn't expect to have to drive a truck around the public streets. At least they didn't ask me any Highway Code questions. I've forgotten most of it.'

Angie took a deep breath. 'You probably realise that I was hoping that you wouldn't get the job. I happen to think that it's a crazy idea. Where are you going to live?'

'I've been in touch with a postgrad who wants to sublet a house off Mill Road for the summer.'

'But won't paying rent on a house defeat the point of taking the job in the first place?'

'That's true. I was hoping that I might persuade you to stay in Cambridge over the summer. With both of us earning, the rent wouldn't be so bad and we'd have a house to ourselves. I know you've got this English language teaching job in Brighton, but maybe you could get something similar in Cambridge. There are tons of language schools here.'

'Steve. It's a bit late for that. I start in three weeks. I don't want to let them down. The people who run the school are friends of my parents. And I've already put down the deposit on a room. Not only that, I need the money before I set off for Edinburgh. Why don't you just come down to Brighton with me? It'd be great to spend the summer together at the seaside. I'm sure you'd get a job in no time.'

'That sounds like a no.'

'And it sounds like you're giving the idea of Brighton a no. You've only just come up with this idea of staying in Cambridge for the summer. I thought that you were going to start work for that German company in the City.'

'I've gone right off that idea. I'm a writer. I don't want to be a suit in the city.'

'Fine. But I don't see how getting a job as a milkman and renting a house down Mill Road furthers your ambitions as a writer.'

'In itself it doesn't, but I know that if I take the city job, I will never write. Being a milkman is just so I don't have to ask my mother for money to settle my college bill before graduation day. Personally I don't care about the degree, but she'll be heartbroken if she can't see me being given a piece of paper in the Senate House.'

Angie was sympathetic to Steve's dilemma. 'Look, Steve, I know that your mother can't help you out. And I know it's been hard for you here, where there are so many people from privileged backgrounds. But I'm sure that if you explained the situation to the college, they'd be accommodating.'

'I don't want charity from a place like St Radegund's. I thought the bank would just let me extend my overdraft for a couple of months. You'd think a Cambridge graduate would be a pretty good bet.'

'It must be something to do with the state of the economy, oil price rises, the miners' strike, three day weeks and so on.'

'Yeah. Just my luck.'

'Wouldn't it be better to find someone you could stay with for a few weeks. And then once you'd got your finances in order, quit the job and come and stay with me. It would be fun for us to be in Brighton for the summer. And then if I get the place in Edinburgh, we could go there together.'

'I know, And that all sounds lovely, but I just feel that I'd be tagging along. You'd be starting your PhD and you'll be getting to know all the other postgraduate students. I would have no reason for being there.'

'Surely, our being together is reason enough. Steve, this last year together has been fantastic. I love you. And I think you love me. We can look forward to enjoying life together.'

'Yes, that's true. But I need to establish myself.'

Angie knew that Steve lacked the easy self-assurance, so evident in their public school contemporaries. 'Steve, I know things haven't always been easy for you. I'm sure your mother is terribly proud of you and your father would have been if he were still alive. And you will do great things, but possibly not in a conventional way. I'm happy with that. And I'm prepared to put up with some of the byways we might travel, so long as we can be together. That's all I really want, but the best way I can help you is by holding steady to the course that I'm on, then you'll always know where to find me.'

Steve was mystified by this speech, but recognised its generosity. He rolled over and gathered Angie in his arms. 'Anj, you're an amazing person. I love you like crazy. I don't want to hurt you, but I need to do this. And I'm afraid that it might hurt both of us.'

'Look, we've got the weekend ahead of us. We can talk some more, but let's try and enjoy it too.'

Steve agreed that that was the best thing.

'Anyway,' she went on, 'Remember we've got the grand end of Finals house party tonight. That should take our minds off things. Once we've had one of Jez's joints or Harry's hash cakes. And then we've got the whole weekend to do nothing. We could walk to Fen Ditton or take a punt to Grantchester.'

Steve's mood lifted. 'Yes, let's do that.'

He picked up his guitar and strummed it idly for a few minutes. The riff he was exploring caught Angie's attention.

'That's nice.'

'Alan's latest, I can't quite get it right.'

'Sounds nice all the same.'

'It's about you.'

'Really?'

'I'm not sure you'll entirely approve of the lyrics?'

'Why not? I hope it isn't inappropriately personal. I have no desire to have my breasts immortalised in one of Alan's ditties. Or any other part of my anatomy for that matter.'

'No, nothing like that. But if I were to tell you that it's called "Hazy Little Lady", you might get some idea of its approach.'

Angie considered this piece of information. She wasn't delighted by the diminutive in the title, and if *hazy* implied she was a scatty blonde, she would have words with Alan. But if the portrait was affectionate, she would be prepared to put up with a degree of artistic licence.

Towards five o'clock, they went downstairs to join the others. Harry was happily at work cooking a large bolognese. He loved to take charge in the kitchen. In fact he loved to take charge, *tout court*. He combined extreme sociability, the capacity for hard work and the ability to recover rapidly from bouts of inebriation in equal measure. He was cut out to be a major in a combat battalion, but given his progressive political views, he was more likely to become head of a voluntary sector organisation or large inner city school. Di and Harry's girlfriend Jackie, who was down for the weekend from her medical school in London, were commis-cheffing for Harry, chopping vegetables and salad materials. Alan was sitting on a stool in the corner of the kitchen, guitar on knee, providing a sinuous soundtrack to the culinary preparations, while Jez, perched on another stool, rolled joints on the windowsill. All in all, a very homely scene; one that was shortly coming to an end.

Harry looked up from his cooking and said to Steve and Angie, 'So nice of you to join us.'

'We just followed our noses,' quipped Angie. 'Smells delicious.'

'How did the interview go?' asked Alan over the top of his guitar.

'Got the job. Start Monday,' Steve replied.

This news was met by a general air of incredulity.

Di paused in her chopping of sticks of celery. 'Monday?'

'Yeah, might as well get on with it, no point in hanging around.'

The housemates understood Steve's family circumstances and so no one voiced what they all thought, that there must be some other way of dealing with his immediate financial needs. Jez took advantage of the embarrassed silence that had developed by holding up a joint and saying, 'In that case we'd better make sure that you have a memorable weekend, meaning if you do remember anything of it, we won't have done our job properly.'

Everyone laughed at what they had come to recognise as one of Jez's stoned Zen koans. Steve took the proffered joint, inhaling deeply. He passed the joint on to Harry, who saw nothing unhygienic in smoking while cooking.

Steve said to Alan, 'I told Angie about your new song. Why don't you play it?'

'I thought you said that the feminists will be after me, if I played it in mixed company.'

'No feminists here,' Harry said, exhaling a large cloud of smoke.

Jackie folded the tea towel she had over a shoulder and gave Harry a smart thwack across his shoulders with it. 'Watch it, Edwards.'

Angie cut in, 'I understand the song is about me, so I think we'd better hear it.'

Alan started retuning the guitar. 'Let's say that the subject of the song bears some resemblance to you, but in other respects is completely different. It would be an elementary error of interpretation to assume that the protagonist of the song and the model on which the protagonist is based are identical. When in fact the model is just the starting point for a fictional character.'

Steve said, 'Okay, we all know you did a paper on modern drama. Just sing the song.'

Alan, having finished retuning his guitar, said, 'Well, I'm just saying . . .'

He then hit a big chord and launched into the song.

Everybody liked it, even Angie.

'Nothing like me, apart from the flowing hair. I've never run in circles for the simple reason I don't run. And as for going nowhere, in three weeks I'm going to Brighton and at the end of the summer I'll be on my way to Edinburgh. Those two places are only nowhere in the stoned ravings of a demob-happy Cambridge undergraduate.'

There was a murmur of approval at this deft response by t posed hazy little lady and the song with its Californian vibe pronounced a hit.

While Alan had been performing the song, Harry had been draining the pasta and declared the meal was now ready. Glasses were filled with beer and wine according to taste and the housemates sat down around the table and filled their plates. Such meals had been a regular feature of the previous year. Everyone knew that an era was coming to an end, but for now they were doing their best to put it out of their minds. The mood was lighthearted and utopian, loving even. Reality was to be held at bay for a little while longer.

After the meal had been cleared away, the gang moved into the sitting room. Jez kept the joints coming and the conversation descended into enigmatic nonsense. Di slipped Joni Mitchell's *Court and Spark* out of its cover and put it on the turntable. As the luscious chords and Joni's soaring voice filled the room, even the enigmatic nonsense petered out. Joni's sound world and bitter sweet lyrics occupied everyone's attention.

When that record finished, Jez who now took over as DJ, asked what people wanted to listen to next. Steve suggested Dylan, but was shouted down.

Alan observed that he thought *Planet Waves* was crap.

Harry countered this opinion with, '"Forever Young", man'.

'Yeah, okay, apart from that track.'

In the end they settled on Captain Beefheart's *Clear Spot*. As the spiky chords of 'Low Yo Yo Stuff' filled the room, Steve picked up the LP's clear plastic sleeve and withdrew a large white card from it. One side of the card bore the album's cover photograph and the other the track and personnel listing. It was typical of Beefheart's art school sensibility that an album entitled *Clear Spot* should have a clear plastic sleeve rather than the more usual cardboard slipcase. Steve was intrigued by the cover photograph. 'Where do you think this photo was taken?' he said, mainly to himself. 'It doesn't really look like part of a recording studio. It looks more like the quarterdeck of an interplanetary spacecraft. And why on earth is Don wearing a coolie hat?'

Di surfaced from her reverie and asked 'Who's Don? And what's a coolie hat?'

Steve pointed to the strange headgear he was wearing in the photograph. 'Beefheart's real name is Don van Vliet.'

from Steve and studied it for a few moments.
have pseudonyms too, but Beefheart uses his
to the composing and performance credits. So
) indication as to the real names of the rest of
clearly subordinates.'

) abandon for a moment his habitual deep
_ workings of the dialectic in history and pro-
, Beefheart's just another capitalist exploiter. He's appropriat-
ing the surplus labour of the band members and adding insult to
injury by not giving them their real names.'

Di was not interested in Harry's Marxist posturing. She was still
contemplating the revelation of Beefheart's real name. 'Don Van Fleet
doesn't sound like a real name to me. It sounds more like a car rental
company.'

They all laughed and Alan said, 'Everyone knows that Americans
can be called anything.'

Several heads nodded until Angie pointed out with an unusual
degree of self-assurance that *van Vliet* was a Dutch name before going
back to her original point 'So, does anyone know Zoot Horn Rollo's
real name?'

Jez, who had remained silent during this discussion while he concentrated on rolling another joint, lifted his head from his intricate
handiwork and said in an even tone, 'Zoot Horn's real name is Bill
Harkleroad, Rockette Morton's is Mark Boston, Ed Marimba's is Art
Tripp and Oréjon's is Roy Estrada.'

For a moment there was a stunned silence until Alan said 'There
speaks someone already in PhD mode.'

Di, who was wary of Jez's deadpan sense of humour, said, 'You've
just made those names up.'

Jez lit the joint, took a long drag on it and said triumphantly, 'Zoot
Horn Rollo, Rockette Morton, Ed Marimba and Oréjon,' before passing
the joint on.

Harry took the joint and said, 'Well, I've certainly heard of Bill
Harkleroad.'

Angie laughed. 'Harkleroad sounds as fake as Rollo. And as for Art
Tripp being Ed Marimba's real name! His real name, if it *is* his real
name, sounds more far out that his pen-name. Or whatever term is
appropriate for a drummer's pseudonym.'

She looked over the list of the names again and said 'I'm beginning to feel sorry for Mark Boston, though. He's the only one who has a regular real name. Poor old Rocket.'

Everyone laughed again at the thought that they should feel sorry for a guitarist in the Magic Band. When the laughter had subsided Jez said 'Rockette. Not Rocket. Stress on both syllables. Spondee not trochee.'

The joint was with Alan now. 'See what I mean?'

The ensuing silence was finally broken by Harry. 'Not really.'

'Jez. PhD mode.'

'No, still don't get it.'

'Spondee not trochee.'

'Al, you're jibbering.'

'Oh, forget it.'

'Your wish is my command.'

The first side of *Clear Spot* came to and end and Al took charge of the hifi. 'Time for a change.'

Soon they had succumbed to Pink Floyd's *Dark Side of the Moon*, Alan and Di entwined on the battered old sofa and the others sprawled on bean bags. There was no conversation and little movement for the next forty-five minutes, during which everyone lost themselves in the *musique concrète* linked soundscapes of the Floyd. As the record faded out over sinister synthesised heartbeats and a spoken word coda, Di sat up and said, 'What does he mean, *there's no dark side, it's all dark?*'

The same thing had puzzled Steve when he had first listened to the LP and he had subsequently done some research in the library. Never slow to share the product of his haphazard reading, he said, 'Both sides of the moon receive on average the same amount of sunlight. It only seems that there is a permanently dark side because the moon rotates once on its axis for every orbit of the earth. In the two weeks that it takes the moon to go from new to full, it also makes a half revolution.'

On the assumption that Steve must be bullshitting, Harry said, 'That's the trouble with you, Percival, you're only half a revolutionary.'

Al joined in the mockery, 'Yeah, you can't imagine John Lennon singing about half a revolution.'

Steve laughed. He should have realised that it was pointless to be serious on such occasions. Switching deftly to the same register, he shot back, 'Is that the same Lennon who said that nothing was going to change his world? Or the one who said we all want change?'

'Cake and eat it, if you ask me,' said Harry.

But Di felt that her question hadn't been answered. 'So, is there a dark side or not?'

Steve tried again. 'Yes, but the side we call the dark side when the moon is full is actually fully illuminated by the sun when there is a new moon, which is also confusingly known as a moonless night, because at that point the side that faces us is now dark so we can't see it.'

Di considered this further explanation and decided that it clarified nothing, a view which was widely shared. Wishing he'd never opened his mouth in the first place, Steve announced that he was heading up to bed. Angie got up too, blowing kisses in hazy little lady mode at the others and followed Steve up to their room.

ON THE ROUND

Co-operative Dairy
Saturday, 1 June 1974

STEVE AND ANGIE TOOK things easy the next day. They spent the best part of the morning in bed, not all of it devoted to sleeping. Eventually hunger of another kind forced them downstairs for cereal, toast and coffee. Having restored their blood sugar levels, they turned their thoughts to what to do with the rest of the day.

The sun was shining from a clear blue sky. It would be a pity to spend such a glorious day inside. Angie returned to her idea of the previous day. 'Let's walk to Fen Ditton and have lunch in a pub.'

Steve was not much of a walker, but he was won over by the mention of a pub lunch, as Angie knew he would be. They got themselves dressed and walked down to the river, crossing it at the Jesus lock footbridge and set off along the towpath in the direction of Midsummer Common. Further along they passed under the Victoria Avenue bridge and walked along Riverside, passing the gasometers and the tall chimney of an old pumping station, before reaching Stourbridge Common, where they sat on a bench and looked at the placid river. Steve felt that he could already do with a lunchtime pint.

'So, where's this pub?'

'A bit further, I'm afraid, but it's a lovely walk across Ditton meadows.

Steve looked at his watch.

'It's one o'clock. We better get a move on then. Otherwise the pub will be closed before we get there.'

They resumed their course and to Steve's relief reached the Ancient Shepherds with time for a pint or possibly two. The pub was notably empty with only one other couple in a corner by the window, deep in conversation and hunched over some lunch.

Angie asked what hot food was on the menu, but the landlord merely shook his head in a pantomime of despair. Sadly, they had no hot food left, but he could offer them a Ploughman's Lunch. Angie reluctantly accepted his offer, but was pleased to discover when the plates arrived that the cheese was a strong, tangy piece of cheddar and the bread was fresh and crusty. She was not keen on pickled onions however and transferred hers to Steve's plate. He reciprocated by scraping the salad leaves that garnished his own plate onto Angie's.

Once they had cleared their plates, Steve felt able to relax a little and, looking around to study his surroundings, realised with a start that the couple in the corner were in fact acquaintances. He nudged Angie.

'It's Jon and Ginny. Not the kind of place you'd expect to find them. Maybe we should say hello.'

Angie wasn't so sure. Whilst Angie agreed that it was not the kind of place with which one might associate this resolutely hipster couple, she was much less sure about acknowledging them. Steve pooh-poohed Angie's reservations. It would be odd not to say hello and embarrassing once Jon and Ginny spotted them. Angie was inclined to think they had already been spotted and ignored. But Steve was already crossing the bar.

'Hey, Jon, Ginny, great to see you. I never had you down as regulars in the Ancient Shepherds.'

Even as he said it, Steve realised this was not the coolest way to announce his presence. The hipster couple swivelled around and, taking a second to place Steve, acknowledged him with minimal rise in affect.

Jon didn't beat about the bush. 'Heavy conversation going on, man. We needed to find somewhere quiet.'

Steve was taken aback by what amounted to a rebuff, the clear implication being that he had breached some kind of *cordon sanitaire*. Covering his confusion, he hazarded, 'Kinda long walk to find a quiet place to talk.'

To judge from the blank looks that met this gauche attempt to keep the conversation going, it seemed that repartee was precisely what was not required at this moment.

Jon narrowed his gaze. 'Came in the VW Camper.'

Steve wilted. No one was going to walk the towpaths of the Cam and its water meadows dressed like this couple were.

'Sorry to interrupt your conversation,' he said weakly. 'Angie and I just spotted you across the room.' He pointed back in the general direction of Angie. 'And I thought I'd just come over and say hello.'

Jon raised his head a little and looking past Steve spotted Angie's golden tresses and honey skin and brightening perceptibly said, 'Cool, man. That's a beautiful chick you've got there.'

Steve acknowledged the indubitable truth of this observation and indicated that he would return to the said beautiful chick right away. Jon and Ginny clearly approved.

But just as he was turning on his heel Jon said, 'Sorry to be so un-friendly man. This is a bit of a heavy scene. But listen, I'm doing a gig with The Doodah Men, my new lineup, at the church hall in St Barnabas Road next Saturday. It's a special gig, a performance really. I'm launching my Dark Star Variations, a homage to the Dead's most iconic track. I'll put you and your chick on the guest list. It'd be a gas, if you could make it.'

Steve thanked Jon for the invitation and scuttled back to his own table, from which Angie had followed proceedings with considerable distaste, only relieved that the encounter had been so brief.

Angie couldn't prevent herself from expressing her irritation. 'Why didn't you listen to me?'

Steve looked crestfallen. 'You were right. But at least we're on the guest list for the Dark Star Variations.'

Angie was puzzled. 'What are you talking about? What are the Dark Star Variations?'

'Jon's playing a gig and he's invited us.'

'And the gig has a title?'

'Yeah.'

'That's a bit odd. What's it mean?'

'Jon is a Deadhead, a devotee of the Grateful Dead. And 'Dark Star' is a track on the Dead's *Live/Dead* album. It's basically a spaced out twenty minute jam. It sounds as if Jon's band is going to perform a series of improvisations based on that track.'

'God, that sounds a bit pretentious, more Soft Machine than Bonzo Dog Doo Dah Band.'

'Well, funnily enough, he said the band is now called the Doodah Men.'

'Weirder and weirder.'

'Yeah, but very Cambridge. It'll be good way to finish the year.'

Angie laughed and said. 'Okay, let's carry on to Baits Bite Lock.'

What with the beer and the ignominious rebuff from Jon and Ginny, Steve was ready to head back home. He was not unfamiliar with the lock. In fact, in his brief rowing career, it had been the outward bound goal of early morning training sessions. But he had never cycled let alone walked there and he saw no reason to rectify that omission right now. But Angie was having none of this faintheartedness. They had spent the morning in bed, and she was keen to make the most of the beautiful weather.

'Come on, Steve. It's not that far. And we can walk back on the other side of the river.'

Steve was unable to see how that was any kind of incentive, but conceded with as much good grace as he could muster. They walked through the village, past a recreation ground and onto a footpath. Before long, as Angie had predicted, they came to the lock. They crossed by the footbridge over the roar of the weir onto the jetty that formed one flank of the lock and then over a second footbridge that spanned the northern entrance to the lock.

'Right. We're on the homeward leg now,' said Angie brightly.

Steve woke early the next morning. It was his last day of freedom, his last day of being a student. He was only too aware that he was going to have to reset his body clock. In order to be at the dairy by five-thirty, he would have to be in bed, or more precisely to be asleep by nine-thirty or so. It was a long time since he'd been in bed at that time for the purposes of sleep. And he wasn't at all sure it was feasible in a house full students who had all just finished their Finals and were looking forward to a few weeks of hedonistic excess before graduation day. So, even though he was feeling bleary-eyed, he thought it best to force himself to get up early and do his best to expend enough energy to help him get to sleep early that same evening.

He untangled himself from Angie's warm body and slipped on a pair of jeans and a tee shirt. He went downstairs and put the kettle on for a cup of coffee. While waiting for it to boil, he made a start on clearing up the debris from the previous night. When the coffee was ready, he fixed a bowl of cereal and sat down to his meagre breakfast. It was a fine morning, so he thought he'd take one of the bikes and go for a ride. When he'd finished his breakfast he let himself quietly out by the back door and took the uppermost bike from the pile resting against the wall of the house. He wheeled the bike along the alley at the back of the house and headed for the city centre. On the way he thought he'd drop into the college to see if there were any letters or messages for him. A few minutes later, he pushed the door of the Porter's Lodge open and went inside to check his pigeonhole. The porter on duty chuckled and said, 'Good Morning, sir. Not often we see you here at this time of morning, especially on a Sunday. If you're coming in for morning service, I'm sorry to say that it's already over.'

Steve grinned somewhat sheepishly. 'I've got a terrible hangover, Stan,' he said. He had no such thing, but he thought it sounded more plausible. 'Going for a bike ride to clear my head.'

Stan nodded sympathetically, 'What you need is a shot of Fernet Branca. Clears the head and settles the stomach, knock it straight back, don't let it touch the sides or you'll throw up.'

'That good, eh?' Steve tucked the piece of advice away for future application.

There were several things in his pigeonhole, mainly flyers, but there was also a card from Beth Rawsthorne suggesting that he come to the house in Ainsworth Street any time after midday on Sunday to discuss the possibility of his having the house for the summer. He hadn't expected such a prompt reply, nor such a prompt interview. He looked up at the clock behind the counter in the Porter's Lodge and saw that it was nearly eleven. He could combine his bike ride along the towpath with a circuit of the streets around the dairy to familiarise himself with the area and get to the house in Ainsworth Street shortly after midday. It was premature of course to make any assumptions as to what area his round might cover. Still, it wouldn't harm to get a better feel for that part of the city.

As he was leaving the Porter's Lodge, he told Stan that he would let him know how he'd got on with the Fernet Branca. He then cycled back towards Jesus Green and picked up the towpath retracing part of the route he and Angie had walked the previous day. It was a beautiful morning and he was in no hurry. He pedalled slowly along the towpath admiring the narrowboats moored on both sides of the placid river. Before long he passed the lido, which he'd occasionally swum in, but which he and his friends had mainly used as a place to sunbathe, since the pool was completely unheated, although impressively long. He passed under the Victoria Avenue bridge onto Midsummer Common continuing to the edge of Stourbridge Common and then turned right into Stanley Road arriving at the dual carriageway section of Newmarket Road.

He hadn't intended to cycle on such a busy road, but time was getting on and he needed to find his way through to Ainsworth Street. After a few wrong turns, he recognised one of the narrow roads he'd gone down on his driving test. Soon he was in Ainsworth Street and found the house he was looking for opposite a small shop called the Empire Stores, which looked as if the window display hadn't been changed since the Empire was at its zenith. The house had a tiny front garden with a low brick wall against which he propped the bike. He pushed his hair back, brushed himself down and then taking a deep breath knocked on the front door.

After a short pause the door was answered by a young woman not much older that himself. He explained who he was and the young woman said that she was Beth and invited him inside. The house was tiny, the narrow hallway leading straight into a living-room with a single bay to the front and a little french window to the rear, which in turn opened into a narrow conservatory and a weed-choked garden.

Beth invited him to sit down. The dusty room was full of books. Beth explained that she was a postgraduate in the English faculty. She and her housemate Sandra would would be away for three months and were looking for someone to cover the rent in that time. Beth asked Steve about his own situation. He felt that he had nothing to lose by telling the truth. Beth seemed to be happy with his explanation. So it boiled down to whether Steve could afford £12 per week and when he wanted to move in. On the latter point she said that she and Sandra would probably be leaving in a week or two.

As Beth told him more about the house, Steve was trying to calculate whether there was scope for a bit of negotiation. The fact that Beth and Sandra only had two weeks at most before they were due to leave Cambridge probably meant that they hadn't got anyone else lined up. Mentally crossing his fingers, he said that the house was perfect for his purposes, but only if he could let the second bedroom and even then he could only afford £10 a week. The people he had in mind were fellow students. Beth was not enthusiastic about this idea, but in the end she agreed, perhaps feeling that she didn't have many other options at that precise moment.

She then showed Steve the rest of the house, which didn't take very long. There were two small bedrooms, and a bathroom on the ground floor beyond the kitchen, an arrangement that was typical of these little Cambridge houses. The main thing that struck Steve was how untidy and dusty the house was. His place in Victoria Road was hardly a model of domestic decorum, but it was nowhere near as chaotic as the scene which presented itself at that moment. Beth seemed oblivious to the disorder and did not try to excuse it.

They went back downstairs and Beth gave Steve a sheet of paper with the main points of information about the house, including her bank account details. She was happy to keep the entire arrangement on an informal level, but asked for a small deposit before Steve moved in. Steve said that would be okay and that he would drop it off at the end of the week. With that they concluded the negotiations and Beth showed him to the front door.

Steve was feeling pleased with the morning's work as he cycled back across Cambridge. The only thing that was worrying him was that Angie had made it abundantly clear that she had no intention of changing her plans for the summer. And as things stood none of the other housemates had plans to stay in Cambridge over the summer either. If Steve's plan to restore his financial affairs was going to have any chance of succeeding by the deadline of graduation day, he needed at least one other person to share the rent of the Ainsworth Street house with him.

Suddenly the feelings of self-satisfaction evaporated as he reflected that the relationship structures that he had taken for granted for the last few years were about to undergo considerable reshaping. At the same time he had neglected to put in place any kind of career structure. And he had also let himself down academically, despite Richard Doyle's best efforts to keep him on the straight and narrow.

The previous year Richard had arranged for him to spend a year at the university in Freiburg. He had even organised a bursary, but perversely Steve had turned down the opportunity. Right now cycling back from Ainsworth Street, it was hard to remember what his rationale had been. He was immensely grateful to Richard for all his efforts and recognised that he was a man of huge learning and a deep thinker. Nor was it that the history of German thought didn't appeal to him. It certainly did. But so did many other things.

When he looked into the magic mirror of his dreams, he saw himself as a creative writer, a poet essentially. In his bleaker moments, he realised that this was a gross overestimation of his talents, especially since he had actually written very little, but he put this down to the demands of the Tripos, demands that he had not been very diligent in meeting. But that would surely change now. Life was going to be a routine of early bedtimes, early rising, paid work over by mid-morning and the rest of the day free for creative endeavour with the bonus that the unsocial hours would preclude large scale roistering. And the way things were looking, he would in any case be deprived of fellow roisterers.

When he got back to the house in Victoria Road, the debris from the night before had been tidied up and everyone was lazing around reading the Sunday papers or escapist paperback novels. He sensed a slight disapproval at his absence from communal duties, but excused himself on the grounds of getting himself ready for the rigours of the outdoor life of the milk roundsman. It seemed to him that only Angie had taken seriously his plan to solve his financial predicament. The others were a little more sympathetic when he explained that he would be getting up the next day at four-thirty. and that while they were sunbathing at the lido or playing frisbee on Jesus Green, he would be slogging around the backstreets of Cambridge delivering red and silver top.

He then gave an account of his meeting at the little house in Ainsworth Street, stressing that he needed to recruit at least one other person or couple to make the project economically viable. He knew that Harry and Jackie were off backpacking around Europe before Harry started his PGCE in London and Jackie started her internship as a junior doctor. And he knew that Jez was off back to his haunts in Spain. But how firm were Alan and Di's plans? Alan said they were planning to go back to the South of France. Steve asked when they were thinking of going. Alan replied that they would be off as soon as they got some bread together. Steve suggested that meant that they wouldn't be off for several weeks and in the meantime they would need somewhere to live. But Alan pointed out that the lease on the Victoria Road house didn't expire until the end of June. He didn't understand why Steve wanted to take on the expense of a new gaff, when he would still be paying rent on his existing accommodation.

Steve admitted it might seem a little illogical, but he just wanted to get things sorted out so he could get on with the job he had lined up and also get back to his writing. Alan said he and Di would think about it, but he wasn't making any promises.

Later when they were alone in their room, Steve asked Angie if she had had any further thoughts about the summer. Once again she parried the question by saying that she would like to ask Steve the same question. They both needed to recognise that Steve's plan which had emerged from nowhere only a few days previously was likely to be a major turning point in their relationship and they should have a proper discussion about it, preferably without any of the others involved and in the absence of alcohol or other stimulants and most importantly before he had committed to taking on the house in Ainsworth Street. Privately, she hoped that once Steve had spent a day or two pretending to be a milkman, he would see the error of his ways. So there was nothing more to be said for now and Steve did his best to get to sleep at what seemed a ludicrously early hour by blocking with a pillow the familiar riffs of *Dark Side of the Moon* rising from the room below. He fell into a shallow sleep which only became pleasantly deep shortly before the jangle of the alarm clock woke him.

For the third time in almost as many days, Steve found himself cycling across Cambridge in the direction of Mill Road, but this time just as the sun was coming up. What had happened? Talk about a crashing change of gears! One moment an undergraduate at an ancient seat of learning, the next a milkman. For a moment his courage faltered. It was not too late to turn back and throw in his lot with Angie. He would soon find a job in Brighton and then he could repay the money that he would have to borrow from his mother. But suddenly the rays of the rising sun flashed across the rooftops and a golden light suffused the trees and buildings. It was as if some kind of magic dust had been sprinkled on the city. He took a deep breath of the sweet air and his mood started to lift. No, he must press on.

In this more positive frame of mind he arrived at the dairy. The yard which had been deserted for his interview was now a hive of activity. Steve parked his bike and went over to the foreman's cabin. The gaffer greeted him perfunctorily and asked him to him to wait until he had finished reading his newspaper. Eventually he pushed his chair back, headed out the door and motioned to Steve to follow him. They crossed the yard to the loading bay alongside which several milk floats were already parked, while their drivers loaded them up with crates of milk bottles. The gaffer made for the float at the front of the queue which was being loaded by a wiry dark-haired man with a small cigar clamped between his lips.

The gaffer caught the cigar-smoker's attention. 'Oi, Ron. I've got yer cover driver here. His name is Steve. Show him the ropes and we'll see how he does on his own in a week or two.'

Ron nodded impassively at Steve and then jerked his head sharply to one side to indicate that Steve should get in the cab. Steve climbed into the cab and a few moments later Ron joined him in the somewhat confined space, having humped the last couple of crates onto the flatbed of the float. He flicked a switch on the dashboard of the float and then manoeuvred the vehicle out of the loading line and towards the gates of the yard. Without removing the cigar from between his teeth, Ron asked, 'Done a round before?' Steve shook his head.

Their first port of call was the fish and chip shop on Mill Road near the old library, but soon they were zigzagging through the network of streets bounded by the railway line to the south-east, Station Road to the south, the south-west side of Mill Road as far as Hills Road, and Parker's Piece to the north-west. Ron had a logbook open on the dashboard in front of him, a pencil behind his ear and the constant cigar clamped between his jaws. Standing up to drive, he would peer at the logbook and then having selected a parking spot, leap out of the cab and drop off the appropriate orders, returning with the empties. Initially, Steve just observed, but soon Ron was barking out particular orders for Steve to fulfil. 'Two silver tops at number 43 and three red tops at 45.' Meanwhile he would take care of a batch of deliveries on his own side of the road. The process was by no means leisurely. Ron seemed to do everything at the double, not quite running, but certainly not strolling.

Nor was he given to chit-chat. His attention was either fixed on the logbook or focused on the road ahead scanning for parking spots. Steve wondered what the hurry was. The streets had been relatively free of traffic and they seemed to be making good progress. But this all changed when they got to Hills Road. Even at this early hour the traffic was starting to build up. And as it did so, parking became increasingly difficult. Ron, however, was a decisive driver and seemed to enjoy the tussle with the other early morning drivers.

Having completed the Hills Road deliveries Ron turned into Union Road and pulled up outside a primary school. He pointed to several crates of third of a pint bottles. Even though it was only just after eight, Ron said, 'Need to get the thirds to the school before nine o'clock.'

Steve nodded and carried the crates into the playground.

The next stop was at a block of flats in George IV Street. Ron nodded at the block and said, 'This one's a bugger. We've got to do those.'

He pulled the float into the flats' carpark, tore off a page from the back of his logbook and jotted down some numbers. 'Right, fill a crate with this lot. The numbers on the left are the flat numbers, obviously, and the ones on the right the order and the kind of milk. With luck you'll get it all into one crate. If not, you'll have to make a second trip. Don't use the lift or it'll take forever. And don't forget the empties. You take that staircase and I'll take this one.'

And with that he was already filling up his own crate. Steve peered at the piece of paper trying to make sense of Ron's scrawl until he heard him say, 'Come on. What are you waiting for?'

Steve found an empty crate and started to fill it. When it was full, he lugged it over to the entrance of the block that Ron had indicated. A crate of full milk bottles wasn't that heavy, but it wasn't an insignificant load either, especially when it came to carrying it up several flights of concrete stairs, as Ron had recommended. When Steve eventually got back to the float, Ron was already there drumming his fingers on the steering wheel.

'You'll have to be bit faster than that. Anyway, were there any changes of order?'

Steve wasn't quite sure what Ron meant.

'You had a couple of full bottles in your crate when you got back. Did you put too many in the crate or did someone cancel?'

Steve thought for a moment. 'Oh, yeah. There were two places they had a *no milk today* message.'

'Right. So what were the flat numbers?'

Steve couldn't remember. He suddenly felt very stupid. Ron looked at him in disbelief.

'Look, if someone changes their order, we need to note it in the logbook. That's what it's for. Otherwise we get in a bugger's muddle and it ends in arguments when it comes time to collect money.'

Steve offered to run back. He thought he would be able to identify which ones had changed because he had left the messages in situ. Ron looked doubtful, but let Steve jog back and disappear into the block. He re-emerged some minutes later panting and gasped out, 'None at 34 and one less silver top at 25.'

Ron snorted. 'I thought so. Those two are always changing their minds. Most people take the same order every day, no matter what, but there are others who are always messing around. Bloody nuisances. And they're the ones who always argue the toss.'

He took the pencil from behind his ear and made an adjustment in the logbook. Steve, who had started to recover his breath, felt slightly aggrieved. If the culprits had been so easy to identify, why had Ron let him run up and down the stairs again? Hadn't the gaffer said that Ron was an ex-squaddie? He supposed it was Ron's version of square-bashing.

They set off again, back onto Hill's Road and then up Station Road. There weren't many deliveries on Station Road itself, but at the top just before the station they swung around the little roundabout, dropped off a full crate, and retrieved a crate of empties from the Station Hotel. It was then back down Station Road and left at the War Memorial. As they trundled along the upper part of Hills Road, Steve noticed two pubs side by side right next to the bus garage, The Osborne and the Crown Inn.

At the junction with Brooklands Avenue they pulled into a quaint set of almshouses and made a couple of deliveries. They then crossed Brooklands Avenue and made several deliveries in Clarendon and Shaftesbury Roads. Ron, who had been lost in thought and smoking furiously since they had finished the block of flats said with a note of satisfaction, 'Just one more delivery and then we're done.' He looked at his watch and then said, 'Not too bad considering the time we lost at the flats.'

Steve thought that was a rather unfair criticism given than it was his first day, but he bit his tongue. Ron spun the float around and they retraced their route. Just before the bus garage, Ron turned sharp left through a set of gates and Steve suddenly found himself in a verdant paradise. Trees, lawns and flower beds stretched as far as the eye could see. Ron propelled the float along a narrow metalled drive until they came to a handsome white building with a portico. Steve realised that this must be the back entrance to the Botanic Gardens.

Soon they were back on Hills Road again. Steve was exhausted. They'd been going for just over four hours without a break or so much as a cup of tea. As they rattled back to the dairy Ron kept looking at his watch. He was obviously running late. When they had turned in through the gates of the dairy, he stopped the float and before getting out told Steve to offload all the crates onto the loading bay, then take the float to the charging station and to make sure not to be late the following day. Without saying goodbye, he turned on his heel and headed off.

A wave of anxiety swept over Steve. Ron had briefly shown him the controls in the cab, but hadn't let him drive and now he wanted him to manoeuvre the float alongside the loading bay and then slot it into the charging bay. Steve moved into the driving seat and, making sure the switch on the dashboard was set to drive, gently pressed the accelerator. The float moved smoothly forward. He hit the brake, flipped the switch to engage reverse and moved the float back a few feet.

Feeling a bit more secure now, he brought the float alongside the loading bay and unloaded the empties before driving slowly over to the charging station. He pulled into a bay and climbed out of the float, unsure of what the re-charging procedure involved. Was he meant to plug it in himself or leave it for someone else to do? There was nothing for it, he would have to ask.

He walked over to the foreman's cabin and knocked on the door. The gaffer was at his desk, still reading *The Sun* it seemed. Steve explained his problem. Folding up the newspaper, the gaffer waved a hand and said, 'You get off home, son. I'll deal with it.'

As Steve was about to leave, the gaffer looked up and, suddenly serious, said, 'Okay?'

Steve nodded, 'A bit knackered.'

The gaffer chuckled, 'Yeah, old Ron doesn't hang around. Don't worry, son, you'll get used to it.'

Steve grinned back at him and thought to himself that there might be a nice bloke beneath the gruff exterior.

NEGATIVE POETICS

WHEN STEVE GOT BACK to Victoria Road, he dropped the bike in the back garden and opened the door of the kitchen to find Angie still having her breakfast. She looked a little startled. 'Goodness me, I didn't expect you back so soon.'

'Yeah, a piece of cake . . .'

He sat down and took his shoes off. '. . . if you happen to have done a Royal Marines training course.'

Angie could see that he was tired. 'Go and lie down and I'll bring you a cup of tea.'

But by the time she got up to the bedroom with the mug of tea, Steve was fast asleep, fully clothed. Angie put the mug of tea on the bedside table, kissed him on the forehead and let him sleep. The impact of four hours in the fresh air delivering milk conducted at Ron's furious pace had been quite a shock to someone for whom the previous three years had been largely sedentary.

Steve woke a few hours later to find Angie sitting at the little desk in the bay window of their room writing. Alerted to his wakefulness by the sound of his stretching and yawning, she turned around from her work and gave him a cheerful smile.

'Feeling better?'

'Yes, much. Sorry, I didn't mean to crash out for so long.'

'Do you think you're going to be able to stick it?'

'I hope so. It was certainly a bit more strenuous than I was expecting. But I think that was partly from trying to keep up with Ron. When I'm doing the round on my own, I can take it at a easier pace, apparently.'

He went on to describe how the morning had unfolded. When he had finished his account, Angie said, 'Well, at least it gives you quite a lot of the day to get on with other things.'

'Yes, that's the idea. But I wish I had your self discipline. It looks like you're already back at work. What are you reading?'

'I'm just taking some notes on Northrop Frye's *Anatomy of Criticism*. It's a brilliant book, but very weird. It attempts to systematise the study of literature by treating criticism like a science. His starting point is Aristotle's *Poetics*, from the first half dozen pages of which he distils an immense critical apparatus. I feel I need to get some of the classic texts of literary theory under my belt before I get up to Edinburgh.'

But Angie didn't want to talk about the *Anatomy of Criticism*. She wanted to perform an analogous operation on their relationship.

'So when are we going to have this talk? I'd rather not do it here. There's too much chance of interruptions and unhelpful contributions.'

Talking things over was the last thing Steve really wanted to do, mainly because he didn't really have a firm grasp of his real aims and motives, but also because he had a high opinion of Angie's debating skills. Playing for time, he said, 'What do you suggest?'

'I suggest we go out for an early evening meal, just the two of us, and no alcohol.'

Doing his best to make it sound as though he wasn't just trying to get the matter over and done with, he said, 'Okay. We could go to the Eros or the Corner House this evening and stay off the booze.'

Angie approved of the idea and returned to her reading, while Steve picked up his guitar and strummed it listlessly, trying to work out what he was going to say later.

They had only known each other for little more than a year, but already he felt that, with the possible exception of his mother, she understood him better than anyone else. That she was from a more privileged background had not been an issue in their relationship, but it seemed to him that it might well become so now.

He had sensed this possibility when he had met Angie's parents for the first time at Easter. George and Viv Barrett had driven up to Cambridge from Kent to take Angie home for the Easter break. Steve and Angie had had to hurriedly rearrange their bedroom to make it seem that they didn't share a room and that Steve's room was in the attic. Despite Steve's irritation at having to resort to this subterfuge, he had warmed to the Barretts and done his best to make sure that they went away with a good opinion of him. Well, perhaps he hadn't tried that hard. Ignoring Angie's pleas to tidy himself up a bit, he had presented himself at the pub, in which they had arranged to meet, in his usual garb: a pair of faded blue loons, a collarless granddad shirt, and a pair of Indian leather flip-flop sandals.

By contrast, Angie's father was extremely well turned-out, wearing a beautiful jacket made of some kind of superior cloth, immaculate collar and opulent necktie, and highly polished shoes. If, on Steve's arrival, Viv had looked a little askance at his lack of good sartorial manners, George hadn't seemed to bat an eyelid, even if he had teased Steve a little bit about his lack of collar or socks. But there was no malice in his teasing and otherwise he operated on a man to man basis.

At one point George had gone to the bar to order another round of drinks. Steve had accompanied him to help carry the drinks back to their table. As they were waiting for their order to be completed, George had turned to him and said, 'I don't mind what you two get up to, not that Viv would agree with that sentiment, but I want you to treat Angie properly and look after her. If you can't do that, I'd rather you went your separate ways.'

Steve had assured him that he loved Angie and that he would always look out for her. George said that Angie was a very special young woman and that Steve was a lucky man. Steve hadn't been expecting this kind of straight talking, as though he and Angie had just announced that they were getting married. Once again he assured George that he would always do the right thing when it came to Angie. He felt rather uncomfortable about making such a blanket promise, but his words seemed to satisfy George, who proffered his hand as if to seal the pact. As they shook hands, Steve was aware of the huge power of George's grip. Back at the table the conversation reverted to the lighthearted mood of earlier.

Steve and Angie had then taken her parents to have something to eat at Arjuna Whole Foods in Mill Road, one of the grittier thoroughfares of the city. What were they thinking of? The expression on Viv's face on entering the premises was one of considerable distaste, as if she were worried about the standards of hygiene they were likely to encounter. Or perhaps it was a reaction to the relentless aesthetic of stripped pine and stoneware pottery favoured by such establishments.

But George had found it hugely amusing. He wasn't entirely ignorant of the vegetarian movement, but he had never personally eaten a nut cutlet or a mung bean salad, both of which featured prominently on the short menu. He was also probably more used to waiter service and a degree of nappery not in evidence in the dining area of Arjuna Whole Foods. Even so they had both pronounced the brown rice and worthy cutlets surprisingly tasty, although they were picking little sprigs of herbs out of their teeth for some time afterwards. As they left the restaurant, George was chortling quietly to himself, already working the details of the meal into an anecdote that he thought might amuse his pals at the club.

So why wasn't Steve doing the sensible thing and throwing in his lot with Angie, a summer together in Brighton and then a move to Edinburgh, by all accounts, a beautiful and lively city? Of course, the need to raise funds urgently was not the real reason for his enigmatic behaviour. It was a kind of alibi. If he put his mind to it there were surely other ways to solve the problem. He knew that he was exploiting the perception of his mother's lack of means to disguise his real motives. But would he be able to explain to Angie, what those motives were? In all likelihood, she already had a good idea, in which case it was just a matter of enunciating what they both already knew. The problem was that he had scarcely admitted it, even to himself. To jeopardise their relationship to buy time to finish the poem sequence he was working on was reckless in the extreme.

And yet that poem had loomed large in his thinking for the last six months. Its working title was *Self/Contained*. Jez and the others were aware that he wrote poetry, a matter of considerable mirth for the most part, but the material they knew about was a collection miniature pieces, knotty haikus. He'd kept *Self/Contained* under wraps and sworn Angie to secrecy. Otherwise, the only other people in on the secret were his friend Rob Williams, a leading light of various Cambridge poetry groups, and Grace Mitchell, his supervisor in French literature, the latter not the most obvious confidant. The reason that this academic personage was privy to the gestation of *Self/Contained* was that Steve had had the temerity to use time spent working on the poem as an excuse for not having delivered an essay, very much an advanced version of the dog ate my homework routine. Unexpectedly his supervisor was sympathetic to his situation.

But neither Grace nor Rob, nor, more surprisingly, Angie had seen anything of the poem and it would be entirely understandable if they doubted its existence. The truth was that this was not where he had expected to be in terms of poetic development by the end of his under-graduate career. He was beginning to doubt that he had anything to say or a convincing way of saying it. And the more he found himself talking about the poem, the less inclined he felt to show it to anyone.

It hadn't always been like that. At school he'd been a member of the poetry society, but where other boys' poems were metrical, stanzaic and rhyming, his were short, obscure and defiantly *vers libre*. His friends were polite but baffled by his contributions. He was polite about their work too, but not in the slightest baffled, unless by the apparent need to retread worn-out poetical fashions. But if he managed to avoid such fashions himself, it was only because of his tendency not to use the first person pronoun, which he said reflected the emptiness he felt inside, the not-being at the centre of his being. Nevertheless this approach, which he airily referred to as his negative poetics, had impressed in the school poetry society and he had arrived in Cambridge, fairly confident in his praxis.

Despite his former affiliation with the school poetry society, Steve was not really one for joining clubs and groups, but poetry was such an underground activity that it was really the only way to find out what the state of the art was in Cambridge. Noticing a flyer about a reading group that met in the Merton Arms, he'd gone along experimentally and had had the misfortune to be the first to read, a decision arrived at by lottery. Somewhat appositely the poem he had chosen to read was called 'Rien Ne Va Plus', which played with the image of a roulette wheel as a compass, the idea that we are guided, whether we like it or not, by chance and that what we like to think of as the self is a kind of needle or pointer that is moved by a powerful and invisible force. Death may be ineluctable, but the route there is not predetermined. Contingency redeems necessity, as it were. It was possible, for example, to create something that only that particular individual could have made, in this case the poem that Steve was reading to the little group of poets, a poem which had emerged from the silence in the same way that that the universe had been created by the utterance of God ('I / utter silence / in the centre / here.') Or something like that.

When he had finished reading, there was a silence, more awkward than utter. Eventually someone said that it was a rather difficult poem to digest, perhaps somewhat obscure. Another person said that she didn't think that the language was particularly poetic, indeed lacking music. Steve muttered something about it being more a poem for the eye, but that the sound of it was important too. He pointed out that *utter* was a homograph, in which one meaning was *absolute* while the other meant to *speak* or *pronounce*. Conversely the final word *here* was a heterograph, with one meaning indicating *this place,* while the sound of the word could be taken to be the imperative of to *hark* or *hear.* He also thought, though refrained from giving voice to the thought, that if the flickering semantics of the *last word* was not enough, in the sense that the poem needed further explication, then the poem had failed.

If anything, the silence following this rationalisation was even more uncomfortable. Fortunately the next reader was ready with a poem about flowers, which enabled everyone to relax. In due course everyone had read a poem, some of which attracted more comment or approbation than others. The woman who had convened the group thanked everyone and announced the date of the next meeting. There was now time for a couple of pints and some chitchat. Steve, furious at having exposed himself in this way, wishing that he'd found out a bit more about the group before joining, had decided not to hang around for the break-out session and slipped quietly out of the pub.

He was already striding purposefully down the road, when he heard a shout. He looked around and saw that another of the participants, a tall, bespectacled man of about his own age, who had been sitting on the other side of the room, had followed him out and was trying to attract his attention. The man caught up with him and said, 'Christ, you were out of the blocks fast.'

'Yeah, I didn't realise that it would go on so late. I'd arranged to meet someone,' Steve lied.

'Oh, that's a pity. I thought that we could get a drink somewhere else. I liked your piece and wanted to talk about it, but not with that lot in there. Which way are you going? We could walk and talk at the same time. By the way, I'm Robin.'

Steve remembered hearing the name and a few fragments of the poem that Robin had read surfaced in his mind. 'Lines, angles, very abstract, microscopic. Your piece, I think. Is that right?'

'Yeah, roughly. A bit more to it, but not a bad summary of the approach.'

'It was good. But I was losing the will to live with a lot of the other stuff.'

'Know what you mean.'

'Look, I'm sorry, I was lying earlier on. I don't have anyone to meet. So, yeah, if you've got time, let's have that drink.'

They crossed the road to the Rose and Crown and found a table. Robin went to get the drinks and when he returned they exchanged notes about their respective colleges and subjects. Rob was already very clued up on the Cambridge poetry scene. Had Steve had any of his work published? Steve shook his head. Did that mean that Robin had? As it turned out, just the one piece. Still, that was a degree of validation that Steve was unable to claim. Robin wondered whether Steve would be prepared to let him read some of his work. Steve thought he could hardly say no, but was relieved that he had only brought with him a handwritten copy of 'Rien Ne Va Plus', which he reluctantly surrendered. Robin, on the other hand, had come professionally equipped, producing from his shoulder bag a slim sheaf of typewritten pages neatly clipped into a plastic folder.

That was the last time Steve went to any kind of poetry group, but he did keep in touch with Rob, who continued to badger Steve into showing him his work in progress from time to time, about which he was invariably complimentary. What little reputation Steve acquired in Cambridge poetry circles was almost entirely down to the hearsay generated by Rob who was also responsible for circulating occasional *samizdat* copies of Steve's work.

Steve was not ungrateful to Rob for his efforts, but it highlighted a difficult dimension to their relationship. Mates they might be, but Steve couldn't help being aware of the fact that they were also competitors. No doubt this perception was simply a function of his own lack of self-confidence in relation to his work, something that Rob apparently did not suffer from. Rob seemed to have arrived in Cambridge fully formed, already familiar with the eddies and currents of contemporary poetry. At times it did occur to Steve that Rob was perhaps not quite as confident as he seemed. Once when they had both drunk more than was good for them, Rob had admitted that he didn't understand how Steve constructed his voice, how he *built the fulcrum of his utterance*, as he put it. That seemed to unsettle him, but if it did, it unsettled Steve much more.

And it was Rob who had introduced him to Jeremiah Flynn's poetry and indirectly to Angie Barrett. Flynn was an English lecturer, who had achieved coterie recognition in the rarefied world of Cambridge poetry by courting extreme obscurity and deploying a range of rhetorical resources, not normally thought of as poetic. Rob lent Steve a couple of slim pamphlets, which he found intriguing. Even though he was neither an English student nor a regular lecture-goer, he decided to attend one of Flynn's lectures. He was not disappointed. Despite the fact that this was not a reading of Flynn's own poetry, but an analysis of Wordsworth's 'The World Is Too Much With Us', Steve had responded to Flynn's gloomy but nuanced environmentalism.

At that same lecture he had squeezed onto a bench next to a pretty girl with long blonde hair, who in a pause in proceedings as Flynn took a sip water and searched for a sheet of paper in his folder, had leaned across to Steve and said, 'He's marvellous, isn't he?' Steve had had no hesitation in immediately agreeing nor in asking the girl as they filed out after the lecture whether she fancied a lunchtime drink in the Granta. That same day Angie and Steve became lovers.

However, whilst he had now acquired a girlfriend, his poetic self-confidence evaporated in the fierce glare of Flynn's poetics. He suddenly saw his own approach as ungrounded and arbitrary. What did his negative poetics actually amount to? Despite the fact that it had given him a reasonably stable compositional platform, it was in reality a flimsy exercise in metaphysics. Not using the first person singular was a trivial response to what had probably been a trivial complaint, teenage existential angst. Aware of the inadequacy of his schoolboy poetics, he had been trying, since arriving in Cambridge, to remap the being / not-being idea onto the Freudian model of the psyche, in which the not-being component became the unconscious and the being component became the self or the ego. Using these new co-ordinates he had generated the original sections of *Self/Contained*. But he was still not happy with the rationalisation and troubled too by his inability to carve out a role for the superego and the id. If he was to make his own work relevant to the force field around Jeremiah Flynn, he was going to have to come up with a more convincing poetics.

Unexpectedly, a solution had-presented itself in the person of Mike Paterson, a young astronomer, who was a family friend of Angie's. Mike worked at the Herstmonceux Observatory where he was hoping to 'observe' a black hole. By definition, a black hole is a region of space where the force of gravity is so intense that nothing, not even light can escape from it, so it cannot be directly observed. But Mike realised that it might be possible to detect a black hole *indirectly* by its effect on nearby bodies. He had zeroed in on a particular star which he surmised from its behaviour was in fact a binary star with the visible component in a tight orbit around a black hole. He had published a paper to this effect and now the claim was to be discussed at a conference in Cambridge, hence his presence in the city and his request to stay overnight. The conference in due course backed Mike's analysis and the binary configuration was recognised as a black hole.

Back at the shared house after the conference, Mike had explained all this to Steve and his incredulous housemates. He had gone on to explain that the star would eventually be sucked into the black hole and that at some point it would start to break up. The visible debris would mark a boundary beyond which escape from the black hole's gravity was impossible. Easy familiarity with matters astronomical was notable by its absence among the inhabitants of the Victoria Road house. None of them had ever heard of a black hole and it didn't help that during Mike's account Jez had rolled and circulated a powerful joint. It was not surprising, therefore, if Steve wasn't sure that he had understood all the details but in any case what really interested him was the idea of a region from which light could not escape. Mike had called this boundary the event horizon.

Steve immediately saw an affinity between this astronomical phenomenon, his negative poetics and his subsequent appropriation of Freudian ideas, with the bonus that it was apparently grounded in hard science rather than metaphysics or metapsychology. Not that Steve was an adept of Einsteinian equations. But he now knew someone who was. It wasn't clear to him at first how to make use of this identification. But as he wrote, the idea of a self created through the act of writing became the event horizon around the black hole of the real self, an invisible zone, dense, compacted and inaccessible to introspection.

In due course the new material that agglomerated around this idea changed the nature of the poem to such an extent that *Self/Contained* became an increasingly inapt title. In a moment of algebraic inspiration he substituted the terms on either side of the pretentious oblique slash with terms from his new lexicon and suddenly he was the poet of *Event/Horizon*. The change of title precipitated a period of intense production, so much so that the work started to assume alarmingly asymptotic proportions. He had hoped to have finished a first draft by the time he needed, belatedly, to apply himself to revision for Finals. But despite all his work, a satisfactory conclusion seemed further off than ever. Finally he tore himself away from it and speed-read his meagre revision notes.

Finals over, he read the poem through again and was plunged into gloom. He found it abstruse and nugatory. How had he deceived himself so comprehensively? Yet when he cast his mind back to the period of composition, it seemed that he had had a sense of lyric power, of afflatus, the words had flowed effortlessly from his pen. How could there be such a difference in perspective? Had he simply been smoking too much dope during the composition phase and, having straightened out for Finals, was now seeing it as it really was and as others would see it? He knew that the subject of the poem was highly abstract, even for what might be called innovative poetry. And perhaps his own reaction to it as a reader reflected that equivocation. Or perhaps it was just that it was still unfinished. A little more work on it and it would all come into focus. Two or three months was all that it would need. He could then decide whether to set it free or to leave it behind. Hence his sudden decision to get a job as a milkman and live in a tiny dusty house near the railway line.

He disapproved of explaining what a poem was about, but perhaps the poem would explain to Angie what he was about. He would give it to her, and perhaps she would then understand what lay behind his decision. He was pretty sure that Angie already intuited most of this, but in a spirit of solidarity had kept it to herself, because she too had her own aspirations as a writer. And indeed, in terms of productivity, where Steve was halting, Angie was prolific. She wrote constantly and with immense fluency.

Steve had become aware of this when he came back to the house one day and found the dustbin overflowing with paper. He gathered up the stray sheets of paper to stuff them more securely in the bin, only to realise that the handwriting was Angie's. He read a few pages and saw that it was part of a novel. Appalled that what looked like a substantial piece of work had been consigned to the bin, and only dimly register- ing that that was also what, on more than one occasion, he himself had done, though in his case with much less paper sacrificed, he carefully extracted all the sheets of paper from the bin and then, marching into the house, confronted Angie in their shared room. Why was she throwing away this work? What was wrong with it? Why hadn't she shown it to him? Even from a cursory glance he could tell that it was good material.

She was taken aback by his fury and said that it was a matter for her. For all he knew, what he now had in his hands was a first draft and she had a new draft in her drawer. She had just been trying something out.

Not everything was intended for an audience. That was not the way that Steve saw things, at least that was what he asserted. Angie scoffed at this and asked Steve why, in that case, had he not shown her his poem. This stopped him in his tracks. Eventually, he said, 'Because it's not any good. I need to fix it.'

She said that he should cut himself some slack. Why was he so cautious? Why didn't he believe in his own work? Steve wasn't sure. She said that she knew, in his reaction to the jettisoned pages, that he was just being supportive and she appreciated it, but she wasn't sure about the best way of supporting him, especially since he actively resisted letting anyone help him. Suddenly he was deflated and rueful.

She had tried to embrace him, but he had pushed her away and thrown himself on the bed, staring mournfully at the ceiling. It had seemed best to leave him on his own for a bit and she went downstairs to make a cup of tea.

Steve was roused from contemplation of this painful exchange from a couple of months earlier by Angie saying they should be getting down to the Corner House. Twenty minutes later, having arrived before the early evening rush, they managed to get a table in the window and, as agreed, didn't order any alcohol, settling for a jug of water to go with the moussaka for Steve and the kebab for Angie, both with the standard student accompaniment of rice *and* chips. While they were waiting for the meals to be delivered to the table, Angie said, 'Okay, I'll start. But let's do our best not to have a row, because I've got a feeling that we're going to be touching on some painful issues. And if we do get into deep water, let's just agree to take a time out.'

Steve agreed that this was a good idea.

'Well, to begin with, we've got the Last Party coming up in just over a week's time.'

'Oh yeah, I'd forgotten.'

'And maybe you'd forgotten that not only is it the last party in Victoria Road, but it has a cross dressing theme.'

Steve sighed.

'Oh come on, Steve. You were enthusiastic about the idea when we all discussed it before Finals.'

'That's probably because I was stoned.'

'Well anyway, it's happening, and we need to give some thought to what we're going to wear. I don't think just swapping clothes is going to work because we're rather different sizes.'

Steve could see the problem. Angie was petite, while Steve was six or seven inches taller.

'What do you suggest?

'Well, if you're prepared to leave it to me. I will get a few things from Tiger Lily, the vintage clothes shop on Mill Road.'

That was fine by Steve. He trusted her judgement in such matters. Left to his own devices for such an event, he shuddered to think what he might look like.

Angie smiled. So far, so good.

She took a sip of her water. 'Okay. The next point is a bit more difficult.'

Steve could only assume that this was the *pièce de résistance* of the conversation, but was wrong footed when Angie said, 'We need to talk about graduation day.'

'Really?'

'Yes. Our colleges have congregations on the same day.'

Steve nodded. This was not news. A congregation was a ceremony at the Senate House, at which those about to graduate, graduands, were formally awarded their degree. Because of the number of students involved, there were multiple sessions. As it happened, Angie's college and Steve's had their congregations on the same day, but at different times.

'You said you've invited your mother.'

'Yes, she's really looking forward to it. And to meeting you.'

'So, that's just the point. I'm looking forward to meeting her. But my parents are coming too and they've suggested we all go for a meal together. My father will pay, but we need to make some arrangements.'

Steve was thoughtful. This was a development, he hadn't anticipated. His mother had already expressed her desire to meet Angie and he thought she would probably be interested to meet Angie's parents too, but she was a proud woman and would want to pay her share. He didn't quite know how to put his concern.

'That's very generous of your parents, but I wouldn't want to embarrass my mother.'

'I know. So what my father has agreed to do is to give me the money and then on the day you and I can settle the bill. My dad's perfectly fine with that.'

Steve didn't know whether to be grateful that Angie had anticipated the potential embarrassment or irritated that she hadn't discussed it with him first. But he concluded that it must have been a tricky conversation to have had and thanked her for her sensitivity.

Angie breathed a sigh of relief. 'Okay. Well, the other thing about graduation day is that we're going to have to indulge in a bit of subterfuge. We'll have to move your stuff out of our room and pretend you sleep in the attic room again.'

'Why do they need to come to the house?'

'Because they're picking up my things. I'll be going back to Kent with them the next day, before going down to Brighton a day or two later.'

Steve looked at her blankly. Somehow he'd thought that he still had time to persuade Angie to change her mind, but clearly the stage machinery was already whirring and the scenery was changing around them. Unsure what to say, he remained silent.

Angie continued with her analysis of the situation. 'They're coming up on the Thursday, the day before graduation day, so we'll have to have moved your stuff by then. We're going to load my stuff into the car that same day and then I'm going to stay in their hotel that night, the following night too. We'll head back to Kent on Saturday morning.'

Things were getting real. They were reaching the parting of the ways. Steve felt an anticipatory pang of regret. Neither spoke for some time.

Angie was the first to break the silence. 'So you're going to take this house in Ainsworth Street then?'

'What else can I do?'

'Come down to Brighton with me. I've got a place to live in from the 24th of June.'

'Angie, I can't.'

'Why not?'

'For all sorts of reasons. I'm just not ready.'

Tears formed in her eyes, but she blinked them away.

'Well I'm just telling you what my commitments are and have been for some time. Just so there's no misunderstanding between us.'

Steve felt a lump in his throat. He reached out his hand and took hers.

'Angie . . .'

But he couldn't get any further. They sat there, both overwhelmed with misery, but somehow incapable of doing anything about it.

After a few moments, Steve said, 'Would you read the poem I've been working on?'

Angie narrowed her gaze and studied Steve's face. Was he serious? Had he not been following the thread of the conversation? Was he just blanking something he couldn't deal with?

'Steve, I don't understand.'

'I think it might explain where I'm at.'

'Yes, of course. I'd love to. I've wanted to ever since I knew you were working on it. But I don't see what the poem has to do with whether we stay together or not.'

He searched for a way to explain the situation he found himself in.

'It's something I've got to do. It's a question of what I'm going to do with my life. I need to do this.'

Angie could see that they were starting to get into dangerous territory and confirmed that she'd read it with pleasure. It was time to move the conversation into less contentious areas. Privately she realised that things were coming to an end, although it wasn't clear who was being the more obdurate.

After their meal, they walked back to Victoria Road in silence, lost in their own thoughts. Arriving at the house they went straight up to bed, too miserable to engage with the others.

HOT CLUB DE CAMBRIDGE

The Portland Arms
Thursday, 6 June 1974

FOR STEVE, THE NEXT couple of days passed in a blur of frantic early morning bike rides across Cambridge and then four hours of trying to keep up with Ron's relentless pace around the backstreets off Mill Road. Ron was not an easy man to get to know or to warm to. Despite the number of hours that they spent together in the cab of the float, Steve had no idea whether Ron was married or not, whether he had kids, where he lived, whether he had really served in the armed forces and so on. But in return Ron did not make the slightest attempt to find out more about Steve's circumstances, so he was spared the ordeal of having to sculpt a narrative that would make sense of his situation. Nor did he have to tiptoe through political or moral issues. Ron seemed not in the least interested in whether Steve was a lefty, young conservative, or anarchist. At least Steve was able to have a bit of a joshing conversation with the gaffer, even if it was pretty much confined to the attributes of that particular day's Page 3 beauty.

Steve and Angie had not spoken much since the conversation in the Corner House. When they were together, she buried herself in her reading and Steve brooded while strumming his guitar. So when he got back from the round on the Thursday morning, he was not surprised to hear her announce that she was going out that evening to have supper with Julie, one of her college friends. Steve concluded that he was not invited. Angie was not the only one with plans for the evening. Jackie had gone back to London. And Di and Jez also had social engagements elsewhere in Cambridge. That just left Alan, Harry and Steve, so the house seemed unusually empty. For a very pleasant couple of hours, they sat in the sitting room, smoking and listening to records. It took them back to their first year when they had met and bonded as friends. At seven o'clock, Harry announced that he was feeling hungry and would make something. Alan and Steve were welcome to join him.

When they had finished eating, Alan and Harry decided they fancied a pint and thought they might go down to the Portland Arms. Why didn't Steve join them for a bit? In fact, they wanted to have a chat with him in the seclusion of a boozer. Steve knew that he shouldn't. But he was intrigued by the suggestion that they had something to say to him that could only be uttered in the confines of a public house and agreed to join them, but only for a couple. He needed to be in bed by nine-thirty.

They strolled towards Mitcham's Corner and went into the back bar of the Portland, which was a venue for live acoustic music, often folk but tonight featuring a jazz band called the Hot Club de Cambridge. Alan went to the bar and got the first round, Greene King Abbot, all round. Uh-oh, the strong stuff!

After they had quaffed deeply, Alan said, 'Glad you decided to join us, Steve.'

'So am I, but I can't stay long.'

'Don't worry, we'll make sure you're tucked up at a not too ungodly hour,' Harry affirmed.

'We wanted to talk to you about this crackpot scheme of yours to work as a milkman and take on the rent of a hovel in the back of beyond or all the way down Mill Road, which amounts to the same thing,' resumed Alan.

'I don't want to have to ask my mother for any money. These last few years have been hard enough for her.'

'So how does doing a crap job and taking on a sublet solve that?'

'Well, it's just a short term fix.'

Harry took up the baton. 'But wouldn't it make more sense for you to go to down to Brighton with Angie?'

Steve looked at him sharply. 'Has she set you two up?'

Harry denied that there'd been any collusion. 'No, there's been no discussion on the subject. It's just obvious that you two are the perfect couple. And it would be a pity to spoil the ship for a ha'pporth of tar.'

'So that's exactly what I'm doing. Pulling together a ha'pporth for the tar.'

Alan decided that was enough preamble, 'Well, what we thought was that we could help you out there.'

'In what way?'

'Between us, Harry and me, we could lend you the dosh. You could pay it back to us by the end of the summer.'

Steve was speechless with gratitude at the generosity of the offer, but also irritated. He didn't need bailing out by his best mates. He took a sip of his beer.

'That's very generous of you both. I'm touched by the offer, but I couldn't possibly accept it. This is a mess I got myself into and I need to sort it out myself. I don't want to appear ungrateful. I'm not particularly dismayed by the situation. There's nothing shameful in being a milkman. I'm quite looking forward to spending the summer in Cambridge. Moving on from being a student. I'm still hoping to persuade Angie to stay with me until she heads up to Edinburgh. I know that she doesn't want to let the language school down. But I'm sure they'd get over it.'

'Yeah, but aren't the people who run it friends of the family?' pointed out Harry.

'So what?'

Both Alan and Harry thought that Steve was being insensitive towards Angie's situation. Alan shook his head. 'I don't think you quite understand how the feminine mind works.'

'I'll grant you that. But then I have very little idea how any mind works, my own included.'

Harry again. 'So you're determined on this course of action?'

Steve wasn't really. There was still time to change his mind, at least until he handed over the deposit on the house, but being put on the spot hardened his resolve.

'Yes, I'm sure about what I'm doing.'

He might claim to be sure about what he was doing, but knowing *why* he was doing what he was doing, was another matter entirely. Neither the mild financial crisis, nor the need to finish the poem by the end of the summer constituted an entirely compelling reason. It was kind of the boys to offer to help out, but he couldn't possibly accept their offer, although perhaps Alan could help in another way.

'What would help, Al, is if you and Di shared the place with me, at least for a few weeks.'

'I told you, mate, that doesn't fit with our plans. We'll stay here in Victoria Road until the end of the month and then we'll be off to the sunny South of France.'

Steve shrugged. 'Fair enough. But if your plans don't come together, you'd be welcome to join me.'

He already knew that Harry had firm travel plans, so there was no point extending the same offer to him.

In the ensuing pause in the conversation, Steve became aware that there was some activity on the small stage at the back of the room as the members of the band providing the evening's entertainment took up their positions. Harry suggested they drink up and he'd get the next round in before the music started. Steve was about to decline taking part in the next round, but Harry was already making his way to the bar. Steve figured there was no harm in just one more pint. It was still early.

By the time that Harry got back from the bar, the little band had started playing. It was a four piece, two acoustic guitars, a double bass and a violin. The music was very old school, with a nice chugging rhythm. One of the guitarists and the violinist took it in turns to take solos, with an occasional solo from the bassist. All three of the house-mates with the help of the second pint of Abbot were soon getting into the music. And before long they had finished the second pint. Steve could hardly walk out without having bought a round. He gestured to the others to see if they wanted another pint and got the thumbs up from both. He would buy them a pint each and head for his bed.

He picked up the empty glasses, put them on the bar, caught the barman's eye and, while waiting to be served, turned to watch the band. When he turned back to the bar a few moments later, he realised that the barman had drawn three pints on the assumption that Steve wanted replacements for the three empties he'd left on the bar and was now waiting for payment. Oh, well, one more pint wouldn't harm and, after all, the music was great. He carried the beers back to the table and caught Alan and Harry grinning at each other. He decided to ignore their ribaldry and returned his attention to the music. He was close to the stage and had a good view of the guitarists' fretting hands. The runs and arpeggios were way beyond anything he could aspire to, but he thought he might be able to attempt the rhythm part. The only problem was that the chord grips were not like anything with which he was familiar.

Shortly afterwards, the band took a break and came across to the bar to get some interval refreshment. Emboldened by the beer, Steve returned to the bar to tell them how much he was enjoying the set.

'What is the material you're playing?'

The band member that Steve recognised as the rhythm guitarist said, 'We just finished the first half with "Sweet and Low" by Fats Waller, but most of it was Django stuff.'

Steve had heard of Fats Waller, not that he could identify any of his music, but the other name was new to him.

'Django?'

'Yeah, Django Reinhardt and the Quintette of the Hot Club of France.'

'Thanks. I play a bit of a guitar myself. I was watching your chord shapes and not many of them are familiar to me. How do you go about learning that kind of stuff?'

'I started out with a book by a guy called Jed Morgan. You should be able to find a copy in Miller's in Sussex Street.'

Steve resolved go to Miller's after work the next day. He thanked him for the information and went back to the table, where Alan and Harry were sitting with even bigger grins on their faces. He was about to ask what was so funny when he realised that there was yet another round of pints of Abbot sitting on the table. He groaned theatrically, but sat down at the table and settled in for a long evening.

The next morning, when his alarm went off, he found himself groaning again, but this time for real.

At the sound of the alarm, Angie had woken too. She looked at Steve pityingly.

'What an idiot you are. I leave you on your own for one evening and you let those two ruffians lead you up the garden path.'

She was very angry with Alan and Harry. Even through the mists of his hangover Steve realised that she might think much better of them, if she knew about their offer, but now was not the time to set the record straight. Perhaps there never would be a time.

Angie's mood softened when she saw the sallow colour of his skin. She got out of bed, put her dressing gown on and said, 'You go and straighten yourself out as best you can in the bathroom and I'll go down and make some strong coffee.'

Steve nodded weakly and thanked her for being so considerate. He then went to the bathroom and did his best to restore his equilibrium. A little while later with the help of the coffee that Angie had made, he was cycling across Cambridge trying to clear his head. It didn't help that he was going to be in the cab with Ron and his vile cigars for at least four hours. The very thought was enough to make him feel that he was going to vomit. At least Ron didn't do chitchat. And then Steve would get back home as fast as he could and spend the rest of the day in bed. The visit to Miller's to look for the Jed Morgan book would have to wait for another day.

Steve felt sure that Ron realised that he was far from being in fine fettle that morning from the way that he kept casting sidelong glances at him, but at least he refrained from asking any questions. So long as Steve kept up the pace that he set, that was fine by Ron. He didn't want to talk to some student tosser anyway.

As Steve cycled back to Victoria Road, he thanked his lucky stars that Cambridge was so flat and he didn't have to put too much effort into the return journey. When he got home, Angie offered to vacate their room and do her reading downstairs. Steve said there was no need and was very soon fast asleep. He woke several hours later, pleased to find that he was almost back to normal. Maybe trying to persuade Alan to share the house with him was not not such a great idea after all. At that moment, Angie re-entered the room, bearing two mugs of tea, 'Glad to see you're back in the land of the living.'

Steve thanked her for the tea and said ruefully, 'I'm such a twat. I should have known better.'

'You should with those two.'

'No, it's my fault. They were just being good mates.'

'A funny way of expressing solidarity.'

Steve thought it best not to pursue the ways in which Alan and Harry were or were not good blokes.

Angie settled herself in the chair in front of her desk and picked up Steve's manuscript. 'So, I finished reading your poem. Do you feel sufficiently recovered to talk about it?'

'That sounds a bit worrying.'

'No, it's a serious piece of work, and I want to do it justice.'

Steve lay back on the bed and steeled himself for Angie's thoughts which he knew would be well-judged, but he also knew that she would not pull her punches.

'The truth of the matter is that I don't know what to think about *Event/Horizon*. It is not what I would normally consider a poem. But if you tell me it is a poem, and I approach it in that frame of mind, which is what I think we do in contemplating any piece of art, then I would say that it evokes some very strange impressions. The language is not poetic in the usual sense of that word. But, of course, what is considered artistic or poetic is a cultural presupposition. Accordingly, if I accept the language as poetic, it releases a whole range of meaning that I would not usually expect to find in that kind of vocabulary or diction. In that sense, it seems to be a kind of metapoetry, the sort of thing that visual and plastic artists have been doing for some time, if not quite a ready-made. It seems to borrow a form of discourse from a domain that is more concerned with the instrumentalities of science than the meditative observations of art. In that respect it is brilliant. But your chances of finding a readership without also manipulating the cultural frames in which your art is embedded are slight. I can't think of any magazine that would publish a section of the poem or the publisher who would be prepared to publish the whole thing as a book. It strikes me that if you want to find an audience, you're going to have to be a facilitator of your own work, both artist and impresario.'

Steve didn't really know what to say. There was an undeniable cogency to Angie's analysis. She was sophisticated enough not to scrabble for some underlying meaning. And she had resisted grappling with the language, merely noting that it was not conventionally poetic. Instead she had zoomed out to consider what the inscribed material represented from a structuralist perspective, a perspective which Steve himself did not as yet possess. But this was not a comfort. He was hurt and angry. He wanted her to like it without reservation. He wanted her to provide a boost to his own flagging self-confidence with a deft encomium.

Of course, if she had actually taken that approach, he would probably have been just as angry, feeling that she was patronising him. In a sense it was an impossible task he had set her. It was expecting too much of those closest to oneself to offer an objective response. However much your friends wanted to like your work, the pre-existing personal relationship got in the way, not just revealing aspects of a hitherto concealed complex of competitiveness and envy but also hinting at the ways in which allowances were routinely made for one's foibles. It was as if one's intimates had a vested interest in obstructing the metamorphosis that turned a reader into a writer.

Mightn't it be better if one's first readers were complete strangers? Perhaps he should just distribute anonymised copies in the Market Square or nail the pages of his poem to the door of Great St Mary's, rather as Luther had nailed the Ninety-five Theses to the church door in Wittenberg. Fortunately this mood of self-pity as it soared through the firmament of his thoughts was more akin to a meteor than a comet, flaring for a second and then fading away, rather than hanging in the heavens in silent accusation.

'Thank you. I will have to mull over the implications of what you're saying. At least you haven't said it's complete rubbish.'

'It certainly isn't, Steve, but it can be a mixed blessing to be too far ahead of the game. On the other hand I've often thought that cultural conventions are like kaleidoscopes. It only takes the slightest movement to completely change the pattern.'

Steve thought that was a rather beautiful image and made a mental note to work it into his own apologia. The one thing missing from Angie's observations was that she hadn't said that she now understood why Steve wanted to stay in Cambridge for the summer and that she approved of his plan and, what was more, had decided to change her own plans and stay with him. Clearly she didn't see the matters as connected. In the meantime he had a little over a week in which to put down the deposit on the house. If they hadn't reached some kind of reconciliation by then, the prospects for their relationship looked poor.

The only time that Steve became aware that there was another dimension to Ron's life was on the Saturday when they were collecting money. As with everything else on the round, Ron had a carefully worked out system. He had a reasonable proportion of his customers trained to leave out the exact amount in an envelope. But for the rest it was a matter of knocking on the door and asking to be paid. Clearly one could not start doing this too early, and even though most transactions were straightforward, some households were thrown into a state of panic as a purse or wallet was hunted for. This inevitably slowed things down.

When he had started the job, Steve had assumed that there would be zero or little interaction with members of the public, but here he was knocking people up early in the morning and asking them for money.

Fortunately the sums of money were small and people, on the whole, seemed to be well disposed towards milk roundsmen, even a total rookie like Steve. His complacency, however, was shattered at one house, when in response to the amount that Ron had asked him to collect, the householder disputed the bill. Steve was nonplussed and said that he'd go and check with Ron, who muttered something under his breath and picking up the logbook said as he walked briskly up the garden path, 'You had an extra pint on Tuesday, love.'

Love denied this, 'Why would I want an extra pint on a Tuesday?'

'No idea, love. Perhaps you had someone to stay, but I've got it marked down in my book,' stabbing his finger on a open page of the book.

'You could write anything in there.'

'Yes, I could, but why would I? There are easier ways to get an extra 5p.

The householder was reflecting on this assertion and wrinkling her brow in an attempt to come up with a proportionate response, when her face lit up and she said, 'You know, you're quite right. Masie came to stay. I'd quite forgotten.'

'There we are,' said Ron, not without a hint of menace. 'The book's never wrong.'

The woman went inside and got her purse and handed over the money. Ron tipped his invisible cap and strode back to the float.

'Poor old dear. She's starting to lose it.'

Steve caught the note of sympathy and thought that maybe after all there was a sliver of humanity in the otherwise rigid persona that Ron presented to the world.

'And that's why it's important to mark all changes to the standard order in the book. Otherwise, you haven't got a leg to stand on.'

Steve nodded.

'Of course, some people just try it on. You can't show a shred of doubt. The book is the bible.'

Steve picked up the logbook and looked at it with renewed respect. As he flipped through the pages, he noticed that some entries were marked with a question mark, others with an asterisk. He asked Ron the significance of the symbols. Ron said that the question marks were his way of indicating those customers who had a tendency to let their bills mount up or were hard to get hold of and needed keeping an eye on and those marked with an asterisk were places where you might get a cup of tea from the lady of the house when you were collecting.

'They know I like it sweet and strong, if you know what I mean?'

Steve thought he probably did, although the idea that Ron was the recipient of sexual favours from some of his customers was distinctly unsettling. As they trundled on their way, Steve stole a quick glance at Ron's profile, finding it hard to envisage him as the Casanova of the Co-operative Dairy. But a man who chain-smoked Hamlet cigars was probably capable of almost anything.

A little later they were working their way along Tenison Road, Ron taking one side, Steve the other. There were still not too many pedestrians about, but just then a young man in full fig came tottering along the pavement towards them, no doubt a survivor of one of the May Balls. His party clothes were not particularly exotic, but around his long, lank locks he was wearing a paisley bandana. Ron expostulated wordlessly, spat a shred of tobacco into the gutter and clearing his throat said, 'Look at that cunt. What a twat!'

Steve thought that Ron was being just a little harsh and that in any case his invective was tautologous. Not wishing to get into semantics, however, he conceded the substantive point. Accessorising a dinner suit with a bandana was probably a sartorial solecism, not that he put it like that. He didn't have anything against montaging different styles. It was something he had done himself. The one time that he'd been to a May Ball he had worn Wrangler jeans, Green Flash plimsolls, and a collarless grandad shirt. His concession to formality had been a tail coat he had found in a vintage clothes shop and a pair of white kid gloves. He would accept that his strategy was not unlike that of the woozy reveller's, with whom they were just pulling abreast, but he felt confident that his own approach had had just that *je ne sais quoi*, although he doubted that it would have got the thumbs-up from Ron.

Now that they were closer to the object of their criticism, Steve realised with a start, that he was in fact an acquaintance. Actually slightly more than an acquaintance. This was a fine how-de-do. The last thing he wanted to do was to have to acknowledge their affiliation. He was sure that at any moment the quondam twat, soon to be revealed as his friend, would look up and greet him cordially. He shrank down in the cab and considered pretending that he had dropped something, but just then Ron parked the float and Steve was able to hop out of the cab keeping the body of the vehicle between him and his friend. In any case the friend paid no attention to the two rude mechanicals delivering the daily pinta and tottered on his way. Steve supposed that light though his disguise as a milkman was, to wit no cap or apron, the mere fact that he was operating a milk float rendered him a generic tradesman.

Whilst it would have been embarrassing had his friend recognized him, with the subsequent exchange of pleasantries taking place within earshot of Ron, Steve was even more troubled by his apparent invisibility during the encounter. He brooded for the rest of the round, to the extent that Ron actually started to look concerned, or at least puzzled. Had he been able to read Steve's mind, he would have realised that Steve was beginning to understand what it meant to pass from the charmed world of the gown, to the quotidian reality of the town. Reality Checkpoint indeed.

Back at the depot Steve's mood lifted, when Sid handed him a small brown envelope, his first week's pay packet. With the envelope securely tucked in the breast pocket of his jean jacket and recovered from the effects of Thursday's overindulgence, Steve felt that a trip to Miller's was in order to try and track down the jazz guitar tuition book that the guy at the Portland had recommended. What was the point of slogging around the streets of Cambridge delivering pints of milk if he couldn't spend a bit of his earnings? This line of reasoning was completely at odds with the idea of saving up to pay his college bill and have enough to put down as a deposit on the Ainsworth Street house, but with the scent of an introduction to the mysteries of jazz guitar in his musical nostrils, Steve ignored any such misgivings.

He chained his bike at the end of the street and went into Miller's. Did they have a jazz guitar tutorial by Jed Morgan? They certainly did. The sales assistant leafed through a rack of music books and handed Steve a bright blue A4 softback book sporting an idiosyncratic layout; title set slantwise at the top left of the cover in a typewriter typeface over a series of mugshots of a black dude in shades fingering improbable chord shapes on an acoustic guitar, below that at the same angle as the title and hugging the right margin some text promising to tell you everything you needed to know to become an accomplished Jazz Guitarist (with initial capitals), all for 95p. For good measure, a red flash, at a disturbingly different angle from title and photos, proclaimed that the contents were new! And completely revised. How could Steve resist? He fished a pound note out of the brown envelope that the gaffer had given him and handed it over. No need to put the book in a bag.

Earlier cycling down King Street, he'd passed Garon Records, noted for its stock of jazz records and almost certainly the best place in Cambridge to find a Django Reinhardt LP. He left his bike in Sussex Street, walked back up King Street and entered the little shop which proved to be a cornucopia of what were to Steve obscure records. He went up to the counter and asked if they had any Hot Club LPs. They certainly did. The friendly gent behind the counter pointed to a section of the display racks. Steve realised that he didn't know the titles of the numbers he'd heard at the Portland. He'd hoped to act as if he were an aficionado, but on reflection no expert jazzer was likely to walk around with a jazz guitar tutor under his arm. He went back to the counter and admitted that he didn't know his way around Django's music. He had heard some played at the jazz club at the Portland a few nights before and would like to get to know the material better. The man was delighted to help. He introduced himself as Gavin and not only did he own the shop but he'd been at the same gig.

He picked a record out of the display bin and said he thought that particular one was a good place to start and had some of the numbers on it that the band at the Portland had played. Steve saw that it was called *Swing '35-'39, The Quintet of the Hot Club of France*. The record was on the Decca Eclipse label and the cover design featured a naïve illustration of a bow-tied violinist and a brilliantined guitarist in front of cartoonish palms all printed in sepia. Clearly none of the care or expense routinely lavished on run of the mill rock records had been deemed appropriate for an album of French gypsy swing jazz. Steve must have looked doubtful, because Gavin said that he could listen to it in the shop if he liked. Steve accepted the offer and was soon sure that it was just what he wanted. He slipped another note from his pay packet and accepted the proffered carrier bag into which he also tucked his copy of Jed Morgan. Gavin noticed the book and said, 'That seems to be where everyone who wants to play jazz guitar starts. It's not as easy as they make it sound on that LP. The key thing is to keep at it. And try and hang out with other guitarists. If you need any introductions, I can help. Come back soon.'

Steve stepped back onto the pavement, delighted with the morning's work. He was impatient to start on the book. Right next door to Garon Records was the Champion of the Thames pub, which had just opened for the lunchtime session. He could have a quick half and leaf through the book without being distracted by encounters back at the house. He entered the pub and felt it unseemly to order a mere half, so went for the full pint. He settled himself at a table and took the book out of the bag that Gavin had given him.

Lesson One was just two pages, five sparse paragraphs on the verso page and 26 chord charts on the facing page, all but two of which he had never encountered before. One of the chords was asterisked and the footnote declared that some chords had two or more names and that this would be explained in Lesson 19. Steve was already lost and without a guitar in his hands could not even attempt to finger the chord shapes. He flicked through the book and was dismayed to see that there was also a lot of traditional musical notation. He knew at once that the road to jazz guitar mastery was not going to be an easy one. Still, you had to start somewhere. He settled back to enjoy his pint. At least that was one thing that didn't need hours of practice. Or to be clear, many hours had already been applied to that particular art.

Back at the house Steve went up to say hello to Angie, who as usual was working at her desk. He came up behind her and kissed the back of her neck. She shivered in pleasure and then said, 'Steve, have you been drinking?'

Steve squirmed. 'I went to Miller's to buy a music book and then to Garon Records to get an LP of the kind of music I want to try and play . . .'

'Do I take that as a yes?'

'Well, the Champion of the Thames was right next door.'

'I'm sure he was, but that is still not an unequivocal answer.'

'I was just trying to explain why I needed to go into the pub called the Champion of the Thames. And you can't go into a pub and not buy a drink.'

'It seems to me that the life of the trainee alcoholic is nearly as complex as the that of the neophyte poet.'

Steve laughed. The two were perhaps more closely connected than she supposed.

'Anyway, let's have a coffee and I'll play you this new album.'

'What is it?'

'It's French swing jazz from the 1930s. It's amazing.'

'Well, it'll make a change from Pink Floyd. When did you get into this obscure branch of music?'

'The other night at the Portland. That's why I stayed so late. Nothing to do with Alan and Harry. There was a band playing this kind of music and I knew that I wanted to hear more. The guitarist on the LP is amazing. He plays an acoustic guitar. The runs are ridiculous and there is a violinist who is equally brilliant. The music is a French gypsy take on swing jazz.'

'I have to say that description doesn't sound any weirder than a lot of the music you're into. What's wrong with the Rolling Stones I'd like to know?'

They went downstairs, made some coffee and took their mugs into the sitting room. Steve took the disc reverently out of its sleeve and put it on the turntable. 'The first track is "Limehouse Blues".'

After some introductory crackles of surface noise a thin and scratchy sound filled the room, quite different to the dynamic range of the contemporary rock music they were used to, but within seconds the vibrant playing had engaged their attention. The violin took the first two choruses, serene to begin with while establishing the melody, guitars chugging in the background, then swinging for the first improvisation on the repeat. A spiky guitar figure at the turn-around for the second chorus hinted briefly at the fireworks to come, which were unveiled in earnest at the start of the third chorus with several bars of rapid strumming, before the lead guitar proceeded to tiptoe and pirouette spectacularly around the chord progression. On the fourth chorus the guitar took a different approach, spraying angular stabbing chords and fast runs at the listener, before violin and guitar shared the honours for the final chorus, with the violin winding proceedings up with another scorching riff.

The subsequent tracks on the first side of the disc maintained the same high level of musical wit and invention. Steve didn't think he'd ever heard anything quite like it. From an audiophile point of view the sound quality was poor, hardly surprising since the recordings dated back to the 1930s, but there was no mistaking the genius of the playing. He turned to Angie for her reaction. She didn't quite know what to think, but she realised that Steve had fallen in love.

'It's lovely, but maybe a little old-fashioned. One thing I find a little odd is that the first track is called "Limehouse Blues", but it doesn't sound like any kind of blues I know. And isn't Limehouse in east London? I suppose there might be some suburb of New Orleans or Chicago called Limehouse, but I can't believe there's anywhere in France called Limehouse. Limoges perhaps'

Steve, not for the first time, was taken aback by Angie's perspicacity. 'You know, you are absolutely right. It's not a blues at all and as for

Limehouse, I have no idea. I will have to look into it. But it's definitely jazz.'

'I wasn't aware that you liked trad jazz.'

'This isn't trad jazz. It's swing. The give away is the LP title *Swing '35-'39.*'

'I don't know the difference.'

Steve wasn't sure he knew the difference either, but decided to hazard a guess. 'That chugging effect from the guitars, with the stress on the offbeats is the signature swing sound. Swing has another meaning too, but that kind of swing is very much a zen-like category. It's hard to explain.'

'It don't mean a thing, if it ain't got that swing?'

Steve laughed, 'Quite. First track on side two.'

'Well, I don't know about the zen aspects of jazz, but maybe the chugging rhythm is a little relentless. That third track is so sad to begin with. The guitar sounds like its weeping and then breaks into a latin rhythm, but just before the end we get a quick burst of the inevitable chugging.'

Steve consulted the track listing. 'St Louis Blues. Yeah, but at least that one is a real blues, the tango section aside. And St Louis is definitely in the USA.'

'But named after a French king.'

'Okay, Miss Clever Clogs. In future I will make sure to do my research before passing myself off as a jazz buff.'

'Steve, I love your enthusiasms. I was just trying to contribute.'

Steve didn't doubt it, but he resolved to take his first steps with Jed Morgan in private.

DARK STAR VARIATIONS

Mawson Road
Saturday, 8 June 1974

DESPITE THE LESS THAN successful encounter in the Ancient Shepherds, Steve and Angie had decided to go to Jon's gig and had invited the rest of the Victoria Road gang. The venue for the gig was a church hall just off Mill Road. The hall had seen better days, but it was an ideal space for a gig, with a high pitched ceiling and a stage at one end. By the time the Victoria Road gang got there, there was already a decent sized crowd of assorted Cambridge hipsters standing around in groups. Steve noticed a screen-printed sign fixed to the notice board outside the hall which bore the legend, executed in swirly, psychedelic lettering, 'Jon Chapman and the Doodah Men present the Dark Star Variations'.

The Victoria Road crew went inside. Little Feat's *Dixie Chicken* was playing over the PA and people were chatting, laughing and smoking. There was no sign of the band, who were presumably backstage tuning their instruments and getting in the mood with a joint or two. The atmosphere was lighthearted, optimistic, anticipatory. Though entry was not free, the event was resolutely non-commercial, more like a happening from the previous decade than the expensive extravaganzas that had consumed the rock world more recently.

There was not anyone ostensibly in charge, no heavy security. It was just a group of young people gathering to smoke dope, listen to electric music and possibly hook up with a partner for later amorous adventures. For the most part people were dressed in flowing clothes, soft fabrics, silk scarves, the girls in long skirts or dresses, some with shawls, the boys wearing flared trousers and tight cotton shirts or tee shirts. For both sexes there was plenty of denim and indian embroidery.

It seemed like the band was never going to come on. No doubt they had slipped into an eddy in the spacetime continuum with one joint too many. But no one in the crowd seemed particularly perturbed. They were having a good time anyway. Eventually there was a disturbance to one side of the empty stage and the band ambled into the performing space and started plugging in. After a precisely calculated pause Jon joined them to cheers from several boys at the front of the hall and plugged his Strat into the stack of Marshall speakers which was nearly as tall as he was. He then moved to the front of the stage and hit an exploratory chord, as the record playing over the PA was faded down.

Jon stepped up to the microphone and spoke a few words. 'Thanks for coming, folks. Tonight's show has a bit more structure than our normal gigs. It's an explicit tribute to the Grateful Dead's "Dark Star". Many of you are probably familiar with the track of that name on the Dead's *Live/Dead* album. But what you might not know is that every time the Dead play it, they play it differently, the number is a launchpad for deep space exploration.

'Because the Dead are not breadheads and are utopian vanguardists they have no objection to members of the audience recording their performances. As a result quite a few of their gigs are circulating on tape. I am lucky enough to have acquired a number of these bootlegs and have made a close study of them. What we are going to do this evening is to present our own versions using riffs from four of the tapes as a starting point. There will be an interval roughly halfway through the evening. Before the interval we will present "Clouds of Delusion" followed by "Reflections of Matter". After the interval we will play "Lady in Velvet" and "Transitive Nightfall". We hope you dig the performance.'

And with that, Jon hit another chord and started to feel his way through the delusive clouds of the first variation, hitting long notes with lots of tremolo and distortion. The bass and keyboard players kept out of the way for the moment, waiting for Jon to establish the riff, while the drummer played the simplest of fills with the hi-hat and bass drum. Steve thought of it as musical fly-fishing. Patience was required as the lure was sent skittering across the sonic surface. And then suddenly there was some ripple in the continuum and Jon pounced, locking onto a riff and spinning it out between his fingers, at which point the bass, keyboard and drums settled in behind Jon's evolving figure, the bass picking it out in the lower register, the drummer injecting bounce into the groove and the keyboard adding in washes of sound.

The audience, who had been swaying gently to the freeform introduction were now galvanised and started spinning around, weaving their arms in tendril-like patterns. Once Jon was confident that the other musicians had locked onto the riff, he then started to improvise around it, producing increasingly abstract harmonies and rhythms. As the music spiralled to a crescendo the dancers became more extrovert chasing the thrill in the music until it disintegrated in a riot of feedback and cymbal crashes, indicating the end of that passage. Jon took a swig of beer and letting the dancers recompose themselves, stepped up to the microphone and said, 'OK. This one is "Reflections of Matter"'. He stepped back and set off again, feeling his way into the new riff, which, once hooked, he reeled in, sharing it with the rest of the band, whipping it up and finally landing it in an explosion of feedback. The crowd were ecstatic. The extroverts span and swayed in the centre of the hall, the introverts leaned against the walls and nodded, eyes half-closed, feet tapping.

After an hour Jon seemed to have run out of inspiration and the band took a break. They went backstage and had some beers and a joint and retuned the guitars. During this time the sound guy put Hawkwind's *Space Ritual* through the PA. After fifteen minutes or so the band came back and played for another hour, showcasing first 'Lady in Velvet' and then 'Transitive Nightfall' until the caretaker made his presence known and indicated that it was time to start winding down. There wasn't much protest, because, in truth, everyone was played or danced out.

Steve and Alan had been standing to one side of the stage for the second half of the performance and as the band's roadies started to unplug the amps, Alan said, 'Despite the new format, it sounded just like a regular Jon Chapman gig to me. I feel sorry for the new bloke he's got on bass. He looked as if he was really struggling. He thought he was joining a blues band and suddenly finds himself in a free improvisation outfit.'

Steve laughed. 'Yeah, he obviously wasn't stoned enough.'

At that point, Jon, who had been prowling the stage accepting plaudits from some of the more enthusiastic members of the audience, spotted Steve and Alan, crossed the stage in their direction and jumped down to join them.

'Hey guys, thanks for coming. You should have brought your axes. You could have plugged in.'

Alan shrugged. 'You were doing fine without us.'

Jon took that as a compliment and then addressing Steve said, 'Hey man, sorry about the vibe the other day in the pub. Ginny and I were in the middle of a heavy scene. You know how chicks can be.'

Steve thought it would be inappropriate to confirm such generalities, but accepted the apology.

Adopting Jon's mode of discourse, he said, 'Cool, man, no problem. I was just trying to find a way of getting out of walking all the way to Ely.'

Jon could dig that and nodded sympathetically. 'So are you guys still up in Victoria Road?'

Alan confirmed that this was the case. 'Yeah, but only until the end of the month when the lease comes to an end. And then we're all going our separate ways. I'm off to the south of France with Di.'

Jon was impressed. 'Cool. Where are you off to Steve?'

'I'm staying in Cambridge. I've got a job here.'

'Groovy. What are you doing?'

'I'm a milkman.'

'Woah, heavy duty. When do you start?'

'I've already started. Up at four-thirty every morning.'

'Crazy. So where are you going to be living when the Victoria Road gaff comes to an end?'

'Angie and I are getting a place in Ainsworth Street.'

'Angie's your chick, right? The beautiful blonde chick in the pub?'

'Yeah.'

Jon suddenly seemed to become distracted and said that he was neglecting Ginny. He should go and find her and with that made his way through the thinning crowd. Steve and Alan exchanged glances, both more than a little surprised by this sudden evidence of gallantry on Jon's part.

When Jon was out of earshot, Alan said, 'So you've persuaded Angie to stay?'

'No, but I'm still hoping she'll come around to the idea.'

* * *

A while later, Steve decided that he ought to be getting home. It was already past his optimal bedtime. What the others chose to do was up to them. But he could hardly leave without checking if Angie wanted to go back with him. He went in search of her and was surprised to find her in conversation with Jon and Ginny, who seemed to be hanging on her every word. At Steve's approach, Jon waved him into the group. Steve found himself standing next to Ginny, who scarcely registered his arrival and continued to focus her piercing gaze on Angie. He had got used to the fact that on the handful of occasions that he had previously encountered Ginny she had studiously ignored him, but he was fazed by the electrical charge that was now crackling between the two women. Jon caught Steve's eye and said, as if he were making an indecent proposal, 'Ginny was just suggesting to Angie that we four go and get something to eat.'

What on earth was going on here? This was a major turnaround from the encounter in the Ancient Shepherds. Whatever it was, Steve needed to head back to Victoria Road and said, 'We'd love to, but we have to get to bed.'

Ginny appeared to experience a frisson of pleasure, '*Ooh!*'

Steve wished he'd chosen his words more carefully, but at least she seemed to have registered something he'd said. Even so he was finding the whole tone of the conversation a little odd. Were they on drugs? Well, of course, they were. They were always on drugs.

'No, nothing like that. I have to get up at four-thirty tomorrow morning.'

This was clearly incomprehensible to Ginny. Jon needed to help her out.

'Steve's got a job as a milkman. He needs to pull some bread together quickly.'

Ginny was not convinced. 'But it's Sunday tomorrow.'

Steve pointed out that the Co-op dairy delivered milk every day of the week and that this was his first week. He was learning the round from an experienced roundsman, so he needed to be on time. Ginny pouted and seemed to be disconsolate. There were hugs and kisses all round.

As Steve and Angie were turning to leave, Jon said to Steve, 'How about you and me having a drink in the Locomotive tomorrow at lunchtime? I assume you've finished your job by then.'

Steve was reluctant to come across as churlish, particularly having turned down the invitation to get something to eat and found himself agreeing to the proposal.

Later on their way back to Victoria Road, Angie slipped her arm through Steve's and said, 'Well, that was an interesting evening, Jon and Ginny are actually quite a nice couple, when you get to know them.'

Steve wasn't so sure *nice* was the right word.

Angie continued, 'I knew you wouldn't be able to go and get something to eat with them. They made the suggestion before you came over and joined us. So I invited them to next week's party. You don't mind, do you? They are your friends.'

Were they his friends? He wished now that he hadn't been so eager to greet them in the Ancient Shepherds. Still, Angie knew what she was doing and had every right to invite whoever she wanted to the party.

Later on as they were going to bed, Steve turned to Angie and said, 'This party next week has a cross dressing theme, right?'

'Yes, you know it does.'

'And you mentioned that when you invited Jon and Ginny?'

'No, it didn't occur to me to.'

'I can't see Jon feeling comfortable in a room with a bunch of blokes in dresses or donning an off-the-shoulder number himself.'

'Oh, I don't know. He carries himself rather well.'

Steve wasn't sure that he welcomed this evidence of Angie's appreciation of Jon's physique. Fortunately he was pretty sure that Jon and Ginny would give the event a wide berth once they became aware of the theme of the party.

The Sunday morning round passed without incident and with scarcely a word exchanged between Steve and Ron. When they were back at the depot Ron ceremoniously handed the logbook to Steve with a far from cheery, 'Don't screw it up.' Steve assured him that he wouldn't. Ron didn't look as if he had much faith in that promise, turned on his heel and disappeared out of the gates of the yard. Steve never saw him again.

Steve was relieved to be free of Ron's glowering supervision and immediately felt more optimistic about the course of the next few weeks. By the following Sunday he would have pulled together enough money for the deposit on the house in Ainsworth Street. And by the time he was due his first week off, he should have sorted things out with the college and the bank and, more importantly, resolved things with Angie about their joint futures. The only fly in the ointment was that he had still not found anyone with whom to share the rent. Surely he couldn't be the only recently graduated student who had decided to hang around in Cambridge for a few more months? He needed to put out some feelers. He wondered what Rob's plans were? Even if he did take on the house, the sublet was only for three months. If his plans to linger in Cambridge turned out to be misguided, there was still time for him to tack around to Angie's suggestion and relocate with her to Edinburgh.

He was about to jump on his bike and cycle back to Victoria Road, when he remembered that he had agreed to meet Jon in The Locomotive at lunchtime, an arrangement he now regretted, since he still had a couple of hours to kill until opening time. It seemed pointless to go home first and then come out again. It would be better to pick up a copy of *The Observer* and catch up with the news in the sunshine on Parker's Piece. He bought a copy from a little newsagent at the bottom of Mill Road and then wheeled his bike across the main road and found a sunny spot on the vast acreage of grass. It was a lovely morning, bright and warm. He sat down on the grass and opened his newspaper. But the combination of a late night, early start and Ron's energetic approach to milk delivery soon made him feel drowsy.

He stretched out on his side and was just about to nod off when out of the corner of his eye he caught sight of an attractive woman in a yellow and brown velour track jacket and very brief shorts in the same material jogging across the green not far away from him. He was admiring her easy gait and the effect it had on her figure, when he realised with a shock that it was Grace Mitchell, who had supervised him in modern French thought and literature.

Grace was one of the younger members of the modern languages faculty and had had a refreshingly informal approach to the pedagogical relationship. She was probably 15 years or so older than Steve, but she was definitely fanciable and had seemed not unaware of the effect she had on Steve, who, from time to time, had shared with Alan some distinctly school-boyish observations on her anatomy. Watching her now, bounding across the sward in her skimpy running kit, he was more than a little gratified to have those observations confirmed. Should he try and catch her eye or pretend not to have noticed her? It might be a little embarrassing to be caught ogling his former teacher. She, however, seemed lost in her own thoughts, oblivious to the concupiscent former student sprawled on the grass at her feet. And so, Steve decided to shrink further behind his strategically placed newspaper and let her pass.

This time he really did nod off and when he woke a little later and checked his watch, he saw that it was only a quarter of an hour before opening time. He gathered up his things and wheeled his bike back up Mill Road, chaining it up outside The Locomotive just in time for the landlord to open the doors. Steve bought himself a pint and one for Jon. He put a few coins in the jukebox and selected several classics, including Dylan's 'If You Got To Go, Go Now', The Stones' 'Honky Tonk Women', Hendrix's 'Cross Town Traffic' and Traffic's 'No Face, No Name, No Number'. He then sat down at a table and returned to his newspaper. It wasn't long before Jon sashayed into the pub and slid into the seat beside Steve. 'Hey, man. Thanks for coming last night.'

Steve pushed the pint of beer towards Jon, who accepted it gratefully.

'It was a great gig. We had a good time.'

'Were you up in time for your round?'

'Yeah, milk all delivered. From tomorrow I'm on my own.'

'Trusting you with the horse and cart?'

Steve laughed. 'Yeah.'

Jon took a mouthful of beer. 'So, that chick of yours is not only hot, but a smart cookie too.'

'Yeah I struck lucky there. When I first met her I thought she was way out of my league.'

'No way. I'm sure you're a bit of a lady killer. Ginny certainly thinks so.'

Steve flinched at the inappropriateness of the term and the improbability that Ginny had any view of him at all.

'I hardly think so, Jon.'

'No man. It's true. Play your cards right ...'

Jon left the sentence unfinished to Steve's relief. It was deeply weird to have someone like Jon more or less implying that if he chanced his arm with Ginny he would probably get some action.

Steve laughed uncomfortably. 'I've rather got my hands full at the moment.'

Jon sniggered, 'Know what you mean.'

If Steve had had any expectations of how the conversation with Jon might unfold, it had not included a frank exchange on the relative merits of their girlfriends. It was all a bit too nudge-nudge, wink-wink for Steve.

But Jon had other fish to fry and, changing the subject, said, 'So we're looking forward to this party. Thanks for the invite.'

Steve was more convinced than ever that it had been a mistake on Angie's part to invite them and seized on the opportunity to put them off.

'Yeah, it should be a gas. It's going to be one of those cross-dressing things. I hope you don't mind making an effort.'

He assumed that Jon, who came across as decidedly macho, would disapprove of the namby-pamby way of flibbertigibbet students, but he couldn't have been more wrong. Apparently that was right up Jon and Ginny's street. Jon would leave the details of his outfit to Ginny. She was great at that sort of thing. Steve struggled to imagine what Jon would look like in women's clothing. Sure, he was slim and had beautiful, long hair, but he was also fairly muscular and far from androgynous. On the other hand Steve didn't have much confidence in his own androgyny. With luck, Jon was just doing his best not to lose face and in the event they wouldn't turn up.

Jon said that he'd get some more drinks in. A few minutes later he returned with two new pints and said, 'I wanted to talk to you about this house in Ainsworth Street you and Angie are moving into. What would you think about Ginny and me sharing with you?'

What Steve thought was that it would be a terrible idea. But he had to admit that it would solve the problem of finding someone to share the rent. On the other hand, Jon and Ginny would have been at the bottom of any shortlist of potential sharers, in fact they would probably not have made it onto a shortlist. He could hardly put it like that though and confined himself to, 'Well, it's a thought, but I'm not sure that Angie will be keen on sharing. She's had enough of that in Victoria Road.'

Jon did not seem in the least discouraged. 'Of course, but there's been quite a lot of you there. It should be easier with just two couples. And it'll make the rent more affordable.'

Playing for time, Steve said, 'The other problem is that I've given Al and Di first refusal.'

He suddenly realised that he'd made a tactical mistake mentioning that Al and Di had first refusal, because it implied that he had nothing against sharing with another couple per se.

Jon was into the opening like a flash. 'Cool. When do they need to decide?'

'Two weeks today.'

That wasn't true, but Steve needed time to sort things out.

'That suits us fine.'

Steve cursed himself. He'd played this all wrong. They were already talking practicalities rather than possibilities. On the other hand if Angie was adamant about going to Brighton, he might need to accept Jon and Ginny as co-tenants.

Wanting to understand Jon and Ginny's situation better, he asked, 'So what's the position with your current arrangements? How much notice do you need to give?'

'None,' was the prompt reply. 'The landlord wants us out pronto.'

Steve was saved from having to ask for further details by Jon adding, 'He's okay. But he's been getting grief from neighbours about how loud the music is.'

That didn't sound like a recommendation and Jon realised he needed to say something to adjust the negative perception. 'I wouldn't be moving the big amps and speaker cabs in. Or at least not for long. I'm going to be playing a few festivals around the country over the summer, so I'll leave them with the roadies. And that also means that we'll be away for quite a few days on the festival circuit.'

That did put things in a slightly better light. Steve thought it might take the pressure off him, if he made out that it was Angie who had the last word on such matters. 'I'll talk to my old lady about it. She's the one who calls the shots when it comes to the home front.'

Jon nodded sagely. 'Don't I know it, man?'

Keen to change the subject, Steve returned to the pieces that Jon had showcased at the previous night's gig and said, 'Tell me some more about the Dark Star bootlegs.'

'It's not just the Dark Stars, the entire sets were recorded by public-spirited deadheads. But there is so much material that you have to have some kind of focus and mine is "Dark Star", as it is for many people. I'm part of a network of people who tape Dead gigs. I've been lucky enough to go to most of their British gigs. The first one I did was at a festival in Stoke-on-Trent in 1970. I was lucky enough to be able to jack into the PA mixer.'

Steve found it hard to associate the Dead with one of the five towns of the Potteries. 'Stoke-on-Trent?'

'Yeah, it was called the Hollywood Music Festival. Crap name, really; but great lineup - Black Sabbath, Free, Mungo Jerry, Family, Traffic among others, and of course the Dead.'

'Mungo Jerry must have felt a bit out of their league.'

'Yeah, you always have to have a bit of pop at these things. But 1972 was the big year. That was the year that they did their big European tour, some of which is featured on *Europe '72*. I got three recordings that year. I was at the Bickershaw Festival, one of the Lyceum nights and one of the two Wembley gigs. I went to the first night at Wembley, but from what I hear I should have been at the next night. Deadheads say that that was one of the best ever versions of "Dark Star", moving seamlessly into "Sugar Magnolia".

'Once it became known that I had these tapes, I began to get offers to swap them for tapes of gigs I hadn't been at, mainly in the States, of course. So now I have quite a collection.'

'Don't the Dead object?'

'No, they encourage it. It reflects their own value system. They're progressives. It's a way for deadheads to enjoy the Dead's music outside the normal market channels. It can't last of course. At some point some real cool trader, some hip marketer will see the potential in the material and commercialise the best recordings. Unfortunately, that's how capitalism works. But in the meantime a few of us get to luxuriate in a prelapsarian musical playground.'

Steve was beginning to revise his view of Jon.

'And you've listened to them all?'

'Yeah, many times.'

Steve couldn't understand why you'd want to listen to what he assumed were poor quality bootleg recordings of gigs by a band as shambolic as the Dead for pleasure. Hardly any commercially released live albums bore repeated listening. But, had he been the headmaster of a school for rock aficionados, he would have given Jon full marks for application.

'Do the performances differ much?'

'Massively. From what I can work out the first phase culminated in the version on *Live/Dead*. The pattern of those versions is that they start with the Dark Star theme and then go into a jam before the vocal, after which they return to the theme, a new jam and then a second vocal before transitioning to the next song in the set. Later versions drop the second vocal but introduce what deadheads call *Space*, a very loose jam which feels like a sonic exploration of inner space, and then increasingly the *Tiger*, which is a passage of very fast play from Garcia and finally one or more jams, based on identifiable tunes or heads as the jazzers would call them. The "Feelin' Groovy" jam is a frequent one.

'Last night, we were trying to do a little of that. The problem is that you need a group of who have played a lot and trust each other. Sadly I can't seem to keep a bunch of guys together long enough to advance very far that way.'

Steve had had no idea that Jon's approached was so meticulous, almost academic. He felt guilty now about his mocking comments to Alan about Jon's playing at the end of the previous night's gig.

'I'd like to understand this a little better. Where do I start?'

'*Live/Dead* is a good start and then *Europe '72*. There's not actually a "Dark Star" on the latter, but it gives you a good idea of the live sound from that period. And then when Ginny and I move in with you, you can listen to some of my tapes. Now, if that's not an incentive, I don't know what is.'

Steve smiled. He'd walked straight into that one.

Soon enough it was two o'clock and the landlord was shouting 'Last orders.' Out on the street he took his leave of Jon who pressed him to get back to them about the idea of the house share as soon as possible. Steve promised that he would and unchained his bike.

Now that Steve no longer had to contend with Ron, he was able to relax a little. And since, unlike Ron, he was not hurrying on to another another job, it was not absolutely necessary to start on the dot, nor complete the round on the double. The only problem was that Ron had never entrusted Steve with driving the float. That meant that Steve had neither internalised the route, nor more importantly the best places to park. Nor, for that matter, had Ron allowed Steve to work out each day's consignment. Consequently Steve had given no thought to that aspect of the job. So on that first day on his own he had to spend fifteen minutes with the logbook working out how many crates of each kind of bottle he needed. To make matters worse he had arrived fifteen minutes after Ron's usual starting time. So he did not get to his first delivery point until more than half an hour after Ron would have done.

To begin with he was not been particularly worried to be running half an hour late. After all, hadn't the gaffer said that precise timekeeping was not required. But by the time he got to Hills Road he began to realise that there was some logic to Ron's approach. That half an hour made all the difference to the weight of the traffic, which in turn made it harder to find optimal parking spots. By the time Steve got to the flats it was nearly the time that Ron aimed to have the round finished on a non-collecting day. But Steve found doing the flats on his own not only took more time but was utterly exhausting. Eventually he limped back to the depot at eleven-thirty, a full two hours after Ron's benchmark time.

When he had offloaded the empties and parked the float at the charging station, he realised that he was going to have to drop off the logbook in the gaffer's cabin. With a bit of luck he had already gone home. He poked his head around the door and cursed under his breath at the sight of the gaffer sitting at his desk with the inevitable copy of *The Sun* open in front of him.

'What kind of time do you call this?'

Steve shifted uncomfortably and muttered, 'Sorry.'

'Not so easy on your own, is it?'

'No, the traffic was awful. Much worse than normal.'

'So, is that what you want me to say to people, when they phone up to complain about not getting their milk before they go out to work?'

'No, but I thought you said it didn't matter when I got back.'

'Yeah, but I didn't mean lunchtime.'

Steve promised to do better the next day and slunk out of the cabin.

Within a couple of days he had improved his running time considerably, mainly by getting much more strategic with his parking. On top of that his level of fitness was improving too, so that he had more energy at the end of the round.

But this mood of quiet satisfaction was punctured when he got back from his round on the Wednesday to find that the Finals results had been published. His housemates had all got the grades that they had expected. There was general rejoicing which of course called for a certain amount of overindulgence. Steve joined in enthusiastically. After all he too had got the grade he was expecting. But the truth was that he had hoped for something better even though the patchy attention he had paid to his studies did not warrant such hopes. Between the completion of the exams and the publication of the results he had slipped into a quantum mechanical situation in which he had both done well and not done well. But now the wave form had collapsed into the 2:2 that was probabilistically more appropriate.

He put a brave face on things, but found it hard to sleep that night and throughout his round the following day he was not able to clear his mind of pointless self-recrimination. He was reluctant to return to the house whilst he was stewing in such thoughts for fear that he reveal his disappointment to his friends. He decided to go to a pub to try and recalibrate his mood by the wholly ludicrous, but time-honoured, means of drowning his sorrows. Conscious of the fact that The Loco was Jon's local and reluctant to go the Perch or any of the pubs frequented by Al and Harry, he dropped in at the Six Bells in Covent Garden, a pub that as far as he knew none of his circle frequented.

He settled himself in a corner, unfolded his newspaper and started to read. He had not got very far with his survey of the dismal state of the world when he heard his name being called. This is exactly what he had been trying to avoid. He looked up, doing his best to conceal the irritation he felt at this intrusion when he was feeling so miserable, to see Robin, his poetry buddy.

Rob sat down on the other side of the table and said,'Haven't seen you for a while.'

Steve didn't really want to go into detail, but Rob was a decent guy. 'I'm working. Needed to pull some money together.'

'What kind of job enables you to be in a pub at eleven o'clock in the morning?'

'I'm a milkman.'

'Steve, you never lose your capacity to surprise. I too start a job here in a couple of weeks, but nothing so exotic.'

'What have you got lined up?'

'Ususal thing. Teaching at a language school. All those lovely French and Italian girls.'

Steve wondered for a moment why he wasn't doing something similar, until he remembered that that was exactly what Angie had suggested, albeit in Brighton. 'I can't be doing with beautiful European teenagers, I'm much more of a middle-aged housewife in curlers and slippers at six-thirty in the morning kind of man.'

Rob laughed at the surreal vision. 'I hope this is all going into your writing.'

'Ha! The chance would be a fine thing. Haven't wielded the bardic nib for months.'

'Well, if I recall correctly, last time we met, you said that you were doing something quite different from your usual jewel-like miniatures, a long poem with some obscure title, which you promised to show me, but the pages never materialised.'

Steve groaned inwardly. That fucking poem! What had he been thinking of, going around talking about it before it was finished?

'Yeah, I'm sorry about that, but I'm not sure it's ready for any kind of public showing yet. What about you? How's your stuff going?'

'I'm rather pleased to say that Intrinsic Spin have just issued my first pamphlet.'

Steve was shocked. It was one thing to have had a few pieces published in small magazines, but to have had a pamphlet put out by an imprint as hip as Intrinsic Spin was something of a coup. He was grateful to Robin for his encouragement, but Steve had always felt that he was one step behind him. Now he felt that he was several steps behind. He did his best to conceal his dismay and offered his congratulations, which Robin waved away.

'As a matter of fact, I have a copy of the pamphlet with me.'

That was so typical of Robin. He was a shameless promoter of his own material. It was not often that he didn't have copies of his most recent work tucked into his capacious shoulder bag.

Steve made a half-hearted attempt to avoid having to take the pamphlet. 'I'd much rather buy a copy. I am sure there are those more deserving of a complimentary copy.'

Robin was not to be deflected, some of the poems had been influenced by Steve, apparently, a suggestion that Steve did not for one moment believe. Robin pulled a slim volume out his bag and, before handing it to Steve, wrote on the title page *For Steve Percival, a brother in iambics*. An inscription, that old trick. How could he now not take the darn thing?

He thanked Robin with as much enthusiasm as he could muster. Looking at the cover he saw that the book was entitled *Soundings*. Good title, damn it.

'And Steve, I mean it, I'd like to see your long poem. I have acquired some good contacts and I might be able to get an extract published somewhere.'

Steve protested that the poem wasn't at that stage yet, but Robin said that the writer was not best placed to judge his own work. Steve conceded the point quietly and then tried to change the subject by opening the copy of *Soundings* and leafing through it. It looked good, crisp layout and a nice typeface. He felt despondent, but had the grace to say that he looked forward to reading it properly. Robin suggested they meet again when he had done so, then said brightly, 'So, how's Angie?'

'She's fine. She did really well in her Finals and is starting a PhD course at Edinburgh in a couple of months' time.'

'Amazing, that's where I'm off to myself.'

Steve was puzzled. 'But I thought you were staying in Cambridge to do your PhD.'

'Things didn't quite go according to plan. But you know, I think it might be for the best. Edinburgh is an amazing city.'

Presumably Robin had not done quite as well in his Finals as he had hoped. To that extent they were both in the same boat. On the other hand, Steve wasn't doing a PhD anywhere. And to make matters worse not only would Angie and Robin be in the same city, but they would be members of the same academic department. Not that he had ever been aware of any signs of attraction between the two of them. In fact so far as Steve knew, Robin had never had a girlfriend. Even so, this was not a development he welcomed.

As he tried to peer into the cloudy crystal ball of his apprehensiveness, he realised that Rob was still talking. 'What about you? How did you get on?'

Steve refocused. *Oh fuck it. Might as well get it over and done with.* 'Bang on target, 2:2.'

'Nicely played, sir. Achieved without lifting a finger. One of that select number who really don't give a toss for grades, all the more remarkable in your case, given that, if I'm not mistaken, you are not the heir to a mighty fortune.'

Steve laughed at Rob's deftness of touch. He felt like giving him a hug and wished he'd been more gracious about *Soundings*. On an impulse he said, 'Hey, Rob, we're having a big party on Saturday, last one in the shared house. It'd be great if you could join us.'

'I'd love to. That's the house in Victoria Road, right?'

'Yeah. Just one thing. There's a cross-dressing theme. Not obligatory, but you know . . .'

'Going out on a high?'

'That too.'

'Count me in.'

Rob stood up and said that he needed to be getting on. He was doing the rounds of Cambridge's fledgling poets before they dispersed for summer, but he'd see Steve and the others on Saturday. He hooked his pamphlet laden bag over his shoulder and left the pub with a cheery wave.

Unaccountably, Steve already felt in a much better mood. He always dreaded encounters with Rob and yet he invariably came away from them feeling better about things and in particular feeling better about himself. Rob was a generous spirit and he also treated Steve's work seriously. Steve could learn a thing or two from Rob.

Back at Victoria Road Steve went up to his room and took Rob's pamphlet out of his bag. He lay on the bed and read it through. In the way of poetry pamphlets, it wasn't actually that long, but to his dismay it really was quite good, not uniformly so, but enough to make him feel downright envious. It was now going to be tricky the next time he bumped into Rob. If it hadn't been very good, he wouldn't have thought twice about saying how much he had enjoyed it. That kind of white lie was entirely acceptable. But the fact that it was impressive, paradoxically made it harder to be generous and calibrate the praise appropriately. He read it again and it held up on a second reading. He put it to one side and brooded.

THE LAST PARTY

Victoria Road
Saturday, 15 June 1974

IF, DURING THE COURSE of his first week with Ron, Steve had improved the way that he negotiated the streets, one thing he had not yet done on his own was collect payment. When he totalled up the takings for his first Friday on his own, he was dismayed to find that it was far less than Ron routinely achieved. That meant that he was going to have to put a lot more effort into the Saturday collection. The gaffer grumbled when he got back to the depot late on the Saturday, but moderated the ticking off when he saw how much Steve had improved on the previous day's amount. But the extra effort left Steve exhausted. He went straight up to the bedroom when he got home and in Angie's unexpected absence lay down on the bed and immediately fell asleep.

He was awakened a couple of hours later by Angie entering the room. She greeted him brightly and said that she had picked up the things that they needed for that evening. Steve didn't know what things she was talking about.

'The outfits for the party tonight.'

In the panic to improve his takings on the round, Steve had completely forgotten about the party. He sighed. He'd rather not have to deal with that right now, but Angie said they needed to sort their clothes out before going down to help the others get the food and drink ready for the evening. She knew that he had been working but it wasn't fair to leave it all to the others.

78

Angie laid the things that she had acquired from Tiger Lily on the bed and added to them a number of items from the wardrobe. Steve watched this procedure from the bed in a mood of uncooperative truculence, a mood that quickly evaporated when Angie stripped down to her knickers. She had bought a pair of trousers that were a close match to the colour of Steve's suit jacket and just about fitted her in the leg, but not around the waist. Steve said he had a belt she could use. He got off the bed and while rummaging for the belt came across a pair of braces. Would they be any good? He tossed them over to her and watched as she attached them to the waistband of the trousers and hooked them over her shoulders and her bare breasts.

Steve let out a low whistle. 'My God, you look sexy.'

Suddenly he felt a little more engaged in the project. He moved towards her, reaching for her breast. She slapped his outstretched hand away. 'Not now. And I am not going to the party topless. Let me try your jacket on.'

Steve was not particularly broad in the shoulders so the jacket was a much better fit. Experimentally, Angie did the middle button up. 'Nah, leave it undone,' said Steve studying her carefully.

'I can see you're enjoying this, which if you don't mind me saying is a bit premature. So you'd better let me try your white shirt on.'

Steve fished out his good white shirt from the wardrobe. The real problem was that, apart from the fact that it was none too clean and rather crumpled, it didn't fit Angie across the bust or around the neck.

'What about if you don't wear a shirt at all, but keep all the buttons done up.'

'Steve, I know what you're getting at.'

'No, seriously. Try it.'

Angie gave it a go and had to admit that it did look much better without Steve's grubby shirt, but insisted that she would have to wear *something* under the jacket. She had a white silk camisole somewhere. Maybe that would do the trick. She rummaged in the small chest of drawers and soon found what she was looking for. She removed Steve's jacket and slipped the flimsy garment over her head, a procedure that Steve observed with considerable pleasure. She then put the jacket back on and looked at herself again in the mirror, deciding that that would do.

The shoes were the next problem. Steve's smart black shoes, which had seen very little wear in the previous three years were far too big, but Angie had a pair of flat brogues. She put them on and then peered at herself in the mirror again. 'What do you think?'

'Perfect. Once you put your hair up. Admittedly you don't look much like a guy, but you look sexy as hell.'

Angie spun around in pleasure. 'Okay, you're turn now. Get those things off.'

Steve stripped off down to his underpants. Angie had bought a long grey skirt at Tiger Lily and handed it to Steve. 'Try that on. I've got a back up if it doesn't fit.'

Despite the fact that the zip couldn't be pulled all the way up, it was a reasonably good fit in the length. Angie found a safety pin in a little pot on the mantelpiece and decided that would solve things as long as Steve didn't dance too energetically. The bigger problem was that, although long, it only came to mid-calf on Steve, revealing his far from glabrous calves.

Angie had a solution. 'You'll have to wear some tights. I've got some which are slightly opaque.'

Steve wasn't keen on wearing tights. Angie told him to stop being so ridiculous and handed him the pair of tights. 'Take the skirt off and put these on.'

Steve did as he was told, but then got himself into a terrible tangle getting them on. Angie couldn't help laughing at his clumsy efforts. It was now her turn to tease him. 'Very nice,' she said, admiring the bulge of his crotch. 'It enhances your manhood. Very Rudi Nureyev.'

He executed what he imagined was a *plié* to cover his embarrassment. Angie laughed at his ungainly attempt. 'Rudi has nothing to fear, when it comes to the terpsichorean arts.'

But he could tell from the look on her face that she wasn't satisfied with the look or the fit. 'The problem is your underpants are creating a very visible ridge. I think you're going to have to take them off or put something less structured on underneath.'

Steve bridled. 'I am not going to wear a pair of your knickers.'

'In that case just wear the tights. They should keep everything under control.'

Steve protested in vain. A few moments later feeling self-conscious with the skirt hitched up, he removed the offending undergarment and struggled back into the tights. He smoothed the skirt down, conscious now that the way it was tailored at the front was not intended to accommodate the male anatomy. Maybe he should wear something a bit looser, but Angie dismissed his worries and handed him a lacy blouse to try on. He put it on. Not only was it far too tight, but the cut, designed to accentuate a cleavage, merely revealed a triangle of chest hair. Angie ran her hand experimentally over his silk clad chest. He felt a familiar stirring in his loins and said, 'See what I mean. About the skirt.'

She kissed him on the side of the neck, 'Well, you'll just have to make sure to control yourself.'

Steve thought it was a bit much to expect that kind of bodily self-control from a twenty-one year old male, but Angie was more focused on the problem of what he should wear on top, not whether the contours of his manhood would be obvious through the thin fabric of the skirt. She searched through the pile of garments and handed him a tight fitting sweater, suggesting he try that instead of the blouse. As Steve swapped the sweater for the blouse, Angie circled him slowly, adjusting the ensemble. 'Not necessarily sexier, from my point of view, but probably more practical. And your hair is fine, apart from the fact that it needs a wash and a brush. But seeing that we've managed to cover up the hair elsewhere on your body, I think you also need to get rid of that stubble.'

So that was the outfits sorted. They started to get undressed, but this time they both felt aroused. When Angie had removed the jacket and camisole, Steve cupped her breast with one hand and kissed her neck under her long golden hair. This time she didn't push him away. She slipped her hand inside the waistband of the tights. One thing led to another and before long they were both asleep in each other's arms. It was the middle of the day and there was a party to cater for.

A couple of hours later, after a post-coital nap and a bath, Steve and Angie descended to a jocular chorus of disapproval. Party preparations were in full swing and the crew were at their familiar stations. Jez was rustling up hash brownies, Di and Jackie were making salads, Harry was eating a thick cheese and ham sandwich and Alan was strumming his guitar.

'Nice of you to decide to come down and join us,' said Di.

Angie attempted an apology. 'We were getting our clothes sorted out for this evening.'

'And we got ourselves in a bit of a tangle,' added Steve with a wink.

Angie elbowed him in the ribs. But Harry had picked up the innuendo. 'A new line in foreplay, eh?'

Angie giggled and tried to change the subject. 'What can we do to help?'

Di suggested that they might push the furniture in the sitting-room back, find some silk scarves to cover the lamps and put out some candles.

By five o'clock everything was pretty much ready. The hash brownies were ready to eat. Jez thought it would be a good time to sample them, because the full effect might take an hour to come on, but warned the others not to be greedy because he thought they might be rather strong. Steve was working the next day and Jez's space cakes, even the everyday kind, were notorious, so, reluctantly, he declined to sample them. But all the others happily snacked on the cookies and after complimenting Jez on his culinary skills, not normally much in evidence, went up to their respective rooms to change for the party. A little later they reassembled in the sitting-room, whereupon a period of hilarity ensued as they considered the relative merits of their respective attempts at crossdressing.

Harry was over six foot and broad in the shoulders. There was little that resembled female deportment in his manner and whilst he was clean shaven and had beautiful long thick hair, his thighs and calves were verging on the Herculean. Meanwhile Alan who was also clean shaven, but somewhat less stocky than Harry was just as devoid of feminine elegance. Both of them looked a little awkward, more like a couple of blokes auditioning for parts as the Ugly Sisters in a panto than David Bowie impersonators. But Steve deployed his long straight hair which Angie had brushed out after their bath to considerable effect and whilst he could hardly be said to be projecting femininity either, there was a definite air of androgyny about his costume. Jez had declined to participate in the project, partly because he wasn't currently in a relationship, so he lacked a female partner with whom he could swap clothes. In any case, his everyday style of dress while not extending to skirts or sarongs was sufficiently exotic to not seem out of place on this particular evening.

But the girls looked great. They were all in dark suits and following Angie's lead had decided not to wear shirts. Steve wondered whether they too were wearing camisoles or had decided to do without. With their hair up they looked like they might be part of an act from a Weimar Republic era cabaret performance. None of them could have passed for a man, but they were enjoying trying out what might be thought of as masculine gestures, swaggering gaits, splayed knees when sitting down and so on.

Jez put the Stones' *Exile on Main St* on the hifi and everyone started dancing, losing themselves in the music and enjoying the sweep and hang of unfamiliar garments. Normally it was the boys who would imitate Jagger's strut, but now the girls joined in too. And the hash cookies were beginning to have a decided effect. The tempo dropped with 'Shake Your Hips' and 'Casino Boogie' giving everyone a chance to catch their breath after the adrenaline rush of 'Rocks Off' and 'Rip This Joint' and an opportunity to demonstrate a more sinuous style of dancing to match the groove. By the end of the side Di and Jackie took refuge on the bean bags. As they sipped drinks and nibbled crisps and peanuts, it was agreed that this was already one of the best parties that any of them had attended.

Then Jez pointed out that not a single guest had shown up. 'That's because it's not seven-thirty yet,' said Di, 'So the party hasn't really started.'

'Wow, man! Massive time dilation,' remarked Alan. 'I thought we'd been partying for ages.'

'Nice cookie, Jez.' This was Harry.

Steve was beginning to regret that he hadn't had one of the cookies, but at least Jez had rolled a joint, and he was soon pleasantly high, even if he was nowhere near as smashed as his friends.

'What a pity we invited other people,' said Angie. 'This is a great party just on our own.'

There was no dissent. Jez continued to spin the records and the gang resumed dancing. Everyone was in the moment, wrapped in his or her own thoughts. But these delirious reveries were soon shattered by the sound of someone knocking loudly on the front door. A tremor of anxiety ran around the room. Jez turned down the amplifier just in case it was a neighbour complaining about the noise. Not that they often had complaints. They were the end of the terrace, but the house on the connected side was occupied by an older couple. Or might it be the police? It was easy to become paranoid when you were as stoned as the housemates now were on Jez's overstrength hash cookies. Since he was not as high as the others, Steve was despatched to answer the door.

He opened it gingerly and peered around the half-open door. A smiling young man stood on the doorstep. 'Hi, I've come to the party.'

Steve was momentarily tongue-tied. He didn't recognise the guy. That in itself wasn't strange, but in his stoned state he didn't have the presence of mind to elicit his name or which housemate had invited him. All he could manage was, 'Oh yeah, man. Come in.'

He opened the door fully and beckoned him in. The new arrival was about to step inside, then halted. He had caught site of Steve in the splendour of his feminine attire and seemed nonplussed. Steve had forgotten that he was somewhat unconventionally dressed and was puzzled by the guy's hesitation. Maybe he'd come to the wrong house. After all there must have been many parties getting going in Cambridge on that particular evening. As they both hovered, one either side of the threshold, Steve found himself saying that there was plenty of food and drink. This seemed to reassure the newcomer and he stepped inside, keeping as far away from Steve as was possible in the narrow hallway. Steve shut the door behind him and followed the guy into the sitting-room.

The newcomer hesitated in the doorway. Steve looked past him into the room and saw his strangely clad friends staring at the door open-mouthed with puzzlement. Not a single one of them greeted the newcomer, because no one seemed to know him. It was beginning to look as if he was a complete stranger to all the housemates. How could that be? Surely at least one of them must know him? Or at least recognise him? It was as if everyone, including the newcomer, was frozen to the spot. Steve could see the funny side of the situation, but also realised that the longer it persisted, the more it was likely to puncture the earlier mood of hilarity.

He pushed the newcomer gently in the back. 'The clothes. Just a thing we're doing for the party,' he said quietly. The newcomer gulped slightly and nodded.

Steve asked him what he'd like to drink.

'A beer, please.'

Steve went into the kitchen and poured a beer. When he came back into the sitting-room, Jez had put something a bit quieter on the hifi. The newcomer was standing by the fireplace looking decidedly uncomfortable. No one was talking to him. In fact no one was talking, period. Steve handed him the drink, at which point there was another knock on the door. The others were still frozen. Steve went out into the hall again and this time threw the door open to reveal a young woman holding a bottle of wine, which she pushed in his direction.

'Oh, thanks,' he mumbled. 'Come in.'

Once again he had no idea who the new arrival was. Had they somehow only managed to invite people they didn't know? Or had the dope somehow destroyed the innate human ability to recognise people? He indicated the door to the sitting-room. As they entered, several pairs of eyes swivelled in the direction of the new arrival, but not one of them seemed to know her. Even more weirdly, no one seemed to have regained the power of speech. What the hell was going on?

The first arrival was still by the mantelpiece sipping his beer nervously. Steve asked the female newcomer what she would like to drink and went out to the kitchen to get her a glass of wine. What were they going to do? This had the makings of a very weird scene. He returned with the glass of wine to find that nothing had changed, except the two guests were now conversing quietly with each other. Thank goodness that Jez was keeping the music going or it really would have been unbearable. He went over to Angie and gave her a sickly smile. 'Who are they?' she asked.

'Haven't got the foggiest,' he replied.

The atmosphere which only a short while before had seemed so light-hearted had now become rather sinister. Steve wasn't sure how things were going to develop.

At that moment there was another knock on the door. Steve couldn't remember having volunteered to be doorkeeper. However, given the state the others were in, he felt obliged to do the honours. But if the next guest also turned out to be a complete stranger, he wasn't sure that he would be able to maintain his composure. He opened the door very slowly, peeped around it and was mightily relieved to see that it was Julie, a friend of Angie's.

'Boy, Julie, am I pleased to see you!'

'Is that some kind of come on?' she said lightly. 'I mean I don't mind, if it's cool with Angie.'

'No, no. It's just that everyone's who's turned up so far has been a complete stranger.'

Julie didn't seem to be able to process this statement, but now that she had had time to look Steve up and down asked, 'Are you wearing Angie's clothes?'

Steve nodded and giggled.

'Oh my God. You're high aren't you?

'Well, a bit,' Steve conceded.

'Is my friend Dave here yet. I told him to be here at seven-thirty. I thought I'd be here before him, but I got delayed.'

Steve had to admit that he didn't know whether Dave was there or not, but when they went into the sitting-room, it became clear from the look of relief on the face of the first guest that he knew Julie and was therefore probably Dave. He came over a gave her a kiss. Busking furiously as if he'd always known Dave's name, Steve said carefully, 'Dave, can I get you another beer, while I'm getting Julie a drink.' Dave nodded and Steve returned once again to the kitchen, deciding before he did anything else to have a drink himself.

It was starting to look as if it hadn't been such a good idea to throw a party. No, the party was a good idea, a celebration of three years' friendship. What had been a bad idea was to entrust the production of the space cakes to Jez. Harry who was an accomplished cook might have been a better choice. Steve perched on one of the stools in the kitchen and let his thoughts drift. It was nice to be out here in the peace and quiet. Why was he the only one doing anything? It was as if the others had become zombies. Suddenly he remembered that he was meant to be getting drinks. He got a beer and a glass of wine and headed back to the sitting-room.

When he stepped through the doorway, there had been a complete transformation. People were dancing and talking and several more people had arrived. He hadn't been aware of hearing further knocks on the front door. How long had he actually been in the kitchen? The more he thought about it, the harder it was to say. He spotted Julie and Dave and took their drinks over. 'Sorry, got a bit tied up.'

Dave seemed much more relaxed and flashed Steve a friendly smile. 'You should have said on the invitation that it was a transvestite party.' Steve said that they hadn't really planned it. It had just happened. As he drifted away from Julie and Dave, he noticed that the girl who had been the second arrival was now talking to Mike, a member of their circle. So, now the connections were accounted for. Steve decided that he had done enough hosting and found a corner where there was an empty chair and sat down and watched the party action. People seemed to be enjoying themselves. Thank goodness.

The music was less dance orientated now and he found himself being sucked into it, marvelling at the way he could hear every detail. What was it that was playing? Oh, yeah. It was *Naturally* by J. J. Cale. Boy, that guy sure knew how to create a vibe. He settled in his corner and got into the groove. The room continued to fill with people. He felt there'd be plenty of time later to talk to the people he knew. After a while he was conscious that someone had slipped into the chair beside him. It was Phil, their next-door neighbour. He was rolling a joint. When it was assembled, he lit it up, toked on it a bit and then offered it to Steve, who took a couple of hits and handed it back.

Having broken the ice, Phil said, 'Great party.'

Steve agreed. 'Tricky to get the mix right.'

They continued the desultory exchange, passing the joint back and forth. When Phil had stubbed the exhausted joint out, he leant across and said, 'Fancy a dance?'

Steve hesitated. He had no real objections to dancing with another guy, but it seldom arose following a formal invitation. It normally just happened on the dance floor. He turned his head in Phil's direction and looked quizzically at him. It suddenly occurred to him that Phil hadn't recognised him in his crossdressed transformation and was trying to pick him up. Steve wasn't sure whether to be appalled or amused. He decided to play it straight, as it were, and said that his feet were killing him and in any case you couldn't really dance to J. J. Cale. Phil seemed to take the refusal placidly and after a few more minutes drifted across to the other side of the room.

Steve went in search of Angie and when he found her, told her that Phil had been trying to pick him up. Angie laughed and said that he shouldn't feel deterred on her account.

Steve laughed at her deft response and pulled her towards him and said, 'Let's go upstairs.'

'But what about Phil?' she answered archly.

Just at that moment there was another knock on the door. Steve had no desire to resume his role as door person, but since no one else seemed to have heard this latest knock he went out into the hall. He readied himself to deal with the eventuality that it was another person unknown to him. But the greeting froze on his lips at the sight of Jon and Ginny standing on the doorstep. It was not so much that they had actually decided to come, it was the extravagance of their apparel. Ginny was dressed from head to toe in black leather, peaked cap to knee high boots. No insignia but an undeniable SS vibe, or a slimmer, slinkier version of Brando in *The Wild One*, with a better cap. But what really took Steve's breath away was Jon's get-up. He was in a full Mr Fish satin man dress and suede boots, a very close copy of the outfit that Bowie had worn on the cover of *The Man Who Sold The World*. It was as if Jon and Ginny had done a complete role reversal, which Steve supposed was exactly what the party was meant to be about.

Steve waved them into the hall and eventually recovered his composure enough to say, 'Glad you could make it.' By comparison with the glamour of the newly-arrived couple he felt distinctly dowdy and far from transgressive in skirt and jumper. At that moment Angie emerged from the sitting room to greet the new arrivals. Steve saw the look of amazement on Angie's face, who defter in her response than Steve, congratulated the couple on the triumph of their respective transformations.

Jon shrugged, 'We're old hands at this game. But you both look pretty cool, if this is your first time. Well, Steve looks pretty and you look cool.'

Angie glowed. 'We had to improvise. We didn't have much to work with. Whereas your outfits look as if they are made to measure. Where did you get the man dress?'

Jon bowed his head in Ginny's direction and opened his palm towards her in a somewhat theatrical manner. 'Ginny made it. There's not much she can't do with a sewing machine.'

Ginny accepted this plaudit with complete equanimity.

Steve pointed to the sitting room, 'The action's in here. I'll get you some drinks. Wine?'

'Sure, man,' was Jon's immediate response.

By the time Steve got back with the drinks, Jon had taken over joint rolling duties and Jez was cueing The Who's *Who's Next*. Pretty soon everyone was back on the dance floor including Jon and Ginny. Normally, they didn't do dancing. They were way too cool. If Jon wasn't playing guitar he tended to stand a little apart observing the dancers with wry amusement, which was Ginny's default mode in any event. But here was Ginny strutting in time to the music and cutting poses, with her hands in the pockets of her leather jacket. Meanwhile Jon was doing a series of pirouettes, letting the skirts of the man dress billow outwards, almost as if he were a slo-mo dervish.

After several more tracks, Ginny had had enough of dancing and collapsed onto the sofa next to where Angie was sitting and soon the two women were deep in conversation. Meanwhile Jon busied himself rolling another joint. Steve went out to the kitchen for some refreshment and found Julie there opening a bottle of white wine. She smiled at him and asked how it was that he was so sober, when his housemates were so smashed. As she filled their glasses, he explained about the ungodly hour at which he would be having to get up the next day, not long after the others were crawling into their beds, he imagined. In fact he'd be going up to bed shortly, if she'd like to come and kiss him good night.

Julie laughed. 'You're outrageous, Steve Percival. Just because you're wearing women's clothes, you think you can get away with anything.'

But she didn't say no and indeed moved a little closer to him. Throwing caution to the winds, Steve pulled her towards him and kissed her. She didn't resist and opened her mouth to his tongue. After a few moments, she pushed him away. 'Steve, Angie's my best friend.'

Steve felt chastened. 'Yeah, I know. I'm sorry.'

'And I'm here with Dave.'

'Yeah, but you have to admit there's a bit of a spark between us. Always has been.'

'It's a bit late to be telling me now, just as we're all going our separate ways.'

'Maybe our paths will cross again.'

'Well, if they do, make sure you're wearing a skirt and I might consider taking things further.'

With that she straightened her hair, picked up her glass and headed back into the heart of the party.

He gave her a few minutes and then followed her in. The Stones' *Sticky Fingers* was playing. There were now lots of dancers on the floor gyrating to the music and even though the french windows were open there was not much of a breeze. Angie and Ginny were still on the sofa chatting earnestly. Clearly it was now too warm in the room for a leather jacket and Ginny had taken it off to reveal a skimpy black lace top, which accentuated the very curves that the jacket had concealed. Angie still had her jacket on but had unbuttoned it. As the strains of 'You Gotta Move' faded away, the knot of dancers threw themselves on beanbags or retrieved their drinks and stepped through the french windows and into the back garden. Suddenly, the room was emptier.

Spotting that Jez had joined the exodus and gone out into the garden with a girl with wild hair and sooty eyes, Jon moved over to the hifi and searched through the pile of albums. A few minutes later the world-weary sound of the Velvet Underground's 'Sunday Morning' with its tinkling celeste figures filled the room. As if on cue, Ginny jumped up and pulled Angie to her feet. It seemed she loved this track and really wanted to dance. She shimmied into the centre of the floor and beckoned to Angie to join her. Angie didn't need much persuading, but before joining Ginny took off her jacket revealing her own camisole clad curves. The two women, one so dark and the other so fair, span and twisted around each other, the only dancers on the floor.

It was by now apparent that Jon had deposed Jez as master of ceremonies and had changed the whole mood, to the clear approval of those that remained in the living room. Their approval may also have had something to do with the floor show that Ginny and Angie were putting on, which had definitely introduced an element of eroticism into proceedings. Was this a foretaste of all tomorrow's parties?

It wasn't often that Jez ceded control to someone else. Normally he liked to be the one in charge of the vibe, but presumably he was getting some action with the girl with the wild hair. Steve wouldn't have minded a bit of action himself. Whilst the sight of his girlfriend smooching on the dance floor with another woman was quite a turn-on, he would have preferred to have been a participant rather than a disenfranchised observer. When 'All Tomorrow's Parties' had faded out, Jon switched to Lou Reed's 'Transformer', whereupon the hot couple were joined by other dancers, forcing them into closer proximity.

A few moments later, Jez appeared in the embrasure of the french windows with his arm around the girl with the wild hair. Steve wondered how he would take to having his role usurped by Jon, but he seemed completely unfazed. It looked like he had other matters on his mind. He guided the girl across the room and a moment or two later Steve heard their footsteps on the stairs. Jez must be taking her up to his room. And why not? Perhaps he should he have been a bit bolder with Julie, especially since Angie looked as if she was otherwise engaged.

These thoughts were interrupted by another knock on the door, but Steve had had enough of answering the door and refused to acknowledge the summons. He was much more interested in where things were going with Angie and Ginny. There was another knock. Alan, who was the only other resident in the front room at that moment, rose from the beanbag in which he was slumped and went out into the hall. He returned a few moments later grinning broadly followed by a tall figure carrying a large carpet bag and umbrella, face made up like a peg doll, a black boater festooned with flowers and cherries perched on an unconvincing wig, a high buttoned, ruffle-fronted blouse with a little red bowtie, and a peplum jacket over an ankle length maxi skirt from beneath which peeped red high heel shoes. It took Steve a moment or two to realise that the pantomime dame was in fact Rob. He went across to Rob and gave him a big kiss on his exaggeratedly rouged cheek. 'Amazing. You take first prize.'

Rob glowed with pride beneath the thick makeup. 'I thought I'd make a bit of an effort. The hardest thing to find was the carpet bag.'

'Did you walk here like that?'

'Of course. What would be the point otherwise?'

Rob never failed to surprise Steve. 'What would you like to drink?'

'Any white wine left?'

Steve went in search of a new bottle of white. As he did so there was yet another knock on the door. This was getting ridiculous. Surely no one could top Rob's get up? Whoever it was, had better be in full Carmen Miranda rig, turban overflowing with fruit, gold lamé dress and bare midriff. Steve threw open the front door to give ingress to the latest drag queen to arrive on the doorstep, but instead there stood a short, balding, middle-aged man, whom Steve recognised as their other next door neighbour. Could he help? The little man looked him up and down quizzically, then, drawing himself up to his full height, said, 'Well, look, Miss, I don't want to be a spoilsport, but it's getting late and the music is really quite loud. I know you young women like your pop music, but my wife is feeling rather poorly. Well, you know.' And then by way of an afterthought, 'I normally speak to Steve or Alan.'

Steve apologised profusely and said that he would turn it down right away, thinking, *He doesn't recognise me or realise I'm a bloke with long hair and a bit of makeup, dressed in my girlfriend's clothes.* But he felt that there was little to be gained from even trying to explain. Best just to carry on as if everything was completely normal. The neighbour beamed. Steve could have sworn that he also winked at him. Was he indicating complicity or that he understood what was going on? Or even worse that it was a brief glimpse of an erstwhile flirtatiousness?

Steve wished the diminutive and misguided gallant good night and closed the front door gently. He went back into the sitting room and turned the music down a little and then burst out laughing. After the protests had subsided, Steve explained that they'd had a complaint from their neighbour. No point in risking him complaining to the police. Angie asked him why he was laughing. He explained that when he had agreed to turn the music down, the neighbour had calmed down, called him Miss and winked at him as if to indicate that he was a bit of alright.

Once the mirth provoked by Steve's account and the subsequent ribald embellishments suggested by Al and Harry had abated, Steve decided that it was time for him to go to bed. He went over to Angie and told her that he was going upstairs to bed and that she could join him if she fancied a bit of stoned hanky-panky. She wasn't quite ready to go to bed yet, it seemed, but would join him shortly.

In the event, she eventually crawled into bed around three o'clock, too late for any amorous activity. Steve, in turn, crawled out of bed two hours thereafter and had to pedal furiously to the dairy. When he got back to Victoria Road after his round, the house was still in exactly the same state that it had been in at five o'clock in the morning. The smell of stale tobacco smoke pervaded the downstairs rooms. Empty glasses and plates littered the surfaces. There was no sign of human activity. Everyone was still in bed.

Steve washed up a couple of mugs and made some tea. He then carried the mugs up to their room where Angie was still buried under the covers. Steve slipped off his clothes and got in beside her. He ran his hands over her body and images of her dancing with Ginny arose in his mind. Angie woke and protested that she was trying to sleep. Steve apologised and rolled away from her.

When he awoke, the other side of the bed was empty. From downstairs came the sound of the house being restored to order. Steve was normally public spirited, but, still feeling utterly exhausted, put his head under the covers, and went back to sleep. Some time later, he became aware that Angie was sitting on the edge of the bed, smiling at him.

'What time is it?' he asked.

'Gone three. This job is playing havoc with your body clock.'

Steve yawned, but could hardly deny that it was so. 'I know I've just got to stick it out.'

'Anyway, it was a great party, wasn't it?

'Yeah, I had enormous fun answering the front door and watching the rest of you get high and I was rather pissed off with the way Ginny monopolised you. I was hoping to spend at least some of the evening with you. We've only got one more week together.'

'Steve. This is not the right kind of job for you. You can't hope to lead the kind of social life you're used to and get up at four-thirty every morning. Something's got to give.'

'It's just because it's the end of term. Things will settle down after next week.'

'I have a feeling that things will never settle down in your life, Steve. You do things the hard way. Look, there's still time to change your mind. You haven't committed yourself to this house yet, have you?'

'No, I'm still hoping that you might change your mind.'

'I'm not going to change my mind. And I think you should know that after you went to bed, Ginny referred to the fact that you and I were considering them as co-tenants, but that apparently I was the one who made the decisions in such matters. When I put her straight and told her that I wouldn't be staying in Cambridge, as I had obligations elsewhere, she looked quite shocked. She and Jon left shortly afterwards.'

A furtive look came over Steve's face. So that was what Ginny had been up to. She had been trying to ingratiate herself with Angie.

He tried to explain. 'I thought it would put them off. I didn't expect them to mount a campaign to win you over.'

'But wouldn't it have been better not to have hidden behind my skirts in the first place?'

Steve bowed his head in shame, but managed a quip. 'I seem to recall I was the one wearing the skirts.'

Angie ignored his heavy-handed humour to gloss over what had been in truth a pusillanimous attempt to deal with Jon and Ginny. 'Well, with luck I've put their noses out of joint so much that they will never speak to either of us again.'

Steve wasn't so sure. Their situation seemed almost as urgent as his own. 'I can assure you that I'd rather not share with them. I've been trying to find a way to avoid that eventuality. But I need someone to help with the rent.'

'Deals done when one's in a desperate situation seldom work out well. And living in close proximity to people like Jon and Ginny might very well take you in a direction you will come to regret.'

'Anj, I can take care of myself.'

'I'm not sure you can, Steve. Or not with people like that. They're hustlers and they've identified you as someone they can pressurise. There's more to this than meets the eye.'

'Anj, that's a very paranoid way of looking at the situation. I think Jez's hash cakes are still affecting your thinking.'

'Very possibly. That guy can't be trusted not to overdo it with recreational drugs.'

'I think he met his match in Jon last night.'

This time Angie was prepared to acknowledge the humour of the exchange with a half-hearted laugh. That was perhaps something they could both agree on.

'Look, Steve, last night was our last hurrah as undergraduates. We graduate on Friday. Things start to get serious now. My parents are arriving in Cambridge on Thursday. I will be staying with them at the Garden House Hotel that night and the following night and leaving Cambridge on the Saturday morning. If we are going to sort things out between us we need to do it in the next couple of days. Now that the bank has extended your overdraft and you have paid your college bill, there is really no need to go ahead with this crazy scheme. Quit the job and come down to Brighton with me.'

Steve felt his eyes pricking. He knew that Angie was right.

GRADUATION

EVEN THOUGH IT WAS Steve's graduation day he still had to get his round out of the way first. He had decided to go straight to the college from the dairy. That meant taking his graduation gear, hired suit and smart shoes in a rucksack which he stuffed in the cab of his float when he got to the dairy. Despite the miserable night he had spent, alone for almost the first time in what had been their shared bed, he had managed to be up betimes and get the round done in good time.

The problem was that all graduands were required to attend a meeting in the Hall at eleven o'clock during which the college Praelector would check that they were properly attired and explain the running order of the ceremony itself. Anyone not attending this meeting would not be allowed to take part in the congregation later on. Steve had arranged to meet up with Alan, Jez and Harry in the St Radegund's JCR at ten forty-five, but he realised as he set off from the dairy that he was unlikely to make the rendezvous. More worryingly it looked like he might also miss the start of the Praelector's meeting. He arrived at the college breathless and sweaty with five minutes to spare. But he still had to change into his suit. He ran into the JCR toilets and stripped off his work clothes and threw on his formal gear, only to realise that his shirt had French cuffs and he had no cufflinks. He ran into the Porter's Lodge and asked Stan what he should do about his cuffs. The only thing that Stan could think of was to tie them up with string. Stan hunted in a drawer and brought out a roll of parcel string. He snipped off two lengths and handed them to Steve. He chuckled as he watched Steve struggle to knot each cuff and said, 'I shouldn't let the Praelector see your cuffs, sir, or you won't be attending today's congregation.'

Steve tugged his jacket sleeves down and regaining his composure said, 'I thought that was why the sleeves of the BA gown were so long.' Then flourishing them like a trainee vampire he dashed to the Hall where the roll call had already started, but fortunately the College Marshal had only reached the letter K. He caught Alan's eye and pursed his lips in a silent whistle of relief. After the roll call, the graduands' formal attire was inspected. Fortunately, it was Steve's hood that seemed to cause the college officials most consternation and some time was spent adjusting it. At no point did they ask to see his cuffs. The graduands were then formed into a phalanx in the main court of the college and marched to the Senate House.

The congregation, large parts of which were conducted in Latin, seemed to go on for ever. Steve craned his neck to see if he could spot his mother, but without success. Eventually it was Steve's turn to be admitted to the degree of Bachelor of Arts. The college Praelector took him by the right hand and led him up to the dais where he was required to kneel and put his hands together as if in prayer whereupon the Vice-Chancellor, clasping Steve's hands, declared in Latin that he was now admitted to the degree in the name of the Holy Trinity. He was then handed his degree certificate and invited to resume his place in the body of the Senate House.

Later, out on the lawn in front of the Senate House he located his mother, whose expression was a mixture of pride and relief. She accosted one of the roving photographers and Steve posed for a formal portrait. Steve's mother wondered whether there was somewhere they could get a cup of tea. She had had to make an early start to get to Cambridge in time for Steve's session in the Senate House. Steve explained that there were refreshments back at the college and suggested they make their way there forthwith.

Back at the college the garden party for the new graduates and their guests was in full swing in the Fellows' Garden. The last few weeks had been so busy that Steve had given little thought to this aspect of proceedings, but he suddenly realised that he was not only going to have to interact with a number of college tutors and officials, but there was also the distinct possibility that his mother might ask to speak with his director of studies. Or vice versa. All sorts of complications might arise out of that kind of encounter. But for the moment, his mother was getting to know the parents of Steve's housemates. Steve grabbed a glass of wine from one of the circulating waiters and knocked it back before getting two more, one for his mother and a second for himself.

Fortunately, the assembled parents were enjoying meeting their counterparts and trying to find out what kind of friends their respective offspring had been consorting with. No doubt Steve's mother had had her reservations when he had announced that he was going to live out of college for his final year. Steve had studiously avoided giving her too much information, so it was hardly surprising that she had assumed that he must have teamed up with a bunch of reprobates. But now, with their degrees safely bagged and with the help of a glass of wine, Steve's housemates were all revealed as fine fellows. The parents were soon getting on as if they'd always known each other.

Under the influence of the wine Steve started to relax and was showing off his unconventional cufflinks to Alan, when, from the corner of his eye, he caught sight of Dr Doyle, his director of studies, heaving into view. Steve detached himself from the group of graduates and parents and did his best to intercept Doyle as far away from his mother as possible. Doyle was his usual gracious self, congratulating Steve with, so far as Steve could tell, undisguised sincerity.

'I'm sure you were hoping for something better than 2:2, but under the circumstances a creditable achievement. I'm sorry I haven't been able to congratulate you before, but I haven't spotted you around college in the last few weeks. Too many May Balls to attend, no doubt?'

The last remark was delivered with a knowing look. Steve confined himself to a nod. He didn't want to go into details, although he had a feeling that Doyle had some inkling of what was going on. He was no fool. But Steve was genuinely fond of Doyle and grateful to him for all his wise counsel.

'So, are your parents here today? I imagine they're very proud of you.'

'Yes, my mother's over there. My father died when I was young'

'Oh yes, my dear fellow, I'm sorry. I should have remembered. Would you introduce me to your mother please?'

'Of course, but first I want to express my gratitude to you for having put up with me for the last three years. You had every right to wash your hands of me. I realise that I let myself down on a number of occasions, but I can assure you that I have learnt a huge amount from you, which I am sure will stand me in good stead in the future. It has been a privilege to be your pupil.'

Doyle looked embarrassed. 'Nonsense, my dear chap. That's what St Radegund's is all about. It is the epitome of collegiality.'

Steve felt guilty and stupid in equal measure.

'I would be delighted to introduce you to my mother, but would you mind not stressing the circumstances of my 2:2. It will only make her worry about what those circumstances were.'

'Of course. I understand completely.' Which no doubt he did.

Not for the first time Steve thanked his stars that he had been lucky enough to be assigned to Doyle. Not only was he a top notch intellectual, but he was also a nice bloke. The two attributes seldom seemed to manifest themselves in the same individual. Somewhat reassured, but not entirely without anxiety, he led the way over to where his mother was standing and made the introductions.

Doyle gave a master class in reassurance. He told Steve's mother that Steve had been one of his more interesting students. His mother beamed on hearing this. Steve couldn't help wincing at the true meaning of this term. Fortunately he was not in his mother's immediate line of sight. Small talk continued for a few minutes until Doyle excused himself for not being able to spend more time with them, but he had a number of families to get around. Taking his leave, he said that he had no doubt that Steve would do very well in whatever he set his mind to. Steve hoped that this was an honest assessment, but he doubted that Doyle had milk delivery in mind.

When Doyle had moved on, Steve's mother said, 'What a charming man! How lucky to have had him as your tutor.'

'Mum, he's not my tutor. He is, was, my director of studies. At Cambridge tutors have a pastoral role, moral guidance, that sort of thing. Preferring not to receive such guidance, I hardly ever saw mine.'

Steve's mother ignored his convoluted joke and asked after the name of his tutor. Steve, with little enthusiasm, revealed that it was Professor Higgins.

'Are we going to meet him too?' his mother wondered.

Steve couldn't think of anything worse. Higgins was a dry old stick. He and Steve had never really hit it off. Higgins would also have been more aware of the issue of late payment of college bills, an issue which he doubted had reached Doyle's ears. Steve was counting on the fact that Higgins had many more families to get around and might not be too sorry if he missed one or two out. But inevitably talk of the devil resulted in the time-honoured outcome of that conjuration with Steve spotting Higgins tottering towards their party. Steve shrank behind the group of parents and turned in a not altogether successful mime of spotting an acquaintance on the other side of the Fellows' Garden. He tensed, waiting to hear his name called, but was relieved to hear Higgins' quavering voice hailing Jez. Steve had forgotten that Higgins was also Jez's tutor. Jez's father was himself a professor at another university.

Under cover of the bout of high academic jousting that ensued with terms like 'iconography' and 'pedagogical' peppering the discourse, Steve suggested to his mother that they take advantage of the buffet and led her over to where it had been laid out. She did not seem to have taken in that the crusty old academic was also Steve's tutor. As his mother was loading her plate with vol-au-vents, Steve checked his watch and saw that Angie's session in the Senate House would have finished by now.

The remainder of the graduation party passed without further anxiety. Steve explained to his mother that he had booked her into the Clarendon hotel, midway between the college and his house. He would walk her back there and she could have a rest before they met up with the Barretts in the evening. They made their way from the Fellows' Garden to the main entrance of the college. While Steve retrieved his rucksack which he had left in the Porters' Lodge, Mavis stood and surveyed the ancient ranges of the main court. When Steve rejoined her she said, 'I imagine you're going to miss this place.'

Steve wasn't so sure about that, but felt it would be churlish not to agree. His mother had made enormous sacrifices to support him through his education.

'Your father would have been very proud of you. Not just the first person on either side of the family to go to university, but Cambridge at that.'

Steve picked up his mother's overnight bag, guided her through the main gateway of the college and unchained his bike from the railings where he had left it. Steve knew he was going to have to tell her that he had decided not to take up the job with the German company. What she might find even harder to comprehend was that he was now planning to stay in Cambridge while he worked on a book length poem and support himself with the kind of job that he could have done without any qualifications whatsoever. He was pretty sure his mother would see this as a waste of the education, which she had supported him through. It was probably better to have that conversation before they met up with the Barretts later that evening.

They walked back across Jesus Green and crossed the footbridge to Chesterton Road. His mother checked in and Steve carried her bag up to her room. When he was happy that she was settled in, he said he'd go back to his own place, which was only ten minutes away and change into something more appropriate for the evening. He would return at four-thirty, so that they could have some tea together before getting a taxi to the Garden House hotel to meet up with the Barretts. That suited Mavis. She could do with a nap. For that matter, so could Steve.

Back at Victoria Road, he divested himself of the ludicrous graduation gear and ran a bath. Having washed the sweat and anxiety from his body, he climbed into bed yearning for the touch of Angie's body. Without all her stuff, the room seemed bare and empty. He fell into a troubled sleep until he woke a couple of hours later to the sound of the rest of the crew returning from their graduation lunches.

Checking the time, he realised that he'd better get a move on and get dressed. He remembered that on the previous occasion that he had met Angie's parents, Angie's father had teased him about his sartorial style. Conscious that the Garden House was a somewhat smarter establishment than Arjuna, Steve decided to take more care with his appearance. He put on a pair of red velvet flares, a pair of Green Flash plimsolls, a Wrangler jean jacket and a shirt with a collar. On his way out, he put his head around the door of the sitting room and announced that he was off to tea with his mother and then they were joining Angie and her parents for dinner.

He walked slowly down to the Clarendon and found his mother in the lounge. She patted the space on the sofa beside her. Steve leant down and gave her a kiss and sat down. 'Did you manage to get a nap, Ma?'

'Yes, quite a comfortable bed and a lovely view of the river and the green from the window.'

'Yeah, this is a nice place, but not as swanky as the one we're going to later.'

'So, tell me about Angie's parents.'

'I don't know too much about them. I've only met them the once. They seemed very nice, quite posh, live in a beautiful house in rural Kent. They've invited me down, but I've not yet got around to visiting them. George is some kind of international businessman, something to do with engineering. Viv is a teacher.'

'Is this place we're eating at going to be expensive then? I want to pay our share.'

'No, Ma. Angie and I are paying. It's our treat.'

'But you can't afford to pay for a posh dinner.'

'I've got a job, Ma. I've been working since I finished my exams.' This was true so far as it went, even if it wasn't exactly how the meal was being paid for, but it was a convenient way of introducing the fact of his menial employment.

'Tell me about the job.'

'I will, but let's order some tea first.'

He signalled to a passing waitress and ordered a pot of tea and some sandwiches. With the tea ordered, Mavis returned to her question.

'So what's this job you're doing?'

'I'm a milkman.'

Mrs Percival couldn't believe what she was hearing.

'A milkman, Steve. Why didn't you ask me if you needed money?'

'Ma, you have given me so much already.'

'But you will soon be earning a good salary and you could repay me.'

'That's something I wanted to talk to you about. I've decided to stay in Cambridge.'

'To continue studying?'

'In a way.'

'To do one of these PhDs?'

'Not exactly, nothing to do with the university as such. I'm writing something and I want to stay here until I've finished it.'

'But what about the job with the German company.'

'I've decided not to take it.'

'But why? What's the point of all this studying, if it isn't to get a good job?

'I know people think you go to university to get a job. I did when I arrived here and to be honest plenty of people do just that. But one of the things you learn is that there are more important things than money. There is knowledge for its own sake, and art and culture. My director of studies whom you met today, Dr Doyle, is the cleverest person I know. You don't think he makes much money, do you? I don't suppose he owns his own house or even a flat. He does what he does because he loves his subject and he loves sharing his knowledge with people like me.'

'So, do you want to do what he does?'

'Yes, part of me does, but he's a critic and I'm an artist.'

'An artist? I didn't think you could even draw.'

Steve laughed. 'It's true, I can't. No, I mean artist in the general sense, someone engaged in cultural production.'

'I don't really follow you.'

'Well, you can use the word to indicate writers, musicians and playwrights and so on. Not just painters.'

'And which of these are you?'

At this point Steve's courage failed him. He realised that his mother was finding it difficult enough to cope with the idea of her son turning his back on a secure job, let alone being able to accommodate herself to the notion of her son as a poet. Fortunately, the tea and sandwiches arrived at that moment giving him time to think how best to put the matter.

Having between them cleared the plate of sandwiches, Steve said, 'You could also apply the term artist to people who write things for TV and for films.'

'Do you mean that you want to work in TV?'

'Yes, maybe, but first I probably need to get some experience in the theatre.'

'Okay,' Mavis said doubtfully. 'I didn't know you were interested in the theatre.'

It was true that he had never talked to his mother about it, but he had actually been involved in a number of productions as an undergraduate. On the spur of the moment he decided to double down on his supposed theatrical ambitions.

'I want to take a production to the Edinburgh Fringe later in the summer and I have contacts here who can help me with it.'

'And then what?'

'Maybe apply to theatre school.'

'What, more study?'

'Yes, but I'll fund it myself.'

'Steve, it's your life, but this all sounds a bit vague.'

Mavis was nobody's fool and she knew her son well enough to realise that this wasn't the whole story. But at the same time, she thought that he was basically sensible. He'd always had a capacity to surprise her, even as a little boy. There was no doubt that he'd worked hard to get to Cambridge. She wasn't sure how hard he'd worked once at St Radegund's, but perhaps he was due a bit of unstructured time in which to find himself.

'Well, all right, dear. I'm sure you know what you're doing. Does Angie know all this?'

'Most of it. She knows I don't want to do the German job. She'd like me to go to Edinburgh with her when she starts her PhD.'

'That sounds like a good idea.'

'And I'll probably do that, but she's not very happy about my staying in Cambridge over the summer. She'd like me to go to Brighton with her. She's teaching there.'

'Steve, I presume you two have been more than just sharing a house.'

Steve blushed. 'Yes.'

'Do her parents know you've been sleeping together?'

'No.'

'I see. I'm looking forward to meeting this young lady.'

'And I want you to meet her. She's beautiful, clever and good fun.'

'So why don't you want to be with her?'

'I do want to be with her, but I don't want to leave Cambridge right now. It's all a bit of a mess and it's all my fault. I should have made it clear much earlier what I wanted to do, but I lacked the courage.'

'Poor Steve, that's not like you.'

Steve suddenly felt like a little boy again owning up to his mother about some infraction.

'So, Ma, there might be the odd awkward moment tonight. If there is, it's entirely my fault. I don't want you to think badly of Angie or her parents.'

'Oh dear, has something happened.'

'I think Angie might be a bit annoyed with me and I haven't seen her since the day before yesterday.'

'You've worried me now.'

'I'm sorry, I didn't want to, but I thought I should explain the situation to you. I'm sure things will be fine. The Barretts are very nice people.'

Mavis hoped that Steve was right in his judgement.

On the way to the Garden House hotel, Mavis turned to her son and said, 'Steve, I do wish you'd let me pay.'

But Steve was adamant. 'Ma, that's why I've got a job, so that I can pay for things myself.'

In an attempt to change the subject, Steve said that the hotel that they were going to was in a beautiful location, not just with a view of the river, but literally on the riverbank. It was also the subject of a certain amount of notoriety on two counts. Firstly, a few years previously it had been the site of a protest against an event sponsored by the Greek right wing military junta. The protest had degenerated into a riot and a number of students had been sent to prison. Mavis listened with interest.

'So this junta is what they call the Colonels?'

Steve nodded.

'Seems they've been at it again.'

'I don't know what you mean, Ma.'

'It was on the news this morning. The Colonels provoked a *coup d'état* in Cyprus last week and yesterday the Turkish armed forces invaded the island.'

Steve was little taken aback, not so much at the propensity of fascists to stage *coups d'état* as at the fact that his mother was more aware of current affairs than he was. Now that he was getting up so early, he wasn't even reading a newspaper every day, nor did he have access to television or radio. He said thoughtfully, 'That's a bit more serious than a student demonstration.'

Just then the taxi arrived at the front of the hotel in Granta Place. As they were about to get out of the taxi Mavis said, 'And what was the second count of notoriety?'

Steve laughed. There was nothing wrong with his mother's brain.

'Two years ago, the hotel burned down. This is a brand new building. It's scarcely been open a year.'

And indeed they were now standing in front of an aggressively modern building.

'It doesn't look much from this side, but it's impressive from the riverside,' Steve assured her.

Before they went into the hotel, Steve said that he had a favour to ask of his mother. Would she mind if he went for a drink with Angie after dinner? They wouldn't be seeing each other for a while. She was leaving with her parents the following morning while Steve was at work. He'd arrange a taxi to take Mavis back to the Clarendon and then he and she could have lunch before her train back to London the next day. Mavis was happy to oblige. She had had a long day and was quite keen to get to bed reasonably early.

They went into the lobby and asked the receptionist where they might find Mr and Mrs Barrett, whom they were meeting for dinner. They were led to a lounge bar with a view of the river. Across the room Steve spotted Angie and her parents enjoying an aperitif. Angie waved to them and came over.

'Mrs Percival, it's so lovely to meet you at last.'

'It's a great pleasure for me too. I've heard so much about you. And please call me Mavis.'

Angie lead them over to her parents' table and made the introductions. George asked Mavis and Steve what they'd like to drink. Mavis asked for a gin and tonic and Steve opted for a beer. When the drinks arrived, George suggested they drink a toast to the graduating couple. Glasses were clinked and congratulations offered. After these brief formalities, the conversation became more general. Mavis was a phlegmatic and good natured person and got on with all and sundry. By contrast Vivienne, Angie's mother, though refined and blessed with impeccable manners, was reserved to the point that some might consider a little haughty. But underneath the polished veneer there was an engaging personality and on this particular evening it was to the fore. The two women were already talking as if they'd known each other for years.

They talked about how beautiful the colleges looked in the early summer sunshine and how impressive the graduation ceremony had been. Mavis said that Steve's father would have been very proud of his son. Vivienne asked tactfully how long had it been since Mavis's husband had died and commiserated at the reply, saying how difficult it must have been to bring up a child on her own. Mavis said she was lucky because Steve had been a well-behaved and studious child. Vivienne said that she and George had been relieved when Steve had appeared on the scene because previously Angie had had one or two unsuitable attachments. From the start of the relationship with Steve she had become an altogether happier person and with his encouragement had concentrated on her studies. She trusted that Angie had had a similar effect on Steve. Mavis said that Steve never stopped talking about Angie. She understood that Angie had got a particularly good grade and was going to do a PhD. George and Vivienne glowed with pride and another toast, this one to Angie's First, was drunk.

Putting his glass down, George turned to Steve and said, 'And what are your plans now, Steve?'

Steve took a deep breath and said, 'I'm hoping to take a production of *The Importance of Being Earnest* to the Edinburgh Fringe, so I'm staying in Cambridge until then.'

George and Vivian nodded at this news, unaware that it had only been dreamed up a couple of hours earlier, but Steve could see that Angie was openmouthed in amazement. Mavis caught the look that was exchanged between the couple and realised that this was news to Angie too. Only too well aware of the consternation he was creating, Steve pressed on. That was why he had got himself a temporary job in Cambridge, while he rehearsed the play. George asked what the job was. Steve divulged that that he was a milk roundsman. On hearing this George let out an enormous guffaw and declared that when three or four years earlier he had learnt that his daughter had won a place at Cambridge, little did he realise that she would end up going out with a milkman.

Given that he had only been mocked and not anathematised, Steve decided to give the fantasy a bit more body and explained that he had been involved in a number of student productions including having directed one. He was planning to apply to the Bristol Old Vic Theatre School to do a master's degree in theatrical direction, but he needed to boost his production credits. Angie's mother asked him how that related to the course that he had just finished. He explained that a large part of his course had had focused on classic French and German drama. He reeled off a number of the dramatists he had read, and some he hadn't, listing Molière, Racine, Corneille, Goethe, Schiller, Brecht, Hauptmann. Oh, the list went on and on. George and Viv looked suitably impressed, which could not be said for Angie or his own mother to judge from their slightly bewildered expressions. At that point the waiter brought their meals and they turned to other subjects of conversation.

As they ate, George was still chuckling about Steve's job as a milkman and asked him what the job was like. Steve told them about the driving test and the gaffer who spent the whole day looking at Page 3 of *The Sun* and Ron who chain-smoked Hamlet cigars. Soon he had them all in fits of laughter, even his own mother, who suddenly seemed amused at the thought of her son working as a milkman. Whether she was actually happy with the situation was another matter.

The meal was coming to an end. Mavis and Angie's parents had made a good connection and promised to meet up again soon. Mavis said that she had had a long day and should probably be getting back to her hotel. Steve caught Angie's eye and pronounced solemnly that he and Angie would like to pay for the meal as a thank you to their amazingly tolerant parents. An approving smile played around George's lips. Steve called the waiter over and asked for the bill and if a cab could be called to go to the Clarendon. When the waiter returned with the bill, Steve realised that he had not pre-arranged with Angie the division of the money George had provided, to make it look as if Steve and Angie were sharing the cost of the meal. His first thought was that he didn't have enough cash in his wallet to cover the cost of the meal, but then he remembered that he had withdrawn enough cash from his account the previous day to cover the deposit on the house in Ainsworth Street which needed to be paid by the Sunday if the house was to be his for the summer. On the other hand if he paid for the meal in its entirety it might be awkward to try and recoup the outlay later from Angie. She saw the hesitation flickering across his face and said, 'Steve, you know we agreed to share the bill for the meal. I'm not going to let you pay for it all on your own, even if you are now a milkman.'

She passed her purse across the table. 'There should be enough to cover my share in there including a contribution towards a decent tip.'

Steve took the purse while trying to look as if he was conceding gracefully. He made an elaborate show of taking some notes from his own wallet, before in fact withdrawing the full amount needed to settle the bill from Angie's purse as had been agreed. After this com-plicated piece of stage business he placed the required sum plus a rounded up amount for the tip on the salver with which the waiter had presented the bill. He looked guiltily around the table but the others had averted their gazes from the unseemly procedure and were chat-ting amiably.

The party rose and made its way to the lobby. Vivienne was saying that she thought that she would probably get an early night too. George on the other hand had spotted that the hotel bar had a good collection of malts and thought he might have a bit of a nightcap. Seizing the moment Steve asked Angie's parents whether they would mind if he and Angie went for a stroll to one of their old haunts for a farewell drink He wouldn't get her back late because he was working the next day and had to be up at four-thirty. That also meant that he wouldn't see Angie and her parents before they set off for home. It was clear to everyone that this was a poignant moment for the young lovers and it was readily agreed. There was a scrimmage of kissing and handshaking. The Barretts waited until Mavis's taxi had arrived and then retired to bed, in Vivienne's case, and in search of a fortifying glass of malt, in George's.

The young couple escaped onto the street and turned right in the direction of Coe Fen. Angie looked as if she was going to explode. 'What was that all about? What on earth are you up to?'

In reply Steve just swept her up in his arms and kissed her hard on the mouth. 'Let's just walk and I'll explain the whole thing.'

As they walked along arm in arm, Steve said, 'My God, I've missed you.'

Angie was still bristling about Steve's performance in the restaurant. 'I'm not sure I believe you.' And after a pause. 'And what was all that nonsense about the Edinburgh Fringe and the Bristol Old Vic Theatre School? *The Importance of Being Earnest* indeed! Who are you trying to kid?'

'My mother, of course. I just made it up on the spur of the moment, because I needed to create a reason why I'm staying in Cambridge and not going back home or planning to start with the German company.'

'But something so elaborate that will be proved false in not many weeks.'

'Yes, but by then she will have got used to the situation. And actually I don't think it's such a bad idea. I know I said it was a production of *The Importance of Being Earnest*, but actually I've always wanted to do *Krapp's Last Tape*. It's a one man piece and really all it needs is a tape recorder and a lot of bananas.'

'Well, you're certainly bananas. So where are we going to have this drink?'

'Well, actually, I thought we could go back to your hotel room.'

'What?'

'I thought we could talk in the comfort of your room.'

'Steve, my parents are at the hotel. My father's still probably in the bar. He might see us. And anyway I don't think you've got talking in mind.'

The fact that she hadn't uttered an outright no gave Steve hope and he said, 'Well, now you come to mention it . . .'

For the first time in their post-prandial walk Angie laughed. 'You really are incorrigible.'

'But you're not saying no?'

'You can't stay all night, though.'

'It's a deal.'

They went back to the hotel and, skirting the bar just in case Angie's father was having a second nightcap, crept up to Angie's room. It didn't take them long to divest themselves of their clothes. Not much talking was done. Having accomplished this pleasurable task they both fell into a deep slumber from which Steve awakened a couple of hours later. He disentangled himself from Angie's embrace and went into the bathroom where he had a quick shower before drying himself and dressing. Angie was still sleeping. He bent down, brushed her hair back from her face with his hand and kissed her tenderly on the forehead. Then he let himself out of the room and walked back to Victoria Road. He too wondered what he was up to.

Steve experienced more than the usual difficulty getting up the next morning. He really was getting into serious sleep deficit. To make matters worse, it was a collection day. Despite that, he somehow managed to get back to Victoria Road after his round with enough time to tidy himself up before slipping down to the Clarendon to meet his mother. She had already checked out and was waiting for him in the lobby. He suggested that they go to the rooftop restaurant at the Arts Theatre. They could then walk through to the Market Square and get a taxi to the station after their lunch. While they waited for their food, Mavis said how much she had enjoyed meeting the Barretts and in particular how much she liked Angie. Steve said, 'And she liked you. She's a great girl.'

'So why aren't you being more careful with her feelings?'

'We've talked about it a lot. She's not happy about my plans, but it's not a reason for us to break up. At least I hope not. Neither of us have talked in those terms.'

'But often what was never said is what actually happens.'

'It's only for a few months and then we'll get back together again.'

'Steve, I'm not so old that I've forgotten how these things work. And I would say that you are at a dangerous moment in your relationship. I also have to say that this business about directing a play and putting it on in Edinburgh doesn't sound like you at all. You're not the kind of person to organise a group of people on a joint project. You are more of a lone wolf. I don't think you've changed that much in three years.'

'I was saying to Angie last night, that it's not *The Importance of Being Earnest* that I'm planning to put on, but *Krapp's Last Tape* by Samuel Beckett, but I thought the title might offend George and Vivienne. The play is a single hander.'

'That's not really what I'm saying. And if Angie didn't know about it, it suggests to me that you haven't been as honest with her, as you're making out.'

Steve had said more than he'd meant to. His mother always had a way of getting at the truth. He felt ashamed of his prevarication.

'I'm sorry, Ma, you know me too well. Angie and I have talked a lot, but we hadn't talked about the idea of my putting on a play at the Fringe.'

'So that means that not only were you not being straight with her, but you were trying to pull the wool over my eyes too.'

Steve hung his head. 'What we talked about was my finishing a poem I'm working on. I thought you and Angie's parents might not think that a good reason for not doing the job with the German company. Angie doesn't mind me not taking the job in the city, but she thinks I should go to Brighton with her and I could finish the poem there.'

'And I think she's right. She's got a job and a place to live. Two can live as cheaply as one. It wouldn't take you long to find a job. And there should be no problem about your living together. If you think that I and Angie's parents don't realise that you two have been living together for the last year, then you're more naïve than I thought. I'm sorry to say, Steve, but I think it might have more to do with the fact that you're not as committed as you say you are. Is there someone else?'

'Oh, Ma, not at all.'

'Steve, If you let that girl go, you will spend the rest of your life regretting it.'

Suddenly, Steve didn't feel hungry any more. He loved his mother, he loved Angie, but he didn't want to be hemmed in just yet. It wasn't really to do with commitment. He had things to do. If he'd started work with the German company and they'd posted him to Frankfurt or New York, people would have accepted that it was a condition of the job. It would not have attracted negative comment or doubt as to his intentions towards Angie. It seemed, however, that if he asserted his own will as to what he did with his time, then he was just being wilful, rather than compliant.

But he didn't want to have a row with his mother. He certainly had no desire to upset either her or Angie. Mavis could see that she had unsettled her son. She didn't really care that he hadn't been straight with her, but she felt that he should treat Angie honourably. More importantly, he should not deceive himself. The conversation reverted to less weighty matters. When the bill had been paid they walked through St. Edward's Passage to the Market Square and Steve hailed a cab. He hugged his mother and promised to think about what she had said. He waved her off and watched the cab turn into St Mary's Street and disappear from view.

In truth, the college bill shenanigans had always been a flimsy pretext and it would hardly be surprising if others, including Angie herself, now interpreted his actions as a lack of commitment to their relationship. That was not how he saw things, but in truth he didn't have a more convincing explanation for his behaviour. Dimly he perceived that it was something to do with his lack of belief in his own talent. But the idea that three months intense work on his poem would decide the matter one way or the other was ridiculous. Even so he felt he owed it to himself to push ahead with his plan. So he was indeed taking a risk with Angie's affections. And now he deadline for him to confirm his intention to take on the house in Ainsworth Street was looming. On receipt of the agreed deposit, Beth would hand over the keys. Until then, it was still open to him to join Angie in Brighton. Sure, quitting his job at the dairy would be embarrassing, but no more than that. Then he and Angie could look forward to a summer on the South Coast together and in the autumn move to Edinburgh. The prospect seemed delightful in so many ways.

He cast his mind back to the start of their relationship. They had moved from a preliminary sense of compatibility to vigorous intimacy in one afternoon. After Flynn's lecture and several drinks at the Granta, they had gone back to Angie's room at Newnham and, without much ado, made love. Several hours later, managing to prise themselves apart for long enough to get some supper in the college cafeteria followed by more drinks in the college bar, they had returned to Angie's room for a reprise. Steve had been starting to assume that he would be staying over, but Angie was not yet ready to take that step.

That had soon changed. They discovered that that they had a lot more in common than the mere ability to trigger the appropriate pheromone response in each other. They shared values and outlook to a considerable degree and were comfortable in each other's company. But staying the night in each other's college room was against college rules and not without its risks. Hence when Steve found out that Al and Harry were looking for another person for a house share, he proposed Angie and himself as a couple.

In Victoria Road their relationship had deepened. By any conventional measure the prospects were good, so why jeopardise things? It was not as if Steve was on the lookout for the next conquest. He was perfectly happy with Angie. That was exactly the point of his plan, if it wasn't too grandiose a term for what he was proposing. It had nothing to do with a negative view of the relationship and everything to do with establishing who he was. But the lease on the Victoria Road house was coming to an end the following Sunday and, in the absence of an alternative, he would need to go back to his mother's or go down to Brighton with Angie. Either of these outcomes would feel like a defeat.

Harmony & Sublation

STEVE SLEPT RIGHT THROUGH his four-thirty alarm the next morning. But even though he was once again running late, his mind had cleared. He was going to take the plunge. He checked the notes in his wallet to make sure that he hadn't done something stupid during his absurd prestidigitation when paying the bill at the hotel restaurant. He was relieved to see that he still had enough for the deposit with a few pounds left over to get him to payday. He attacked the round with considerable energy, impatient to get things over and done with.

In the event, the transaction with Beth was perfunctory. She took the little wad of notes and gave him the keys. She made it clear that she expected Steve to have vacated the house by the 31st of September. Steve said that was fine because he would probably be heading up to Edinburgh around then. He tucked the key in the breast pocket of his jean jacket and did the rivet button up. He was simultaneously excited and apprehensive.

As he was cycling past The Locomotive, he noticed that it was just opening its doors for the lunchtime session. He felt that he could do with a pint to steady his nerves. He dismounted and chained his bike up. He went into the pub and ordered a pint. He found a table and as he sipped his beer registered that he had certainly crossed some kind of Rubicon. *Alea jacta est* or something and look what had happened to

113

Caesar. Even so he felt quietly satisfied, a mood that quickly evaporated, as he saw Jon and Ginny sweep through the doors of the pub. They spotted him instantly and came over to his table.

'All hail!' said Jon portentously. Ginny draped herself elegantly on his shoulder and stared into the distance, a considerable achievement in the restricted confines of the Loco. But at least she seemed aware of his presence.

'Can we join you, man?' Jon was already slipping into the chair opposite Steve.

'Ginny was just about to get some drinks. Would you care for another?'

Fuck it. Why not?

'Same again?'

Steve nodded. While Ginny was getting the drinks, Jon said, 'So what are your thoughts about the house?'

Steve hadn't anticipated that he would have to deal quite so soon with the fact that Jon and Ginny now knew that Angie wasn't going to be staying in Cambridge. What was he going to say? He certainly wasn't yet ready to admit that he had secured the Ainsworth Street house. He was still finding it hard to come to terms with the fact that he had no choice but to accept Jon and Ginny as his housemates. He knew there was really no other solution to the financial implications, but he wasn't sure he had the emotional energy to make two irreversible commitments in one day.

'I've been tied up with this graduation malarkey. I also had my mother come to stay. I hope to sort things out in the next couple of days. As soon as I have, I'll come round to your place and let you know.'

'Well, listen, man, I can tell you before Ginny gets back with the drinks that we're getting desperate. It's seriously affecting her state of mind. She's prone to bouts of depression.'

Steve made sympathetic noises, but that piece of information was not exactly an incentive to accommodate the groovy couple.

Catching sight of Ginny returning with the drinks, Jon changed the subject. 'That was a great party, man. Haven't had such a crazy time for ages. That Jez is a monster. Beat me at my own game.'

Ginny put the drinks on the table and took a seat. She took a sip of her drink and fixed Steve with a piercing smile.

'I was sorry to hear that Angie is not staying in Cambridge for the summer. You must be rather disappointed. I know I am.'

'Yes, I am. And I'm feeling rather guilty. I didn't realise that she'd made a commitment that she couldn't break. The job she's got is through a family connection.'

Ginny continued to hold his gaze. 'So what does that mean for your plans?'

'I'm not sure yet. I'm still reflecting on the situation.'

Jon seemed happy to let Ginny do the talking. 'When do you need to make a decision about the house?'

'By next weekend,' Steve lied.

Ginny considered the matter. 'I imagine our contribution to the rent will be all the more welcome, now that she's not staying.'

Steve was reluctant to concede the point, confining himself to a slight nod of the head.

Jon decided to summarise the situation. 'So it looks like we could move in on 1 July. That would make things neat and tidy.'

Steve realised that that was the implication of what he had said.

'Yes, but, as they say, there's many a slip 'twixt cup and lip. I'll come around to your place and let you know as soon as I have the keys.'

Ginny clearly was keen to cut off the escape route that Steve was trying to construct by his resort to proverbs and was determined to get a stronger commitment from him. 'You don't really want to share with us, do you?'

Steve choked quietly on his beer. Had Angie been even more candid with Ginny than she had admitted to Steve? His courage failed him. 'No, of course not. I'm sure we'd all get on well.'

Ginny inclined her head to one side. 'It's understandable if you have some reservations. You probably think we're a bit unconventional, but you might be surprised to discover how ordinary our way of life is, and that we have high standards of tidiness and cleanliness.'

Steve didn't really know what to think. Untidiness hadn't been top of his list of concerns and it was possible that his own record in that respect didn't bear close scrutiny.

Jon's thoughts, however, were elsewhere. 'That reminds me. Who was the Mary Poppins dude?'

Steve had to think for a moment what he meant. 'Oh, that was a friend of mine, Rob Williams. He's a poet.'

'I have to admit he made a big effort, stole our thunder, but he took the sexuality out of crossdressing. That's not taking it seriously. He was just playing. Some poet!'

* * *

Without Angie around and with graduation out of the way, Steve felt at a loose end. He could move into Ainsworth Street now, although he still had to work out a way of getting his things over there. The remnants of the gang needed to be out of the Victoria Road house by the end of the week. But Steve felt becalmed by the knowledge that this was the end of his student days. The others meanwhile were making arrangements to tidy the house enough to stand a chance of getting the deposit back from the landlord. Considering how scuffed and gritty the house was Steve thought it unlikely.

The front door slammed and Di and Alan came into the sitting room and threw themselves on a couple of beanbags. They had been moving their stuff to Di's mother's in Di's battered old Hillman Minx before setting off on their French adventure. Alan could see that Steve was feeling despondent. 'Cheer up, mate. How about a drink later? Last chance, we're off tomorrow.'

Steve could do without another hangover, but he didn't fancy an evening on his own.

'Yeah, okay. But let's make it the Portland. I don't want to hack all the way into the centre of town.'

Later, sitting in the back bar of the Portland, Alan said, 'So that's it then.'

Steve looked mournfully over the top of his beer. 'Yeah. It all went by so fast.'

'Well, we'll always have the Portland.'

'Yeah, and the Merton.'

'And the Fort St George.'

'And the Eagle.'

'And the Loco.'

'So it wasn't so bad.'

'It wasn't bad at all.'

'Fare forward.'

'Don't look back.'

Having temporarily exhausted their powers of repartee, they both fell silent. Steve took a big swig of beer. 'So what are you going to do when you get back from France?'

'Who said anything about getting back?'

'You're going to stay?'

'I thought I might teach English as a foreign language. I've got some contacts at a place in Nice.'

'What does Di think of that?'

'She's fine with it.'

Steve's face fell. Alan was unsentimental about these things.

'Steve, I'm moving on. You should too.'

'I'm going to, but not just yet.'

'So, are you going to take the house in Ainsworth Street?'

'I already have.'

'Who's going to share it with you?'

'Well, I've pretty much agreed that Jon and Ginny can.'

'Steve, you're crazy. Those two are trouble.'

'Maybe trouble is what I'm after.'

'I don't think you have to go looking for it though.'

'Maybe. But I think I get where Jon's coming from. I admit that Ginny is a bit of a fruitcake, even if she does look amazing. But I think Jon has her pretty well sussed out.'

'Look, but do not touch. When are they moving in?'

'Next Monday.' Steve made it sound more definite than it was.'And I'll probably move in this Wednesday.'

'Di and I are going tomorrow. Harry's leaving on Wednesday and Jez is leaving at the end of the week. He said he'd drop off the keys at the landlord's.'

'It's been a good year,' said Steve thoughtfully.

'Don't start that again. There'll be more good times.'

Alan remembered that the last time the two of them had been sitting in that bar was the night of the jazz session, when he and Harry had got Steve pissed. A day or two later, Steve had shown Al the Jed Morgan book. Now in an attempt to divert Steve's millenarian brooding, Al asked 'How are you getting on with the jazz guitar book?'

'It's slow going. I can finger most of the chords he introduces at the beginning of the book. I just don't know how to use them.'

Alan asked Steve to give him an example.

'Well, he has these progressions that move back and forth between G major seventh and sixth, then between A minor seventh and A minor sixth, then B minor seventh and B minor sixth before returning to the G major. I can play that. It sounds nice and very old time, but I don't understand why he chooses those chords.'

'It's the harmonised scale, mate.'

'I don't know what that is.'

'Well, you need to find out. Essentially, it's the relationship of triads and triads with sevenths and other extensions in a chord progression. The sequence of triads in a scale is expressed numerically, typically in

Roman numerals, capitals for major and lowercase for minor triads. Those chords you just mentioned are the tonic or I chord of G major and the minor ii and iii of the same scale. You should try and analyse a Beatles' song, say, 'I Want To Hold Your Hand'. That song is in G major. But the bridge, you know where it goes, "And when I touch you I feel happy inside" is in C major, which is what the boffins would call a subdominant tonality. The clever thing is that the G major chord, at the chorus end ("I want to hold your hand") is the tonic, obviously, but in the bridge, it acts as the dominant or V chord. If you get your head around that, the rest falls into place.'

He might as well have been talking in code, but it gave Steve some idea of why Alan hadn't enjoyed his brief stint as Jon's bass player. Unfortunately, Steve had neither the primitive panache that Jon brought to his playing, nor the musical understanding that Alan brought to his. Still, at least he now had an inkling of what he should be doing if he wanted to advance his own guitar skills. Alan suggested another pint, which Steve declined. And indeed Alan had made the suggestion, in the hope that it would be rejected. He too needed to be up betimes and grooving on the morrow. He and Di had a cross channel ferry to catch. The two friends walked pensively back to the house they had shared for the previous year. There was nothing more to be said, for now.

When Steve got back from his round the next day, he found a note from Alan in his room. It was the chord chart for 'I Want To Hold Your Hand', and at the bottom the words, *Fare Forward*. Steve folded the sheet carefully and put it in his guitar case.

And then there were three. He went downstairs and found Jez and Harry chatting in the kitchen, while Harry chopped vegetables. He looked up. 'Al said that you're moving your stuff to Ainsworth Street tomorrow.'

Steve nodded.

'So I thought I'd do a supper for the survivors, but Jez has an Aikido lesson. What about you? I don't think even I can eat a whole lasagne on my own.'

Steve said he'd love to join Harry. He'd go out and get a bottle of wine later.

'Make sure it's something decent, none of your Mateus Rosé or Blue Nun.'

Steve objected to the implication that he was a serial Blue Nun imbiber. He certainly didn't have Harry's knowledge of wine, but nor was he entirely ignorant. He may not have attended to his studies as closely as he should have, but he had made sure to note the kinds of wines that were served on those occasions when he dined in hall. St Radegund's had a decent cellar and routinely served good wine even to undergraduates. The real point of being the bursar, it was whispered, was to manage the college's cellar.

After a brief nap, Steve walked down to the local off-licence and picked up a nice claret for £2, double what he would normally expect to pay. Harry was impressed, but not as much as Steve was with the wonderful lasagne that Harry had made. No shortcuts for Harry when it came to cooking. While a ragu of fresh vegetables and prime beef mince from the local butcher was sweating gently in olive oil, plenty of garlic and what tasted like a bottle of wine, he had whisked up a silky nutmeg and bayleaf infused béchamel sauce, before layering both ragu and sauce between sheets of lasagne. The only thing he hadn't produced from scratch was the pasta, but Steve had little doubt that before long Harry would be making his own pasta too. The two of them ate their fill and despite being noted trenchermen managed to leave enough for Jez to have a decent plateful when he got back from his Aikido session.

Harry pushed his plate away and topped up their glasses.

'So, this is the moment we have all been waiting for.'

'I'm not so sure I've been waiting for it,' said Steve.

'I mean moment in a dialectical sense.'

'Of course you do, Harry. You mean everything in a dialectical sense. But are you referring to the German neuter noun "Moment", which means something like aspect or the masculine noun which is to do with time?'

'Your trouble is you're too clever by half . . .'

'Which has not been half clever enough . . .'

'Well, the 'aspect' aspect which incidentally, we do have in English, when applied to the physics of torque . . .'

'That's a Beatles song isn't it? *Torque about a revolution . . .*'

'Ha, very ha. Anyway, to continue with my dialectical analysis, we are experiencing a moment of sublation, in the sense that graduation both abolishes our status as undergraduates and raises us to the state of being graduates. It is just another step on the path of becoming.'

'Oh come on, lay off that Hegelian twaddle.'

'I'm surprised that as a Germanist you aren't better disposed to old Georg Wilhelm.'

'I find his work impenetrable. He tortures language. The situation is not improved by the way that his German is translated into English. I mean *sublation* indeed. What a dreadful Latinism. In German, or modern German anyway, *aufheben* means both to keep and to abolish as much as it means to raise.'

'Well, that is almost a perfect description of the dialectic, the old state is cancelled, but preserved in the new elevated form.'

Steve, as ever was impressed with Harry's rhetorical skills, but was reluctant to concede the point.

'But I don't think that one could assume that things are always getting better, as is implied by the image of being raised up. Progress is surely a projection of the human mind. Evolution is not necessarily a case of the chain of being reaching its inevitable apotheosis in man or indeed in the Übermensch. There is no guaranteed path in evolution to some kind of perfection. Evolution is not teleological, homing in on some end. It is open, driven by mutation, coding errors in the genes, which in most cases will be lethal, but in a few cases, advantageous to the offspring of the affected individual. If there is any necessity in all this, it is the necessity of the contingent.'

Harry was thoughtful. 'So, you don't think we've reached a turning point.'

'I don't know. I can't read the future as well as you seem to be able to do.'

'Only because you refuse to take one of the well-worn paths away from this august institution. It seems to me that you're inviting the contingent into your life instead of trying to minimise its influence.'

'I don't believe that well-worn paths minimise the likelihood of contingency. Nothing can remove the effect of chance, not even the throw of a dice, to borrow an idea from Mallarmé. Even god has to accept contingency.'

Harry laughed. 'I don't think that bringing the deity into it is going to help your career.'

'Well, of course I don't believe in a god, but if, for the sake of argument, we assume that the world was created by a god, did he have a choice in the matter?'

Harry was not going to accept this line of reasoning. 'God is supposedly omnipotent. He can do anything.'

'But his omnipotence is at odds with his omniscience. If he knows everything, he can't change things.'

'When you say things, you mean events in time, but the god we normally have in mind in these kinds of discussions isn't subject to time. Time for him is just another spatial dimension.'

Steve was instinctively an immanentist. 'Creation on this view is something separate from god himself, but god is supposedly perfect. Why did he feel the need to create the world? Perhaps he had no choice in the matter.'

'I'm not sure you can equate choice and contingency, especially when talking about the prime mover. In any case you're getting your registers tangled up. Speculations about the nature of god are not a good way of planning a career, unless you were thinking of becoming a priest.'

'On the other hand you seem to have no problem with the idea of a career even though a career is any mode of work relations condoned by the ideologies of late capitalism, the very thing that you're working to overthrow in your political activity.'

'Well, which side are you on? Capitalism or Revolution?'

'Harry, These terms don't mean what they used to mean. Everyone, including the revolutionary, is a capitalist now, in the sense that everyone participates in the capitalist system of exchange. There may well be people who want to overthrow the system, but they quite likely have a mortgage, a steady job and a nice collection of consumer durables. In the developed world and increasingly in the developing world, there is no space outside capitalism. The socialist is just a capitalist with a guilty conscience.'

'Steve, you're just a cynical old bastard. Well, young bastard.'

'Perhaps, but maybe you're just utopian.'

'I'd say optimistic. I know we're never going to agree on this, but I'd say our interests are closer than you seem to be suggesting.'

'I'm sure you're right. And I'm going to miss these crazy discussions. It's been one of the great pleasures of the last three years.'

The two men embraced and promised to stay in touch. Steve headed for his bed to ready himself for the rigours of the morrow. He might be up for allowing contingency into his life, but he was starting to get fed up with the necessity of the milk round.

Summer's Lease

Complete the Cycle

ONCE HARRY AND ALAN had gone, Steve knew that it was also time for him to go. Jez was happy to close up the house and drop the keys off with the landlord. Then he was heading off to Granada. Steve booked a taxi and Jez helped him load all his things into the boot and the back-seat of the cab. Twenty minutes later, he was unloading his bags and his guitar onto the pavement in front of the little house. As the cab drove off, he fished the house key out of his trouser pocket, unlocked the front door and ferried his things into the front room.

He wandered around the house, which in truth he hadn't really taken in on his two previous visits. Beth had made little or no attempt to put her things away and make it suitable for the sublet. The sitting room was full of books. There was a battered sofa and an armchair and on a shelf by the fireplace a Dansette Major portable record player with a collection of LPs leaning against the wall on the floor beneath it. It was not the kind of hifi set up, Steve had become used to in Victoria Road, Jez's Videoton Minimax speakers, Trio amp and Goldring Lenco deck, but it was better than nothing, given that Steve had no hifi of his own. At the back of the room, there were french windows that, via a narrow conservatory, gave access to the back garden, which appeared to be choked with weeds.

Steve went through into the none too clean kitchen. Under a window, looking out onto the space in front of the conservatory, was a sink, containing unwashed crockery from a hasty breakfast, and a draining board over which there was a small gas heater for hot water. On the other side of the sink, was the back door and beyond that the internal door into the bathroom. Just inside the door from the hallway was a tiny fridge which proved to contain little but a pint of milk, a block of bright yellow Anchor butter and a couple of eggs in the plastic egg holder.

The room also contained a small kitchen table with four wooden chairs and a 1950s kitchen cabinet with a fold-out work surface. The two upper cupboards in the cabinet had oval windows and white curved bakelite handles. Through the windows Steve could see that there were brightly coloured earthenware bowls, plates and mugs on the left, and pots and pans on the right. Below these cupboards were two drawers which housed cutlery on one side and cooking utensils on the other. The space, that the fold-out work surface gave access to, contained painted enamel canisters for flour, sugar, tea and coffee, a breadboard, a bread knife, and a Brown Betty teapot complete with knitted cosy. In the corner of the kitchen was a grimy cream coloured gas cooker with an eye-level, grease-caked grill and a battered kettle on the hob.

The paraphernalia for making tea and coffee made Steve realise that he could do with a cup of coffee. He and Beth had not discussed whether he could use her things. Somehow he had assumed that the house would be emptied, which was absurd given that he was only taking it for three months. Still, he was sure she would have no objection to his using household supplies, as long as he replaced them. He ran some water into the kettle from the cold tap and lit one of the burners on the stove. He washed a mug and looked around for a tea towel, but rejected the one that was hanging from the hook as too grimy. He spooned two teaspoons of Nescafe into the mug and a few minutes later when the water had boiled, filled the mug and gave the dark liquid a quick stir with the spoon.

While the bitter brew cooled, he opened the door to the bathroom and looked inside. The room was tiled to shoulder height and contained a chipped enamel bath, a white ceramic sink with a mirror-fronted green cabinet over it and a lavatory with the cistern high on the wall and a long chain hanging from it. A plastic-covered metal clothes rack was perched over the bath still displaying items of female underwear.

Steve went back into the kitchen, sat down at the table and sipped his coffee. He hadn't anticipated having to undertake a major spring clean on moving in. If he'd been the only one involved, he'd probably have camped out in the hastily abandoned chaos, but he was already starting to accept that he would have to accept Jon and Ginny as his housemates. He assumed that all that stuff about tidiness and cleanliness that Ginny had given him a few days earlier in The Loco had been designed to soothe Steve's anxiety. But if there was an element of truth in it, they, or more probably, Ginny might have second thoughts about moving in once she'd seen the state of the place. There was also the possibility that Angie might visit and she would certainly be horrified.

There was not much that he could do about the sitting room, other than run a duster over the surfaces and a vacuum cleaner over the carpets, not that he'd actually spotted any such device. But the kitchen and bathroom, though horrible by any standards and undoubtedly the most shocking rooms in the house from the point of view of cleanliness, were also the rooms that would respond to the vigorous application of cleaning fluids. These vaguely comforting thoughts were shattered when he went upstairs to examine the two bedrooms.

The one at the back of the house contained a bed, which if not a single, was certainly none too wide. There was a desk under the window with piles of books on the floor to the left of it. The surface of the desk was overflowing with folders and notebooks. Steve picked up an envelope from the pile of papers in the centre of the desk and saw that it was addressed to Miss E. Rawsthorne. So this was Beth's room. To the right of the desk was a two-drawer filing cabinet. In the alcove to the left of the narrow fireplace was a chest of drawers, from an open drawer of which spilled a profusion of tee shirts and jumpers. In the other alcove was a shallow built-in closet, which when he opened one of the doors revealed a hanging rail crammed with coats, blouses and dresses. The floor of the closet appeared to be cluttered with several pairs of shoes and boots.

Steve went through to the front bedroom, Sandra's presumably. It was larger than Beth's and was dominated by a proper double bed. There was also a desk, a chest of drawers, a small bookcase and a rickety armchair. A quick inspection of the freestanding wardrobe revealed that it was every bit as full of clothes as the one in the front room and contained many more pairs of shoes than any one person could make use of.

Steve sat on the edge of the bed in dismay. Somehow he had imagined that the bedrooms at least would be left in a state such that the incoming summer tenants could fit out those rooms with their own clothes and a few belongings. Steve travelled light and didn't really have many possessions. He didn't actually mind living out of bags and boxes for a few months, but a drawer or two in which to store his clothes and a bit of hanging space was surely not too much to expect for the rent that he was paying. If he were to take Beth's room, he wondered whether it would be acceptable and not an invasion of privacy for him to re-arrange things in the room so that he could at least unpack a few of his clothes.

The more worrying aspect of the situation was how much stuff Jon and Ginny might have. Neither he nor Jon had gone into that kind of detail in their brief discussions. Steve had no idea what their current arrangements were. He thought it unlikely, given their nomadic lifestyle, that they had any furniture of their own, but they probably didn't have as few possessions as Steve. What, though, if they decided that camping out in the midst of Sandra's stuff was not something they were prepared to do? They might decide not to move in after all and then Steve would be left shouldering the whole rent. On the other hand the thought of sharing with another couple, especially a pair of freaks like Jon and Ginny, was not one to relish. Nor was the layout of the house, with the bathroom and the toilet on the ground floor, access to which was via the kitchen, ideal in that respect. Angie had been right to urge caution.

He was starting to feel despondent. He had only been in the house for a few minutes and already he was beginning to think that he'd made a serious mistake. He could see that he would have to have a proper talk with Jon and Ginny. In the meantime he would bring his things up to the back room, go out and get something for supper and some basic supplies for the next few days, then get an hour or two of kip.

He had noticed on his first visit the little grocery shop across the road, and decided to see if he could get the supplies he needed there. He crossed the road and pushed the door open to the cracked tinkle of a little bell connected to the lintel over the door. An elderly man wearing a brown khaki warehouse coat and a collar and tie emerged from the room at the back of the shop. He smiled at Steve and said, 'I believe I saw you moving your things into Beth's place. She told me someone would be staying in the house while she was away. I'm Bert.'

Steve hadn't been expecting to be a person of interest for the neighbourhood watch. 'Pleased to meet you, Bert. I'm Steve. I thought I'd just pick up a few supplies.'

'That's what I'm here for. Been serving the local community since before the war.'

Steve was about to ask which war, but decided that the joke was in bad taste. He glanced around the shop and couldn't help noticing that not only was it not well stocked, but that some of the items on the shelves might indeed be pre-war. The interior reminded Steve of what corner shops had been like when he was a small boy. There was little in the way of refrigeration. The small deep freeze was devoted primarily to ice cream, ice lollies and some cartons of fish fingers, while the small glass-fronted chill cabinet housed a few pints of milk, some Anchor butter and a couple of packs of Wall's pork sausages. Apart from a few blocks of tired cheese and a piece of dubious looking ham resting on a marble slab beneath a perspex cover, Bert's stock seemed largely comprised of packaged goods: screw-top jars, cans and cardboard packets of various kinds.

But now that he was on first name terms with Bert, it would have been impolite not to make a few purchases. Steve reeled off a list of the things that he needed and Bert fetched those items that he could supply, totting up the bill with a stub of pencil on a sheet of wrapping paper. As he gave Steve his change, he said, 'Lovely girl, Beth. The man who captures her heart will be doing very well for himself.'

Steve could only agree, but hoped that Bert didn't think, on the basis of five minutes' conversation, that he was a suitable candidate, or even worse, that Beth had given Bert to understand that she fancied Steve. He said that he looked forward to getting to know Bert better over the next few months and carried the supplies back to the house. He stowed them in the kitchen and then went upstairs for the nap he had promised himself.

When he woke a couple of hours later he still had not shaken off the feeling of disquiet. Maybe he'd feel better after a bath and something to eat. He went down to the bathroom and speculatively ran the hot tap, which coughed once or twice and then delivered a trickle of water, which at least proved to be hot. He lifted down the clothes drying rack that straddled the bath, faintly amused that Beth and Sandra, even though they knew that they were going to have a male tenant, had not thought to put away the underwear that was draped over the bars of the rack before they went off for the summer. But reflecting on the state of the bedrooms, Steve concluded that putting things away was not a top priority with those two. And perhaps it was also the case that many women found it difficult to understand the significance of women's underwear for the male mind, particularly those males of a prurient disposition.

Steve's own approach to tidiness involved a practice which he called completing the cycle. This largely involved putting things back where they came from. One might not finish a project, but at least one should tidy up the things involved in the activity. The practice, that he thought of as being vaguely zen, but which Angie thought of as a mild version of obsessive compulsive disorder, also implied that he extend this responsibility to others' things. Don't just put your own stuff away, put your partner's stuff away too. In the spirit of the extended version of this spiritual practice, he felt that it would be wrong to leave the underclothes dangling from the rack for the whole of the summer. He would return them to their owner's room. But as he folded them into a small pile to take upstairs, he realised that, of course, it was quite probable that some of the items were Beth's and some Sandra's. Whose were whose? Surely it should be possible to separate the garments into two smaller piles based on size or style. This was exactly the kind of problem that Steve relished, even when unrelated to women's underclothes.

Without thinking of the wider implications of what he was doing or questioning his motives, he picked up the bra that was on top of the pile of clothes and examined the label, which though faded revealed that it was a size 30B. He put that bra to one side as the first item on a pile for woman one. He then picked up a second bra. The label of this one was completely illegible, but in style it was very similar to the first bra, unstructured and unadorned and really rather grubby. He decided on the strength of stylistic analysis to add it to the pile for woman one. By contrast a third bra was a lacy affair and its label clearly showed that it was size 32B. Steve's intuitive impression was that this bra belonged to woman two and he started a new pile for her items of clothing.

Almost immediately he wanted to resolve the issue of whether Beth was woman one or woman two. To judge from his samples, woman two was slightly fuller on top than woman one, but since he hadn't met Sandra, it was impossible to form a mental comparison of the two women's figures. In truth he didn't even have a strong impression of what Beth looked like. He was normally quite attentive to the female upper torso and since he had not been particularly struck by Beth's figure when they had met, he presumed she was quite slim in that regard. On the other hand there wasn't much between a 30B or a 32B. Or was there? The latter was presumably more of a handful, if that wasn't an inappropriate way to put. But in fact he only had the vaguest idea how women's clothing measurements worked.

Lowering his sights, he wondered if there might be some correlation with knicker size. He picked up the topmost pair of knickers, surprised at how silky they were, and looking at the label, saw that it indicated that they were size 10. He moved on the next pair which were briefer and lacier, which also proved to be size 10. The remaining two pairs of knickers, both in a pale flesh-coloured cotton jersey, which he felt must be much more comfortable and practical to wear, were also, irritatingly, size 10. Here was a conundrum. Did that mean that the all the knickers belonged to one women? Or that, while having different bra sizes, the women took the same size in knickers, and certain of the knickers belonged to one and some to the other? It seemed counterintuitive that a woman would put a bra into wash, but not, at the same time, a pair of knickers, or indeed more than one pair. So he felt that he ought to attempt to divide the knickers between the 30B pile and the 32B pile. Once again *faute de mieux*, he decided the matter on stylistic grounds, allocating the lacy ones and the silk ones to the 32B pile and the jersey knickers to the 30B pile.

Tolerably pleased with the results of his underwear sleuthing, but aware that he had not yet identified whether Beth was 32B or 30B, he took the two piles of underwear into the kitchen and placed them on one of the chairs with the intention of repatriating them upstairs later on. He then went back into the bathroom, stripped off his clothes and climbed gingerly into the bath and, pondering how he was going to put names to the bra sizes, wallowed happily in the tub until the water became tepid.

He reached for the towel that was hanging over the towel rail and was not entirely able to suppress a grimace of revulsion on discovering that it was not only damp, but was also impregnated with an unfamiliar scent. This was hardly surprising given that it was Beth or Sandra's towel and not his own, which he had not thought to unpack before getting into the bath. He was normally quite fastidious about matters such as using another person's towel. In the shared house in Victoria Road, he had taken to keeping his own towel in his room and carrying it back and forth to the bathroom. As he dried himself he was dimly aware that by using the heavily scented towel he was anointing himself with his landladies' scent. He padded upstairs naked, with the clothes, he had been wearing earlier in his arms. He opened his case, pulled out a set of clean clothes and got dressed.

Later, as he sat down to his supper, a Fray Bentos steak pie, mashed potatoes and Batchelor's peas washed down with a glass of Marks and Spencer's Vin Superieur Rouge, a bottle of which he had found in the kitchen cabinet, food and drink a considerable step down from the meal he had shared with Harry the previous night, he returned to the problem of what to do about the bedrooms and Jon and Ginny's expectations. These intractable thoughts were interrupted by his gaze falling on the two neat piles of underwear on the kitchen chair beside him. Complete the cycle.

He finished his meal, washed up the two pans he'd used to prepare the meal, his plate, cutlery and glass and put them in the rack on the draining board. He put the tin that had contained the steak pie in the pedal-bin, and then picked up the two piles of underwear and went up to the back bedroom with the single bed, which he had now designated as his own. He was determined to do two things: establish who 30B and 32B were so that he could repatriate the underwear from downstairs correctly, and make some attempt to reorganise the room.

He started with the chest of drawers. The top row was divided into two drawers. He opened the one on the left. It contained knickers and tights. Presumably, they were size 10. If not, something odd was going on. He picked up a pair and checked the label size—10. Okay. Style? Simple, unfussy. He opened the drawer on the right. As he had assumed it contained bras and slips, with a noticeable absence of flimsy or sexy bras. He picked up one and checked the label—30B. Just to be sure, he checked another. It was the same. It looked pretty much as if Beth was was Miss 30B. But the only way to be absolutely sure, within the parameters of his experiment, was to check the underwear in the other room.

He went next door and checked Sandra's chest of drawers. The knickers, as expected, were size 10 and scattered among the sensible pairs were several fancier pairs. So far, so good. But the clincher would be the bra size. He opened the bra drawer and took out the first bra that came to hand, a lacy black number. He checked the label and took a moment to realise that it said 30C. That immediately falsified his hypothesis. He picked up another, 30C again. He checked several more, all 30C. Finally he found one that was 32B, and then a second one. He sat on the bed surrounded by bras, five 30Cs on one side and two 32Bs on the other. He was glad no one could see him just at that moment. He was not sure that they would believe that his motives were well intentioned, that all he was trying to do was to apply forensic principles to the situation.

Uncertain, he picked up the bras and put them back in the drawer. Despite the presence of several 30C bras, he felt that his hypothesis was still viable, if only on the basis of stylistic analysis and the fact that two of the bras were the same size as his bathroom sample. He went back to the other bedroom and for the sake of completeness checked all six of the bras in Beth's chest of drawers, relieved to find that they were all 30Bs. Had a 30C turned up, or even worse, a 32B, his theory would have been in tatters. He put the bras back in the drawer and then, taking a deep breath, added knickers from the 30B bathroom pile to the lefthand drawer and bras from the same pile to the righthand drawer. He then went into Sandra's room, and did the same with the 32B pile. He felt exhausted, but satisfied that he had completed the cycle. And he now also had a more intimate understanding of Beth's and Sandra's underwear than he had of Angie's, although he couldn't help feeling that this was a form of illicit knowledge.

Cycle complete perhaps. His purpose, however, was not to conduct an anthropological study of late 20th century women's underwear, but to create some space for himself and for the pair of freaks he had somehow agreed to have as his housemates. He didn't actually have that many clothes that needed to be hung up, but in order to accommodate even those few, he was going to have to take some of Beth's things out of the closet. He opened it and looked more closely at the garments that were hanging there, coats, dresses and blouses, the kinds of thing that if not hung up would crease. Was there an easy way of deciding which ones could be sacrificed? And what would he do with them in the meantime? Maybe he should leave the closet for now and direct his attention to the chest of drawers. He was by now more familiar with the contents of the top two drawers than he would care to admit to. But what about the two lower drawers? He opened the middle one to find it stuffed to the gunwales with tee shirts and jeans. Such garments hardly needed the same kind of care as the clothes hanging in the closet. But even so, where would he put them? To have them lying around on the floor was no solution. He went next door and was reminded that the problem in that room was even more acute.

He was stumped. Maybe he was being too optimistic or extending the cycle beyond its natural boundaries. The cycle in question had been to repatriate the stray bras and knickers, not to solve within his first few hours in the house how to accommodate the stuff that Jon and Ginny would be bringing with them. If completing the cycle was an important principle, getting things in the right order was an even more important principle. He needed to talk to Jon and Ginny first, put them in the picture about the storage problems and see what their response was before he did anything else. It would be absurd to empty their room and then for them to decide that they couldn't move in. He resolved to go and see them after work the next day.

Having sidestepped the immediate problem, he went downstairs and decided to see if Beth and Sandra had anything worth listening to in their collection of LPs. He poured himself another glass of wine, wincing as he sipped it and flipped through the pile. He picked out Joni Mitchell's *Court and Spark* and put it on the Dansette.

Something about the intelligence and sensitivity of the lyrics reminded him of Angie. He imagined that she must be settling into her flat and her job in Brighton. He had an urge to speak to her, but neither of them had domestic access to a phone. When they had been separated in the past they had had to schedule calls, Steve invariably phoning from a call box. Otherwise they had written to each other, sometimes several times a week. Steve decided to write to her now, because surely moving into Ainsworth Street was a milestone, even if it was one that Angie didn't really approve of. He fetched his notepad and started writing.

He described the state of the house and how angry he was with Beth and Sandra for not having made any attempt to tidy up or to make the place suitable for other people to live in. He decided that it was probably better not to go into the rigmarole with the underwear. But he did express his concern that even Jon and Ginny might not find the state of the house acceptable. He would let Angie know how things turned out. He told her that he missed her terribly. He knew she was angry with him, but he hoped that she would understand that he needed this space to get himself sorted out. It would be great if she could write to him soon and let him know how she was getting on.

After work the next day Steve set out for Jon and Ginny's place in Argyle Street, the other side of the railway line but not too far away. It might be a little early in the day for a couple of night owls, but that was too bad. It was his best chance of finding them in. He had never been to their place before and wasn't sure if he had remembered the street number correctly, but the presence of a flamboyantly painted VW camper van parked rakishly in front of the street number he had in mind, reassured him that he had found the right place.

He knocked on the door and after a prolonged pause the front door inched open to reveal a suspicious Jon Chapman.

Steve said, 'Sorry to come around so early. We need to talk about this house share business.'

Jon brightened and opened the door wider. 'Hi, man, Good to see you. Come in.'

Ginny was not in evidence. Jon took Steve into the little front room and Steve said, 'I've moved into the Ainsworth Street house now and there are some issues with the house that I need to discuss with you.'

The brightness, that Jon had affected, clouded over.

'That sounds ominous. Unfortunately Ginny's unwell. After we saw you last, Ginny came down with one of her bouts of depression. She calls it her black dog. She seems a lot better today, but she's still in bed.'

Steve commiserated and said that in that case he'd put Jon in the picture and he could discuss the situation with Ginny when she was feeling better, but just at that moment the door opened and Ginny walked in and sat in a chair opposite Steve without saying a word. She was in a flimsy nightdress, her long, black hair in tangles. Jon picked up a shawl that was draped over the back of a chair and put it around her shoulders and said gently, 'What can I get you?'

Without looking up, she said, 'A cup of tea, please.'

'Coming right up. Steve's come around to talk about a problem with the house share.' Having clarified the matter Jon went off to the kitchen to make a pot of tea.

Ginny didn't seem to react to what Jon had said. She just sat shivering in her chair, her head bowed, her arms folded across her chest. In an attempt to break the silence, Steve said, 'Sorry you're not feeling well. Depression is a terrible thing.'

Ginny raised her head and looked at him directly for the first time since she had entered the room and said in a monotone, 'It will pass. Everything does.'

Steve nodded noncommittally.

In the same enigmatic manner, Ginny continued, 'I can tell you still have reservations about the house share. Are you afraid of us?'

'Well, I don't really know you.'

'And you think we'll lead you astray or harm you?'

'Angie thinks I'm easily lead astray.'

'Is that what you think too?'

'I don't think that I really know myself.'

Why had he said that? Was that what he really thought?

Ginny continued with her interrogation. 'Do you want to know yourself?'

'Yes, of course.'

'You say of course, but the truth is that most of us really don't want to know ourselves. We would rather do almost anything than be brought face to face with ourselves. But if you really do, I think I can help you.'

Steve was beginning to resent being cross-examined and attempted to switch the dynamic. 'What makes you think you can do that?'

'I can't go into details now, but it is something that I have some experience in. Look, it's okay to be scared of us. It's sensible, but I promise you that you will come to no harm. I will look after you.'

Steve was finding this exchange very freaky. He didn't feel that he needed looking after and if he did, he wasn't sure that he would commit himself to Ginny's care. But rather than ignore what others might have taken as a throwaway comment, Steve said, 'How can you say that with any certainty?'

Ginny suddenly stood up and cast off the shawl that Jon had put around her shoulders. She looked a lot bigger and not in the least poorly as she took two or three smooth strides across the room and, standing just inches from him, said, 'Give me your hand.'

He started to stand up, but she pushed him back into his chair, took his left hand and turned it over, palm up. She ran her fingers expertly over his palm and then lifted it up to look at it more closely. Steve felt powerless, and, powerfully conscious of the scent of her body, stared at the ground, unable to meet her gaze. Why was he letting her do this? After a few more moments studying his hand, she released it and placed her own hand on his forehead as if taking his temperature. He finally dared look up and was dazzled as the afternoon sun poured through the front window bathing her in gold. He shut his eyes against the dazzle and when he reopened them, she was back in her chair, smiling at him. He felt amazingly relaxed.

'You'll be fine,' she said, 'You're strong and loving.'

He finally found his tongue and said, his voice seeming to come from a great distance, 'I'm afraid I don't have much faith in palmistry, if that's what you were doing.'

Ginny continued to smile at him serenely. 'Not believing in electricity doesn't stop you being struck by lightning.'

Steve, struggling to regain some initiative in the exchanges, said, 'Ginny, if you're trying to make me feel more positive about our sharing a house, this is not the best way of going about it.'

'If you don't want us with you, all you have to do is say so. Now's your chance. There'll be no hard feelings on our part.'

That was precisely what he wanted to say, but the words stuck in his throat. He felt paralysed. Where was Jon? He was taking the devil of a long time to make a pot of tea. Ginny, sensing his discomfort perhaps, leaned forward and said, 'So, what's the problem with the house?'

At that moment, Jon re-entered the room, bearing three mugs of tea and put them on the side table. Steve realised that he had now passed the point of no return and that the state of the house was not a reason for them not to join him, but a problem for them to solve collectively. For the first time for weeks he relaxed and submitted to the momentum of the situation.

Steve described the conditions in the house and explained that whilst he himself could put up with the lack of personal storage, because he had little in the way of possessions and the sub-let was only for three months, he assumed that Jon and Ginny had much more stuff and were probably looking for a longer tenure.

Jon shook his head pensively, 'We don't have a lot either. None of this furniture is ours. I suppose we'd better come around and suss things out. But not until Ginny's kicked the black dog.'

That wasn't exactly the response that Steve had been hoping for, but there was really no alternative but to play out the current hand of cards, Tarot cards, it would seem.

Steve sipped his tea. He was going to suggest that they didn't come around before midday, but decided that that was probably unnecessary. In any case Ginny had withdrawn once more into herself and Jon was staring into space. Steve finished his tea and said he should be going.

He spent the rest of the afternoon in his room reading and dozing. Towards six o'clock he strolled down Mill Road, giving The Locomotive a miss, on the basis that it was Jon's regular haunt, and choosing instead the Six Bells in Covent Garden, an altogether staider establishment. Steve settled himself in a corner and, sipping his beer, opened his book, registering the gentle murmur of the early evening conversations around him. He was reading Elias Canetti's *Crowds and Power*, which he'd picked up in David's, the secondhand bookshop in St Edward's Passage. It was a dense book about the behaviour of people in groups and the effect of those groups on the individual. Steve wasn't quite sure why he was reading it. As he'd leafed through it in the bookshop, he'd been fascinated by the anthropological details that caught his eye. He resumed reading it now at a point marked with a buff coloured Eastern Counties bus ticket. Soon he was absorbed in his reading and scarcely lifted his eyes from the book until his glass was empty. He went to the bar, ordered another pint and some food and resumed his reading.

When he had finished the second pint, he decide that it would be sensible to go home. It wasn't a good idea to drink too much on a work night and annoyingly every night at the moment was a work night. He was lost in this deliberation, when he spotted a familiar face across the room. It was Grace Mitchell, who had supervised him in modern French thought and literature and whom he had last seen a couple of weeks previously jogging across Parker's Piece. On that occasion he had taken evasive action, but it was rather more difficult to pretend he hadn't noticed her in a bar as snug as that of the Six Bells.

Grace, however, had already spotted him and came across to his table. 'Hello Steve. Well, this is a surprise. I thought you'd be holed up in a taverna in Naxos putting the finishing touches to the magnum opus.'

'Not quite.'

Steve hadn't meant to be quite so terse. He was actually feeling distinctly guilty about not having thanked Grace for her efforts in getting him through his Finals. He'd intended to, but he'd had his mind on other things. There was nothing for it, even if it called his sincerity into question, he would have to do it now. 'I wanted to say how much I appreciated everything you did to prepare me for the exams. Without your help I wouldn't have got through. You are a brilliant supervisor. I meant to write . . .' His voice tailed off.

She smiled at him. 'Don't be ridiculous. That's my job. Actually I think of myself more as a coach than a supervisor. But thank you. Anyway you got a good mark for that paper, so well done the both of us.'

Steve felt hugely relieved that he'd got that out of the way and said the least he could do was buy her drink. Grace said she'd have a gin and tonic, if he didn't mind her joining him for a bit. When Steve got back with the drinks, Grace said, 'So, what brings you to the Six Bells? Waiting for your girlfriend? Angie, isn't it?'

Steve shook his head and explained that Angie was in Brighton. Grace, sipping her drink asked, 'How are you getting on with your writing?'

Steve winced at the memory of having used his poem as an excuse for not getting an essay in on time. He now regretted that particular hostage to fortune.'Thank-you letters are not the only thing that haven't got written in recent weeks.'

Grace tilted her head to one side and said, 'Maybe you just need a coach for your creative writing too.'

Steve laughed. 'Yeah.'

'I'm not joking Steve Percival. You let yourself off too easily.'

'Well, Angie used to encourage me, but, as I was saying, she's down in Brighton and then she's off to Edinburgh to begin a PhD.'

'So, there's a vacancy?'

Steve looked carefully at Grace. He wasn't sure where she was going with this.

'Vacancy for what?'

'For a coach. You need someone to hold you to account, to make sure you do the work. If I recall correctly, you were going to let me see your poem, once Finals were over.'

'Did I say that?'

'You certainly did.'

'I thought you were just being polite.'

'For goodness sake, man, we worked on Mallarmé together. Did you think that I wouldn't be interested in your poetry?'

'I was embarrassed. I'm not sure if it's any good.'

'How could you find out without letting other people read it?'

'I wanted to be sure of it before I showed it around.'

'You can never be sure. Do you still have hopes for this poem?'

'Yeah.'

Steve took a deep draught of his beer and wiping his mouth with the back of his hand said, 'So, is this your local?'

Grace chuckled at this blatant attempt to change the subject. 'Yes, as a matter of fact, though I don't come in here very much. I've been stuck in the house all day, working, and I hadn't the energy to make myself any supper, so I thought I'd have liquid one.'

More comfortable posing the questions, Steve asked her what she was working on.

'I suppose you think that academics just put their feet up once the students disappear or spend all the summer in the pub knocking back the gin and tonics. But the fact is that this is when we do our real work. I'm writing a book on Sartre and Camus. It's already well overdue and the publisher is chasing me.'

Steve saw his chance to even the score. 'Sounds like you're the one who needs a coach.'

Grace saw his call and raised him. 'Are you offering your services?'

Steve pulled his horns in. 'Sorry, stupid joke.'

'Well, maybe not so stupid. You did some good work on existentialism. And the fact is, I could do with someone to read over the current draft. Pete is far too busy at the moment to do that.'

'Pete?'

'My husband. He's a publisher, although not *my* publisher unfortunately, not in that sense anyway.'

She finished her drink. 'So, are you up for it then?'

Steve looked puzzled. 'For what?'

'Reading my manuscript.'

'Well, okay,' he said hesitantly.

'But you've got to take it seriously, Steve. Student days are over. This is the real world. There's about 200 pages of typescript. You should be able to get through that in a week, but to be on the safe side, let's say two weeks. Ideally you'd put your thoughts in writing. Doesn't have to be long. Two or three pages. What do you say?'

Steve didn't actually know what to say.

'The quid pro quo is I'll offer my thoughts on your poem, however much there is of it. I will give you an honest opinion. And if I think it's any good, I'll let Pete see it. He's the publishing director of Inflexion Books.'

Steve gulped. This was deeply weird. He felt that he had entered an alternate reality, in which his student obligations were being reprised, but in a slightly different key. The whole idea of his staying in Cambridge was so that he could get on with his own work. At least that had been the general idea. Okay, he hadn't done much in the previous few weeks to that effect. But now, just as he was ready to get down to work on the poem, he seemed to have agreed to read the draft of an academic book by one of his former supervisors on a subject that he thought had been consigned to oblivion along with his undergraduate gown. Not only that, he was on the point of letting her see *Event/ Horizon*. It was one thing to talk to Angie about the ideas behind the poem, quite another thing to let Grace, who was an expert in modern French poetry, see it. On the other hand it might be the fast track to getting it seen by a professional publisher.

But time was getting on. Steve said, 'I'm sorry Grace but I need to be getting back.'

'Of course. And so do I. Pete will be back from London soon. Which way are you going?'

'I'm living in Ainsworth Street, just off Gwydir Street.'

'Well, if you don't mind making a small detour, you can pick up the manuscript now. I live in Glisson Road.'

It didn't take them long to reach Grace's house. He waited in the hallway while she went upstairs to where he guessed she had her study. He glanced through the open door of the front room and admired what he could see of an elegant sitting room lined with books and paintings. A short while later Grace came back downstairs with a manilla folder and handed it to him.

'Two weeks, remember. My telephone number is on the front cover. Do you have a phone where you're living?'

Steve shook his head.

'Well, phone me from a call box when you're ready with your report. You'd better give me your address, just in case I need to rescue my manuscript.'

He wrote his address on the pad she gave him.

'And drop off your poem, in the next day or two,' she continued. 'I mean it. Otherwise I'll be up ...' She glanced at the pad he'd handed back to her. '... I'll be up to Ainsworth Street to prise it out of your grubby little hands.'

She pushed him towards the front door. 'Now, scoot,' and leaning forward gave him a quick peck on the cheek, an unexpected token of no longer being *in statu pupillari*.

When he got back to Ainsworth Street he threw himself onto his bed, pulled Grace's manuscript out of his bag and started reading. It wasn't so much that he was keen to get on with the job, more that he was curious to get a feel of Grace's prose. It was certainly an odd sensation to be, to some extent, assessing the work of someone who until recently had been his own supervisor. But before long he was immersed in the world of Camus and Sartre and any incongruity in his situation evaporated.

Later as he drifted off to sleep, images of his own first visit to Paris in 1969 in the uneasy calm after *les évenements de soixante-huit* filled his thoughts. Squads of CRS officers, the much hated riot police, had still been occupying key intersections of the city. But despite their unsmiling presence, Steve, like countless others before him, had been captivated by the Parisian combination of elegance and frankness, epitomised by the aromas of the city; Gitanes, coffee, red wine and piss. The stylishness of Parisian dress and the openness about sexual matters and bodily functions, contrasted strongly with the fustiness and prudery of Anglo-Saxony. Paris might be only 300 miles from London, roughly the distance to Newcastle-Upon-Tyne, but the atmosphere couldn't have been more different.

TRANSFORMATION

FRIDAY WAS ALWAYS A difficult day on the round because it was a collection day. Steve was aware that his weekly take was once again not as good as it might have been and, now that he was living closer to the dairy, decided to spend the extra time available to him trying to catch up a bit. The gaffer was impressed when he got back to the yard and said that they might make a milkman of him yet. Steve was strangely proud of the pat on the back and decided to celebrate by having a nap when he got back to the house. As he drifted off to sleep, he reflected that graduation had been just a week ago. And it was also a week since he'd last held Angie in his arms.

He had not been long asleep when he was roused from his slumbers by a loud knocking at the front door. He pulled on his jeans and tee shirt and went downstairs to see who was at the door. He was only a little surprised to see Jon and Ginny standing there.

'Ginny's feeling a bit better, so we thought we'd come around and see what you were talking about,' explained Jon.

Steve invited them in and took them through to the kitchen, waving his hand at the inadequate arrangements.

Ginny shrugged, 'I've seen worse. Actually there's something authentic about it.'

Steve pointed through to the bathroom. 'That's another problem. No facilities upstairs.'

Jon let Ginny do the inspection. She emerged and said, 'Yes, well that is a little primitive, but it can probably be improved with a bit of elbow grease.' Which had been Steve's own view, even though he had not actually applied any of the said grease yet.

They then walked through into the sitting room. Ginny made no comment. She went over to the french widows and peered through the grimy windows into the little conservatory and out into the tangled garden. Steve thought he heard her say, 'Sad.'

Clearly the downstairs while unlikely to win any ideal home awards, even in the shabby chic category, did not appear to be a no-go area as far as Ginny was concerned. Jon, who had refrained from comment since greeting Steve on the doorstep, would be guided by Ginny, it seemed.

He led them upstairs and took them into Beth's room, now his. 'I thought I'd take this one, since it has the single bed and is the smaller room.'

Ginny asked if she could look in the closet and chest of drawers. Steve could hardly refuse since he himself had spent a whole evening doing exactly the same thing. Ginny opened the closet and ran her fingers expertly over the hanging clothes. She then went over to the chest of drawers, opened the top lefthand draw and took out the topmost pair of knickers and held them up to inspection. Steve was shocked, partly because it seemed an entirely unnecessary thing to do, but mainly because they were one of the pairs that he had spent so much time analysing himself. Ginny laid the knickers back in the drawer and smoothed them down with the palm of her hand. She didn't look impressed. He hadn't expected the house to be subject to such minute scrutiny. It would be slightly weird if they decided not to move in with him on the basis of the kind of knickers his landlady wore. She gestured at all the papers and books on the desk, 'Those are hers?' Steve nodded.

They went next door to the front room. 'I thought you could have this room,' Steve said needlessly.

Ginny repeated the same procedure checking the closet and the chest of drawers. She seemed to be particularly interested in the number of pairs of shoes that covered the base of the wardrobe and once again pulled out individual items for closer inspection.

Wanting to bring this bizarre procedure to an end, Steve offered his guests a cup of tea. They trooped down the narrow staircase, Ginny running her forefinger along the banister and scowling at the amount of dust it accumulated in this way. Steve put the kettle on and got out three mugs, while Jon and Ginny sat down at the table.

'As you can see there's not even any space to unpack my things and you probably have considerably more gear than me. I spent the first evening here contemplating taking all the clothes out of both wardrobes and chests of drawers, but then where was I going to put all their stuff? I'm quite annoyed really. When you pay rent, you expect to be able to put your things away.'

Jon seemed incapable of constructing any kind of equation between rent and expectations and shrugged equivocally, whereas Ginny was completely uninterested in Steve's limp-wristed annoyance, but approved of the plan that he had balked at. 'Of course we need to get their stuff out of the bedrooms. Nothing we can't fix over the weekend,' she declared emphatically.

'But where are we going to put them?' Steve asked plaintively.

'We'll sort that out tomorrow. First we need to clean the place up. It really is unbelievably filthy.'

Steve found himself agreeing, but had no idea what she had in mind.

'I presume there's another key that we can have, so that we can make a start while you're at work.'

'Tomorrow?'

'Yes, tomorrow,' Ginny said sharply.

Steve took one of the keys of the keyring and handed it to Ginny, feeling that things were slipping out of his control.

When Steve got back from his round on the Saturday morning, he found Ginny standing in the Ainsworth Street kitchen dressed in dark blue dungarees, her hair put up in a scarf and her hands encased in rubber cleaning gloves, but still managing to look decidedly sexy. She pushed an unruly lock of dark hair out of her eyes and greeted him dispassionately. She was getting to grips with the grease that caked virtually every surface in the kitchen. Steve asked what he could do to help. Ginny said that he could make a pot of tea and when they had had their tea, he could vacuum the sitting room, the hall and the stairs.

Steve put the kettle on and asked whether Jon would want one.

'Jon's not here. He's got a gig today.'

Steve was not surprised at this piece of information, but he was surprised that Ginny seemed not in the slightest bit resentful that he wasn't helping out. Steve made the tea and put the mugs on the table. Ginny pulled the rubber gloves off and sat down beside him.

'How was work this morning?'

'Being a milkman is not exactly complicated. In fact it's quite straightforward. You go at your own pace and for the most part you don't have to engage with people. But Fridays and Saturdays are different. It's when we collect money. So everything takes longer and suddenly you are dealing with the public and they can be surprisingly difficult about relatively small sums of money.'

Ginny nodded knowingly. 'Money changes everything.'

She took a sip of her tea, 'So, who are the women who live in this place and have let it get in this state?'

'Beth and Sandra. I don't really know them. In fact I've never met Sandra and I've only met Beth twice, both times very briefly. I found them by answering an ad.'

'Can you believe that two women could live like this? What do they do?'

'Beth's a postgraduate student. I don't know anything about Sandra.'

Steve didn't really want to reflect on Beth and Sandra's lack of cleanliness.

Ginny nodded and drank her tea thoughtfully. Uncomfortable with the awkward silence that had arisen, Steve said, 'I'm glad to see that you're feeling better today.'

Ginny made a sideways movement with her hand as if she was drawing a line under something. 'I'd rather not talk about it.'

Not sure how to continue the conversation, Steve finished his tea. 'Right, I'll get on with the vacuuming. By the way where did you find the vacuum cleaner? I looked for one when I moved in.'

'I brought it from the other house, so do a good job, because we'll have to take it back.'

She also suggested that he vacuum the soft furnishings and to make sure to move the furniture.

Steve set to. He had to empty the vacuum cleaner bag several times and felt that he had inhaled almost as much dust as he had sucked into the cleaner itself. His eyes became red and he coughed and spluttered. In the meantime Ginny transferred her attention to the bathroom. The chemicals in the cleaning materials seemed to affect her almost as badly as the dust affected Steve. They reconvened in the kitchen for another cup of tea and for a period of recovery.

'What now?' Steve asked.

'Clear the little conservatory. Move the junk into the garden. None of it looks as if it is of any use or value. Hoover up the dirt and the grit. Then get the mop and bucket and make sure that the floor is a clean as can be.'

Steve was at a loss as to why Ginny thought the conservatory should be cleaned up. It just seemed to be used to store broken furniture. But he did as he was told. Ginny was most definitely in charge. An hour later he returned to the kitchen and found Ginny still scrubbing furiously.

Steve wished she would finish for the day and go home. He was tired and hungry. With some trepidation, he said, 'Ginny, I don't want to sound defeatist, but it's nearly half past six. I've been working since half past five this morning. I need to get myself something to eat and get to bed by nine-thirty. We can hit this again tomorrow.'

Ginny did not immediately reply. She continued rinsing out the sink she had been scrubbing. Steve sensed his suggestion had not gone down too well. He was just about to reiterate how tired he was, when Ginny turned around, peeling off the rubber gloves and smiling at him and said, 'Of course. You must be exhausted. Why don't I run you a bath and while you're having your bath, I'll make some food?'

Steve found the sudden change of mood from tight-lipped briskness to cheerful kindness and the accompanying offers, as welcome as they were, unsettling. The only problem was that he had neglected to do any shopping.

'I'll nip across to the Empire Stores and get some sausages or something.'

Ginny went across to the fridge and brought out two bottles of beer. 'No need. I brought some supplies with me.'

She put the beers on the table, pulled open the drawer in the kitchen unit, found the bottle opener, flipped the caps off the bottle and handed one to Steve. They clinked bottles and Steve took a big swig. The cold beer tasted delicious.

'Ginny, this amazing. Thank you.'

'Least I could do,' she said. 'I know you'd rather not have us here, but it won't be so bad. I promise you. I'll go and run that bath.'

Steve protested that he could do it himself, but she was having none of it. He didn't have the energy to struggle and sat back to enjoy the beer. She returned a few minutes later. 'All yours. No rush, though. The bath's going to take a while to fill.'

Ginny lit a burner on the stove and heated a small amount of oil in a frying pan into which she scraped some diced onion, garlic and pancetta. A delicious aroma filled the room. Steve watched her work. This was not the Ginny he had previously encountered. After her performance two days earlier he had been dreading being alone with her, but but the weird sister who had read his palm had somehow been replaced by a more nurturing personality. She seemed almost happy, a quality that Steve had not previously associated with her. At the same time she had lost none of her poise or beauty. She sensed his gaze, turned and smiled.

Embarrassed, Steve said, 'Why did you ask me to clear out the conservatory? It just seems dead space to me.'

'Because that's where we're going to put all the stuff from the two bedrooms.'

She could tell from the look on his face that he didn't think this was a good idea.

'Don't worry, we'll do it all properly. Jon has been locating some storage items and he'll bring them over tomorrow. Everything will be carefully packed and labelled. Trust me, I've done this before. And cleaned up worse places.'

Steve thought that unlikely, but didn't dare question the assertion.

'Anyway, are you going to have that bath or not?'

Steve finished his beer and went next door into the little bathroom. He stripped off and climbed into the bath. The room already seemed more wholesome as a result of Ginny's hard work. As he soaked the aches out of his tired limbs, he wondered whether if it was true that Ginny had cleaned up other dismal temporary digs. He had a feeling that she might have underestimated how much stuff Beth and Sandra had. There didn't seem any point arguing the toss, though. Ginny had the bit between her teeth.

In the meantime the smells emanating from the kitchen were delicious. Steve was on the point of nodding off, when Ginny put her head around the door and said, 'Come on, slowcoach. The meal is ready,' and threw a towel at him. Steve was disconcerted by this mild invasion of his privacy and said he'd be right out. Ginny went back into the kitchen, neglecting to close the door. Steve climbed out the bath awkwardly, trying not to expose himself. This was exactly why he was apprehensive of sharing a small space with a couple of far-out bohemians. He had also neglected to bring down any clean clothes, so he dressed himself hurriedly in his work clothes and re-entered the kitchen to find the table set with two plates of pasta, together with a green salad and two more bottles of beer.

'Ginny, this is fantastic. I didn't expect you to do all this.'

'Don't be ridiculous, we both need to eat.'

Steve sat down and started to eat. The food was delicious. After a couple of mouthfuls, he said, 'I'll do the washing up and put the supper things away.'

'Thank you, Steve.'

'You must be pretty tired. You've been at it all day.'

'No, I feel good. I'm planning to go to Jon's gig a little later. Do you want to come?'

'I'd love to, but I really need to get to bed.'

'Of course. I'm not planning to stay long. I want to get a good night's sleep, so we can finish getting this place straight tomorrow. Then Jon and I will bring our stuff around in the camper van on Monday.'

They finished their meal. Ginny plucked at the dungarees she was wearing and said, 'I can't go to a gig looking like this.'

Steve thought she probably could. Even dressed as she was, she would turn heads.

'Would you mind if I had a bath here? It would save me going back to Argyle Street. I brought some clean clothes with me.'

How could he refuse? 'Of course help yourself.'

Ginny went through to the bathroom, neglecting to close the door. Steve started to clear the table but couldn't help noticing through the half-open door Ginny stepping out of her dungarees and pulling her tee shirt over her head. She didn't seem to have noticed that she was undressing in his line of sight or perhaps she didn't care. For a moment he was transfixed by the unexpected glimpse of her naked torso, but fearful that she might look up and catch his eye, he moved over to the sink and started to rinse the plates. A few moment later he heard the flush of the cistern and then Ginny calling out, 'Steve, are you running the hot water?'

Trying to sound not too flustered, he said, 'Oh, yes. Sorry. I'll finish the washing up later.'

'Thank you. I won't be long.'

Steve dried his hands and went through to the sitting room. He was already finding the proximity to Ginny troubling. What had Al said? *Look, but do not touch.*

Right now, he wasn't even sure that looking was a good idea. Soon he could hear the sound of gentle splashing and Ginny singing to herself. He was about to go up to his room, when he heard her calling out, 'Steve, I've left my straw bag with my towel and other things in it somewhere. Could you look for it, please?'

He stepped into the hall and called back, 'Any idea where it is?'

'I think it's in the kitchen somewhere.'

Steve re-entered the kitchen and eventually found the bag hanging on a hook on the back of the kitchen door. He tapped on the bathroom door and waving the bag in the opening of the door said, 'Is this it?'

'Of course it is. Bring it in.'

Steve did as he was asked. Ginny was lying in the bath with the water up to her chin.

'Thank you. The towel's at the bottom of the bag. Put the clothes on the lid of the loo and give me the towel, please.'

Steve took the blouse, skirt and underclothes out of the the bag and having deposited them as requested, held out the towel. Ginny stood up, water streaming from her body, and took the towel. Steve made a somewhat exaggerated but wholly inadequate attempt to avert his gaze. For a moment he was frozen to the spot, but as she started to step out of the bath, he turned, saying over his shoulder, 'I'm going up to my room. I hope the gig goes well. See you tomorrow.'

Ginny laughed. 'My, you are a shy chap. Don't worry I'm not going to eat you. I'm sorry, I thought you were cool with nudity.'

But Steve was already on the far side of the kitchen. All he could manage by way of response was, 'Up to a point.'

Without turning again, he went up to his room. After a while he heard Ginny close the front door. When he was sure the coast was clear, he went downstairs, cleaned his teeth and got himself a glass of water. He then switched off all the lights and returned to his room. He undressed and got into bed and tried to quieten his thoughts by reading, but the sense of the words would not cohere. He put the book down and turned over, the image of Ginny's glistening body rising from the little bath seared onto his mind's eye. Before long he fell into a fitful sleep.

He woke a few hours later and thought that he could hear someone moving around downstairs. And then he heard the cistern in the bathroom flush. He looked at his clock. It was just gone midnight. Who was moving around downstairs? Surely Beth hadn't come back? He put on his jeans and went downstairs to find a shivering Ginny sitting at the table in the kitchen with her head in her hands.

Steve said, 'Ginny, what's going on?'

'Jon's got involved in something. I didn't know what to do, so I came back here.'

Steve couldn't imagine what it might be that Jon had got involved in, but decided to accept the statement at face value. Ginny looked ashen, the lighthearted person of a few hours earlier had vanished. She looked up imploringly at Steve. 'Would you mind if I stayed the night? I'll sleep in the front room.'

Steve could hardly object to the proposition.

'Ginny, are you okay? Can I get you anything?'

'No, I'll be okay. Go back to bed. You have to get up soon.'

Steve went back to bed. After a while he heard her stumbling up the stairs and go into the other room. At least he could now get some sleep. He turned over and was drifting off, when he heard the door to his room creak open.

'Steve, are you still awake?' It was one of those questions, where whatever he said confirmed the supposition.

'Yes, is there a problem?'

'Can I get into bed with you?'

'Ginny . . .'

'Just for a few minutes. I'm not feeling too good. I need someone to hold me.'

'I'm not wearing any pyjamas.'

'Please.'

Without waiting for his reply, she slipped into the bed and pressed her own naked body against his. She was shivering so much that Steve wondered whether she'd taken something. He put his arm around her and felt the silkiness of her skin and the improbable angles of her body. She buried her face in his chest and her body was wracked with sobs. He pulled her towards him and held her tight. 'Ginny, what's going on?'

In response Ginny slid down his body and took him in her mouth. Steve groaned in pleasure, but pulled her up towards him.

'Ginny, this is crazy. We can't do this.'

She pushed him down and straddled him, guiding him inside her. She pinioned his shoulders to the bed and rocked her hips slowly up and down He was about to come. She sensed it too and said fiercely, 'Don't . . .'

* * *

Sometime later, exhausted, they lay in each other's arms. Steve was in unknown territory, untethered from his familiar coordinates, unsure at what point the affective scenery had changed, or what had triggered this movement in life's tectonic plates. What he needed to do was to talk to Ginny and understand what this meant for her. Was this an aberration, the result of a crazy impulse, or was it something more complex? On the assumption that it was a terrible, if briefly ecstatic, mistake, he needed to know how they were going to extricate themselves from the situation. But Ginny just put her finger, still fragrant with their sexual effusions, to his lips and said that she would go down and make them both a drink. She rolled out of bed and padded downstairs, returning a few minutes later with mugs of chamomile. Steve sipped his drink and said, 'Ginny, we really need to talk.'

'You need to sleep. We'll talk later. Don't worry, it's all under control.'

From Steve's point of view that was the last thing it was. She saw the fear in his eyes and drew him to her, cradling him in her arms, kissing his face and eyes. 'Go to sleep. Don't worry.'

She rocked him gently, his head pressed against her breast, her heart beating evenly. Soon he was asleep.

For a moment, as he came to consciousness at the sound of the alarm clock, Steve was surprised by the presence of another body in the narrow bed with him. As the realisation of what had transpired just a few hours before swept over him, he groaned. Ginny too had been wakened by the jangle of the alarm clock. She rolled over and kissed him. 'It'll be okay.'

Steve felt a stirring in his loins, but knew it would be madness to resume amatory relations now. He untangled himself from her embrace and got out of bed. 'Ginny. I've got to get to work. I'll be back by eleven, I hope. I have to say, I'm worried about how we're going to deal with this. Presumably Jon will be around later. I need to know how we're going to handle the situation. What are we going to say?'

'We're going to say nothing. Nothing happened. Relax. Just play it cool. We'll find time to talk. Go to work now.'

Steve went downstairs and cleaned himself up a bit in the bathroom, then made some tea. He took the teas back up to the bedroom. But Ginny had gone back to sleep. He dressed quietly and a few minutes later, pulled the front door shut behind him and walked the couple of hundred yards to the dairy. He was grateful that it was a Sunday and that therefore there would be only a limited number of interactions with others. He did the round in a kind of daze, reluctant to pursue the implications of last night's events too deeply. Even so, it seemed to him improbable that Jon wouldn't sense something, some change in the atmosphere and Steve was apprehensive of getting on the wrong side of Jon's infamous physicality. He also felt guilty *vis-à-vis* Angie.

When Steve got back from his round. He was dismayed to see Jon's camper van outside the house. He let himself in, and went through to the kitchen to find Jon and Ginny sitting at the kitchen table having a cup of tea and chatting. Ginny was back in dungarees and headscarf, and had reverted to the chilly hauteur, that he was more used to, while Jon greeted him with elaborate affability.

'Hey, man. Good to see you. Sorry I was not much in evidence yesterday. Have guitar, will gig. And then there were afters, if you know what I mean.'

Steve didn't, but went along with the innuendo.

'Anyway, I'm here now and the plan is to complete the transformation of the pad today and to bring in our stuff tomorrow.'

This was not exactly news to Steve. He pulled out one of the chairs and sat down. Ginny poured him a coffee.

'So, what would you like me to do?' he asked, addressing Ginny.

What she wanted was for the two men to bring the clothes down from the two closets and hang them on the rail that Jon had assembled in the little conservatory. They were to make sure to hang them in the order that they had been in upstairs and on no account to get things from one room mixed up with those from the other room. She would carry on putting shoes, books, papers, and smaller objects in the boxes that Jon had also brought. Every box would be labelled. When everything was boxed up, they'd bring all the boxes down to the conservatory as well. If they stacked the smaller boxes on the big ones they should get everything in. They'd also have to bring Steve's things downstairs temporarily, so that they could give both bedrooms a deep clean. Then she and Jon would head back to Argyle Street to finish packing up their own stuff. When Steve got back from work the next day they hoped to have moved in with everything shipshape, and then they could all look forward to a nice summer in what was really quite a charming little house.

And indeed, that was exactly how things unfolded. When Steve got back from work on the Monday morning, it was almost impossible to recognise the house as the one he had moved into less than a week before. The dust and the grime were gone, surfaces and panes of glass sparkled. There were vases of cut flowers in the sitting room and in the kitchen. A homely smell of baking suffused the spaces of the house. Colourful Indian throws adorned the battered old sofa and armchairs. Candles had been placed on the mantelpiece in the sitting room. Beth's books had been tidied away. The grease that had caked the kitchen surfaces had been removed. Stains and limescale had been scoured from the sink and draining board in the kitchen. Even the battered old gas cooker gleamed. The sanitary ware in the bathroom was as white as it was ever likely to be. An aromatic fragrance from an essential oil burner masked the smell of bad drains that had hung in the damp air.

Upstairs Steve's clothes were neatly stowed in the closet and the chest of drawers in the back room. His books were in the little bookcase beside the desk and his papers were neatly stacked on the writing surface of the desk. His guitar was propped in one corner of the room and his bags had been put on top of the closet. A similar miracle had been wrought in the other room, but where Steve's room retained its essential austerity, Jon and Ginny's room had been transformed into a hippy boudoir, tricked out with bright cushions and pillows, a large cream macramé tapestry gracing one wall, the desk draped with a fringed and tasselled throw.

One thing that did unsettle Steve was the amount of music equipment that Jon had brought into the house, a couple of big speaker cabinets and several guitars and effects boxes. Perhaps Jon had forgotten that he had assured Steve that he would be keeping his gear elsewhere. It wasn't so much the space that it took up or the fact that Jon chose to store the equipment at the back of the sitting room, but the fear that he might be inclined to plug in and fire it up at inappropriate times of the day or, more worryingly, night, an eventuality not likely to foster good relations with the neighbours or to ensure that Steve got a good night's sleep. That, and the unfortunate entanglement with Ginny aside, the transition to shared living with Jon and Ginny in Ainsworth Street had been surprisingly straightforward. It had to be admitted this had little to do with Steve or for that matter Jon, and was largely down to the effort that Ginny had put in. Steve couldn't help being impressed with, and a little perturbed by, Ginny's organisational abilities.

Jon and Ginny were in celebratory mood and said that they were planning an inaugural meal, to which, of course, Steve was invited. On the basis of the meal that he had shared with Ginny on the Saturday evening, Steve was more than happy to accept the invitation. He asked if he could help, or if there was any contribution he could make. Jon said that he and Ginny would handle it, which seemed to mean that, Ginny would handle it. Furthermore she seemed to have returned to studiously ignoring Steve, a state of affairs he felt more comfortable with. Seeing as his offer to help had been rejected, he made himself a cup of coffee and went up to his room, marvelling once again at the way in which it had been transformed. He noticed that a letter had been propped on the mantelpiece and recognised Angie's handwriting. He threw himself on the bed and opened the envelope.

Angie's letters were both expressively emotional and novelistically detailed. She had the enviable ability to reproduce in writing her spoken style, so that Steve could almost hear her voice. But her tone in this letter, while not unfriendly, was at best cordial. She couldn't pretend to be happy with the situation. She had been hoping that he would decide not to take the house in Ainsworth Street or that the arrangements would fall through. But it seemed that he'd gone ahead. Given the nature of their jobs, that meant that they were unlikely to see much of each other over the next few months. Perhaps it was for the best, but she feared that he was heading into uncharted territory.

It was unclear to her at the time of writing, whether Jon and Ginny would be joining him in the house. She couldn't decide which would be the worst outcome, their not joining him and his being responsible for the entire rent or their moving in and setting the tone in the shared house. She apologised for being less than enthusiastic and hoped he would write back soon. She signed off affectionately and said she would tell him something of her life in Brighton in her next letter.

Steve was unsettled by the letter. He had hoped that Angie would forgive him and accept their temporary estrangement. He also objected to her assessment of his character. It was true that Jon and Ginny did seem to have taken over. As impressed as he was by the transformation that they had effected in the condition of the house, he had to admit that the net result was that it felt like their place and not his. Goaded by Angie's comments, he resolved to stake out his right to the communal spaces and also to raise the matter of the rent that same day.

After a short nap, he went downstairs and found Jon and Ginny quietly smoking and reading in the sitting room. Confounded by the demureness of the scene, his resolve faltered, reducing him to asking if anyone fancied a cup of tea. They both accepted the offer. Ginny said that she'd baked a fresh loaf, if he'd like to help himself. Steve said he was fine. But when he went into the kitchen and smelled the delicious aroma of the freshly baked bread, he changed his mind. While he waited for the kettle to boil, he cut a couple of slices and buttered them. He looked in the fridge and found a block of cheese and cut a hunk of it off. He wolfed down the bread and cheese, while he waited for the tea to brew and then carried the three mugs through to the next room. He sat in the free armchair and confessed that the smell of freshly baked bread had changed his mind, and that he'd cut himself a couple of slices. He declared it to be excellent. Ginny accepted the praise without emotion, while Jon twinkled. 'Yeah, Ginny is a woman of many talents. As you are already no doubt aware.'

Steve was taken aback. There was enough backspin in the delivery for it to mean something other than that she had sorted out the house brilliantly. Surely, Jon didn't know or suspect what had transpired between Steve and Ginny on Saturday night? Steve struggled to regain his composure.

'I think the government ought to enlist Ginny to sort out the economy.'

Jon laughed, but whether at Steve's inept return of service, or the idea of Ginny running the economy was not clear.

'Hey man, what about a number?'

The last thing that Steve wanted at that moment was to get ripped. 'I've got some important milk to deliver tomorrow.'

The joke was lost because Jon had already reached down his stash box and was assembling a joint on an album cover. If Steve was going to raise the matter of the rent, he'd better do it now. He'd probably be too stoned to tie things down later. Affecting an air of nonchalance, he said, 'So, we'd better sort out the rent situation. It's handy that not only is today a Monday, but it's also the first of the month. I'm sorry to have to raise the matter of filthy lucre.'

Jon didn't bat an eyelid. 'Cool, man. The thing is, we can't pay you right now. We haven't got our deposit back from Argyle Street yet. And the whole move has had costs too. But how about we contribute in other ways, until we can catch up. We're happy to cook in the evenings and get provisions, and I'm sure there are other ways we can compensate you.'

At which point he handed Steve a fully loaded joint. Once again, Steve's guilty conscience detected a subtext in Jon's words. Reluctant to get too smashed while they were talking turkey, he dragged only shallowly on the joint, then offered it to Ginny, who declined. Steve handed it back to Jon.

'So, when do you think you might get your deposit back?'

'No idea man, but we'll do our best. Don't worry, we'll see you right, one way or another.'

Steve wished that Jon would stop talking in this way or was it that Steve was already stoned? It was not often that Steve smoked in the middle of the day.

'I'm sure you will, Jon, I just have my own money hassles.'

'Life's a bitch, man.'

Steve was aware that Ginny, though silent, was paying close attention to the exchange. Jon picked up the acoustic guitar which was propped against the sofa he was sitting on and started to play. Steve was initially irritated by what he saw as a blatant attempt to shut down the discussion, but through the prism of the dope he reconnected with Jon's music and discerned an unexpected affiliation with *Event/Horizon*. The riff he was playing was in a stable orbit around its own resolution. No, that wasn't quite right. The orbit wasn't stable, the riff would founder before it resolved. But Jon was connecting to something powerful, hooked into the nothingness at the centre. Steve felt himself drowning in the whirlpool of sound. His petty concerns about the rent evaporated. This obsession with money was poisonous. He should lighten up. Money was just a means of making diverse things equivalent, but somehow it had become an end in itself and a trivial one at that, rather than a means of facilitating exchange. It was entirely wrong to relate income and outcome. It was process that counted. Perhaps not the best way of putting it. But then ideas of numbers and storytelling were hopelessly entwined. Despite having toked only lightly, Steve was now very stoned. But so what? He leant back and gave into the music.

Jon played until he judged that he had pacified Steve. Then he held the neck of the guitar towards Steve. 'Here, you play.'

Steve shook his head, 'No, man. I can't follow that. I'm not in your league.'

'Don't be ridiculous. It's not football. It's expression. Everyone has something to say.'

Steve wasn't convinced. 'But some people have something worth saying.'

Jon was not taking no for an answer and put the guitar in Steve's hands.

Steve wasn't sure which was more pathetic, not to have the courage to play, or to play and disappoint his audience. The truth was that he hadn't played in public for a considerable time now. Something happened to his brain as soon as he tried to perform. The thinking process got in the way of the music. It was true that his technique was not much to talk about. But, from time to time, especially if he were not trying to do anything in particular, the music just flowed. It was as if someone else, or another part of him, had taken over. Steve fingered a chord and strummed the guitar. It was a very nice instrument, much more resonant than his own guitar. He played the same chord several times, letting it ring out and fill the room. Unfortunately the dope seemed to have affected his memory. He was unable to remember the simplest chord sequences of the pieces he habitually played.

But something that Alan had said the previous week surfaced in his mind. He started to improvise a sequence based on a harmonised scale. Nothing complex, just sticking to triads, but it sounded okay. He relaxed a little and started to embellish the sequence. Jon and Ginny appeared to be getting into it. He rode the riff for as long as he could. He was starting to feel pleased with himself. Maybe he could do this, maybe he should play stoned more often. But as so often, the access of self-consciousness ejected him from the source of the music. He lost his way and the piece collapsed. This always seemed to happen, he found it hard to remain in the groove and shelter the spark of inspiration. He was annoyed with himself and handed the guitar back, disconsolate.

'Sorry, I can't seem to maintain the vibe,' he muttered apologetically.

But Jon was having none of that. 'Don't apologise. Never apologise. It was great. We should play together.'

Steve was grateful to Jon for his encouragement. He returned to his chair and caught Ginny's eye. As he did so, he thought he detected, in a slightly raised eyebrow, the faintest approbation, but he was probably kidding himself.

Later over the meal, Jon said, 'Seriously, man. We'll be cooking for ourselves most evenings. It's no problem to include you. Nothing formal. If you're around, join us.'

'Okay, but you must let me make a meal from time to time.'

'Fine. It's a deal.'

Steve took a sip of the wine that Jon and Ginny had also provided.

'You probably realise I work crazy hours. I get up at five, and I'm out the front door by five-thirty. I will be as quiet as I can. Unfortunately, that also means I need to try and get to sleep by ten o'clock. So I won't be hanging out much in the evenings.'

'Cool, man. We won't be ripping up the joint,' Jon said with a wicked grin, 'well, not often.'

Steve laughed uncomfortably.

Jon switched to a more serious tone. 'But surely you get some time off?'

'Not for another couple of weeks.'

'Sounds like a heavy gig.'

'Yeah, it's a bit of a drag, but it pays good money, although to be honest, I'm getting a bit fed up with it. Still, I can't really think of getting a job with better hours until I've paid off my overdraft.'

Jon sympathised. 'Banks are bloodsuckers.'

Ginny, who had contributed very little to the conversation, said, 'Do you have another job in mind?'

'Not really, I'd rather not do anything quite so mindless, but beggars can't be choosers.'

Ginny was not impressed by this approach. 'What would you do, if you had a completely free hand?

Steve was still feeling mellow from the effects of the joint and now the wine and consequently was less guarded than normal about expressing his ambitions.

'Well, I see myself as a poet. But, of course, there's no money in that.'

Jon tutted, 'Steve. You're not a breadhead, you should do what you want to do.'

'Yeah, but we all have to pay our way.' Steve felt mean about what might be taken for a veiled reference to the missing rent, but only slightly.

Jon ignored the implication. 'Money is one of those things, like happiness. You don't get it by aiming for it. It's a byproduct of what you do.'

Privately, Steve thought that was a bit glib. And the equivalence between money and happiness clumsy. But he got what Jon was driving at.

Ginny said, 'Is that the only kind of writing you want to do?'

Steve shook his head. 'But that's where I feel most comfortable. Actually, I'd like to write plays too. But I feel I need to get more theatrical experience.'

'Get a job in the theatre, then.'

'Yes that's occurred to me. And as a way of doing that, I thought I'd put on something at the Edinburgh Fringe. Easier said than done, though.'

Jon asked, 'What do you have in mind?'

'*Krapp's Last Tape* by Samuel Beckett.'

'I know the name, but I've never seen it.'

'It's a one-man play, involving a tape recorder. Some parts of it are pre-recorded. I thought I could produce it and perform it myself at the Fringe.'

'Cool.'

'But I've got to work out how to do the pre-recorded part. I don't know much about the technicalities of recording.'

'Well, I could give you a hand there perhaps. That's exactly my bag. And I've got a decent tape recorder in that pile of gear in the sitting room.'

Steve thought some technical help from Jon on the recording front might well be a better form of compensation for the late rent than whatever else he had had in mind with his earlier suggestions.

'Are you sure?'

'Yeah, let's do it when you've got some time.'

Steve went up to bed thinking that life with Jon and Ginny might not be quite as bad as he had at first feared. Even if he did end up being a bit out of pocket and out of his depth in sexual relations.

Later on he was wakened by the sound of footsteps on the stair and the door to Jon and Ginny's room creaking shut. He looked at his watch and saw that it was only just gone ten o'clock, so he could hardly complain. He went back to sleep, but was wakened again a half an hour later by the sound of sobs coming from their bedroom. Was something unpleasant happening? Had Jon worked out that he and Ginny had fucked? Was he hurting her? Maybe he should intervene. As he lay there, all his senses straining to make sense of what was going on, he heard what he judged to be Jon's steps on the stair and a few seconds later the front door slamming. If he was right in his assumption, maybe he should go and check that Ginny was okay. But supposing that he was wrong and it was Ginny who had gone out. Or if Jon came back as he was checking on Ginny. He lay there in an agony of indecision until he finally fell asleep again.

Box Office

THE NEXT DAY AFTER he had finished his round Steve thought he'd make further inroads into Grace's manuscript. But it seemed a pity to confine himself to his room for another afternoon, especially as the weather was so glorious. He thought he might go to one of the riverside pubs and have a pub lunch. He put the manuscript in his bag and made his way to the Fort St George. He went inside, ordered a pint and some food and then went out to a table on the patio overlooking the green.

He took Grace's manuscript out of his bag and resumed reading. He was soon absorbed in the intellectual and social ferment of postwar Paris. He was by no means an expert on the period, but he had read a number of works by both authors, *La Nausée* and *Les Mots* by Sartre and *La Peste* and *L'Étranger* by Camus. However, he had given Sartre's *L'Être et le Néant* a wide berth and had only dipped into Camus' *L'Homme revolté*. As for Sartre's *Critique de la raison dialectique* reason, forget it.

In Steve's mind Jean-Paul and Albert were the Butch Cassidy and the Sundance Kid of the *rive gauche*. But, as he read through Grace's manuscript, he started to appreciate that their relationship was very far from what this facile analogy suggested. Indeed not only was there a good deal of antagonism and rivalry between them, but to a very real extent they didn't even share the same values, Camus' absurdism diverging in numerous ways from canonical existentialism. And as the years went by the split widened.

As public intellectuals and long before they had even met the two men were aware of each other through the pages of the journals, in which they reviewed each other's work, not always in an approbative register. When they did finally meet during the Occupation, however, they were drawn to each other, proceeding to booze and wench their way around Paris. At the same time Camus was holding down the post of editor of *Combat*, the underground newspaper of the Resistance, commissioning articles from many leading intellectuals, including, of course, Sartre. They might not have been involved in the armed struggle, but had their involvement with *Combat* become known through betrayal or bad luck, it would most probably have resulted in torture and execution. After the exhilaration of the Liberation, Camus used his position as editor to arrange for Sartre to go to New York in January 1945 as *Combat*'s American correspondent.

But thereafter as life in Paris normalised and they were no longer bound by a common enemy the underlying tensions in the relationship resurfaced and the friendship fractured. It didn't happen immediately, but by the time of the publication of *L'Homme revolté* the gloves were off. Whilst Sartre and de Beauvoir never actually joined the Communist party, they had become decidedly *anti* anti-communist and *Les Temps modernes*, which Sartre edited, carried a lengthy hatchet job on the anti-historicism and the anti-revolutionary tendencies in Camus' book. Camus was permitted to respond, but his response elicited a bitter *ad hominem* attack from Sartre himself. The relationship was over.

Steve put the manuscript down. Clearly his view of their relationship was wide of the mark. It was more like the Lennon and McCartney story, a creative relationship between two individuals of genius which had soured and eventually foundered on mistrust and jealousy. But he doubted that was the kind of remark that Grace would find useful in the report she had asked him to write.

As he let his thoughts drift he noticed that someone had left a copy of the *Cambridge Evening News* lying on a nearby table. He reached over, picked it up and started leafing through it. The digest of international and national news was pretty grim, while the local news was hyper-parochial. He soon came to the classified section and his eye was caught by an ad for the Arts Theatre. They needed someone to work in the box office for six months to cover a maternity leave. The pay was not great and the hours were somewhat unsocial, but it was only a five day a week rather than the seven day a week schedule he was on at the dairy. Some evening work was involved and the successful applicant would be expected to work two Saturday evenings a month. On the plus side, from Steve's point of view, there were no early starts and no Sunday shifts. He resolved there and then to go and see if the job was still available.

Finishing his pint, he made his way to the Market Square and then up the ludicrously named Peas Hill, one of the least hill-like inclines in a notoriously flat city, to the foyer of the Arts Theatre. He presented himself at the window of the box office and asked the young man sitting there, filing his nails, who he should speak to about the box office vacancy advertised in the evening paper. The young man yawned and said Steve should speak to Mike Wallace, the front of house manager. How did Steve find this person? He'd be in the admin office. Which was where? Steve felt that the young man was not being very helpful. Reluctantly it seemed, the young man suggested that he go to the stage door in St Edward's Passage and ask there. Steve was about to act on this painfully extracted piece of information, when the doors to the auditorium swung open and a man only two or three years older than Steve himself passed in front of the window of the box office heading towards the street doors of the foyer.

Suddenly the smooth young man in the box office seemed to change his unhelpful approach and said to Steve, 'That's him there, Mike Wallace.'

Steve turned around and just as the front of house manager was about to push the door open, said 'Mr Wallace, could I have a quick word? I've just seen your ad for someone to help out in the box office.'

Mike Wallace turned around and said, 'Oh, good. How soon could you start?'

Steve wasn't sure. He did a quick calculation and said, 'Three weeks.'

Mike nodded. 'In that case, let's go upstairs to the office.'

Steve followed him back through the auditorium and up several flights of stairs, until they came to the administrative offices of the theatre. Mike's desk was in one corner. He invited Steve to sit down, pushed a form towards him and asked him to fill it in. As Steve did so, Mike asked Steve a number of questions about his education, what he was currently doing. Had he ever done a job dealing with members of the public? Had he ever dealt with cash? Steve's answers seemed to satisfy him. He was amused but also impressed that Steve was working as a milkman. When he realised that Steve had just graduated, he asked him what his subject had been. Steve's answer provoked a laugh. 'Same as me. I graduated a few of years ago. Who supervised you for German.'

'Richard Doyle.'

'Oh, yeah. Bright guy.'

'French?'

'Grace Mitchell.'

Mike laughed again. 'Me too. Looks like you got the job.'

He opened his desk diary. 'Let's see. Could you start on Monday 29 July?'

Steve said he could. Mike explained the hours and how the shift system work. He'd put a contract in the post. Then he led him back downstairs, this time to the exit in St Edward's Passage. As they were taking leave of one another, Steve asked the name of the young of the guy in the box office.

'Oh, that's Seb. Don't take any notice of him. He doesn't like the general public.'

As Steve made his way up St Edward's Passage to the Market Square, he shook his head. It looked like he'd just got a new job, thanks to the invisible influence of Grace Mitchell and without yet having resigned from his current job. He needed to think about this carefully. When he got home he went straight up to his bedroom and threw himself down on his bed and tried to think through the implications of quitting the dairy job and starting a theatre job paying him considerably less. He still had a sizeable overdraft and what with Jon being flaky with the rent the financial impact would be significant. On the other hand the job was almost exactly what he felt he needed. But if he was going to leave the dairy, he would have to tell the gaffer in the next couple of days so that he could give a full week's notice in order to be paid up to the end of his scheduled week off. Later when he judged that Jon and Ginny had vacated the kitchen, he went downstairs and made himself a drink.

He was still turning the matter back and forth in his mind next day on the round without coming to any conclusion. Once again when he got home he went straight up to his room without going into the kitchen to greet Jon and Ginny, even though he could hear them quietly chatting.

He wished he could speak to Angie about the situation. She would have a clear view of the matter. Which reminded him that he owed her a letter. As promised, she had sent him a second letter describing life in Brighton. She had filled it with cameos of some of her students and one or two of her colleagues. There was the German boy Heinz who knew everything and wanted his teachers to recognise this fact and felt so empowered that he had asked Angie out for a drink even though she was a good five or six years older than him. It was only with considerable difficulty that she had persuaded him that fraternisation between students and members of staff was inappropriate. Among the colleagues the two with leading roles were droopy Janet, whose emotional state hovered only inches above full-blown depression and stolid Declan, with whom Angie had had the occasional drink. She had ended the letter with a brief rant about how dank her basement flat was, how irritating most of her colleagues and students actually were, winding up with a reprise of her disappointment in Steve. He re-read the letter, feeling slightly aggrieved. No doubt he was guilty of not committing to arrangements for Edinburgh, but how did she expect him to get down to Brighton when he had to work every day including weekends? One way or another he would soon have some time off. He would visit her then and they could talk everything through in detail.

He went over to the little desk in front of the window and opened the pad of notepaper and started writing. He might not have any new tales from the dairy, but his week had already produced quite enough for him to fill a lengthy letter. He started with the fact that Jon and Ginny had moved in and completely transformed the place. They had managed to sort out all the junk the girls had left and the house was now sparkling clean. That was the thing, scratch a hippie and underneath as often as not was a solid bourgeois. Possibly living with them wasn't going to be as problematic as he had feared. Even better, Ginny was an excellent cook and at least so far had no objections to cooking for the household. As with hippies, so with feminists. He thought it better not to mention the rent problem. Or the clinch with Ginny.

Then he moved on to the visit to the Arts Theatre and the offer of a job in the box office. This had put him in a bit of a quandary. It was of course a much more amenable job, but the pay was not great and there was still the rent to pay on the Ainsworth Street house. Even so, he had pretty much decided to take it. He was planning to see the gaffer in the next couple of days and hand in his notice, a meeting he was dreading. Since the new job didn't start for nearly three weeks or so, it meant that he could now visit Angie and stay for a few days, if that was okay with her.

He folded the sheets, tucked them into an envelope, sealed and and addressed it and propped it on the mantelpiece for posting the following day. Before he had started writing the letter, he hadn't actually been sure about the Arts Theatre job, but the process of unpacking his thoughts in a letter to Angie had helped him clarify the situation. It was definitely the right move. He tumbled onto the bed for his afternoon nap and was asleep within a few minutes.

He was roused from his sleep some time later by a tap at the door. Jon put his head around the door and asked Steve if he'd like to join them for supper. Steve was touched by how considerate Jon and Ginny were being, especially since he had been distinctly standoffish for the previous two days. More to the point he was very hungry and the chance to quieten his rumbling stomach was hard resist. He accepted the offer with alacrity and said he'd be down in a jiffy.

When he entered the kitchen a few minutes later, there was a large plate of chilli con carne and rice in his place. He took his seat and by way of apology for his earlier failure to greet his housemates explained that he'd been knackered. The other two received this information without comment and resumed eating. Steve loaded a fork and transferred the contents to his mouth. The food was delicious. All three ate in silence for a few minutes, until Jon, who had now cleared his plate, pushed his chair back, belched quietly and asked Steve how work had been that day. Steve said it had gone okay, but that he was getting seriously fed up with it. In fact he had been offered a new job the previous day, which he had accepted but he couldn't decide whether it was a good idea to take it seeing as it paid a lot less than his current job.

Ginny asked what the job was and Steve described the brief interview and the coincidence of the house manager having had the same supervisor for French. Ginny said he should take it, an opinion that Jon shared. And all the more reason to get the play together that he had mentioned the other day, the one with the funny title. Jon was serious about helping with the recording. Why didn't they have a go at it after his round on Monday? He couldn't do it before then because he was going to London the following day for an audition and then was going to stay with a buddy. He wouldn't be back until Sunday. Steve said that would be brilliant. It would give him a few days to go over the play and get the lines straight. He thanked Ginny for the delicious meal and insisted on doing the washing up.

Later back in his room, he got out his copy of *Krapp's Last Tape* and started working his way through the text, marking with a pencil the words and phrases that he felt should be stressed. He had also been planning to mark pauses, but close reading of the text revealed that it was already liberally freighted with such directions. Steve knew that Beckett had a reputation for being a very precise director of his own material, but now, working slowly through the text with a view to performing it himself, he was starting to come to the conclusion that Beckett was in fact a bloody control freak. He read the speeches aloud a couple of times and recognized that his acting skills were not up to sustaining an Irish accent. More worryingly he was going to have to differentiate old Krapp's voice from young Krapp's voice. Fortunately the taped sections were of the young Krapp. He could bother about simulating the voice of a man in his sixties another time.

As he was going to sleep he reflected that he must be a very bad judge of character. He had completely underestimated Jon and Ginny. They were a decent and organised couple, very far from being the dangerous, badass hipsters he had described to others.

Walking back from the dairy after work on Friday, Steve remembered that this was the day that Jon was going to London. That meant that he and Ginny would be alone together for the next two days. He wasn't sure what to expect or how he wanted things to develop. If it turned out that the events of the previous weekend turned out to be a one-off consequence of Ginny's mood swings, he would certainly be disappointed, but also to a considerable extent relieved. A return to the status quo ante would in all likelihood enable him to preserve his relationship with Angie, not to mention his sanity, and save him from finding out exactly how tough Jon really was.

When he arrived back at the house he was relieved to find neither Jon nor Ginny in evidence. He got himself a drink and went up to his room, where he stayed for the next couple of hours. Towards the end of the afternoon he was beginning to regret that he hadn't been braver and established himself in the communal spaces, when there was a tap on the door, and before he could answer, Ginny entered, hands on hips, and said, 'Are you avoiding me?'

Steve was momentarily lost for words. 'No, I just didn't want there to be any unpleasantness.'

'But how do you think that makes me feel?'

'Ginny, I don't know, I'm not sure what the situation is. You and Jon have been great. I don't want to fuck things up.'

'Jon's not here.'

'But he'll be back.'

'So, we shouldn't waste the time we've got to be alone together.'

'I didn't realise we were having a scene.'

'What do you think Saturday night was?'

'An accident?'

'You think I just throw myself at any man who happens to be around?'

'No, but sometimes, mood, proximity, stress, opportunity result in, you know . . .'

'You don't think that I didn't come back here on Saturday night on purpose?'

'I didn't think about it. I didn't really think you had any interest in me. You're with one of the coolest guys around.'

'Don't be ridiculous. Anyway, are you going to keep me standing here?'

'What do you want me to do?'

'What do you want *me* to do?'

Steve could think of several things that he'd like her to do, but was reluctant to give voice to his desires. She sensed the struggle going on inside him and said, 'If you can think it, I can probably oblige. Don't be shy.'

But still he hesitated.

She started to unbutton her blouse and said, 'Are you going to make me guess? You won't get this kind of offer too many times in your life, perhaps never again. So take advantage of it.'

Half an hour later they were lying next to each other drinking the tea that Ginny had made on her way back from the loo. If it were possible, the sex this time had been even more transcendental than previously. The only thing that troubled him was that the neighbours might be concerned at the shrieks that Ginny had produced at key moments in the proceedings. But this concern was balanced by an immodest surprise at his own stamina in contributing to those shrieks.

As she sipped her tea, she said, 'You chose wisely. For a moment I thought I'd misjudged you.'

Steve wasn't sure which parts of the preceding carnal interaction he'd chosen and which he'd been guided towards, but he was childishly pleased to have passed whatever test she'd set him. He was, however, apprehensive that as soon as she'd finished her tea, she would demand another bout, just to make sure that it hadn't been beginner's luck. In the hope of heading off further developments in that direction, he said, 'Ginny, can we talk now? Properly.'

'Go ahead,' said Ginny.

Steve didn't really know how you started this kind of conversation. Perhaps it wasn't a good idea.

'I don't want to screw things up between you and Jon.'

'Don't you think they're pretty screwed up already?'

'No, I wasn't aware of that. I've always thought you two looked pretty cool.'

'It's not about how we look; it's about how we are. It's a fake. He looks after me; I enhance his image.'

Steve was shocked, but not totally. 'So it's a relationship of convenience?'

'You could put it like that.'

'But why do you need looking after? You seem more than capable of looking after yourself to me.'

'Yes, but sometimes I just crash and Jon's cool with that. And when I'm okay, it means I'm not being pestered by guys who just want to go to bed with me. Jon can be a very effective bodyguard.'

Steve didn't doubt it and wondered again how it was that he'd slipped under the net. 'There must be more to your relationship than that, companionship, physical intimacy?'

'Companionship, yes, to an extent, but nothing really physical.'

'What, you don't have sex?'

'Not like you and I have just had.'

'But why? Has the relationship got stale?'

'Surely it's obvious?'

Steve was struggling to make sense of this. 'Do you mean he's gay?'

'Let's just say he's not reactive to me. But I have reason to think it's not just with me.'

'I don't know what that means,' said Steve, feeling like a naïve teenager.

'Okay, well, when you're with me you seem to have a permanent hard-on. Of course, I don't know whether it's just me, or whether you're like that with other women. But Jon is definitely not like that with me. He can get a hard-on, but it doesn't happen easily. It's hard work, hard work for both of us, if that's the right expression.'

This was more information than Steve really wanted.

Ginny continued. 'I didn't realise at first. I just thought it was something else, the drugs, the booze, maybe something medical. And he wouldn't level with me, so we couldn't really talk about it. And maybe I was a bit insensitive. I kept making him try. At least at first. The few times we were successful, there was no sense of elation, no satisfaction for either of us. Both of us would be exhausted and upset.'

'So, that's why I heard you crying the other night,' Steve said, as if all had been revealed.

'That's wasn't me. It was Jon who was crying.'

Steve was shocked. Jon and tears didn't correlate. Ginny pressed on. 'He couldn't do it. We hadn't tried for ages. He wanted to try again, but he couldn't do it. He couldn't get a hard-on.'

'I was wondering if I ought to have intervened. I thought he might be hurting you, but then someone left the house. I couldn't work out if it was you or him.'

'He went out to find someone he could have sex with. I could smell it on him when he came back.'

After contemplating this piece of information, Steve said, 'So, does that mean that although you're a couple, you take sexual partners outside the relationship?'

'That wasn't the plan, but it seems to be what happens from time to time. You must have done the same.'

'No, I haven't.'

Ginny immediately zeroed in on the contradiction. 'Until now.'

'Er, yes, I suppose so.'

'Does that make you feel uncomfortable?'

'Yes, it does.'

'Don't you think that Angie would understand?'

'No, I don't think she would.'

'So, you're not going to tell her?'

'No.'

Ginny received this piece of information without comment, while Steve tried to work through the implications of the situation he now found himself in.

'Does that mean you'll tell Jon?' he asked uncertainly.

'No, I don't think that would be helpful.'

Steve was relieved. Even if Ginny was right about Jon's proclivities, Steve didn't want to put his complaisance to the test.

'So we're in the same position?'

'It would seem so. How are things with Angie?'

'Good question. I seem to have upset her.'

'By staying here in Cambridge?'

'Yes.'

'You said the other night that you were a poet. Is that connected with the reason you're staying in Cambridge?'

'Yes. I know it sounds a bit pretentious, ridiculous even, but I've always thought of myself as a poet.'

'It's only ridiculous, if you don't actually write poetry. Do you?'

Steve wanted to say that he wasn't sure that was actually true. Being a poet was a matter of attitude, not of output, but even he knew that his chances of succeeding with such an argument at this precise moment were decidedly slim.

'Well, yes, a bit.'

'Have you had anything published?'

'No, but I'm trying to finish a long piece called *Event/Horizon*.'

'Can I read it?'

'I'm not sure it's quite ready yet for others to read it, but now that I've got a base for the next few months I hope to make progress on it.'

'Come on, Steve. You've got to be a bit more determined than that.'

Steve was silent. He knew that Ginny was right.

After a while he said, 'OK, we've analysed me, we've analysed Jon. What about you?'

Ginny, reverting to her more usual dispassionate mode, gave a highly compressed account of herself. She was a few years older than Steve. She had grown up in Norfolk, gone to a girl's boarding school. Got a place at Hornsey College of Art in time for the student protests and the sit-ins of 1968. Dropped out at the end of that year, partly because she had been spotted by a fashion photographer and subsequently signed up to a model agency.

But she soon found the fashion world to be a sordid environment. She had been coerced into sex with her mentor and thereafter with a number of other powerful men in the industry. There was little consent in it. She had also got messed up on drugs, to the extent that she had been dropped by the agency and had ended up in a squat in Finsbury Park, selling her body at an even more sordid level until she had met Jon who had helped her get clean and stabilise her life. Jon didn't abuse her and he was too tough for most other guys in the squats they moved through to take on. They spent the summer touring the festival circuit in the VW camper van. They made a glamorous couple albeit in a ramshackle hippy mode and things were looking up.

They moved to Cambridge in 1972 and became fixtures on the local music scene. Ginny owed Jon a lot, but it soon became clear that he was gradually coming to terms with his own sexuality. They were fond of each other, but the relationship was coming to an end and then Steve had entered their lives.

Steve was trying to figure out how he had suddenly become a character in their much more visceral story. They both seemed more heroic figures. By comparison he was a mere neophyte, a callow apprentice. Steve sensed that he had reached a major fork on a road he had not realised he was travelling. He didn't know what to say and in the hope that Ginny would absolve him from having to make a choice right now confined himself to a noncommittal, 'What now?'

But Ginny wasn't about to provide a neat solution and simply replied, 'I don't know. We just play it cool.'

Steve was thoughtful. He was impressed by the dignity with which she had recounted her story, all the more so given some of the less than edifying details. His own account seemed little more than frivolous posturing. At the same time it was a terrible warning about what could happen if you left the beaten track. He was playing a dangerous game in which he might lose everything, in particular Angie, through an act of sexual madness. But wasn't all sex a form of madness? He was beginning a relationship with this powerful, beautiful, enigmatic woman and yet absurdly he felt sorry for himself. He sobbed a couple of times despite his best efforts to retain his composure.

Ginny rolled over in the bed and wrapped him in her arms. 'You'll be fine,' she said. 'You've got a strong soul. I saw that in your palm when you came around to Argyle Street. That doesn't mean that everything will work out. But you'll be able to bear it.'

She covered his face in kisses and stroked his hair. 'We'll be alright.'

Steve let himself be embraced. Just at that moment he didn't feel strong at all. He knew he was deceiving a number of people, who deserved better of him. But worst of all he was deceiving himself. Ginny seemed to have seen right through his pretentiousness, with an uncanny clarity. A powerful sense of vertigo and loss overwhelmed him. Suddenly there was no ground to his being. Ginny held him in her arms and rocked him gently. Where had this self-pity come from?

He wasn't normally like this. He considered himself a resolute person, capable, level-headed. It was true that on occasion he had had reason to doubt that this was the full picture, but on the whole he had managed to maintain the comfortable illusion of an integrated personality. Now this carefully constructed persona was disintegrating in the incandescent power of Ginny's sexuality.

They lay there entwined in each other's arms for some time until Ginny said she'd make some more tea. She extricated herself from his embrace, put on a long pink satin robe and disappeared downstairs, reappearing some minutes later bearing two mugs of tea. She put Steve's on the bedside table and said she'd take the first bath. Steve stayed under the bedclothes and tried to recompose himself. Soon Ginny returned with her hair wrapped in a towel and another knotted over her breasts. Steve watched her carefully. He thought her sexier then ever. He wanted her to come back to bed and for them to fuck again and again until he had emptied his entire being into her. He felt unhinged, intoxicated. Ginny let him watch her get dressed and brush her hair. She moved with an exquisite precision, finally smoothing her skirt over her hips. She turned around, hands still on her hips and said, 'Right, that's the end of the show. Time for you to have your bath.'

They had talked, but things were not that much clearer. In fact they were more complicated than ever. Still, one thing he was certain of was that he was going to give in his notice the following day.

That Saturday morning Steve's mind wasn't really on the job. Not that the job, needed much of a mind. His thoughts were occupied with the awkward conversation he would have with the gaffer at the end of the round and also the precise nature of his relationships. He knew he had been careless with Angie's affections in refusing to commit to her summer and Edinburgh plans, but this had not reflected a fundamental lack of belief in their relationship. Okay, if he was honest with himself, he hadn't ruled out the odd fling, but nor had he planned the summer hiatus with that in mind. If this scene with Ginny was just a fling, then he had time to decide whether and when to confess to Angie. But if Ginny had something longer term or more established in mind, what then? That would require much more careful handling and a considerable reconfiguration of arrangements. Nor did it make sense that Ginny had fallen for Steve, even if it had given his self-esteem a considerable boost.

Maybe he was overthinking things. Perhaps all Ginny wanted was a little uncomplicated sex from time to time. On the surface nothing would change. Jon and Ginny would still be a couple, even if their arrangements were a little unconventional. Steve could decide how to settle his conscience *vis-à-vis* Angie in due course. In the meantime, the next three months in Ainsworth street would involve plenty of home cooking, a surprisingly civilised living environment, considerably better than the accommodation he had taken on and occasional bouts of energetic sex. When viewed like that, what was not to like? As Ginny had implied, he was just being too uptight. He should play it cool. For the moment, that was what he resolved to do once he had got the awkward discussion with the gaffer out of the way.

After he had parked up he went over to the gaffer's cabin and asked if he could have a word. The gaffer looked up from his paper and waved him in.

Steve stood in front of the gaffer's desk feeling like an errant school-boy in the headmaster's study. The gaffer viewed him steadily. 'Well?'

'I don't quite know how to put this, Sid . . .'

'. . . but you're handing in your resignation?'

'Yes, how did you know?'

'It was obvious, son. This is not the job for you. I've got someone else lined up.'

'I'm sorry, Sid.'

'Don't be.'

'Er, will I get paid for my week off? After all I've earned it.'

'I don't see why not, but it's not up to me.'

And that was it. No ranting. No insults.

He walked back to the house in a daze, amazed at how easy it had been. Maybe he was starting to get used to making dramatic moves. He let himself into the house and went through to the kitchen to get a drink. There was no sign of Ginny, but the back door was open. He stepped through it and found Ginny, once more in dungarees, hacking down the gigantic weeds in the garden with a rusty pair of garden shears. She came over and gave Steve a kiss and said, 'How did it go with the gaffer?'

'Fine. He said he wasn't surprised. Took it very calmly.'

'Congratulations. It was the right thing to do.'

'What are you up to?'

'There's the bones of a lovely little garden here. I thought I might try and tidy it up. Found these old shears in a little shed at the back.'

'Ginny, you don't have to do this.'

'Of course I don't *have* to. I want to do it. It seems a pity to have a garden and not to be able to use it. You might as well say there's no point in our having a relationship, because it's not going to last for ever.'

Steve wasn't sure whether to be pleased that the situation between them was just temporary, or outraged that the termination of the relationship was already factored in, albeit *sine die*.

'But we're only going to be here for three months.'

'I wouldn't be so sure about that.'

'I am sure about it. That's the agreement I have with Beth.'

'We'll see. Anyway, three months is plenty of time for me to tidy things up in the garden. The weather's going to be good for another couple of months at least. It will be nice to be able to sunbathe out here and maybe do a barbecue.'

'Ginny, you're amazing. Where do you get all the energy from?'

'It's not as if I'm doing anything else.'

Which was true and another matter that Steve had wanted to talk to her about. How did she survive financially? Was she on the dole? Why didn't she get a job? But in the spirit of playing it cool, an approach that did not come naturally to him, he suppressed the desire to pursue that particular line of thought.

Steve fancied a nap, but thought he really ought to give Ginny some help and show that he was not quite as negative as she had alleged. 'I'll give you a hand. What would you like me to do?'

'Steve, you don't have to help.'

'No, I know, but I'd like to. We've only got a few more hours alone together. I want to make the most of them.'

She smiled at him. 'Now you're talking.'

They toiled in the garden for several hours. Steve rummaged in the shed and found a sickle. He also found an old whetstone and put a better edge on the sickle and the shears that Ginny was using. With the two of them working, they managed to clear the area that had once been the lawn. Then Ginny made a start on cutting back the tangle of jasmine, honeysuckle and old roses that had once formed graceful borders to the garden. Steve found a rake and raked all the cuttings into a big pile. He was dog tired, but didn't want to give up while Ginny still had energy. Eventually, she called time. They stopped for a cold drink, both now covered with little cuts on the backs of their hands and their arms.

As Steve tried to get a thorn out of the flesh of his thumb, he said, 'What are we going to do with the cuttings?'

'We'll have to have a bonfire, but not today. The next thing on the agenda is a bath. Then you'll get your reward. I'll let you give me a massage.'

After the bath and the massage, which developed in a rather obvious direction they had something to eat and then they moved into the sitting room. Ginny handed Steve Jon's stash box and suggested he roll a joint. Steve might be shagging Jon's missus, but he was a little reluctant to help himself to Jon's stash. Ginny laughed at his diffidence and assured him that it would be okay. He rolled a small joint, fired it up and took a couple of drags, registering that it was very strong. Must be good hash. What the hell! He dragged deeper on it and then passed it to Ginny. Pretty soon they were very stoned.

Ginny got up and said she'd be back shortly. When she returned she had a large photo album in her arms. She settled herself on the sofa and patted the space next to her for Steve to join her. She opened the album and spread it across her lap. It was a collection of photos from her modelling days. They were not snaps. Many of the images had been shot by some of the best known photographers of the era and were undeniably iconic. Not many years had passed, but these photographs already exuded the lustre of a golden age. Steve knew that this was the whole point of the culture of fashion. It was intended to evoke longing. But seen through the fragile mood in which he now found himself, these artful images just filled him with an intense feeling of regret, regret that he had not known Ginny when she bestrode the catwalks. He knew that this was stupid, because the real woman in those pictures was actually siting right next to him, apparently in love with him.

Krapp's Last Tape

STEVE SLEPT SOUNDLY THAT night, exhausted by the varied exertions of the day. As he tumbled out of bed at the sound of the alarm clock, Ginny woke and reached out to pull him back. They kissed and then Steve said, 'Sorry. Gotta go.'

Ginny pouted, rolled over and promptly went back to sleep.

Steve rattled around the sleepy Sunday streets, enjoying the fresh air and birdsong until his thoughts turned to his situation. Had he been premature in handing in his notice? Might it not result in financial disaster? Was his judgement being swayed by forces he didn't understand? He had a general sense of anxiety. And on top of all that today was the day of Jon's return. He found it hard to believe that Jon wouldn't sense something, even though Steve and Ginny had confined their lovemaking to Steve's bed.

When he got back to the house Jon was already there. Steve braced himself, but Jon was bonhomie personified. He and Ginny were in the sitting room, drinking coffee and Jon was rolling a spliff. Steve thought it was a bit early in the day to get blasted but Jon seemed in an expansive mood.

'Hey, man. Good to see you. Ginny tells me you've given your notice in at the dairy. Absolutely the right thing.'

Steve was reluctant to share the sense of trepidation that he was really feeling and said, 'Yeah, just one more week to go, and then a couple of weeks off before I start at the Arts.'

'What are you planning to do with your time off? Go and see your chick?'

Steve wasn't sure how to reply. On the one hand the question implied that Jon was oblivious to what was going on between Ginny and himself, which was good. On the other hand, Ginny might not be entirely delighted with his public affirmation of that idea. Hoping that she would realise that he was just playing things cool as she had advised, he said, 'Yeah, that's the idea.'

Jon finished rolling the joint and held it up for public admiration. It was a monster. By way of explanation Jon pronounced, 'To celebrate my new gig.'

Steve thought that another gig in a Cambridge church hall hardly warranted a major toke in the middle of the day, although technically the sun was now over the yardarm. But for Jon any time was a good time to roll a spliff. Jon lit the monster and toked deeply on it before passing it to Steve, who, as he took it said, 'Where's the gig then?'

'I use the term gig in the most general sense, man. I think you know that I was in London for an audition. Well, I got the job. I'm replacing Rusty Blades in Alien Hand Syndrome.'

Steve had been about to draw on the spliff, but paused at this improbable news. He didn't really know the Syndrome stuff, but they were certainly a well-established act with several albums to their credit. Rusty Blades was a handy guitarist, but the word was that he was pretty messed up on smack. Even so he would be quite an act to follow. If he'd received this information two minutes later, once the hash had done its work, Steve might have doubted what he was hearing, but, right at that very moment, he was completely straight. 'Wow. That's incredible. Congratulations. Where's the first gig? I'd like to be at it.'

'New York,' said Jon with undisguised pride.'

'What!' Steve had still not toked on the joint.

'Yeah, I'm joining them for their North American tour.'

Even straight, Steve was finding it difficult to deal with the news and decided that there was no point in delaying taking a hit any longer. He dragged on the joint twice before passing it to Ginny. For a moment, their eyes met and a current of unspoken meaning ran between them. Steve turned back to Jon.

'So, when does this tour start?'

'We fly out next week.'

The information was not getting any less improbable.

'Rusty's too messed up and can't do the tour. Syndrome's management is trying to get him cleaned up, but they also want this tour to go ahead. So they need someone to stand in for Rusty. And they and the other members of the band decided that yours truly fits the bill. It's not a permanent gig. Well, not unless Rusty sparks out. But as temporary jobs go it's one of the best and well paid.'

'How long does the tour last?

'Well, that's what I wanted to talk to you about.'

Steve suddenly realised that the purpose of the early joint was not so much celebratory, as a way of softening Steve up for whatever was coming next.

'It's a massive tour. There are 30 dates with a lot of travelling in between. But first, there's an intense period of rehearsal. I've got a lot of new parts to learn, although they're happy to let me put my own mark on the material. I don't have to play all Rusty's licks. But all in all, I'll be away for three months and I'll be joining the band for rehearsals in London later this week.'

Steve was stunned. 'Wow! That's all a bit sudden.'

'Yeah, but thank goodness, I can leave Ginny in your hands.

Steve blenched. 'I don't know what you mean,' he said nervously.

'Well, I probably won't be back before the sublet on this place runs out. So I wondered if you'd mind helping Ginny find a new place when it does. And help her move our stuff there.'

Steve was so relieved that Jon wasn't condoning the idea that Steve should take care of Ginny's sexual needs in his absence that he found himself agreeing to the proposition.

'Good man, I knew you would. The other thing is that you won't have to worry about the rent. I'll be earning plenty, and I'll send you the lot as soon as I get an advance. And since time is short, we should start on this recording of your play before I leave. Let's try and do it tomorrow. Is that okay with you?'

Not wishing to puncture the feelgood atmosphere surrounding Jon's news, Steve found himself saying, 'Cool. Here's to Alien Hand Syndrome,' with a brightness that did not reflect his true feelings. Needing time to digest the implications of Jon's announcement, Steve confessed that work had been a bit of a slog that morning, so he thought he'd have a nap. In fact, what was actually getting to him was not only the effect of the powerful joint, but also the previous day's exertions, both horticultural and amatory. As Steve headed for the sitting room door, Jon said, 'I hope you'll join us for supper. I brought a nice bottle of wine back from the Smoke, courtesy of the Syndrome. That's how they rock.'

Steve said he'd love to. Up in his room he tried, not very successfully, to order his thoughts. So Jon was effectively jumping ship, leaving Ginny in his care. Rent had been promised, but so far not a penny had changed hands. And on top of that he had allowed himself to be talked into giving up the one reliable and reasonably substantial source of income that he had, for a job that only paid 60% of that amount. The paranoia, that he sometimes felt when he was stoned, suddenly flared up. He'd been set up. They were in on this together. He needed to have a serious talk with Ginny, but that was not so easy with Jon around. And what was Angie going to say when she discovered it was just him and Ginny living in the house? This was not going to go down very well.

He drifted off into an uncomfortable sleep, from which he was awakened a little later by noises from the back garden. He looked out the window and saw that Ginny had resumed her garden tidying activities. Jon did not appear to be with her. Steve opened the door of his room. From the gentle snores emanating from Jon and Ginny's room he inferred that Jon had also decided to have a nap.

He went downstairs as quietly as he could, doing his best not to make the stairs creak. He went out into the backyard. At the sound of the back door opening Ginny looked up from her work and smiled at him. When he was beside her, she said, 'Magic. Things seem to be opening up for us,' in a tone of voice that suggested she discerned in recent events the operation of occult forces, rather than the unfolding of contingency, or, even more worryingly, design.

Right at that moment Steve was struggling to see those same things in a positive light.

'Aren't you pleased?' she asked, suddenly serious.

'Yes, of course,' he affirmed, not entirely convincingly. 'But I'm a bit shocked too. Things seem to be moving very fast. Did you know that this might be the outcome of Jon's trip to London?'

'I knew he was going for an audition. He does that quite a lot, but I didn't expect him to get the job, not for something like this.'

'But you knew the tour was for three months?'

'Yes, but Jon has never pulled off anything like this before.'

'You could have mentioned it.'

'Why what difference would it have made? Are you saying that you wouldn't have fucked me, if you thought that you'd be stuck with me for three months?'

'No.'

'What then?'

'There's the question of money.'

'Jon said he'll give you the rent.'

'But can I trust him?'

'So, it's only okay if I come with a dowry.'

'No, Ginny, don't mock me. I feel like I'm being manipulated.'

'What a strange boy you are. I give you my warm body and then when, against all expectation, events develop in such a way as to enable us to be together, you cavil.'

'No, no, it's just I feel like I'm in some kind of fairy story.'

'As I said, magic. I'm sorry, Steve. The fate of someone bearing your name is to learn to not ask questions.'

'Ginny, I haven't got the foggiest idea what you're talking about.'

'Steve, you're safe with me. I'll look after you. And I'll return you to real life better armed. I'm not stealing your soul. I'm here to help you.'

Steve felt very stoned. Ginny took his hand with one hand and passed her other hand across his brow as she had done in Argyle Street. 'Stop worrying, stay out here with me, and we can work together on the garden. You'll see, even though we're starting late in the season, we'll make something beautiful of it.'

Steve felt his fears lift and went in search of the sickle.

When Steve got back from work the following day, he found Jon in the sitting room setting up the recording equipment. Steve said he'd go and get his copy of the text and would be right back. Jon carried on plugging in cables. 'In my experience, recording always takes much longer than you think. And even though we're not recording music and we've only got one microphone to worry about, I guarantee it'll take us the rest of the day and maybe some of tomorrow too.'

Steve had never done any recording himself, but what Jon was saying made sense. He went up to his room and found his marked text. When he got back Jon said that he needed to get some levels to make sure the recording wasn't clipping, which he explained meant losing the top frequencies. He asked Steve to read or recite something into the microphone. Steve selected the first verse of The Jabberwocky from the small number of poems that he knew by heart. He cleared his throat and recited,

> Twas brillig and the slithy toves
> Did gyre and gimble in the wake
> All mimsy were the borogoves
> And the mome raths outgrabe.

'Far out, man,' said Jon as he peered at the VU meter on the tape recorder and adjusted a number of knobs on the amplifier. He then wound the tape back and flicked a couple of switches and Steve's recitation of the Jabberwocky filled the room. Steve was appalled at the thinness of his voice. He felt that it wasn't really his voice. Jon dismissed his concern. Everyone felt like that on first hearing a recording of their voice. More worryingly there was quite a lot of extraneous noise, something that Jon called popping, caused by the way that Steve enunciated his plosives. Jon had forgotten to rig up a pop shield. He rummaged through his gear and found a disc which looked like a small, flat sieve which he fixed in front of the microphone. He then asked Steve to recite the poem again. They listened to the new recording and even Steve could tell that the popping had been substantially reduced. He was impressed. Jon clearly knew what he was about.

Jon said that he'd now try and give a bit of body to Steve's voice. He asked Steve to recite the poem again as he adjusted a series of knobs and sliders. Once he had got the right tone, he said they were going to do one more take of the poem. They listened back to the three versions and Jon said he thought they were good to go.

Steve picked up his text, while Jon wound the tape back and then counted Steve in with his fingers. Steve took a deep breath and then read out 'Thirty-nine today, sound as a —' and lost his place in the text. He waved his free hand for Jon to stop the recording and said to Jon, 'Immediately after those words there's a long stage direction and I've only just realised that at that point I have to stop the on stage tape recorder and wind it back to listen to the words again. So the question is do we record them twice, bearing in mind that it will probably be impossible to get it exactly the same each time. Or is there some studio trickery we can use to copy the first part and repeat it?'

Jon considered the problem and said there was a technical solution, which would involve splicing sections of a copy of the tape into the original tape, but it was not something they could do now. Why not just read the speeches for tape straight through as one take with appropriate pauses and use that as the blueprint? Steve was doubtful, but he was in Jon's hands. Jon wound the tape back and they began again.

On stage *Krapp's Last Tape* runs for roughly 30 minutes, but it took Steve and Jon until early evening to capture a complete take of all the taped parts of the play, by which time they were both exhausted. Steve had completely underestimated how much concentration it took to read a text aloud without errors. He seemed to fluff his lines every other sentence, or lose his place or even on occasions his voice. Jon would have to wind back, find a convenient place to resume, all of which took time and then record that passage again.

At one point Steve almost gave up. There were a number of passages that he managed to get wrong several times, the worst offender being the line 'A small, old, black, hard, solid rubber ball'. He kept stumbling over the sequence. In the end he lost track of how many takes they did of that one phrase, but eventually, after many such difficulties, the recording got done. Jon started unplugging the equipment and putting it away. 'Bloody hell, that was a job.'

Steve was feeling more than a little dismayed at how amateurish his performance had been and apologised.

'No problem, man. Happy to help. But that's some weird play. I don't think I really got it. Krapp is a bit of an old goat, isn't he? Got an eye for the chicks. Likes a bit of nooky in a punt. We all do, I suppose. "I lay down across her with my face in her breasts and my hand on her." On her what?'

Steve laughed at Jon's juvenile humour. At that moment Ginny came in with a couple of mugs of tea. She had obviously heard Jon's final words and gave him an old-fashioned look. 'I'm getting some food together. How much longer are you two going to be?'

'We're done. We'll come through in a moment,' said Jon neatly winding an audio cable. Returning to his thoughts on the Beckett play, he asked, 'Is that the kind of thing that people watch at the Fringe?'

Steve shrugged. It was a moot point.

'So when was it written?'

'Just over 15 years ago.'

'No disrespect, but it's not very contemporary, is it?'

'Well, it does look back to a period before the war, it's true, but after all Krapp is using a tape recorder.'

'Yeah, that's another thing. I know a bit about audio equipment. Krapp says the recording is 30 years old. If the play was written in

1960 or thereabouts, then 30 years before was 1930. I'm pretty sure there weren't any tape recorders then, or not what we would consider a consumer device. The first Ampex machines only became available after the war in the late 40s. So I don't know what Krapp was using in 1930 to make his recording.'

'Jon, I think you're being a bit pedantic here, the tape recorder is a dramatic device, but it's a fair point.'

'So, why choose this play?'

'Partly because it's a one man piece, also a lot of it is pre-recorded. It doesn't need much of a set, so it's very portable. I could do it anywhere, so long as I have a tape recorder.'

'You'll need two, won't you? A dummy one on stage and one off stage connected to the PA system. And you'll need to rehearse with the off stage tape operator.'

'Yes, Jon. You're right. I haven't thought it all the way through, perhaps.'

'If you ask me, you'd be better off doing something else. Ginny says you're a bit of a writer. I reckon you could write something yourself that was better than this.'

'It's kind of you to say so, but Krapp is regarded as a masterpiece. And Beckett was awarded the Nobel prize for literature a few years ago.'

'Quite. You only get that hall of fame stuff when you're over the hill, got nothing left to say. Getting the Nobel prize ought to be a warning sign, a vote of no confidence. I mean you couldn't imagine Hendrix or Dylan getting a Nobel prize.'

'Yeah, I know what you mean.'

Jon had finished tidying up the equipment and handed Steve the reel of tape he had used for the session.

'It's best if you hold on to this otherwise it might get used for recording one of my practice sessions. No need to preserve anything else that's on the tape.'

Jon and Steve went next door to the kitchen where the table was laid with a green salad, a potato salad and a homemade quiche lorraine. Steve was, as ever, starving and would have happily eaten a dodgy kebab, but hunger only heightened his growing appreciation of Ginny's culinary skills, not that she seemed to eat very much herself, confining herself, as far as Steve could see, to a few leaves of lettuce.

* * *

For the next couple of days the housemates were each absorbed in their individual projects: Jon getting his gear ready for the tour; Ginny continuing with her work on tidying up the garden, which was already starting to look like a space that one might want to spend time in; and Steve out on his round in the early part of the day and writing his report for Grace in the afternoon, on which, in truth, he was not making much progress.

Over the evening meal on the Wednesday Jon announced that the Syndrome management were sending a van to pick him and his stuff up the following day. He'd been planning to drive down to London in the VW camper van and leave the VW with a friend, but it was better this way. The only snag was that that he'd be leaving the van parked in Ainsworth Street. Ginny didn't have a licence, but he'd be happy for Steve to use it. He slid the keys across the table. Ginny said that was good from her point of view because it would enable her, with Steve's help, to get rid of the garden waste and the broken furniture that they had moved out of the conservatory. Jon approved of the idea. Steve was not sure he wanted the responsibility of having a vehicle to look after, but also thought that it might come in handy for his own purposes. And it was, after all, an iconic vehicle.

He took the keys and said, 'I probably won't drive it much, but I'll make sure to look after it.'

Jon waved away his assurances. 'I know you will. The other thing I won't be able to take is the tape recorder. Hope you don't mind, but you're welcome to listen to my tapes. Some great stuff on there.'

Steve doubted he'd be making a close study of Jon's prize collection of Grateful Dead bootleg recordings, but said he'd be happy to look after the tape recorder too.

When Steve got back from work the next day, conscious that he had only three more days on the round, he walked into a scene of considerable commotion. Two burly blokes were loading Jon's speaker cabinets, amps and guitars into the back of the van. Jon, leather jacketed and booted, was keeping a close eye on proceedings. Once all the equipment was stowed Ginny made everyone a cup of tea. The roadies gulped theirs down quickly and asked to use the toilet. They were keen to get on. There were several days of rehearsals before the band flew out to the USA.

Jon slung his bag over his shoulder, checked that he had his passport and said he was ready. He gave Steve a double thumbs up and

Ginny a cursory hug and said that he'd try and write from time to time. Steve wished Jon well and said that he'd look out for reviews in the NME. Then Jon marched out without a backward glance. Ginny silently watched him go. The front door slammed shut and an awkward silence descended. On an impulse Steve offered to do the supper that evening. It was the least he could do after all the meals that Ginny had produced. His repertoire of dishes was far from extensive, but he'd been known to produce a reasonable macaroni cheese. Ginny said that would be great. In the meantime she would resume work on the garden.

New Skin for the Old Ceremony

AROUND SIX O'CLOCK, STEVE descended to the kitchen, switched on the radio and started to prepare the meal. Although it was a simple dish, Steve's approach to cooking required an inappropriately extensive range of kitchen equipment, but in due course the meal was ready. He laid the table and stood back to survey the scene. Deciding that the jumble of used pots and utensils did not convey the best impression, he threw himself into a preliminary bout of washing-up. Once the surfaces had been cleared, he called up the stairs to Ginny to say that the meal was ready. He cocked an ear for a response, but was unable to detect any sound or movement. Perhaps she was having a nap. He went upstairs and tapped on the door of her room. There was no reply. He pushed the door open. Ginny was sitting up in bed hugging her knees to her chest, with a duvet pulled up to her chin. She hardly seemed to notice Steve at all. He apologised for the intrusion and said that supper was ready. Ginny seemed to come out of her trance, smiled at him and threw the blankets back, saying, 'Sorry, just recharging my batteries. I'll be down in a few minutes.'

Steve went back downstairs and after a short while Ginny, now dressed in a beaded kaftan dress joined him. As Steve was serving the pasta, Ginny remembered that there was a bottle of white wine in the fridge. Did he fancy a glass? He certainly did. A little alcohol might counteract the nervousness he felt at producing a meal for a person of

Ginny's advanced culinary abilities. Ginny got the bottle from the fridge and asked Steve to open it. While he struggled with an elaborate corkscrew that was meant to make opening a bottle of wine easier, but in fact made the task much more difficult, Ginny found two wine glasses. Eventually he managed to extract the cork and he poured them a glass each. Steve raised his glass and said, 'Here's to Jon's tour,' to which Ginny responded, 'Here's to those that remain behind.' They clinked glasses and began to eat.

Steve muttered something about the dish lacking flavour. But Ginny thought it was fine, nothing that couldn't be fixed by adjusting the seasoning or using a different kind of cheese for the sauce next time and at least it was one more meal than Jon had ever managed to cook. Steve hadn't been fishing for a compliment or seeking to compare himself to Jon. They finished the meal in silence. Ginny then washed the plates and Steve dried and put them away.

Drying her hands, Ginny mentioned that she'd just bought the new Leonard Cohen LP and suggested they go into the sitting room and listen to it. They carried their glasses through to the next room and Ginny slipped the disc out of its sleeve and put it on the turntable. Steve asked to see the cover, which Ginny handed to him before sitting down.

Steve studied the cover. '*New Skin for the Old Ceremony*. Weird title, eh?' The illustration on the front showed two winged and crowned lovers engaged in sexual intercourse. Steve guessed that it was a reproduction of an old alchemical woodcut. He handed the cover back and, carefully avoiding any attempt to analyse the title, said, 'Visually quite a departure from his previous albums.' The record started to play and Steve thought it also sounded different from Cohen's earlier work. As usual with Cohen, the lyrics were strangely resonant. Steve wondered if Ginny was using the record to make an indirect comment on their situation.

It was nice to have Jon's musical gear out of the sitting room, but Steve was surprised to find that he already missed him. Maybe he was attracted to scoundrels. Whatever the drawbacks of life in Jon's orbit, he was easy to talk to and absurdly positive. By contrast he and Ginny might be lovers, but they were not yet friends and they had not yet found a way of talking about inconsequentialities. Steve shifted uncomfortably in his chair. Ginny realised that she was going to have to move the conversation along.

'What were you doing this afternoon when I was in the garden?'

'I was reading the manuscript of a book that one of my teachers is writing. She asked me to do a reader's report. It's on Camus and Sartre. She asked me to provide her with a three page report by tomorrow.'

'Have you written it?

'Not yet. I've read the manuscript, but I don't know what to say and I'm regretting having taken on the task.'

'Why did you?'

'As a favour. She was a good teacher and was very patient with me. I was not a good student.'

'There must be more to it than that.'

'Well, her husband is the editorial director of Inflexion Books. I thought she might show *Event/Horizon* to him.'

'Has she seen the poem?'

'No, but she knows about it.'

'And when are you going to give it to her to read?'

'I don't know. I'm not sure it's ready to be seen yet. I need to write some more. Then it needs editing.'

'When was the last time you worked on it?

'Not for weeks maybe months.'

Ginny was not impressed.

Steve tried to explain. 'I know, I know, but other things seem to get in the way.'

'It seems to me, you're using this idea of yourself as a poet as an excuse for the way you deal with people and situations. If you were serious, you'd be out there with it.

'Jon was the same. He didn't play in public. He sat in his room and took acid and played the guitar for hours a day, but didn't play for, or with, others, because, in his own view, he didn't play well enough, or as well as Hendrix. But eventually he understood that he should play like himself and not someone else. And then everything started to come together.'

Steve found it hard to believe that Jon had lacked confidence in his playing. In the time that Steve had known him he just seemed to exude immense self-confidence.

Ginny had a suggestion. 'Why don't you go upstairs now and write your report before we go to bed? Write it off the top of your head. Make it a Steve Percival piece, not an imitation of someone else. Three pages shouldn't take you too long. You can take it around to her tomorrow after work. If it's not what she's expecting, too bad. And why don't you give her a copy of your poem at the same time?'

Steve had an objection. 'I'm tired. I've had too much to drink.'

'Don't be absurd, push yourself.'

Steve had another objection. 'The problem with giving her the poem is that it's handwritten and really quite long. I definitely don't have time to copy it out.'

Ginny considered the situation. 'OK, I didn't realise that you didn't have a typewriter. Isn't that a basic tool of the trade?'

'Yes, I was hoping to save up for one this summer.'

Ginny nodded. 'Okay, new plan. Let me read the poem. I'll tell you what I think of it tomorrow evening. I'm not going to be able to give you the kind of critique that Grace can give you. But I will approach it in the way you should approach writing your report for Grace.'

Steve realised that it was pointless to argue and nodded weakly. But Ginny wasn't finished. 'A couple of other things. Let's sleep from now on in my room. I've changed the sheets and and you can move some of your things in tomorrow, but I'd prefer it if you kept most of your clothes in the back bedroom, which otherwise will be your workroom.'

Steve nodded again. 'But what happens when Jon gets back?'

'He won't be back.'

'How do you know?'

'I know. Trust me. And now you'd better get on with your assignment, if we're going to have enough time to make love.'

Suddenly Steve seemed to have two assignments. He went up to his room and sat down at the desk. He had been trying to write something that would impress Grace. But Ginny was right. That was exactly the wrong way to go about the task. He certainly did not know more about existentialism and its attendant literature than Grace did. He could hardly sit down and speed read *Being and Nothingness* before putting pen to paper. Nor was he her supervisor. He was not marking an essay, the best he could do was to give his response as a general reader.

His facetious thoughts about Sartre and Camus being the Butch Cassidy and the Sundance Kid of the *rive gauche*, whilst wide of the mark, was the way to go. It was anathema to the Cambridge approach, but rather than just concentrating on the works, he felt that the biographical material should get equal billing. After all, the existentialist cast list was in itself utterly fascinating, and arguably the movement itself had had little intellectual progeny. It was almost as if it had expired in the mutual antagonism of its leading exponents. The intellectual spotlight had moved to the structuralists.

Steve had preferred Camus, partly no doubt because reading Camus did not require a background in phenomenology, but also because he was the better novelist and the more glamorous figure, right down to his Humphrey Bogart looks and his tragic death in a Facel Vega, one of the least beautiful French cars ever built. The preference had no intellectual underpinnings. It was more along the lines of the playground conversations back in the early 60s about who your favourite Beatle was. Steve had been a Paul man. The tougher kids went for John; the musos for George. He wasn't sure if he could categorise those who tended to Ringo, but he certainly had a strong female following.

He could hardly apply the Beatles typology to the existentialists, fun though it might be to try and fit de Beauvoir and Merleau-Ponty into the scheme. But the key thing was that the movement was as much a cultural phenomenon as an intellectual one. Camus was obviously the outsider, Sartre an implacable contrarian, Merleau-Ponty the purist. As the reputations of these three waned, de Beauvoir's was increasingly in the ascendant. Certainly she had ably assisted Sartre in much of his intellectual and sexual strong-arm tactics, but her book *The Second Sex* had also, almost singlehandedly, inaugurated the feminist movement.

Short though the piece was, by the time Steve had finished writing, it was well past his regular bedtime. He put the kettle on and while it was boiling re-read his piece. Grace had said that she didn't want a dissertation, but how would she respond to the flippant sketch he had just thrown together? There was only one way to find out.

Steve made two mugs of chamomile and took them up to Ginny's room. She was still awake reading and smiled at him enquiringly. He told her with a degree of self-satisfaction that he had finished his report for Grace. He had taken Ginny's advice and done a Steve Percival piece. He'd take it around to Grace's tomorrow after work. Ginny asked whether he had enough energy for his reward. Steve asked if they might postpone it until the following evening. She laughed and said that she hadn't realised that Steve's appetites were so easily satisfied. Under that kind of provocation, Steve said he felt he might be able to rise to the occasion, as it were, and removed his clothes.

When Steve was walking to Glisson Road the next day, it occurred to him that Grace might not be in. They had not actually fixed a time for the rendezvous and he doubted that the manuscript of her book would fit through the letterbox. In the event his tentative press on the doorbell was answered by Grace swathed in a dressing gown and with her hair wrapped in a towel. She seemed surprised to see him. 'Steve, I wasn't expecting you.'

Steve was confused. 'You asked me to do a report on your book, and you gave me two weeks to get it back to you.'

'Yes, but I expected you to ring me to make an appointment.'

Steve was embarrassed. 'Sorry. We don't have a phone where I live. I can come back another time. I'll just leave my report and your manuscript.'

He pushed the bundle of paper towards her.

Grace sighed wearily. 'No, no, come in. But you'll have to forgive my state of undress. I've just come back from a run.'

She invited him in and led him into a big open-plan kitchen and dining room at the back of the house. Steve was already feeling nervous enough about the tenuity of his report. It didn't help to be made to feel that he was also *de trop*. Grace went across to the big Aga and put a kettle on to boil. Steve stood in the doorway of the room and said, 'Look, why don't I just leave this with you and we can talk about it another time.'

But Grace's mood had softened. 'Steve, this is the first time you've ever got a piece of work in on time. You don't think I'm going to send you away on such an auspicious occasion.'

Steve shifted nervously from foot to foot. Grace laughed at him. 'For God's sake, man, sit down. What would you like to drink, tea or coffee?'

Steve put the manuscript on the big stripped pine kitchen table and took a seat, 'Coffee, please.'

As Grace made him a mug of coffee, Steve said. 'The report is not very long and I'm afraid it's handwritten.'

'You may recall that I'm quite used to reading handwritten scripts.'

Grace handed him the mug of coffee and said, 'But before we talk about your report on my book, let me remind you of the second part of the deal. You were going to give me your poem to look at.'

'Yes, I was. And you definitely can read it, but I'm afraid I haven't brought it today, because my girlfriend said she'd like to see it and I only have a single handwritten copy.'

Grace laughed. 'At least the dog hasn't eaten it.'

Steve blushed. He knew it seemed improbable. That was the problem with the truth when you were a serial disappointer.

'I'm going to make a copy in the next few days and will give you that copy next week.'

'Well, I do accept that Angie has priority in the matter of this poem, though I am surprised that she hasn't read it already.'

Steve had forgotten that he had told Grace about Angie, had indeed sung her praises on more than one occasion.

'Angie has read it, but she and I are no longer together.' Steve wasn't entirely sure that that was actually the situation, but he didn't want to go into too much detail. 'I'm living with someone else.'

This was the first time that he had publicly admitted that he was now with Ginny. Giving voice to the relationship felt weird and exhilarating at the same time.

Grace was intrigued. 'Oh, is that recent? You and Angie sounded as if you were in for the long haul.' Grace had unerringly put her finger on the contradiction.

'Well, it's all a bit confusing actually.'

'Sorry to pry.'

But Steve needed to unburden himself. 'No it's okay.'

Grace listened carefully.

'I wanted to stay in Cambridge to write, but Angie had a teaching job lined up in Brighton for the summer and then she's heading up to Edinburgh in the autumn to start a PhD and suggested that I move up there with her. I think I mentioned that much when we met in The Six Bells. For all sorts of reasons I didn't feel that I was ready to commit to that right now. I certainly didn't rule it out, but she was a bit frustrated with me. And then through a somewhat mysterious sequence of events this new relationship developed. To be quite honest I haven't sorted it all out yet and I'm afraid that I'm screwing things up.'

'Since I am prying, does this woman have a name?'

'Her name is Ginny.'

'And what does Ginny do?'

Good question. What does she do? 'She used to be a model. But that was some years ago. She's kinda between jobs at the moment.'

Grace seemed to be impressed. 'Ooh! That sounds glamorous.'

Steve nodded mournfully. 'She is.'

'And it sounds as if she might be older than you?'

Steve nodded again.

Grace was thoughtful. '*Hmm.*'

Steve couldn't hold back. He needed to tell Grace the truth.

'It's all a bit of a mess really. Ginny and I are a very new thing. She's only just found out that I write and she's encouraging me to take it more seriously. She actually wanted me to give you my poem today, because she thought I had typewritten copies. So she's reading it while I make another fair copy that she wants me to give you.'

'Good for her. I can see that I'm going to have to meet this young woman.'

It wasn't at all clear to Steve why that should be necessary. Grace's pastoral responsibilities had surely lapsed.

'She says that I should stop being so half-hearted. She doesn't like the way that I express doubt about the poem. She gets impatient with me when I say that I don't know whether it's any good or not. And the fact is that I suspect that it's not.'

Grace nodded sympathetically.

'It may surprise you to know that I feel exactly the same about the draft of the book you've just read. I feel that I am a good teacher. I know my field and I enjoy doing research. But there is increasing pressure on academics today to publish. That seems to be the way to enhance one's professional standing. But my God, it's leading to a plethora of virtually identical monographs. I am not sure that my book has anything new to add. It is really being driven by my publisher having to pad out his series on modern thinkers.'

Whilst this display of mutual solidarity was helpful *vis-à-vis* Steve's poetry, it now made him anxious about how Grace might respond to the flippancy of his report. He had assumed that she was secure enough in her intellectual approach to the subject that she would be indulgent towards his suggestion of focusing on the personalities and treating the movement as a cultural rather than intellectual phenomenon. Now he wasn't so sure.

But he wasn't getting out of it so easily. Putting to one side her own self-doubt she asked Steve to show her his piece. Let her have five or ten minutes and then they could talk about it. As she read Steve let his thoughts drift. He was no longer a student, but this felt just like a supervision. *Plus ça change . . .*

She sat down and started to read. Steve sipped his coffee and looked around the room, noting how well-appointed it was. From time to time his eyes drifted back to Grace. As she read she unknotted the towel from around her head and with her free hand unconsciously teased out one or two damp locks of hair. The process had loosened her dressing gown a little and Steve realised that she was showing a considerable amount of cleavage. She felt his eyes on her in that psychic way that people have when they are being watched. Her eyes met his for a moment and she smiled, apparently oblivious to the illicit glances that Steve had stolen. Embarrassed, Steve looked away and did his best not to allow his gaze to drop to her gaping dressing gown.

At one point Grace seemed to backtrack in her reading going back to an earlier sheet, but eventually she finished and put the report down on the table, collected her thoughts and then said, 'Steve, this is fantastic. It is exactly the kind of thing I wanted and hoped you might be able to provide. You've resisted the temptation to quibble about this or that detail of existentialist philosophy, the standard approach of most academics, and you've suggested looking at the movement as a cultural phenomenon and what we might nowadays call a scene. These people were fucking each other and fucking each other up and all the while documenting it in an avalanche of writing. I think this is exactly what is missing from my book. And it's not as if I don't know a lot about all this stuff. It will allow me to extend the discussion to include figures like Boris Vian and Juliette Greco. I could even smuggle in something about Serge Gainsbourg's early work.'

Apart from the surprise that Grace had embraced his hastily cobbled together report so comprehensively, Steve was apprehensive that he might have subverted what, as it stood, was a solid piece of work. He was even more surprised at the mention of Serge Gainsbourg. So far as Steve was concerned French rock music was a contradiction in terms and *Je t'aime, moi non plus* a piece of sonic soft porn. If Gainsbourg had produced anything else of note, it hadn't troubled the UK music charts.

'Does Gainsbourg qualify as an existentialist?'

'Perhaps it's pushing it to say that he was an existentialist, but he was championed by Boris Vian, who definitely was. Serge was a composer of classic *rive gauche* chansons before he was a pop star. He is older than you might think. He was actually born in 1928 and started writing songs in the 1950s. By the time I was doing postgraduate work in Paris in the early 1960s he had had three or four albums out, which, I think, evoke that era very well. The lyrics are amazing. Full of baudelairian spleen. He actually called one of his songs *Le Chanson de Prévert* and got the great man's permission to use his name in the song. I still have the original LPs. If you have time, I'll play you a couple of tracks.'

They went through to the living room and Grace hunted through her extensive collection of LPs until she found what she was looking for and put the disc that she extracted from a rather battered sleeve on the expensive looking hifi system. Before she lifted the tone arm onto the disc she said, 'Look, I can't sit around all day in my dressing gown. People might get the wrong idea.'

Steve wasn't sure who these people were. And he was rather enjoying the idea that Grace was inappropriately dressed. Grace put the record on and said she'd be back in a few minutes. What emerged from the loudspeakers was a curious combination of jazz, pop and chanson, with foregrounded lyrics and sophisticated arrangements. Very *recherché* from his perspective and not immediately compelling.

As the strains of late 50s French chanson filled the air, Steve looked around the room. It was an opulent space but managed to retain an understated informality. The loudspeakers from which the music flowed were positioned either side of a white marble mantelpiece with two elegantly sculpted corbels supporting the ornamental overmantel framing a black cast iron fireplace. Ranged in the alcoves on either side of the chimney breast were built-in bookcases full of books, in front of which were a pair of wingback chairs. In one corner of the room stood a large glass-fronted drinks cabinet and in the bay window a low sofa.

Along one wall was a chesterfield, upholstered in green velvet, above which a large semi-abstract female nude hung. The head of the figure was in the upper left quadrant of the picture space, the buttocks and the curve of the upper hip dominating the lower centre of the canvas, with the legs curled up beneath the torso tapering away to the lower right. The head of the figure was resting on her left arm staring away from the viewer. The image was composed of bold red and bluish-green brush strokes, with the figure dissolving into abstract washes of colour, occupying a space between figuration and abstraction. Steve thought that it was the kind of image that you could live with for a long time.

Steve refocused on the music. He had assumed that he would have little difficulty in picking up the lyrics, but discovered, to his embarrassment, that his command of colloquial French was not quite good enough to catch all the lyrics. What the hell was a *poinçonneur*? Something to do with stamping? And wasn't *lilas* the French for lilac? Was this some other test that Grace was setting him? He thought he caught references to Miami and the Reader's Digest, which seemed unlikely in a chanson. Things became a little clearer with the final lines of the first verse and the refrain of the chorus *J'fais des trous.* It would appear that the job of the song's protagonist was to punch holes in tickets. He must be a ticket collector. Wasn't Porte de Lilas a métro station? Steve was relieved than he hadn't totally lost his ability to unpick a French lyric, but he wasn't sure if he was sufficiently taken with the style of music to try and decode the remainder of the songs on the the first side of the LP. Did a song about a ticket collector qualify as an existentialist text? Admittedly, the fact that by the end of the song the protagonist was planning to put a hole in his own head gave the song an absurdist slant, albeit in a somewhat jaunty mode. He had to admit though that the song's main riff was a bit of an ear worm.

Grace, now attired in a cream silk blouse and navy blue slacks, was back by the time the third track was playing. 'What do you think of the music?'

Steve didn't want to disappoint her and said, 'Well, it's fascinating but nothing like I expected on the basis of *Je t'aime moi non plus.* I found it hard to pick out the lyrics. They're extremely colloquial. I probably shouldn't admit that to someone who used to teach me French.'

'You're right. I think a good translation of some of these songs would be a challenge, even to someone with advanced French. Apart from the colloquialisms, there is a lot of elision going on. There are also a number of English loanwords, but pronounced in extreme Gallic fashion. Gainsbourg's music at this stage is essentially cabaret music. But he evolved his style record by record, borrowing from British and American popular music styles.'

Grace sensed that Steve wasn't immediately hooked and decided not to turn the record over when the first side had finished playing. Meanwhile Steve thought he'd better be getting back. He'd done his assignment and it seemed to have been well received. But, now that she was properly dressed, Grace wanted to keep things going. 'How about a drink? It is Friday after all. A little early to start maybe, but what the hell!'

Steve didn't think this was a great idea. 'Unfortunately, I've got work tomorrow.'

'Ah, yes. I forgot you're a milkman. Don't you find that messes up your social life?'

'Yes, it does a bit. But fortunately, I've found a new job. I finish at the dairy on Sunday.'

'And what will you be doing then?'

'I've got a job working in the box office at the Arts Theatre. I start in a couple of weeks. I believe you know the front of house manager, Mike Wallace. It seems you supervised him too. I think that's the only reason I got the job.'

'Well, what a coincidence! Mike Wallace, yes. Nice chap. Very bright. You two will get on well.'

What the hell! Steve thought he would have that drink after all. Grace was delighted. She fetched a cold bottle of wine, two glasses and a corkscrew from the kitchen and asked Steve to open the bottle. Steve pulled the cork out without too much difficulty and filled the glasses. Grace proposed a toast. 'Here's to your new job.'

Steve raised his glass and said, 'And to Camus and Sartre.' He took a sip of the cold, dry wine, savouring the first mouthful. As the cold alcohol did its work he caught sight of the the big canvas over the chesterfield again and asked who the artist was. Grace waved a hand. 'Oh, that's one of Pete's. He's done several life studies of me over the years. This is the most recent one. It's his take on the Rokeby Venus. I'm not sure that I want my backside on such prominent display, especially when he's made it so fleshy.'

Steve didn't know what to say. He wanted to say that Grace's bottom was much perter than the one in the picture, but it seemed inappropriate to refer directly to her anatomy. He took a sip of his wine and said desperately, 'I thought Peter was a publisher.'

'He is, but he studied at the Slade and was highly thought of. Somehow he just slipped into publishing and turned out to be very good at it. But he still considers himself to be a painter. He'll be pleased you like it.'

Without thinking, Steve said, 'Before Ginny was a model, she was an art student. She studied at the Hornsey School of Art.'

Grace was thoughtful. 'I have an idea. We're having a small dinner party next week. Why don't you and Ginny join us? If you're free. The other guests are Gary, one of my oldest friends from my own student days and his partner Matt, who is a writer. Not your kind of stuff. He writes for television. You'll be able to meet Peter too. And I'll get to meet this lady who has entered your life.'

Privately, Steve doubted that Ginny would be up for the encounter, but he said he'd talk to her and see if she was free on that evening. He didn't mention that, so far in their relationship, Ginny always seemed to be free.

Grace seemed pleased with her machinations and asked Steve to let her know in the next couple of days whether he and Ginny could make it. He could phone or drop a note in. Steve finished his drink and said he really must be getting back now. Grace accompanied him to the door, 'Thank you for your work on my book. I hope you and Ginny can join us next week.'

As he reached the garden gate, Grace called after him. 'And when you come, you can bring a copy of your poem.'

She blew him a kiss and shut the front door.

Portable Olivetti

WHEN STEVE OPENED THE front door of the Ainsworth Street house the first thing he noticed was the heady aroma of baking and the next was the sound of Ginny singing. He went into the kitchen and greeted her with an embarrassed peck on the cheek. The relationship was so new that they hadn't yet established a routine way of greeting each other. They could do intensity, but had not yet established a mode of quotidian affection. Ginny had her hair up and was wearing an apron dotted with smudges of flour. She was clearly in domestic goddess mode today. He was relieved that the ice maiden and sibylline personas had been parked for now, but he hoped that Ginny as odalisque was not too far away.

'That smells delicious. What are you making?'

'I thought I'd do a lemon drizzle cake.'

Steve approved. Ginny said she'd be done shortly and then she'd make some coffee. Steve went up to his room and put his report on Grace's book into a ring binder. When he came back downstairs, Ginny had cleared away the baking paraphernalia but was still wearing the flour smudged apron. She had laid the table with a mug of coffee and a slice of the new baked cake for each of them.

'So how did you get on with your supervisor?'

'It went well. She liked what I'd written. She liked the idea of paying more attention to the personalities.'

'Will she show your poem to her husband?'

'I don't know, but I think so. In any case, she has invited us to dinner next week. We'll get to meet him then. She suggested next Friday. Is that okay for you?'

Ginny frowned. 'I'll just check my very full diary. Oh yes, I can squeeze that in.'

They both laughed.

'So tell me about these people that we're going to have dinner with. I need to work out what I'm going to wear.'

Steve was glad that Ginny had got her priorities in the right order.

'Well, to begin with, they have a lovely house, beautifully furnished and decorated. They're quite a high flying couple. She's a university lecturer in 19th and 20th century French literature. I guess she's about 35 . . .'

'Oh, so she's younger than I thought. I'm not sure what I think about that. I thought she was a lady of more mature years.'

'Ginny, don't be ridiculous. Anyway, she's married.'

'The history of human relationships suggests that the fact that a person is married seldom means much when certain forces are at work.'

Steve reflected that it didn't take much for the cynical aspects of Ginny's personality to surface. He was glad he hadn't mentioned Grace's state of undress when he had arrived, nor their discussion about the nude canvas for which she had been the model.

'I haven't met her husband. His name is Peter Newman. He's the editorial director of Inflexion Books, one of the big figures in British publishing. If I could get on his scanner, it would be very useful to my career as a writer.'

'Do publishers accept handwritten submissions?'

'I don't suppose so. I'll have to do something about that.'

Ginny stood up and took off her apron. 'I might be able to help you there. I'll be back in a moment.'

She returned a few minutes later with a large carrier bag. She put it on the table and said, 'It's for you.'

Steve wrinkled his brow and pulled the bag towards him. Inside the bag was a light blue plastic case. Ginny urged him to open it. He undid the catch and raised the lid to reveal a portable Olivetti typewriter. He looked at it in confused amazement.

'It's secondhand, but I think it's in working order. I tested all the keys. I got it this morning from a junk shop on Mill Road, when you were at work.'

'Ginny, you shouldn't have. You can't afford . . .'

She cut him off. 'You don't know what I can and can't afford. If you're going to be a real writer, you need a typewriter.'

Steve ran his hand over the machine. The absence of even a single scratch on the gleaming paintwork suggested to Steve that the typewriter was far from being secondhand, but he thought it better to keep his thoughts to himself. 'It's fantastic, Ginny. Thank you. It's such a thoughtful present. I don't deserve this.'

'It'd be a pretty poor way to run a relationship, if things were only done on the basis of just desserts. It's what you need to do your work. I can't make you do your work, but if I can provide some of the tools you need for your work, I will be happy.'

There was also a ream of typing paper in the bag. Steve opened the packet and put a sheet into the typewriter and typed a few experimental words. It seemed to work perfectly.

Ginny watched him proudly. 'So now you can give this Peter Newman a typed up version of your poem, which, by the way, I have now read.'

Ginny was full of surprises today.

'What did you think of it?'

'It's an amazing piece of work. It reminds me of an experience I had on acid a few years ago, a crazy trip through deep time. I presume you must have had a similar experience.'

Steve was pleased with her response. He didn't think Ginny did dissimulation. He did slightly object to the implication that the writing was drug-induced. It was not that he disapproved of drugs, far from it. He enjoyed the strategic joint, but he had never taken LSD, although he did not rule out trying it at some point. The poem had in fact been painstakingly pieced together from his haphazard reading and from a process of severe editing.

'I've never taken acid,' he said, almost apologetically.

Ginny was surprised. For many of the people in her circle, acid had been a rite of passage. She reflected that Steve was a few years younger and in that time the relentless demonisation of LSD and the high profile given in the media to a number of so-called acid casualties had had the effect of calling into question its reputation as a safe recreational drug. She regretted introducing acid into the discussion. She hadn't been trying to suggest that Steve had in some way cheated.

'What I meant was that it conveys a wide-screen sci-fi vision, something like *2001: A Space Odyssey*.'

Steve found that association more apposite.

'I do have one negative thought about the poem. I hesitate to mention it. I'm not particularly tuned into contemporary poetry. I'm more at home with Keats or Wordsworth.'

'You have to tell me now. I'm not that fragile. It would be useful for me to have a response to it that wasn't a programmatic response from one or other tendency of the Cambridge poetry scene.'

He braced himself now for proof that Ginny had in fact completely misunderstood the poem. But he also readied himself to be as generous as possible to her contribution.

'It seems to me there's no space in your poem for the personal and the human. The poem, beautiful though it is, is too cerebral. It's lacking emotion, lacking heart. It's not that you lack heart yourself, it's that you seem reluctant to reveal yourself. All art involves self-revelation. You need to be braver.'

Steve was thoughtful. 'I don't really agree that one has to reveal oneself to create a work of art.'

'If you're not prepared to reveal yourself, you'll remain blocked.'

'But I don't feel that I am blocked either. I feel that I write in a particular mode.'

'I'm speaking here as someone who is proposing herself as your muse.'

'Ginny, I'm enormously grateful for the typewriter and for your comments, but that's not the way I work. I don't invoke a muse.'

'Are you sure, Steve? If you're not prepared to risk your heart, this poem won't work. Being my lover has cost you nothing so far, not even your relationship with Angie, but it can't go on like that.'

Steve was troubled. Ginny had apparently liked the poem, but her minor reservation rather undermined his entire approach to writing. She seemed to see the poem as the product of his relationship with Angie and it was as if now that she was occupying the role that Angie had played in his life, she expected his writing to change too. So her comments were only tangentially about his poem and actually about their relationship. So much for playing it cool. Nevertheless he resolved to respond as positively as possible.

'Thank you for being brave enough to tell me these things. I am not sure if I can change the way I write just like that, but I agree that I need to sort things out with Angie.'

'What do you propose?'

'I'll write to her and tell her about you and me.'

Ginny was thoughtful. 'Are you sure? I'm not putting pressure on you to do this. It has to be your decision.'

He did rather feel that she *was* putting pressure on him. But perhaps she was also uncovering something else, something that he had been hiding from himself.

'I don't want to hurt Angie, but I think we've been on different tracks for a while.'

Ginny reached out and took his hand a smiled at him bleakly.

'I know you'll do it properly. And thank you for letting me see your poem and submitting to my negativity. I know it's painful, but it's meant to help.'

Steve decided that it would probably be better to write to Angie before it got too late. He went up to what was now his work room and carefully placed the Olivetti on the desk. He wasn't sure what he was going to write, but this was certainly not a letter that would be improved by being typed. He got out his notepad.

Dear Angie,

I'm writing to you with some difficult news. There is no easy way to say this. I'm now in a relationship with Ginny, something you perhaps foresaw. Jon has joined a successful rock band, that is touring the United States and won't be back before we are due to move out of Ainsworth St. Ginny's view is that they're finished. There is more to it than that, but this is not the place to go into all the details. I am sorry to be sending you this news by letter. I would have preferred to have told you in person. But I think it only fair to everyone concerned to make the position clear as soon as possible to avoid further hurt.

I'm very sorry. I have loved our time together. You are a lovely, intelligent person. I'm simply not in your class academically or ethically. I seem to have strayed into a darker part of the wood. It would be unfair to expect you to wait until I return to my senses. I have no doubt that you will succeed in whatever you do, nor do I have any doubt that you will find someone who can give you the support that you deserve.

I feel horrible, sad, unworthy. I'm not sure where I'm heading. I feel I need to go on this journey, if I am to become a writer. It is not a place I can ask anyone else to follow me to, particularly someone I care as much about as you.

Please forgive me and know that I will always love you. Even if this is a love that will be of little consolation to either of us.

Please stay in touch. And when your anger has subsided somewhat, let me know how you're getting on.

In sadness and with love, Steve

He wasn't sure if he had struck the right tone and decided not to seal the envelope so that he could re-read it the next day before sending it. He then went next door to the other bedroom and joined Ginny in bed.

The Saturday round passed without incident. Steve was conscious that he needed to get his letter to Angie in the post. When he got back to the house, there was no sign of Ginny. He went up to his room and was about to look over his draft from the previous night, when he noticed that a letter was propped on the little mantelpiece. He recognised the handwriting as Angie's. Normally the sight of her handwriting aroused in him a pleasant sense of anticipation, but this time the feeling was one of trepidation, a feeling which turned out to be fully justified. She had beaten him to the punch.

Dear Steve,

Thank you for your letter informing me of your decision to visit me in Brighton. Unfortunately it is too late for such gestures. I have been thinking about our relationship since graduation, the ludicrous performance that you put on for my parents that day and your subsequent reluctance to commit to being with me at any specific point in the next year or so. These are not the actions of a person committed to a relationship. I can only assume that you are too cowardly to tell me that you no longer want the relationship to continue. I have therefore decided to take the initiative and to let you know that I consider the relationship over. Please do not try to phone me or come down to Brighton this weekend. I will not be here. Declan and I are going to visit some old friends of his in Oxford. Take care of yourself. I am sorry it ended this way. It was a great year.

Angie.

Steve felt completely winded. The letter was brutally decisive, in contrast to the tentative tone of his own draft. But the thing that really rankled was the presence in the letter of Declan. Wasn't he the colleague she'd mentioned as a drinking companion? He sounded as if he was a little more than that now. He was not oblivious to the fact that he had no right to feel aggrieved.

He was annoyed with himself for having failed to take the initiative. He would now have to rewrite his own letter. He was mulling over how to frame his response when the door opened and Ginny came in. She could see the troubled look on his face.

'What's the matter? You look as though something terrible has happened.'

Steve took a deep breath.

'I've just got a letter from Angie. She's finishing the relationship. She's pre-empted my own letter. I was just about to take it to the postbox.'

'Steve, I'm not going to say I'm sorry, because I'm not. Angie is a strong woman. You're going to have to learn to be more decisive. If you don't make decisions, they'll be made for you. But don't be angry, least of all with Angie. The end point is the same regardless of who made the decision. This is where we wanted to be. We'll get through this together. I'll help you.'

Steve didn't say anything. He just kept looking at the floor.

'Steve, look at me. You've got to start taking responsibility for situations. Angie's just acting on what you had already decided to do, but couldn't bring yourself to tell her until yesterday.'

'I was just doing my best not to hurt her.'

'I think you're not being honest with yourself. You overthink things. Actions and their absence speak louder than words. You didn't have to tell Angie. She got the message. She understands you better than you understand yourself. She's helping you. Stop feeling sorry for yourself.'

* * *

Even the fact that he only had one more day on the round was not enough to dispel the gloom into which Angie's letter had sunk him. On the Sunday morning he rattled around the streets between Mill Road and Hills Road for the last time. At the end of the round he crossed over to the gaffer's cabin to pick up his cards and his last pay packet. The gaffer looked up from his study of Page 3 and slid a brown envelope across the table, and in return took repossession of Ron's log book. He could see that Steve was troubled. 'Blimey, you don't look too bright today. Don't tell me you're having second thoughts.'

Of course, he was referring to Steve's decision to quit the milk round, but, for Steve, regret was colouring everything he looked at. He managed a weak smile and said that he had problems at home.

'Her indoors giving you a hard time, is she?'

'Yeah, you could say that.' As ever it was easier to go along with the gaffer's assumptions, than attempt to explain.

'You've got a nice bit of dosh in that envelope. Buy her a bunch of flowers on the way home. Always works.'

Steve was amused by the idea of the gaffer as a couples counsellor, but thought he might follow his advice, even though it was not Ginny who was the reason for his mood, or at least not directly.

Steve spent much of the next two days in bed, not all of it with Ginny. He told himself that he was catching up on sleep and trying to shift his sleep pattern back to something like what it had once been. But in fact he was brooding. He was thinking about Angie. He had not yet acknowledged her letter, because he still didn't know what to say.

There were, however, compensations to this unstructured time. Ginny had not yet exhausted either her culinary or libidinal repertoire. For Steve the latter in particular was a voyage of discovery. Under her tutelage he was becoming a more attentive and imaginative lover. When Ginny was not cosseting or instructing Steve, she busied herself improving various aspects of the house, touching up the paintwork here and there and fixing door catches that didn't work properly. She also continued to tidy up the garden. At these times Steve hid himself away in his room and made a sustained effort to get to grips with the Olivetti. He typed up several copies of *Event/Horizon*, putting one in the post to Rob. By Wednesday, Ginny had clearly come to the view that Steve had had enough time moping about. It was now time for him to pull himself together. She needed his help. She would like to get rid of the garden waste that she hadn't been able to burn on a bonfire.

She had found out where the municipal dump was and would like Steve to help her load the van and drive it there.

She had generated so much material that it took them three trips to get rid of it all, but when they had done so, the garden looked twice as big. It was too late in the season to do much about the planting, but after they had dropped the last load of garden waste at the dump, she persuaded him to drive to the garden centre at Coton. She clearly knew about plants and had soon filled the van with geraniums, pansies, pinks and alyssum and a number of pots and bags of potting compost.

The physical activity had the positive effect that Ginny had hoped for. That evening as they sat and listened to records, Steve decided that he couldn't put off writing to Angie any longer. His entirely unjustified anger had burned itself out and he was feeling contrite now. He didn't blame Angie for her decision. No doubt the whole sorry mess was his fault. He had contrived it through some kind of passive aggressive mechanism. He picked up his note pad and started writing. Ginny looked up from her book and asked if he was getting back to the poem. His first impulse was to lie and say that was exactly what he was doing, but he was fed up with the knots that dissimulation and prevarication were tying him in and decided to tell the truth.

'I'm writing to Angie. I haven't replied to her letter telling me that the relationship is over. I thought I ought at least to acknowledge her letter and let her know that I have no hard feelings. You can see it if you want.'

Ginny smiled and said. 'That won't be necessary.'

It was a difficult letter to write. Steve had been intending merely to acknowledge Angie's letter and express his sadness at her decision. Any blame should be laid at his door. He had been behaving in a ridiculous way and she was perfectly entitled to get on with her life. He hoped they could stay in touch. Perhaps they could even see each other before she left for Edinburgh. But Angie still didn't know about Ginny and it would be wrong not to allude to their relationship, even if Angie might have already surmised something of the sort. He had set out that information in the letter he had drafted on the Friday night, but the letter remained unsent, having been overtaken by the arrival of Angie's own letter on the following morning. After a number of false starts he managed to pen a coy admission that he and Ginny had become lovers. He read the letter over. The confession of infidelity, expressions of regret and protestations of undying affection did not make for comfortable reading. He very much doubted that Angie would be convinced by his rationalisation or sincerity. He folded the letter, put it in an envelope and addressed it. He decided to take it to the postbox there and then.

When he got back, Ginny was sitting on the sofa with her legs curled up under her. She was doing some kind of needlework. Steve was impressed by her dexterity and her power of concentration. He sat and watched her for a few minutes. Casting his mind back to the day of Angie's graduation, he must have had some kind of image of how things were likely to develop over the summer, but the situation he now found himself in wasn't it. Everyone had plans he assumed, but wasn't there some military adage about plans not surviving first contact with the enemy. Not that it seemed a particularly positive *modus vivendi* to consider life the enemy. He had always assumed that one made choices and that led to certain outcomes, but perhaps one was also the object of others' choices. The sum of the others' choices might easily overwhelm one's own choices.

Was that the situation he was now in? And if it was, was that such a bad thing? There was no saying that this situation with Ginny was going to last. Why not enjoy it while it lasted? She was beautiful, more sophisticated than his original callow impression of her allowed. Her cooking was amazing, the sex too. No doubt she wasn't as intellectual as Angie, but then nor was Steve, if he were honest. And no doubt there were different kinds of intelligence. The thing to do was to learn as much from Ginny as he could whilst they were together. Perhaps she could help him discover the heart that was apparently missing from his writing.

He was also intrigued by her comments about tripping. He was wary of drugs, but he also appreciated that attitudes to intoxicants were culturally based. It was hard to think of a more dangerous drug than alcohol. It ruined countless lives and was a contributory factor in a lot of low-level violence. It was also clear that the health impacts of tobacco were disastrous. In comparison the negative consequences of marijuana consumption were trivial. Might it not be the same with acid? Perhaps Ginny could help him there too.

On an impulse he said, 'Ginny, if I took some acid, would you trip with me?'

She looked up from her needlework, surprised at the sudden introduction of the topic. 'I don't know. It's definitely a worthwhile experience for the right person. But I haven't done any myself for a few years.'

'Of course. But if I could get some, you could just be with me. Look after me. If you didn't mind.'

'Yes, that might be the best way. Let me think about it.'

'The question is how to source reliable acid.'

'Well, if you're serious, I could probably help there.'

'Thank you. It's just a thought. I'm not sure I have the courage.'

Ginny nodded and returned to her needlework.

Steve's thoughts returned to his poem. He went upstairs and fetched one of the newly produced typescripts. Back in the sitting room he read it through in the light of Ginny's earlier comments. It now seemed clever but lifeless. He threw it on the floor. It seemed fundamentally broken. Was there any point in persisting with it? Might it not be better to start something completely new. The central idea was both ponderous and pretentious, the information in it was not well integrated. It felt like it was an assemblage of notes from his reading without any internal dynamic.

Ginny could see that he was troubled and asked him what was going through his mind. He explained that he had promised to take a copy for Grace when they went to her dinner party later in the week. But now, in the light of Ginny's comments, he had lost any confidence in it. In fact it wasn't very good. Ginny got angry with him. If she'd thought he couldn't take a bit of criticism, she wouldn't have said what she said. He should trust himself and give a copy of it in its current state to Grace, but he should also get back to working on it.

As they ate a late breakfast together the next morning, Ginny announced that she had had a letter from Jon, which was very similar in content to the one that Steve had received from Angie.

Steve was surprised, but mainly at the idea that Jon was a letter writer. 'What does he say?'

'Essentially, because of the amount of time he's going to be away touring and because of "other developments in his life" as he puts it, but which he doesn't want to go into in writing, he thinks it makes sense to call time on our relationship.'

Ginny waved the letter around theatrically, but didn't offer to let Steve read it.

'Oh, Ginny, I'm sorry. I feel it's all my fault.'

'Don't be ridiculous. This is the best outcome for all of us.'

Steve wasn't yet ready to see things in that light. In the hope that this was merely some elaborate tiff, he said, 'But we've still got his camper van and his tape recorder.'

Ginny smiled thinly. 'Easy come, easy go with Jon.'

'Maybe he'll come and pick them up.'

'I doubt it. As far as I'm concerned, they're yours now.'

Ginny brandished another piece of paper. 'At least, he's had the decency to send me a cheque for our share of the rent for the full three months. When it's cleared into my account, I'll transfer it to you.'

Steve's disquiet at the synchronicity of Angie and Jon writing within days of each other, to much the same effect, was only somewhat allayed by the inclusion of a cheque from Jon. He'd not had him down as someone who settled his debts. It must be some measure of how much Jon was now being paid by the Syndrome management to deputise for Rusty Blades.

'Wow! That's amazing. Solves the immediate cashflow problems. Good old Jon.'

Ginny smiled again and screwed the letter up.

Life Class

COSMOPOLITANS

Glisson Road
Friday, 19 July 1974

STEVE SPENT MOST OF Friday working on his poem. When he came downstairs at six o'clock, he found Ginny pacing around the sitting room, wrapped in towels and filing her nails with an emery board.

'You'd better get a move on. I've run your bath but you might need to top it up with some more hot water.'

Steve was not sure that he wanted to be treated like a naughty schoolboy, although he hadn't objected to it during their lovemaking. He went through to the bathroom and climbed into the tub. As he soaked in the bath, he heard Ginny padding around upstairs. He got out of the bath, dried himself and joined her. She was dressed in a more formal style than he had come to expect in their short relationship. But there was no doubt she looked absolutely stunning. She was wearing a very short black dress and dark tights which showed her long, shapely legs to advantage. A leather belt with a big brass buckle was artfully slung on her hips and she had knotted one of her Indian silk scarves around her neck and draped it across her bosom. Steve still dripping from his bath looked at her openmouthed. But Ginny was not one for lingering even if it was to receive homage for her styling.

'Come on. Get some clothes on,' she chided.

Steve went to his room and dug out a cheesecloth shirt with a collar, the red velvet flares and the Wrangler jean jacket. If that outfit had been okay for Angie's parents, then it should be okay for Grace's dinner party. But when he went back into the shared bedroom, he could sense that it was not okay for Ginny. He got the distinct impression that he was letting her down.

'Help me out here, Ginny,' he said plaintively.

She made him take the jean jacket off, undid an extra button on his shirt and then got another of her scarves, somewhat shorter than the one she herself was wearing and knotted it loosely around his neck. She then rummaged in her wardrobe and brought out a tiny brown leather bomber jacket. Steve protested that it would never fit him. She brushed his protests aside and urged him to try it on. It fitted him like a glove. Then she put a little kohl around his eyes, brushed his hair out and quickly sprayed it. She stood back to study him. She was pleased with her handiwork. She turned him around so he could see himself in the full length mirror. He had to admit, it was an amazing transformation. But he wasn't sure it was quite him. He'd almost felt more comfortable on the cross-dressing night.

But he didn't have the heart to question Ginny's styling, so he did a little Jagger swagger in front of the mirror and pouted chin up. She accepted the accolade with her default impassivity and said, 'While it's polite to be a little late, it's very impolite to be more than a little late.'

Steve thought he detected a formality or decorum in her comment that belied Ginny's wild child disguise.

Twenty minutes later, as they stood on the doorstep of Grace's house in Glisson Road, Ginny adjusted Steve's jacket and brushed a lock of hair out of his eyes. Steve's irritation with this fussing was snuffed out by the front door being opened by a broad shouldered middle-aged man with dark good looks and dangerous eyes.

'Welcome. You must be Ginny and Steve. Come in. I'm Peter.'

Ginny stepped into the hall to be kissed on both cheeks by Peter, who offered to take her coat. She slipped out of it with a flourish and handed it to Peter, letting him fully appreciate her figure. Steve was uncomfortably aware of the way in which Peter's gaze devoured Ginny's body. Peter indicated that Ginny should go through to the big room at the back of the house and then he turned and shook Steve's hand with a little sideways nod of the head as if to congratulate Steve on his good fortune. Or more likely to marvel in amazement at the blatant mismatch. Peter took Steve's jacket and ushered him through to the back room saying as he did so, 'So, you're the young genius I've heard so much about from Grace. I've been looking forward to meeting you.'

Steve was not warming to Peter. He did not appreciate being patronised in this way and shot back, 'I'm sure any comments were much more likely to involve terms like lazy, indolent or pretentious.'

Peter's twinkling silence suggested that this was closer to his own assessment.

When he and Steve arrived in the back room, Ginny had already been introduced to the other two guests. Grace made the additional introductions. 'Gary, Matt, this is Steve, one of my former students, and a promising young writer. Steve, Gary is involved in the theatre. He's worked in the West End for a long time, but he has just moved back to Cambridge. Gary and I go back a long way. We were friends as undergraduates. Gary's planning a new thetarical venture in Cambridge, but it's all a bit hush-hush at the moment. And Matt is a screen writer. You have undoubtedly seen some of his work.'

Peter asked the new arrivals what they'd like to drink. Ginny requested a gin and tonic and Steve asked for beer.

Grace came over with his beer and said, 'I'm so glad you and Ginny were able to come. By the way, did you bring a copy of the poem?'

'It's in Ginny's bag. I'll give it to you before we go.'

Grace smiled. 'Don't want me peeking at it while you're here, eh?'

Meanwhile Peter had latched onto Ginny. 'So what do you do, Ginny?'

Ginny didn't answer immediately. Steve wondered whether he might have to answer for her. But what was the answer? At the moment, she wasn't doing anything. She lived on the dole. But Ginny replied smoothly, 'I used to be a model, until I got fed up with being gawked at. I haven't entirely severed my links with the fashion industry. And I might return in some capacity in due course. At the moment I'm in remission from superficiality, but I'm sure it'll catch up with me again.'

It was not the kind of answer that Steve had expected, but the others seemed to think it made complete sense. No doubt, Ginny's looks bore testimony to her former occupation. Ginny could clearly speak for herself, but for some reason Steve added, 'And Ginny is also a very talented fine artist.'

Ginny threw him a withering glance. 'I was briefly an art student, but preferred to do something which required no talent and therefore paid more money. Don't you think there's an inverse relationship between talent and income?'

Grace agreed. 'Well that's certainly the case in the academic world.'

'And in television,' said Matt.

'I'm sure Ginny's observation is a universal truth,' added Peter. He turned to Steve. 'As a poet, Steve, do you see yourself at the popular end of things, or at the talented end, but with a tiny readership?'

'Well, I'm at the unreadable *and* untalented end. I'd probably be better off composing clues to cryptic crosswords. Everyone would have much more fun, including me.'

It was Ginny's turn to answer for Steve.

'Steve's problem is that he undercuts everything he does.'

Clearly Ginny was paying him back for his revelation of her art student past.

'He immediately adopts a defensive posture,' she continued. 'It's as if he doesn't trust himself or believe in what he's doing.'

Matt, sensing the underlying tension, asked Steve whether he'd had any of his poetry published.

'No, nothing published,' he admitted.

Grace smoothed over the awkward silence consequent upon Steve's straight bat. 'I believe that Steve has brought with him this evening, but for my eyes only, the manuscript of a long poem that he has been working on for some time, including when he should have been producing essays for me. I have great hopes for this poem and will certainly be showing it to any publishers I know, if I think it has any merit.'

Matt was chortling. 'Surely, you don't know any publishers, Grace.'

'None that publish innovative poetry.'

Peter knocked back his glass of wine and said, 'God save me from innovative poetry. Steve should stick to the composition of cryptic crosswords.'

Grace bridled. 'You're not the only publisher in town, Pete.'

'But I bet I'm the only one that makes any money.'

Steve hadn't expected to be caught in a tussle between Grace and her husband. While he was trying to formulate some appropriate riposte, Gary came to the rescue. 'Take no notice of Pete, Steve. He affects to be a philistine, but he knows more about modern poetry than he lets on. However, it's certainly true that there's not much money in poetry. So how are you planning to support yourself in the meantime?'

'I'm a milkman,' Steve said, a reply which, as he had hoped, provoked considerable mirth among the guests. Technically, of course, he was a former milkman and not yet a box office assistant at the Arts

Theatre, but while the latter was mundane, a kind of nobility attached to the former.

Peter chose this moment to suggest they take their places at the big farmhouse table. Ginny and Steve sat next to each other on one side of the table opposite Gary and Matt with Grace between Gary and Steve at the head of the table and Peter between Ginny and Matt at the foot. Grace put a big plate of watermelon and prosciutto on the table and invited people to help themselves while Peter went around the table filling up glasses with wine white or red according to taste.

The conversation broke up into small groups. Gary said to Steve that he regretted the merriment that had greeted Steve's statement about being a milkman. He was sure that most of the people around the table had done curious jobs before they had got their start in their careers. That had certainly been the case for him and Matt. Gary himself had done all sorts, bus conductor, washer-up in restaurants, bar work. You name it.

At the other end of the table, Peter was keen to know more about Ginny's modelling career. Steve caught one or two fragments of the conversation; *Vogue, Harper's, Queen. Biba*, Ossie Clark, *Cosmo*. Ginny was clearly being more forthcoming about her past than she had been with Steve. Or was it because Steve was so wrapped up in his own situation that she hadn't had the opportunity?

Grace noticed Steve's attention was down the other end of the table. Taking advantage of the fact that Gary had turned to convey some piece of information to Matt. She put her hand on Steve's and said quietly, 'Pete's incorrigible. He's a terrible flirt. I'm sure Ginny knows how to take care of herself.'

Steve flashed a grateful smile at Grace and said, 'Yes, I'm sure you're right. We haven't spent much time together in company. I'll have to get used to it.'

'And we need to talk about your writing. Once I've read your poem. And I'll try and convince you again that Serge Gainsbourg is worth listening to.'

When everyone had finished their first course, Grace cleared the starter plates and brought a large orange Le Creuset casserole to the table. The main course was a chorizo and cannellini bean stew with a green salad and hunks of sourdough bread. Grace started ladling the stew onto plates and asked Steve and Gary to pass the laden plates up the table. Steve realised that he and Ginny hadn't exchanged a single word with each other since they'd sat down at the table. As he passed a plate to Ginny he said to her under his breath, 'I'm sorry I mentioned that stuff about your being an artist.'

Ginny didn't reply, but leaned across and kissed Steve on the side of the neck. He took it that he'd been forgiven. At least he hoped so.

Under the influence of the wine, with which Pete kept replenishing the diners' glasses, the conversation became more relaxed. There was less sounding out and more reflection on the current political situation and the delights of being in Cambridge in the summer, when there were few undergraduates around and a considerable proportion of the permanent population had escaped to the beaches of the Mediter-ranean. By the time the cheese course arrived, the topic was the latest films and TV programmes, which was where Matt came into his own, being hugely knowledgeable in that department.

When the meal was finished, Peter suggested they go into the sitting room. He had a couple of nice malts and they could *spin some discs.* Steve winced at the outmoded expression, but fancied some whisky. In the sitting room Grace and Ginny occupied the chesterfield beneath Peter's Rokeby Venus, while Matt and Gary bagged the wingback chairs on either side of the fireplace. Peter asked Steve to help him with the drinks, having first checked that everyone was having whisky. Once again, Ginny surprised Steve, by saying she would. The choice was Glenfiddich or Lagavulin. She chose the Lagavulin. Steve didn't know one malt whisky from another, so he decided to follow Ginny's lead.

Peter poured the drinks, saying as he did so, 'I assume that everyone takes it with a splash of water.'

He handed the charged glasses to Steve, who distributed them. Peter then fixed his and Steve's drinks and handed Steve a large tumbler of the pale liquid. Steve took a sip and was pleasantly shocked by the smoky taste. Peter took a large gulp from his own glass and said, 'I'm sorry I teased you a bit when you arrived. Grace has talked about you a lot, even when she was supervising you. She said you had an interesting take on things. She doesn't usually get these things wrong. And she was delighted with your reader's report on her book. It sounds to me like you have the makings of a publisher. We should talk at greater length. If you're good at reader reports, you can prob-ably do some work for me.'

Steve was embarrassed. 'That's very kind. I'd be very happy to do some reading for you, but the truth is I had a head start with Grace's book. It was a subject we covered for Finals.'

Peter seemed in no hurry to sit down.

'Grace taught you French, but she tells me you were also reading German. Which do you prefer?'

'Well, I probably probably speak better German. I worked in Germany for the year before I came up.'

'Where did you work?'

'In Frankfurt-am-Main for a company called Metallgesellschaft.'

'Ah, Frankfurt. I lived there for several years when I was a small boy.'

This was an aspect of Peter, that Steve hadn't suspected. 'Really?'

'Yes, I was born in Berlin, in 1929, but we moved to Frankfurt when I was still an infant. I am of Jewish descent. My immediate family was lucky enough to get out to Switzerland in early 1939. And from there we flew to London. I was brought up in Edinburgh. My extended family were not so lucky. I didn't speak a word of English until I was ten years old.'

'Do you ever go back to Germany?'

'I go back once a year for the Frankfurt Book Fair. I used to visit Germany more frequently when my parents were still alive. They returned not long after the end of the war and lived out their days in Karlsruhe.'

'That must have been terrible for them when they went back.'

'Yes, of course. In all the obvious ways. But the family on both sides had been assimilated for a couple of generations. In fact my parents were both devout Lutherans. Indeed, strange as it may seem, my father was a Lutheran theologian.'

'That is surprising.'

'It's a somewhat convoluted story. I'd be happy to share it with you, but perhaps it'd be better over a pint or two, just the two of us. We'll fix an evening drink soon. I'm a bit tied up at the moment. We've just bought a flat in one of the new towers in the Barbican, so that I don't need to commute to London every day.'

'I'd like that.' Despite his initial antipathy towards Peter, especially his blatant flirting with Ginny, the conversation over the previous few minutes had uncovered a seam of mutual attraction.

Peter took a sip of his whisky. 'So what area of Frankfurt did you work in?'

'The Metallgesellschaft offices were in Reuterweg, just behind the alte Oper.'

'Sadly, now just a ruin. My parents used to go there frequently before the war. And where did you live?

'I lodged with an elderly couple in Georg-Speyer Strasse near the Botanic Gardens, the Reicherts, lovely people.'

'And not from far from where I lived when I was a boy. We seem to have a lot in common despite the difference in our ages. But I'd better not monopolise you or I'll be in trouble with Grace. We'll continue this conversation soon.'

Peter strode over to the centre of the room and positioned himself in front of the fireplace.

'Apologies for neglecting you. Steve and I have just discovered we have a link with my hometown.'

'Reminiscences of Auld Reekie?' hazarded Gary.

'As a matter of fact, I have two hometowns. The other one is Frankfurt, where, it appears, Steve spent a year before University.'

Steve perched himself on a ladderback chair to the one side of Matt. The conversation returned to more general topics. Grace was asking Ginny about her experiences as an art student. Steve thought this was likely to end in a conversational car crash, but Ginny seemed to accept Grace's blandishments. They were talking about life drawing. Grace was a bit of an artist herself, not trained of course, but she loved life drawing. She ran a small life class, nothing formal, just a few like-minded people who got together once a month or so to draw the human body and discuss their work over a glass of wine. Would Ginny be interested in joining them? Grace understood that as a trained artist Ginny might not want to rub shoulders with a bunch of amateurs, but it was a supportive group, mainly women, of course. Steve was not surprised to hear Ginny demur, but she didn't reject the idea outright.

Gary asked Peter whether they could have some music. The whisky was definitely making him feel mellow. Peter went across to the hifi and a few moments later the strains of some latin jazz were to be heard issuing from the Celestion Ditton speakers. Grace protested, 'Oh, Pete. You'll be giving our guests entirely the wrong idea about our musical taste.'

Pete performed a little mime of incomprehension. 'What's wrong with Wes Montgomery?'

He was rescued by Matt saying, 'Oh no. Speaking for myself I love jazz guitar. If I could do a fraction of what this guy can do on a guitar, I'd die happy.'

Steve turned to him. 'So, you play jazz guitar?'

Matt laughed, 'Well, not like that. But, yes. It's what I do when I can't write, which, to be honest, is most of the time.'

Steve thought he'd share his own recent conversion to the genre. 'I know next to nothing about jazz guitar, but I bought a Django Reinhardt LP recently after hearing a local band play 'Limehouse Blues' at the Portland Arms.'

Matt nodded. 'Yeah, Django's fantastic. I actually heard Stephane Grapelli play last year in the back room of a pub in Royston with Diz Disley on guitar. Of course Diz, even with a complete set of working fingers was not a patch on Django, but it was still a great occasion.'

Steve found it hard to believe that Grapelli was not only still performing, but was playing small town pubs. Matt seemed like a sympathetic guy and Steve thought he could reveal his own hesitant steps towards playing jazz guitar.

'I play guitar a bit myself, but I don't really understand how jazz harmony works, especially when implemented on the guitar. I bought a book a while ago by a guy called Jed Morgan, but I'm not really making much progress.'

'Ah, so you've found your way to Jed Morgan?'

'You know his book?'

'Yes, a lot of people start with that book, though not many finish it. I've used it myself. But Morgan does manage to give you a lot of options with relatively few chords. The trouble is he doesn't really explain how the progressions are derived and so it's difficult for the student of his system to put together a harmonic toolkit. We should jam some time. Maybe I should revisit it. I might be able to give you a few pointers.'

Steve couldn't believe his luck. He asked Matt what he should work on in the meantime. Matt suggested that he get the material in the first half of the book under his fingers and they'd start from there.

The first side of the record came to an end. Peter offered more whisky, but there was now a general move to bring proceedings to a conclusion. Coats were fetched. Steve remembered to get the copy of his poem out of Ginny's bag and discreetly handed it to Grace.

She smiled at him. 'I wasn't going to remind you. I thought perhaps you hadn't brought it or you were going to chicken out. So thank you. I look forward to reading it.'

Steve said, 'I very nearly did lose my nerve. I am very unsure of what I've written.'

'I understand completely. Please trust me.'

Steve managed a weak smile. 'But it was a lovely evening, thank you. I really enjoyed meeting Matt and Gary.'

'Yes, they're great guys.'

'And Peter, of course.'

'You don't have to say that. He can be an acquired taste. Rather like the Lagavulin.'

'He suggested we have a drink. He said he'd tell me more about his German childhood.'

'Well, you're honoured. He doesn't open up like that to many people.'

In the hallway there was a little fandango as kisses and handshakes were given and received and the guests spilled out into the night.

On the way back to Ainsworth Street having taken their leave of Gary and Matt, Steve asked Ginny what she thought of the evening. She turned to look at him with narrowed eyes, considering her response. After a moment she said in an even voice that she'd enjoyed herself. She really liked Grace. She hadn't really got a handle on Matt and Gary, and she thought Peter was a pompous bore and a failed Lothario to boot, but he served good whisky and they had some very good pieces of art on their walls. The canvas she'd been sitting under was particularly good. She was impressed that Grace ran life classes. It was not often that one came across such sophisticated people.

Steve was pleased that Ginny had enjoyed the evening. He agreed that Peter did seem to have a bit of a wandering eye. Ginny scoffed, 'The older they get, the worse they are. But I could see that you two bonded.'

'I had no idea about his German background.'

'I missed that. Peter sounded Scottish to me.'

'He was born in Berlin. His parents were of Jewish descent and they only just managed to get out in early 1939 when he was ten years old. He then grew up in Edinburgh, hence the slight accent. He mentioned it when we getting the whiskies. He said that he'd like to have a drink some time and he'd tell me more.'

Ginny was thoughtful. 'Well, that is unexpected. But perhaps not completely.'

PURPLE MICRODOT

Elsewhere
Sunday, 21 July 1974

THE NEXT DAY GINNY suggested they go to the Fitzwilliam Museum. Steve wondered whether the previous evening's talk about art school and life drawing had sparked something in Ginny's mind. At the Fitz they wandered slowly through the Impressionist gallery. Ginny was obviously familiar with the layout of the museum and homed in on certain paintings. She spent a considerable time in front of a Monet, a delicate image of two women in a springtime orchard foaming with blossom. Then she moved on to another Monet, with a similar quality to the representation of the sky, but this time an image of a snaking row of poplar trees. She didn't just glance at the paintings, she seemed to drink them in. Next she chose a tiny painting by Seurat, titled the Rue St Vincent in Spring. The image was dreamlike, a sunlight dappled lane, empty of human figures and arched over by trees. There was something deeply mysterious about it, a path leading somewhere undefined. Finally she stopped at a Cezanne, which looked to Steve as if it was unfinished and which was verging on the abstract or cubist.

She then led him into the modern British gallery. She seemed drawn to a brace of Augustus John portraits and a pretty Philip Wilson Steer picture of children on the beach at Walberswick. But what detained her for the longest time was a Stanley Spencer self-portrait of the artist painting a nude of a woman, who Ginny said was Spencer's wife. The thing that struck Steve was that it implied that Spencer himself was

225

naked. Certainly he was shirtless, but since the representation of the artist was from the rear with his face in left profile and cut off just below the shoulders, it was not possible to confirm this supposition. Steve also briefly wondered whether Spencer had had to rig up an elaborate arrangement of mirrors in order to paint a portrait of himself from the rear. Finally Ginny took him to an exhibition of drawings and works on paper. Once again Augustus John was prominent in her choices, but also Matisse and Eric Gill, all of them representations of female nudes. By now they were exhausted and found their way to the tearoom.

Over tea and cake Steve asked Ginny about her experience as an art student.

'I was a fine artist and loved drawing, particularly life drawing. But this was a period when the tutors were keen to get us to transcend the flat surface of the canvas or the sheet of paper. And figuration had become a dirty word. But that's what I liked best. What I love about those drawings by Augustus John and Matisse that we were looking at earlier, is the cleanness and the economy of the line, the energy of execution. But what our teachers wanted was conceptualisation and expressiveness. They seemed to despise the traditional skills of observation and representation.'

'So, you dropped out?'

'Not immediately. For a while to make a bit of money I worked as a model for life classes at the college. One of the tutors put me in touch with a modelling agency. He thought that if I looked good with my clothes off, I'd look okay clothed. Once the money started coming in from the modelling, I lost touch with the college completely.'

'Do you ever think about picking up a brush or a piece of charcoal again?'

'Occasionally. I found my old portfolio a while ago and I thought some of the work wasn't too bad, if a little naïve. But what would be the point? The contemporary art world is even less interested in traditional skills than it was when I started as a student.'

'For your own satisfaction. If you have a talent, isn't it worth using it, regardless of what other people think about it? Or whether you can make a living. Would you be prepared to show me your work?'

'I'm not sure about that. The stuff in the portfolio is really quite old now.'

'Well, do some new work. I'd pose for you.'

Ginny smiled. 'Be careful. I might hold you to that offer. It's harder than you think though, holding a pose, switching your mind off and submitting to the gaze of others.'

'I'm not offering to pose for others. Just you.'

When they'd finished their cups of tea, they walked back across Cambridge. Ginny suggested that they take a detour through the Kite. As they passed Solstice bookshop she said she wanted to go in. Steve knew of the shop, but had never been in. The shop specialised in books and magazines from the so-called alternative scene. A large bearded man emerged from the back of the shop and greeted Ginny warmly. She was obviously a regular customer or a friend. She made the introductions and Steve discovered that the guy with the beard was called Tom. She explained that Tom was active in the movement to halt the redevelopment plans for the Kite, as that part of Cambridge was known. He was also the moving spirit behind a number of underground magazines, always ready to help and advise those who wanted to get something unconventional printed. Whilst Ginny and Tom chatted, Steve leafed through some of the magazines. He bought a copy of *Cambridge Dissent* because he liked the chaotic improvised layouts and the use of colour. Tom was delighted, because that was the magazine that he edited and produced. He said that he hoped to see Steve again.

Ginny and Steve continued on their way. When they got back to the house Ginny said, 'Your trip's on.'

In reply to the look of puzzlement on Steve's face, she explained, 'I scored some acid from Tom. He assured me it's good.'

Steve hadn't noticed any kind of transaction going on. He was grateful to Ginny for her thoughtfulness, but was also now a little apprehensive. He hadn't been entirely serious when he'd said he like to take some acid. He kept these reservations to himself, but as if able to read his thoughts, Ginny said that he shouldn't feel any compulsion. It had to be his choice. But if he was up for it, the next day would probably be a good time to take it.

When he woke the next morning Steve found that he had decided overnight to go ahead and drop the acid that day. It was something that he had wanted to try for some time, but an innate caution, ignorance of how to go about acquiring reliable acid and the absence of a guide he trusted had prevented him turning that ambition into reality.

Now, until his new job started, there was no one requiring anything from him. In Ginny he had someone who knew what she was doing and would look after him. And when it came down to it, he trusted himself. His abiding mode might be apprehensiveness, but paradoxically he was relaxed about radical initiatives. There could hardly be a better conjunction of circumstances. He went downstairs and made some tea. By the time he got back to the bedroom with the two mugs of tea Ginny was awake. He told her of his decision. She approved.

They had a leisurely breakfast and then Ginny said that she needed to go to the shops to get some supplies. She suggested that Steve take it easy, get himself into a calm but focused state. Steve normally didn't need much encouragement to take it easy. It was only when she seemed to have been gone longer than an expedition to the local shops might entail that he started to feel a little on edge. When she got back she was carrying a bag full of shopping and a large bunch of flowers. To Steve's way of thinking, flowers were not normally categorised as household supplies, but he had already noticed that Ginny had a high regard for cut flowers. Ginny found a vase for the flowers and took them through into the sitting room.

Over a cup of tea she produced a tiny purple tab from her purse and handed it to Steve. It didn't look big enough to be capable of having much effect. Ginny told him not to think about it, just to put the tab in his mouth, which he promptly did. He let it dissolve. It was effectively tasteless. Ginny said that now might be a good time for him to decide what kind of music he wanted to listen to over the next few hours and line up a few albums. The thing was to try and set the mood of the trip in advance, something calm, expansive, positive would be best until he had got his bearings. They went next door and Steve flipped through the LPs. He picked out some of his favourites, but obedient to Ginny's mood recommendations decided to start with a recording of Bach's *Brandenburg Concertos*.

She said that it might take up to an hour before he felt the full effect. She then surprised Steve by saying that she had been thinking about his request to show him her portfolio and now was as good a time as any. Steve was touched by this gesture. He knew the secret places of her body fairly well by now, but in some ways exposure of her old artwork required her to invest more trust in him. Ginny went upstairs and returned some minutes later with two large maroon portfolios.

She laid them on the floor and opened the first one up. On top was a large female nude executed in charcoal. Ginny was slim and delicate, but the image on the paper was of a powerful woman, portrayed in decisive broad strokes. There was nothing delicate about this particular female figure. But then he supposed that Ginny was in her own way monumental.

They worked their way through the pile of images. There were many charcoal and pencil drawings, mostly nudes, mostly of the female form. There were also a number of still lifes, predominantly of flowers, some in pastel or conté crayon. As with the female form, the flowers seemed gigantic, almost predatory. And finally there were many portraits, including some self-portraits, which particularly attracted Steve's attention. The work seemed to him of a high order.

Ginny then opened the second portfolio which contained watercolours and prints, again many of vases of flowers, but also a number of landscapes and interiors. Her use of colour in the watercolours was exquisite. The only thing missing were works in oil or gouache. Not surprisingly in the light of Ginny's earlier comments about her difficulties with those media, neither of the portfolios contained any examples of that kind of work. But she said that she had in fact done plenty of work in those media. It was just that they were more difficult to store and transport. She had become separated from them in one of the many moves she had made. She didn't like to think about whether they still existed or not.

Steve was overwhelmed by the richness of what Ginny had produced in her short career as an art student. 'When was the last time you did a drawing or painting?'

She wasn't sure, 'Four or five years ago, perhaps.'

'Ginny, you must start again. These are fantastic.'

'Maybe, but I need to sort things out first.'

'If there was anything I could do to help . . .'

'You have already helped . . .'

Steve wasn't sure how he had helped, but he was encouraged by her response.

Side one of the *Brandenburg Concertos* came to an end and the tone arm of the turntable swung up with a clunk and parked itself. Steve went over to the deck and flipped the disk over. As it started playing, he noticed that the disk was not completely flat and seemed to undulate as it rotated, the tone arm riding up and down the waves of warped vinyl. He'd noticed this phenomenon before, but had never really thought about it. Had the records not been looked after? Or were some records made of thinner vinyl than others? Surely it must make a difference to the music. He listened more attentively. Could he detect the motion in the music? He wasn't sure, partly because the music was both so complex and so fascinating. He noticed the way that the musical lines chased each other, the same patterns repeating in different registers and timbres, as first one section of the orchestra then another came to the fore. While the music was not without emotion, the predominant impression was one of courtly serenity.

He suddenly realised that he had been standing peering at the record deck for some time listening to the interplay of instruments. He turned and saw that Ginny was watching him carefully. She asked him if he'd like a cup of tea. He thought that sounded a marvellous idea. She said she'd be back shortly and went out to make the tea. Puzzled by the thought of the undulations in the record he sat on the sofa and pulled out one of the nudes from the first portfolio and studied it closely. Ginny's style was very spare. She was economical with her lines. Her gestures when drawing must be free and confident. He tried to follow the line that formed the flank of the figure from upraised arm around the curve of the breast down into the waist out at the pelvis and then the downward sweep of the thigh. How did one manage that in a single gesture? And what were the fewest number of gestures that it took to represent a human body?

Ginny returned with the mugs of tea and asked him how he was. *Ah, yes. How was he feeling?* Fine, so far as he could tell. If the acid was having an effect, it was very subtle. As he now examined his own internal state listening to the sublime music of Johann Sebastian he became aware of a slight anxiety shadowing his thoughts, but his predominant mood was one of calm anticipation. Once again he noticed that Ginny was silently watching him. She was like a cat, centred in her own being, inscrutable. Clearly she was all-knowing and powerful, but she was also overwhelmingly beautiful. Her eyes deep pools of mystery, the curve of her cheek bones echoed in the curves of lips, eyebrows and the strands of dark hair that fell across her face, almost as if they were lines of music rearranged in her features. Her head was turned towards him, the tendon furthest from him that plunged towards her collar bone prominent, accentuating the slenderness of her neck. He wanted to tell her how beautiful she was, even though she must surely know it, and that her beauty was in some way reflected in the music. Or was it the other way round?

While he struggled with the relationship between the music and Ginny's looks, he suddenly noticed the flowers that she had bought earlier and that now stood in a delft jug on the mantlepiece in front of the overmantel mirror. They were completely improbable. He moved closer and examined them closely. They were more than improbable, they were inexplicable. How could the slender green stems result in the incredible explosion of shape and colour? Was it possible that he'd never really looked at flowers properly before? He certainly didn't know what they were called. He gestured helplessly at them.

Ginny came over to him and put her arm gently round him. She pointed to one of each kind and named them, 'Pinks, freesias, dahlias.'

He shook his head slowly. All he could say was, 'Beautiful.' She took him by the hand as the music spun around his head and the scent of the freesias enveloped him and said, 'You're there.'

And he was. *There* was the little sitting room in Ainsworth Street, but it was also another time and place, an intersection between worlds. He looked around the room. It was no longer the slightly shabby room, Ginny's efforts notwithstanding, that it had been an hour earlier. The objects that filled it now were burnished and artfully placed, the very dust sparkled, motes danced in the beams of sunshine shafting through the front window. The jasmine that straggled over the broken fence in the back garden writhed in the gentle summer breeze and tapped at the french windows. It was indescribably lovely, but it made Steve feel very sad. It was overpowering. He wasn't sure he could take the intensity.

He managed to tell Ginny that he felt very weird. She stroked the back of his hand and told him not to worry, to enjoy the sensation, nothing bad was going to happen. Everything was under control. He said his mouth felt dry. She told him to try and relax his jaw, not to clench his teeth. She'd get him a glass of water. She arose as if levitating, glided across the room and disappeared into the kitchen.

For a second he felt bereft, but then his eye fell on a book that Ginny had been reading and had left open on the sofa. He picked it up. The pages were fringed with rainbow colours and the text was set in some exotic typeface. He started reading:

> They shaped him in her arms at last
> A mother-naked man;
> She cast her mantle over him,
> And sae her love she wan.

What did all that mean?

At that moment Ginny came back with the glass of water and handed it to him. He sipped it and it tasted delicious. Did water always taste that good? He took another sip and watched Ginny open a pad of drawing paper and a box of pencils and marker pens. She suggested he draw something. He was puzzled by the request but went over to the little side table and picked up a red pen. He moved it slowly across the paper and let out a gasp of delight as the colour emerged from the whiteness of the paper in the wake of the pen. He wanted to trace the curves he had seen earlier in her face, but he could not summon them from the red pen. He tried another colour, blue this time and wove blue lines over and around the red shapes he had produced. Finally he took a green marker and filled in some of the spaces. Something was emerging but it wasn't entirely clear what it was. It kept changing, as if it were struggling to come alive. He was quite proud of his creation, but also worried about how inchoate it was. He put the pens down and held the sheet of paper at arm's length to view it better. Still it resisted.

Ginny suggested he try to draw an image of himself, but she made it clear that she didn't mean a self-portrait. It should be an icon or even a cartoon. He took a fresh sheet of paper and a pencil and started drawing very thin lines on the paper. Nothing emerged. He did not know what he looked like. Ginny took the pencil out of his hand, gave him a piece of charcoal and said, 'Don't try to draw a likeness. And don't work so tentatively. Make big marks, at random, don't force the image. Let it appear. But keep thinking of a human figure.'

He preferred the feel of the charcoal in his hand to the pencil and the way it went onto the paper. He made some big, sweeping gestures and immediately seemed to discern something in the marks. There was a face in there. He made some more marks, but it seemed that instead of adding something, he was removing the white paper to uncover the image that lay beneath it. His marks were chaotic, but the emergent face became more solid, followed by marks that suggested the neck and shoulders, then long hair framing the face. He continued with his paradoxical uncovering, until it coalesced as a rudimentary female torso. At that point he felt exhausted. He handed the sheet to Ginny and said, 'Who is it?'

'It's you.'

'But it's a female figure.'

'Yes.'

He dropped the sheet and asked Ginny to draw something. Ginny took the charcoal from him and worked for a few minutes. She then handed the sheet to him. It was an image of a male torso with well-defined pectorals and abdominals. She had not developed the image above the shoulders nor below the pubic area. It was like a fragment of an ancient Greek statue.

Steve still mulling over the meaning of his own clumsy attempt asked, 'So is that you, then?'

'Perhaps.'

Steve took the sheet and studied it. It was magical. He would have liked to be able to draw something himself, but was clearly lacking in confidence and ability. Ginny could sense his frustration. 'Why don't you do a sketch of your poem?'

Steve was puzzled. 'A sketch of a poem?'

Ginny tried again. 'As I understand it, the central image is of an astronomical configuration.'

Steve wasn't sure this made what she was suggesting any easier. 'But not only is that configuration three dimensional, in fact four dimensional, but the central part of it, the organising point of energy, is something you can't see.'

'Well, all drawing is a reduction of an object to two dimensions. I don't see why the same principle can't be applied to higher dimensions. And the idea of perspective in drawing depends upon a so-called vanishing point. So, maybe sketch is the wrong word. What about a diagram, a simplification of what's involved.'

Steve was thoughtful. 'Well, I'd need to show material spiralling into a central vacancy.'

Ginny beamed at him. 'There you are, you've done it in words. Now do it with lines on a sheet of paper before the impulse fades.'

She gave Steve a piece of charcoal and a clean sheet of paper. Without more ado, he made a series of marks on the paper, lines curving from the edge to the centre and handed the sheet to Ginny. She studied it for a few seconds, counting the lines. 'Okay, I think I see what you're getting at. We've got lines of force streaming in to the centre, converging on a point where they disappear.'

Steve wasn't sure. As instructed he hadn't thought about what he was doing. 'I don't know.'

Ginny took the stick of charcoal. 'Would you mind if I added a few marks?'

'No, go ahead.'

Ginny lightly shaded the space between every other pair of curving lines, creating four arms spiralling into the centre of the page. 'There are four parts to your poem. Each of the shaded areas represents one of the parts of the poem. They are all linked at the invisible centre.'

'Yes, that's exactly it. Thank you. You understand it better than me.'

'I'm not sure I do understand it, but I can see the shape of it.'

Even though Steve was a little perturbed by what she was saying and what she had done, he wanted to see more examples of her graphic ability, which right at that moment seemed entirely magical. 'Would you mind drawing something else for me?'

'No, of course.'

She spent a few moments looking around the room and then picked up her sketch book. This time she used a selection of marker pens and worked with a speed and precision that amazed Steve. Before long he saw that an image of the vase of flowers was emerging from the whiteness of the paper. When she had finished she handed him the image. He had never seen anything so lovely. What magic was it that enabled her to transform a vase of real flowers into these beautiful images?

Steve wanted to see more. 'Could you draw something else for me?'

'Of course. What about if I did a drawing of you?'

Ginny noticed the look of concern on his face. 'Don't worry. You won't come to any harm. Just sit in the armchair and listen to the music. What would you like to hear?'

Steve flipped through the albums that he had selected earlier and handed Ginny a copy of *Astral Weeks*.

'Good choice.'

She took the Bach off the turntable, slid the Morrison disc out of its sleeve and cued up the needle. As the opening chords of the title track struck up, a look of delight crossed Steve's face. Reassured that Steve was caught up in the music, Ginny resumed her sketching, this time working with a piece of charcoal.

Steve had listened to the album many times previously and had always found it magical, but he was struck now as never before by the musical arrangement: flute, violin and vibes weaving in and out of the urgent strum of the guitar and the imperious strut of the double bass, Morrison's improbable voice demanding to be born again in another world, in another time and place. He had never really understood the lyrics. And if he was now hoping that the acid would unlock the meaning, it seemed that he was likely to be disappointed. Indeed he found a number of the phrases somewhat unsettling. He was glad that Ginny was on hand.

The title track faded out on a splash of vibes and a bowed final note from the double bass and after a moment's silence the delicate beauty of 'Beside You' filled the room. The lyrics of this track were no less enigmatic than those of 'Astral Weeks', but it seemed easier to relate the title and the repeated refrain to his current situation with Ginny. He listened through to the end of the first side and then looked over at her and saw that she was still busily sketching. She seemed to have covered several sheets in the time that he had been listening to the record. She noticed his change of posture and looked up at him, her smile filling him with an unbearable feeling of sadness.

He stood up slightly unsteadily and went over to her. She kissed him and said, 'Would you like to see them?'

Steve sat down beside her and she handed him the sheets of paper. Her ability to capture his posture and mood was uncanny. It seemed more truthful than any photograph. In one of the images he was holding his head in both hands as if burdened by the woes of the world. A sense of infinite pity came over him. His eyes filled with tears. Ginny said, 'That was when you were listening to "Beside You". You reacted to each track differently. Do you want to hear the other side?'

'No, I don't think so. Maybe later.'

'Do you want to tell me what you're feeling?'

'I'm not sure I can. The colour of the wall is changing all the time – ebbing and flowing. The colour is three-dimensional. It was changing a lot when the music was playing, but it's changing even now, flowing and warping at the edges. Things look strange . . .'

'Does that worry you?'

'No, it feels amazing. I feel warm inside. I was worried that I might lose control, but I now realise that there wasn't anything to control.'

'So you feel okay about yourself?'

'I feel fine. Actually, I don't even know what my self is. It seems to be an illusion. I'm trying to let it go and I already feel much better. I feel like I'm merging with things, merging with you. I feel at one with things. It's actually a relief to jettison the ego. What's the good of it?'

'What did you think of the music?'

'Well, *Astral Weeks* is amazing, but I hadn't realised how the patterns of sound are related to what I'm seeing. There's really just one pattern and everything is related to that pattern. I'm seeing the pattern everywhere. It's in the carpet and in the walls. I'm not sure why I've never noticed that before. And when I tried to draw I was just uncovering the pattern.'

'Suppose you weren't uncovering but projecting?'

'I'm not sure what you mean.'

'Are you seeing through things and seeing the pattern beneath reality or are you projecting the pattern onto reality because things are actually opaque?'

Steve was troubled by this. 'I don't know. Is reality transparent or opaque?'

'Perhaps it's both. Depending on how you look or the state you're in.'

Steve wasn't sure what Ginny was saying. How did he look? He stood up and caught sight of himself in the mirror over the mantelpiece. He was intrigued. He took a step closer and looked more carefully. He knew that he was looking at a reflection of himself, but it didn't feel like the person he knew himself to be. And indeed what made him so sure that the idea he had of himself was in fact himself? The image he saw in the mirror seemed much older than he was. And at the same time much younger. He saw lines around his mouth that he had never noticed before. He became fascinated by his hair. It seemed alive, moving in the thick air like the tentacles of a sea anemone. His face seemed to change all the time. Suddenly he had the unpleasant feeling that someone else was looking out at him, through his own reflection. He turned away. Ginny drew him back to the sofa.

'It's not a good idea to look for too long. Mirrors are fascinating but they can be dangerous too.'

They sat for a while in silence until Ginny asked him how he was feeling.

'Do you feel happy or sad?'

'I feel both. I feel so happy that I want to cry.'

'You can cry. What do you think is making you cry?'

'It's because I'm being given birth to the universe.'

'Does that mean you're being born or you're giving birth?'

'Both.'

'And it's painful?'

'Yes. I'm not sure if I have the strength.'

'It's hard being both subject and object, being yourself and another. But I'm here to help you. Think of me as a midwife.'

In the suggestible state he was in, Steve started to feel that he was having abdominal contractions. He moaned quietly, rubbing his stomach. Ginny suggested he have a pee and led him out to the bathroom. She said she'd stay with him, if he didn't mind. He freed his cock and pointed it at the lavatory. Initially nothing happened and then he felt his urinary sphincters open and the urine gushed out. The feeling was very strange. He wasn't sure that having started he would be able to stop. But it was also a huge relief. Ginny smiled at him.

'Let's go and lie down.'

They went up to the bedroom and Ginny said he would feel more comfortable with his clothes off. He stripped off and laid down on the bed. Ginny removed her clothes too and laid down beside him.

When he reflected on the experience afterwards, even the moments of anxiety and sadness seemed positive. He wasn't sure if the stomach cramps had been real or imagined, he only knew that it was like being turned inside out. Being born or giving birth was the closest he could get to describing the sensation. Or perhaps it was like when a butterfly emerges from a chrysalis. He wondered what kind of butterfly he had turned into, large and flamboyant or modest and shy?

Ginny's suggestion that they go to bed had been well judged. Sex with Ginny over the previous few days had been explosive to say the least, but on this occasion it was so gentle, so trusting that he felt that he and Ginny were merging. It was not so much that his ego was dissolving, as that it had expanded to accommodate another. The acid enhanced the perspectives and close-ups of their entwined bodies. When they had recovered from their copulatory exertions, Ginny ran a bath and somehow they had both managed to fit into the tiny bathtub. They dried themselves and Ginny put on her sheer robe and handed Steve a kind of kimono to wear. They then went back downstairs and had a cup of tea by which time Steve was feeling decidedly calmer, almost mellow, no longer feeling as if he were strapped to a rocket. Or if he were, the rocket had entered a stable orbit. He went over to the record player and cued up the second side of *Astral Weeks*, which, as he turned the disc over, he noticed was subtitled 'Afterwards'.

As the vibes and strummed guitar of the opening bars of 'The Way Young Lovers Do' played, Ginny asked Steve how he felt about going out. They needn't go far and if he felt anxious at any point they could come straight back. Steve wasn't sure. He felt secure in the protective environment that Ginny had created in the Ainsworth Street house despite the distortions to his sensorium, but when Ginny suggested a visit to The Locomotive for a drink and to play a few records on the jukebox, Steve was persuaded and headed for the front door. Ginny said that perhaps they should change into clothes more suitable for the public realm. Even the laid back clientele of The Locomotive might find a couple of spaced-out groovers in kaftans a bit *de trop*. A few minutes later, more suitably attired, they stepped out onto the street.

In the capsule of the little house Steve had completely lost track of time, but out on the street with the dome of the late summer sky above him it was apparent that it was early evening. It was also apparent that he had stepped into a Tintoretto painting. The clouds were piled up in outrageous pink hued crests. He had never seen anything so ridiculously beautiful. Ginny followed the direction of his gaze and realised the effect the sky was having on him. She squeezed his hand in affirmation. After several moments' absorption in the glowing firmament, the couple resumed their progress towards Mill Road.

For the previous few hours, so far as Steve was concerned, he and Ginny might have been the only two inhabitants of the planet, but now it became clear that there were countless others, many of whom looked like figures from a Tolkien saga. Even more disquieting were the cars that thronged Mill Road, growling and belching noxious fumes. Steve shrank back from the edge of the pavement and pressed himself against a building. Ginny told him it was all quite normal and he'd soon adjust to the noise and the proximity of others. With Ginny steering him, they crossed the road and walked along beside the shops which lined that side of Mill Road. The enigmatic displays in the shop windows they passed soon distracted Steve from the four-wheeled monsters patrolling the carriageway. He found it difficult to relate the exhibits to the ostensible service or commercial activity being advertised.

Before long they arrived at The Locomotive and Steve was relieved to go inside and get off the street. Fortunately, the pub was by no means full. Ginny found them a table and went to the bar to get the drinks. She was soon back at the table with a pint of bitter for Steve and a gin and tonic for herself. Steve took a sip of the beer and realising that he was very thirsty followed the sip with two large gulps. Ginny said she'd put something on the jukebox and wondered if Steve had any change on him. Change? Ah, yes. What a curious word for money. He put his hand in his trouser pocket and pulled out several coins placing them on the table. He picked up one of the coins and, examining it closely, asked, 'How does this work?'

Ginny laughed, 'That's a good question. No one really knows. A matter of belief perhaps. These are just tokens really, which makes them surprisingly difficult to acquire. As a consequence many people put a lot of effort into hoarding them.'

She picked several coins out of the small pile on the table and went over to the improbably fluorescent jukebox and selected several songs. As she came back to the table the opening cowbell hits of the Stones' 'Honky Tonk Women' filled the room. Steve was delighted, 'Wow! That sounds great.'

Steve started to relax and to get into the vibe of the bar. Ginny had selected a number of tracks including Rod Stewart's 'Maggie May', Roberta Flack's 'Killing Me Softly with his Song', and Joni Mitchell's 'Help Me'. She could see that Steve was enjoying the playlist and she allowed the conversation to drop so that he could get into the music. When they had finished their drinks Ginny suggested that they head back to the house. She said that Steve had handled the outside world well, given that it was his first trip and he was still pretty high.

Back at the house the first thing that Steve did was go upstairs and get his acoustic guitar. He settled down on the sofa and got into one of his familiar riffs. Normally his approach was to overcomplicate things, but under the influence of the acid it was timbre and simplicity that attracted him. Ginny sat and listened to him, nodding her head in approval. She went over to Jon's stash box and rolled a joint. She took a couple of drags and then offered it to Steve, but he didn't want to break the flow of his playing and in any case he thought he was high enough and didn't want to muddy the acid experience with a blast of dope and nicotine. Ginny said his playing was really great, much more like the kind of thing that Jon played. Steve had obviously picked up a few things from him. Maybe it was better to go by feel than his usual more programmatic approach. Eventually he had exhausted the riff he had been playing and before he put his guitar away jotted down the chord sequence.

When he got back to the sitting room, Ginny was reading a paperback. Steve joined her on the sofa and sat quietly for a while going back over the impressions of the day. After a while he said, mainly to himself, 'What happens now?'

Ginny explained that it was a gentle glide down now, normally a very nice feeling as more familiar perspectives returned. But Steve said he meant in their relationship. How did Ginny see things developing? She put her book down and said with a serious look on her face that she wasn't sure this was a good time to visit that subject.

Steve spent the next few days trying to capture something of the acid trip in words. His first attempt was a fairly straightforward account, but when he read it back later, it seemed to bear little resemblance to the profound experience it had been. He wished he'd had the presence of mind on the day itself to take some notes. His second attempt was more impressionistic. It was better but still not adequate. The nub of the experience had something to do with the feeling of being transported to another house, identical in every respect to the Ainsworth Street house and yet very different, his home, but not his home, literally *unheimlich*.

But if he didn't have any notes, he did at least have his entirely unsatisfactory attempts to draw an image of himself and the sketch, no, the diagram of his poem. The self image was childish scribble, but the other piece representing his poem was more intriguing. The four shaded areas that Ginny had added to it gave it a solidity that she said reflected the structure of his poem. It was not clear to him in which way this was so. After all each part of the poem contained many hundreds of words. It was true that there were four parts to his poem– 'Flatland', 'Underpinnings', 'Obliquity' and 'Dis/Quiet'–but each part comprised hundreds of words. How could he boil down all that material so that it fitted into each of the four shaded sections? He wasn't even sure that the sections were significantly different from each other. There was only one way to find out.

A couple of hours later, he had produced a list of 40 or 50 words and phrases for each section. He took a clean sheet of paper and laid it over the sheet that Ginny had shaded, tracing the curved shapes lightly in pencil on the new sheet. That done, he fed the new sheet of paper into the typewriter and carefully typed items from each list into one of traced sections. The task was curiously satisfying, much more enjoyable than the initial composition had been. He took the finished page out of the typewriter and held it up. It wasn't really a sketch or diagram. Perhaps it owed more to Lewis Carroll's 'The Mouse's Tail' than to Mallarmé's 'Un coup de dés'. Even so, he considered it *sui generis* and was rather proud of it. He took it downstairs and showed it to Ginny.

'Here's the sketch of the poem you asked for the other day.'

Ginny held it up, in the same way that Steve himself had done, as if viewing an image rather than reading a poem.

'Steve, this is fantastic. It's a kind of map of the journey you've been on. And perhaps also shows where you're going.'

'Way out, then? Or *way out?*'

'Who's to say? Maybe they're the same thing. Don't try to analyse it too much. Just enjoy the achievement.'

'As a matter of fact I am curiously pleased with it. But I don't really know what it is. In terms of journeys I'd be very reluctant to see this single sheet of paper as way out of the compositional labyrinth I've been in for the last few months. Talk about going around the sun to get to the moon.'

'Perhaps that's what you have to do until you work out a better way of getting to where you want to be. Does it have a title?'

'No. It doesn't seem to be the kind of thing that warrants a title.'

'A diagram of *Event/Horizon* seems a rather cumbersome way of referring to it. I suggest the words at the top of the page have volunteered themselves as the title. So let's call it, *Solar Wind Shuttle.*'

Steve felt that honouring the piece with a title was according it more importance than it deserved. It was, after all, just a squib. 'So what do I do with *Event/Horizon*? Just abandon it? Throw it away?' he said, a little irritated now.

'No one's suggesting that. But maybe it's a launch pad for something else.'

Steve's earlier elation now gave way to pensiveness. He wasn't ready to give up trying to make *Event/Horizon* cohere.

'Anyway, it's for you, a little thank-you for looking after me the other day.'

'And thank you, Steve. I'll look after it until you need it.' Ginny seemed genuinely touched.

Steve, unable to imagine a situation in which he might need the product of what had really only been light relief from the self-imposed task of trying to record his impressions of the acid trip, went back up to his room and, deaf to all that Ginny had said, resumed the intolerable wrestle.

By the Thursday he'd run out of steam and needed to clear his head. Ginny said he could help her in the garden, but he said that he'd prefer to walk. He'd be back in an hour or so. She shrugged and got on with her gardening.

When he got back, Ginny said, 'You had a visitor.'

Steve was surprised. 'Really, who?'

'He said his name was Rob. He's read your poem and would like to talk to you about it. He's going to be in The Six Bells from six-thirty this evening.'

'He could have given me more notice. Would you mind if I met him?'

'Steve, thank you for checking, but as I've already said, you don't have to get clearance from me to meet your friends.'

A couple of hours later, Steve pushed the door of The Six Bells open and saw Robin installed at a table in the corner buried in a book. He went over and greeted him.

'What are you drinking?'

Robin downed the remains of his pint and said, 'The IPA.'

Steve returned a few minutes later, bearing two pints and slid Robin's across the table to him. Robin raised his glass and said, 'Congratulations, Maestro. *Event/Horizon* is the real deal.'

Steve clinked glasses with him and said, 'Robin that's very generous of you, but it's not true.'

'Sure. It's not finished and it needs more work. But there's something there.'

'Don't you think it's a bit too abstract, maybe lacking emotion, a bit too impersonal?'

'No. I thought people like us preferred to operate on the abstract level.'

'Well, yes, but is that what readers of poetry want?'

'Who knows what they want. Anyway, the general reader doesn't read our stuff. It's only read by other practitioners.'

Steve thought that was a fair point.

Rob was concerned. 'Who's been getting at you?'

'No one in particular,' Steve lied.

'Your women?'

'I don't have women. I have a girlfriend.'

'And an incredibly beautiful one at that, if you're referring to the lady who opened the door to me at your digs. To follow the previous beautiful lady. Or am I putting two and two together and getting five?'

'Well, no, you're right in that Angie and I have broken up and now I'm with Ginny.'

'I don't know how you do it.'

'I don't do anything. It just happens.'

'That's what all the lover boys say.'

'I don't want to go into all that right now. It's all very new and in some respects quite painful. But getting back to the poem, I just feel that the thing has gone dead on me. I've lost my way and when I read it, I just feel that it's too schematic.'

'That's why you need to let more people see your work. You're too protective.'

Steve conceded the point wordlessly. Rob was not the first person to say this.

Rob took another mouthful of beer. 'That's what I wanted to talk to you about. I'm on really good terms with Martin Lockwood, the editor of *Outwrite*. We got to know each other well, when he was editing *Soundings*. I think I could persuade him to take an extract from *Event/Horizon* for the next edition, but I'd like you to let me select the extract.'

Steve was shocked. 'I don't think it's ready yet.'

'It's a work in progress, and it's you who are not ready. This is a very common form of literary stage fright.'

Steve laughed bitterly. 'Yeah, pathetic, I know.'

He was pensive. Right at that moment, the thing that he wanted most was to have a long talk with Angie. There was so much to tell her. Despite things having ended badly between them, he thought that she would be pleased by Robin's reaction to *Event/Horizon*, and his generosity in trying to get an extract published.

Robin could see that his last contribution to the conversation had plunged Steve into a fit of introspection.

'Ground Control to Major Steve. Are you okay, mate? You're look pretty spaced out.'

Steve refocused. 'Yeah, I think I'm still a bit high. Sorry.'

'Been at the wacky baccy again, eh?'

'Well, actually I dropped some acid on Sunday. And I think it's still having a bit of an effect.'

Robin was startled. 'I didn't know that was your scene.'

Steve wished he hadn't mentioned it. Why had he done that?

'It was the first time the opportunity arose, and I thought it was something I'd like to try before other things got in the way.'

'How was it? Pleasant? Scary? Useful?'

'All those things. But mainly just amazing. Very hard to put into words. Although I have in fact been trying to.'

'So, can we look forward to a mantic strain in your poetry?'

'I hope not, but I have been trying to incorporate the experience into *Event/Horizon*. Tripping is like landing on a new planet, although it's actually the same planet we all live on, of course. But suddenly familiar objects look new or strange. It's uncanny. Or *unheimlich* in Freudian terminology. It seemed to me that the *heimlich/unheimlich* antinomy of the trip was similar to the horizon/singularity antinomy in *Event/Horizon*, two opposing aspects of the same thing.'

'Far out, man, I think I'm meant to say. One hears of people having a bad time with LSD, the so called bad trip.'

'It's intense no doubt, but I didn't feel that I was in danger. I did feel that my ego or sense of self was dissolving. I expect some people might find that threatening. I found it intriguing. Of course I was lucky to have Ginny guide me through it.'

'Was she tripping too?'

'No, but she has in the past. So she could anticipate the kinds of things I might be feeling. She was able to structure proceedings for me. Set and setting she called it.'

'So not only is she beautiful, but she's a shamanic guide too.'

'And a brilliant fine artist.'

'There must be a downside.'

'Perhaps she's a little damaged, maybe more than a little.'

'From the drugs?'

'No. From relationships or maybe family. I don't really know that much about her, whereas I had got to know Angie and her family very well. I think that her folks, while not entirely approving of me, had accepted me. As much as anything, I feel I've let her parents down.'

'Oh dear, it sounds like you're having second thoughts.'

'Not that so much. I just didn't expect things to develop in this way. All I wanted to do was get a bit of writing done.'

'We all have to make sacrifices for our art.'

'Do we? Do you feel you've made sacrifices?'

'No, but then I'm not sure I'm the real thing.'

Steve was shocked. 'Rob, that's crazy. You're the best poet I know. And the cleverest critic. And not just because you like my poem.'

'That's kind of you to say so. But even without chemical stimulation you seem to get to places that are inaccessible to me.'

'That's nonsense, Rob. It might look like that. It sure doesn't feel like it.'

'I think my forte might be identifying and promoting other writers.'

'A latter day Pound? That wouldn't be so bad. The bloke Eliot called *il miglior fabbro*? And I'm not suggesting that you assign me to the Eliot variable in that equation.'

'Without doing that, are you going to let me choose an extract from your poem and send it to Martin? And secondly, I hope you and Ginny can come to my farewell-to-Cambridge party a week on Saturday.'

'Your party will be crawling with the Cambridge poetry glitterati. How could I show my face at such such an event?'

'Bring Ginny, and then no one will be the slightest bit interested in you. All eyes will be on her.'

Steve couldn't help laughing. 'You know how to make a chap feel wanted. No seriously, thank you. Yes to both. You're a real pal. I'm very grateful.'

'Okay. It's a deal. And now if you don't mind me asking, what did you think of *Sounding Off*?'

'Oh, Rob. I'm so sorry I haven't responded to you yet. I read it immediately the day you gave it to me. Twice. It's really good. I had intended to rustle up a little epistolary laurel wreath, but I had to give the muse a good seeing to first.'

'That might be a way of putting it. I'm not sure the periphrastic mode suits you though.'

'It's funny you should say that. The acid blasted through the hebetude the other day and I was thinking of a section of that very stanza, about the pattern being new in every moment. I didn't just understand those lines for the first time. I could see the bloody pattern in everything.'

'Including in my poems?'

'Well, I'd read your poems a few days before I dropped the acid, and I'm sure that was part of it. Your poems are great, Rob. They made me feel depressed. If they hadn't been any good, I would have showered you with praise. But they troubled me, because what you're writing is serious stuff.'

'Well, that's the nicest backhanded compliment I've ever received. And I'll accept it in the sincere spirit in which it was offered.'

'Rob, I'm sorry I'm such a stupid cunt.'

'Steve, you're a poet. All poets are cunts.'

Steve emptied his glass, 'Too true.'

'Good. Well, things will be kicking off about eight. You've got my address. I hope to see both of you then.'

With that, the two dreadful bards embraced and headed back to their respective gaffs. Steve, for another night of passion with his muse. And Robin, to continue with his editing of Steve's poem, which, in fact, he had already begun without mentioning the fact.

Steve felt considerably buoyed by Rob's reaction to *Event/Horizon*. He was not sure, however, whether Ginny would want to come to a party featuring the Cambridge poetry mafia, or at least those who weren't still island-hopping in the Aegean. In the event she said she'd like to go. In fact, Steve was probably more apprehensive about the encounter than Ginny was. Steve wasn't sure whether he was in the right frame of mind to have to deal with Flynn's acolytes.

Why was he so lacking in confidence when it came to his writing? Rob didn't seem to suffer from the same disability and yet he had admitted that Steve's work had something that his lacked. Rob seemed to know what he was doing, whereas Steve was pretty sure that he had no idea what he was doing. But knowing what you were doing was an aspect of craft, not art. The manipulation of what you only knew, could only produce the already known. Expectation was already built into the process.

But maybe because Steve didn't know what he was doing, he occasionally produced something original, or at least unexpected. At such times he somehow managed to operate in a mode of expectancy rather than expectation, open towards the results. It was not unlike finding something you didn't know you were looking for. The problem with his method, however, was there was no guarantee of an outcome, let alone success.

Folk Festival

Cherry Hinton Hall
Saturday, 27 July 1974

STEVE WAS STILL GETTING flashes from the acid. An image or a piece of music would suddenly capture his attention and hint at the magical world he had entered a few days previously. Ginny could see that he was still responding to things in a heightened way and wondered whether she could organise something that might resonate for Steve in his sensitised state. While they were having supper on the Friday evening, she said, 'I bumped into Tom today. He reminded me that the Cambridge Folk Festival is on this weekend. He's going and has a couple of spare tickets for tomorrow, so I took them. Do you fancy it?'

Steve wasn't really a folk music enthusiast. He certainly liked Fairport Convention's *Liege and Lief*. Sandy Denny had a wonderful voice, but he wasn't so keen on the hand in the ear stuff or what he called diddly-dee music. But it was thoughtful of Ginny to get the tickets. So the next day they cruised down the Cherry Hinton Road in the van, eventually finding a parking spot and entered the grounds of Cherry Hinton Hall, which had been transformed into a tented city and was already thronged with shaggy-haired youth.

Ginny's aim was to hook up with Tom. She didn't think he'd be particularly attracted by the headline acts. He was more likely to be found in one of the marquees. Normally at such events there was a notice board. He might have left a message for them saying where he was. As they made their way through the crowd towards the informa-

247

tion centre, they encountered knots of people gathered around ad hoc groupings of musicians sawing away on fiddles and picking on banjos and mandolins. Meanwhile from the marquees that flanked the main performance area came the sound of amplified music. They arrived at the field in front of the main stage which was crammed with a large crowd responding enthusiastically to the band on stage, the Pigsty Hill Light Orchestra, who, to Steve's mind, were little more than a folk version of the Bonzo Dog Doo Dah Band. But the audience seemed to love what they were doing. Steve and Ginny paused in their quest for Tom to listen for a few minutes. Steve had an aversion to music involving kazoos and washboards, although it had to be admitted that the Pigsty Hill percussionist was something of a washboard virtuoso.

Ginny did not share Steve's qualified admiration and wanted to move on. Steve pointed out that Arlo Guthrie was on next. Steve had heard one or two of his albums. They hadn't particularly impressed, but nor had they been completely objectionable. It might be interesting to hear him live. There was a chance he might do 'Alice's Restaurant', the 20 minute long protest against the Vietnam War. This was decidedly not something that Ginny wanted to hang around for. She considered it lightweight compared to Dylan's 'Masters of War'. Arlo might be Woody Guthrie's biological son, but it was surely Ramblin' Jack Elliott or Dylan himself who was Woody's spiritual son. There was something essentially vapid about Arlo's music. Ginny's disapproval seemed so uncompromising that Steve decided that it was better to defer to her judgement and they moved on, looking for the noticeboard.

As they passed one of the large marquees, Steve heard some rather lovely acoustic guitar playing emanating from inside it, not exactly Django, but certainly very groovy. He said to Ginny that he'd just like to check it out for a few minutes. He ducked into the tent and saw a black dude in shades playing some pretty nifty shapes. Ginny followed him in, somewhat reluctantly. Steve had a weird feeling that, not only did he recognise some of the riffs, but that something about the guitarist was familiar too. He asked a bearded youth, standing near the entrance to the tent, nodding his head enthusiastically to the music, the name of the performer.

'Jed Morgan, man. Ace stuff.'

What the bearded guy was saying didn't make sense. Jed Morgan? Surely not *the* Jed Morgan, whose guitar jazz tutorial Steve had been laboriously working through? But yes, he realised as he looked and listened, that it was the very same. Steve whispered to Ginny that he needed to stay for this performance. Ginny, without recognising what was involved, could see that something had clicked and said that was fine. She'd leave Steve there, find Tom and return. So, on no account was Steve to move away from the tent until she was back. Steve readily agreed. Making his way closer to the front, he found a spot where he could watch Jed's hands. He marvelled at the way that he moved smoothly from one shape to another, not the frantic scrambling of fingers that was Steve's style. He was getting thoroughly caught up in the music, recognising one or two of the riffs that he had been prac-tising, when he was startled to hear a voice behind him, addressing him by name. 'Hello, Steve, I wondered if I might find you here.'

It was Matt Parker, Gary's boyfriend.

'Hi Matt, did you know that Jed Morgan was playing? Or did you get here by chance?'

'I saw his name on the poster and thought I'd check him out. Not often you get to hear a bona fide legend live.'

'It's a pity he didn't release any records.'

'Oh, he did and does. It's just not current hit parade stuff. Although he played on lots of hits in the past. He was a major session player. Mind if I join you?'

Steve made some space for Matt and they grooved to the music together. After a few numbers, Jed said he was going to take a break, but would be doing another set after the break. Steve saw him step out of the tent and light up a cigarette. Matt nudged Steve in the ribs.

'Shall we go and speak to Jed?'

Steve wasn't sure that was a great idea. He didn't like the idea of fandom, but Matt had no such qualms. He pulled Steve up by the arm. 'Leave it to me, I'm shameless.'

They went out of the tent and saw Jed drawing deeply on his cigar-ette surveying the hirsute, bedenimmed youth through his shades. Matt marched up to him. "We're a couple of devotees of your jazz books.'

Jed turned his gaze on them. It was hard with the shades to judge whether he was irritated or pleased to be accosted in this way.

'Pleased to meet you. Glad to extend a hand to other guitar players.'

Steve was grateful that Matt had not differentiated their respective levels of ability, but felt a bit of a fraud.

By way of clarification, he said, 'I've only recently started, your tutorial, that is, and I have to admit that I'm not finding it easy going.'

'It's not easy, kid. You've got to work your way through it. Don't give up. Your fingers will get there. But you've got to work on it everyday.'

'I don't understand why you play the chords you do and how they go together.'

'You have to walk before you can run. A lot of the theory is explained in lesson twelve, but it's better to learn the chords, licks and riffs in the first eleven lessons and get the sound of the them in your head. That's what the examples are for, get them off by heart. By all means start with the harmonic theory first, but I don't think that's the best way of becoming a guitar player.'

Matt said, 'I've been playing guitar a lot longer than Steve, I imagine, but I'm still struggling with a lot of the stuff in part two of the first book.'

'You have to take part two very slowly. None of us ever stops learning. There's always new things to learn.'

Matt nodded. 'Have you got any other gigs before you go back to the States?'

'I'm not going back to the States. I live in France and have done so for several years.'

Steve was excited by the thought that Jed might have teamed up with Django.

'Did you ever get together with Django?'

'Not in France. He died before I moved there, but we did hook up in New York City on one of his trips. The guy was an out and out genius.'

At that moment, Ginny hove into view accompanied by a stately plump gentlemen with luxuriant beard and long hair, whom Steve recognised as Tom from the Solstice bookshop. Jed was impressed. 'Jeez, that's one amazing chick. I hope she's the old guy's daughter, and not his girlfriend.'

Steve wanted to point out that the amazing chick was *his* girlfriend, but was unable to find a suitably flip way of making the point, before Ginny and Tom reached them. Ginny nodded at Matt and shot Jed a quizzical look. Steve made the introductions, 'Ginny, this is Jed Morgan, the great guitarist. He was playing in the marquee earlier, but he's on a break between sets now.'

Ginny smiled at Jed, and introduced Tom. Jed, who had been merely cordial in dealing with Matt and Steve, now became more animated. He had an eye for a pretty girl and he was on the road. Not unreasonably, he wondered whether he might get some action with this dark haired goddess, if he could pull some guitar *droit de seigneur*. She was way more alluring than the majority of the pasty-faced chicks sprawled across the lawns of Cherry Hinton Hall. In the pause following the introductions, Matt offered to get some drinks and Steve, oblivious to what was going through Jed's mind, said he'd give Matt a hand.

When they returned with the drinks, Jed was talking about the music scene in the States in the 50s. Jazz was his thing, but the blues paid the bills. The great thing about France was that he could do both, and the French chicks had that *je ne sais quoi*. The beers were handed around and Jed said, 'You guys don't look as if you're camping here for the weekend.'

Matt was first into the conversational breach. 'No, we're all Cambridge residents and we'll be heading back into town later.'

Jed nodded. 'So what do you guys do?' Then, indicating Steve, 'The only one of you who looks like a student is my young friend here.'

Matt laughed. 'Yeah, the rest of us didn't get the memo about the demographic. I can't speak for the others, but I write for TV.'

Jed was impressed. 'Cool.'

'What about you, kid?'

Steve was becoming irritated with being patronised. 'I work at the local theatre.' It would have been truer to say that he was about to start a job at the local theatre, but he hoped the others wouldn't call him out.

Ginny, sensing Steve's irritation, said, 'Steve's too modest to say it, but he's a writer too, a poet.'

Jed digested the new information. 'All struggling artists could do with a big sister like you.'

Steve wished that Ginny hadn't tried to boost him. But there was no stopping her now. She gave Jed a withering look. 'We're lovers actually.'

Jed laughed. 'Let me rephrase that. Every struggling artist could do with a muse like you. Hats off to the kid. Hats off to both of you. And what do you do when you're not inspiring lover boy?'

'I'm in the fashion business. I'm a model.'

Jed nodded. 'That figures. I'm starting to see Steve in a new light.'

This encounter wasn't unfolding as Steve might have hoped.

Jed focused on Tom. 'What about you, Tom?'

'I run an alternative bookshop, selling everything from underground magazines and books on earth mysteries to books of beat poetry and cult fiction. I am also active in the local community's resistance to misguided civic redevelopment plans.'

Suddenly, Jed dropped his bantering tone. 'Well, I'm flattered to have attracted such an interesting group of people to my gig. I'm back on stage soon. I hope you're coming back in.'

How could they refuse? Clearly even a battle-hardened road warrior like Jed still cared about getting a good audience. The group re-entered the marquee and got a good spot to one side of the stage. The second part of the set was a sequence of coruscating blues numbers, played with verve and élan, to which the crowd responded enthusiastically. Even Ginny seemed moved by the music, gently grooving to the thrum of the guitar. At the end of the set when Jed had put his guitar safely in its case, he came over to where Steve's group were sitting. The other members of the audience looked around enviously at the group of people who were obviously friends of Jed. After accepting their plaudits, including a congratulatory kiss from Ginny, Jed asked, 'Are you guys lining up to hear anyone else?'

Steve had hoped to take in a couple of more acts, but if what was being proposed was the opportunity to spend some more time with Jed Morgan, then he was all for it. So it seemed was everyone else.

Tom said, 'Speaking for myself, I'm going to go back into town and get something to eat. Where are you staying Jed?'

'I'm staying at a little hotel near the station. I'm heading back to France tomorrow. And I could sure do with something to eat.'

Tom, with old world courtesy said, 'You'd be very welcome to join us. There are a number of places near my shop. And that's not too far from the station.'

'How do we get back to town?' Jed asked.

'Ginny and I have got a VW camper van. We could probably get everyone in.'

Matt, however, had come in his own car. He'd go home and pick up Gary and then meet them in an hour's time at Waffles in the Kite. When they got to the VW it was decided that because of his girth Tom should sit up front with Steve, while Ginny and Jed could stretch out on the mattress in the back of the van, an arrangement that Steve thought was less than ideal now that Ginny had retracted her claws enough to give Jed a congratulatory kiss at the end of his set.

As they rattled back into the town centre, Steve kept angling the rearview mirror to make sure a seemly distance was being maintained between Jed and Ginny. He also did his best to catch their conversation, but very little of it came through the roar of the air-cooled VW engine. Soon his absurd worries were interrupted by Tom asking how the trip had gone. Up until that moment Steve, focused as he was firstly on Jed's guitar playing and subsequently on his reputation as a ladies' man, had neglected to thank Tom for the acid.

'It was an amazing experience. It opened up so much for me. Thank you.'

'Well, if you want some more, just let me know. Ginny was the right person to have as your guide. She is very wise. She tells me you're writing some big poem.'

'Yes, although I think I might have bitten off more than I can chew. I kind of wish that I hadn't mentioned it to anyone until I finished it. And I don't really know if I have the courage to finish it. It seems to me that to do it, I've got to go to some kind of dark place. But the trouble is I lack courage, or at least that's what I've been told.'

Why was he telling Tom this? He hardly knew him, but something in his gentle, courteous manner, made Steve want to confide in him. He realised that on the whole, he was very guarded with other men, and seemed to prefer to open up to women. But perhaps because Tom was so much older than his other male acquaintances, he didn't seem to pose such a threat. Suddenly, Steve realised that mention of the acid had triggered another flash. He looked across at Tom, who caught his eye and smiled. Steve knew he knew.

'You're in the right place to undertake that kind of quest. And I think you have the right person to show you the way out, the way back, I mean.'

Tom's words rippled out across Steve's thoughts like two pebbles dropped into a mountain pool.

'I hadn't thought of what I was doing as a quest. The truth is that I don't really know what I'm doing or why.'

'That seems to be a sensible place to start from. Even if you know what you want, the chances of success are slight. And wanting is not enough. Often enough what we think we want, is not what we *really* want.'

Tom wasn't making himself any clearer, although Steve felt that he was being told something important.

When they got back to Cambridge, Tom suggested they park in the New Square car park. As they clambered out of the camper van. Tom pointed across to the corner of the square and, addressing Jed, said, 'That's my shop.'

'Cool, man. Could I leave my guitar and overnight bag there? I don't want to carry them around, but I'm not sure that this old crate', indicating the VW, 'is very secure. This is a very precious guitar.'

Tom was happy to oblige and they trooped over to the shop. He got his keys out and let them in. Jed laughed when he saw the interior. 'Crazy, man.'

Tom took that as a compliment. What would be the point of carrying the same stock as Heffers or Bowes and Bowes? Jed wasn't entirely sure what heifers or ribbons and bows had to do with books. He smiled anyway. Tom stored Jed's things in the backroom of the shop and locked the internal door. Then they resumed their walk to the Kite, making their way to Waffles, a trendy eatery, where they found Matt and Gary waiting outside for them. Gary was introduced to Jed and the party went inside to occupy the table that Matt had reserved.

Gary had not met Tom before, but he was aware of Solstice bookshop. Matt said that he'd like to treat Jed to the meal in recognition of the hours he had spent going through his books. Jed was not going to argue against the proposal. Even though he had already literally sung for his supper earlier, he now proceeded with the metaphorical equivalent and regaled them with stories of the West Coast jazz scene in the 50s, Tin Pan Alley in the 60s and, more recently, the Blues scene in France. He gave good value and clearly enjoyed the attention.

They finished the meal and settled the bill. Jed said that he ought to be getting back to his hotel, but first he needed to pick up his gear from Tom's shop. When they reached the shop, Tom invited the party in for a nightcap. Jed, at the mention of a nightcap decided that he didn't need to get back to his hotel quite so urgently. Gary and Matt declined the invitation, but said it had been a nice evening. Matt asked Jed, whether he would be prepared to give Matt his address in France, so that they could stay in touch. Matt was always looking for tips and suggestions to help him improve his playing. Jed said he'd be happy to. He had some business cards in his guitar case.

Tom let him into the backroom of the shop, from which he re-emerged a few moments later with a handful of cards, which he proceeded to distribute to the group. Gary and Matt took their leave, whereupon Tom invited Steve, Ginny and Jed up to his living room above the shop, which seemed to contain even more books than the shop itself.

The nightcap turned out to be a gigantic joint. As Jed toked on it, he said, 'I've never seen so many weird books and magazines.'

'And many of them produced on the premises, not the books, but a lot of the magazines and pamphlets. We have our own print room out back. I'd be happy to show you around.'

Jed was not interested in printing equipment. 'If you don't mind, I'll sit this one out. Y'all take a look though. I've had a long day and I think I'll just sit here and dig the vibe.'

Ginny shared Jed's lack of interest in printing technology. Steve, on the other hand, had always had a fascination for the way printed matter was produced and said he'd like to take a look at the Solstice print room. Addressing Ginny and Jed, Tom said, 'We won't be long. Make yourselves at home. There's some beer and a bottle of white wine in the fridge. The record deck is over there.'

Tom took Steve back downstairs and through to the extension at the back of the shop. He pointed out the IBM Selectric typewriter, the Gestetner 230 duplicator, a guillotine for cutting paper, a large stapling machine and various other things. He showed him how stencils were made on the typewriter, and then put on the drum of the Gestetner. The stencils were a kind of silkscreen, which the raised surface of the typewriter printhead cut, allowing ink to be squeezed through onto the sheets of paper. The Selectric was one of the newer kind that had a self-correcting tape. It had cost a pretty penny, but it meant that Tom's little print room was much more productive. It was also possible to use different coloured inks to produce interesting effects and to use a stylus rather than the typewriter to include hand-drawn illustrations.

Steve was entranced. It occurred to him that if he pulled enough money together, he could publish *Event/Horizon* under his own imprint. He had been flattered that Martin had wanted to run an extract of his poem in *Outwrite*, but he had been irritated by the idea that edits that were being proposed. Nor did he feel that an extract would give an accurate impression of the way the poem developed. He explained his misgivings to Tom, who, of course, knew Martin quite well, because Martin sometimes used Tom's duplication facilities to produce his own pamphlets. But they were also rivals. Nor did Tom particularly favour the kind of poetry that Martin championed, being more of a beat aficionado.

'I'm all in favour of DIY publishing, but it would cost more than you think, even if I were to help you. And then you've got to distribute the material and make sure to get paid. That's what Martin's good at. He's hooked into all the main networks in the poetry world. That's not my scene at all.'

When they got back upstairs, Jed was playing his guitar. He paused in his playing. 'I've had an idea for a song based on the nice time I've had in Cambridge over the last couple of days. I was just trying to get the riff down and some guide lyrics. Ginny's been a great help. She's a very discriminating listener.'

Steve was disappointed to have missed the process of composition, even though his trip to the Solstice print room had been fascinating. Tom, sensing Steve's disappointment, said in his most courtly manner, 'I know it's somewhat importunate, but you wouldn't consider playing it to us, would you? The precincts of Solstice bookshop are not often honoured to be the incubator of new songs.'

As far as Jed was concerned Tom could have been speaking in Martian, but he got the gist and inclined his head towards Ginny. 'Well, only if Ginny doesn't object, since she is the dedicatee of the song.'

Ginny opened her arms wide. 'Go ahead.'

Jed picked up his guitar and started into a slinky minor blues riff. For an improvisation, the lyrics were already expertly structured. They told of a weary traveller from a distant land, who's been on the road for days, getting shelter wherever he can, busking his way through life. Just when he can scarcely drag his weary body another step further, he stumbles upon an inn and goes in for food and drink. He is served by a dark-eyed beauty, the daughter of the innkeeper. He can't afford to spend the night in the inn itself, and asks her if there is somewhere else he can stay. She says there's plenty of dry straw in the stable. The wanderer thanks her and before he leaves the warmth of the inn says if she visits him later in the stable, he will thank her in song. The last verse was wordless and Jed scatted through it, before bringing the song to a close. He put his guitar down to enthusiastic applause from the little audience.

'I need to do some work on that last verse, I'm not sure how it ends yet.'

Steve found it hard to believe that Jed had cooked that up on the spot. But then he supposed that was the way that traditional forms worked, they lent themselves to improvisation. The other troubling thing was that not only was Ginny the dedicatee, but the lyrics were a blatant come-on. It wasn't hard to identify the models for the weary traveller and the innkeeper's daughter. Steve wasn't quite sure how to react. While he temporised, Jed ruthlessly pressed his advantage.

'Okay, kid. Your turn. You give us something.'

Steve protested. 'I can't follow that.'

'You told me earlier you play the guitar and Ginny told us that not only are you her boyfriend but you're also a poet. So show us what you've got.'

Steve squirmed. 'No, I'll only make a fool of myself.'

'Show some courage, kid. You're among friends.'

Steve wasn't so sure that he was. He was very stoned in fact, and still getting flashes from the acid. It had been a very weird day, not only hearing the person, whose jazz book he was following, play live, someone, who up until a few hours earlier, for all Steve knew, was still working the jazz dives of New York City, or even, for that matter, dead, but then spending the rest of the day with that same jazz luminary, including sharing a meal with him at Waffles. And now, here Steve was, in the upper room of Solstice, having just heard the hoary troubadour serenade Steve's own girlfriend and being challenged to follow suit. Something very odd had happened somewhere. He struggled to make sense of it. He tried to catch Ginny's eye in the hope that she would come to his rescue again, but this time she had withdrawn into her familiar sphinx-like impassivity. Steve glanced around desperately at Tom, who smiled blandly back at him, while Jed just stared directly at him from behind his shades, one eyebrow raised and a slight smile playing around his lips.

Steve was adamant. 'I'm no singer, and I'm not a very good guitarist.'

Jed put his guitar down and rose from his chair seeming to fill the room with his sinister bulk. He took Steve by the arm and dragged him into the next room. He shut the door and glared at him from behind his shades. He took a hit on the joint he had carried through with him and handed it to Steve.

'Listen, son, if you can't perform when you're called out, you're not entitled to go around calling yourself a guitar player and a poet. And that means you don't get to join the guild and you don't get to hang out with people like me.'

Steve was shocked by the vehemence of the assault. He dragged absentmindedly on the joint, realising that it was yet another over-strength one, which briefly left him spluttering impotently, his head spinning. When he had regained his composure he managed to say, 'Jed, you're a brilliant player. I can't come anywhere near you. I wasn't really calling myself a guitar player. It's just something I have in common with the people I've met lately.'

Jed was right in his face, huge, lowering, exuding primal aggression. 'Like your chick's ex and nancy boy Matt?'

This was vile. It seemed Ginny had filled him in on quite a lot.

'I don't know whether Matt's a good player or not, but he was the first person I met who knew about your book, which I only discovered myself in the last couple of months. He's been very supportive. I'm only just getting to work. If I tried to follow you with a song, I'd just humiliate myself.'

'Humiliate yourself, then. Otherwise you're going nowhere. All that pride is just cowardice. Humiliate yourself, feel the hurt and fight back. When I was your age, I was a purist too, perfect Bebop progressions, but I was starving, sleeping on the street. I heard this guy busking the blues and spoke to him. He was making a packet. Juilliard trained, but busking in Frisco. A year or two later, he was on every hit record you could think of. I thought, I'll do the same, get my blues chops together and head back East. The rest is mythology.'

'Jed. I don't even know what a Bebop progression is.'

'Okay. Let me put it this way. If you don't go out there now and play something, anything, I'm gonna lay your chick. She's mine already, anyway.'

Steve was angry now. 'If you lay one finger on her . . .'

Looking at Jed's meaty shoulders and strong hands, Steve wasn't sure what might be a credible threat.

'What?' Jed sneered, poking Steve hard on the sternum. 'You'll do exactly what? That chick's too hot for you anyway. She's lost, and there's nothing you can do to rescue her.'

'She's not. She's amazingly talented and strong and wise.'

'Like I said, too hot for you.'

'So, what? I should just abandon her to people like you?'

'She's mine. You have to take her off me. You've got to sing.'

Recently, plenty of things hadn't made sense. But Jed must surely be off his trolley. He'd only met Ginny a few hours previously.

'Fuck you, Jed, you don't get to tell me what to do, just because I'm reading your fucking book. You were playing a sideshow at the festival. I don't suppose Arlo and Loudon had to bum a lift back to Cambridge.'

A big smile spread across Jed's face. 'That's more like it. Now go out there and just pick my guitar up. Oh, and one more thing, take another hit on this.'

He handed the joint back to Steve, who took a tentative drag and then opened the door to Tom's living room and swayed unsteadily across to where Jed's Martin rested in its case. He lifted it out, feeling the coiled energy in the gleaming wood and slivery strings. He sat down on the chair Jed had used and rested the curve of the guitar's body on his right knee. Tom's eyes were smiling and Ginny's earlier disinterested cool was now replaced with something approaching expectancy. Jed stood in the doorway filling the frame.

Steve ran his fingers experimentally across the strings. It was a beautiful guitar, resonant bass, detailed midtone and crystal clear treble. The action was perfect, not too high, but not rattling against the frets either. A guitar like that practically played itself. He started into 'Stormy Monday Blues'. The version he knew was based on the T-Bone Walker changes with sliding semitone shifts, and a pattern of minor seventh chords before the final couplet of each verse which gave it a nice jazzy feel. This enabled him to show off some of Jed's shapes. Even so he kept it real slow. When he had played through a set of changes, he embarked gingerly on the lyrics of the first verse. 'They call it stormy Monday, but Tuesday is just as bad.'

That didn't go too badly, but he was far from feeling secure in his ability to get through the whole thing without blowing up. He kept it tight for the second verse before letting rip on 'Lord have mercy on me' in the third verse, pouring his soul into the final couplet, 'I'm trying to find my baby / Won't somebody please send her back to me' and then riding the song home on a full set of changes without any vocals. He let the last chord fade before hitting the 12th fret harmonics, cheesy he knew, but irresistible.

There was a moment of silence before his small audience broke into applause. Ginny was beaming at him. Jed came over, put his big meaty hand on Steve's shoulder and said, 'Welcome to the guild, son,' and leaning forward whispered quietly into his ear, 'She's yours. You deserve her.'

Steve felt weak. He couldn't believe he'd got through a song in public with Jed Morgan himself in his small audience. The memory of the brutality that Jed had unleashed earlier hadn't entirely faded, but was being overwritten by an altogether more positive vibe. Jed had been helping him, but he still felt bruised by the encounter. He handed the guitar back to Jed.

'That's a beautiful instrument.'

Jed got out a cloth and ran it over the strings. 'One day your own instrument will find you. Don't rush it. An expensive guitar is not necessarily the best one. And the right guitar might take time to reveal itself. Some need a lot of playing in. But be careful not to take the fire out of it.'

Jed put the guitar back in its case and said he really ought to be getting back to his hotel now. It had been a great day. He refused to let Steve drive him. He was in no fit state drive, a view with which Ginny was in agreement. They should be heading home too. They could pick up the van the following day. The visitors thanked Tom for his hospitality and made their way towards Mill Road, parting with Jed at the corner of Parker's Piece. Jed said that he would let them know when he had another gig in Britain and if they were ever in Toulouse they should look him up.

The goodbye kiss between Jed and Ginny was a little too full-on for Steve's liking, but he had reason to be grateful to Jed, and extended his hand. Of course, Jed was not the sort of guy who simply shook hands. Not for him the conventional gentleman's handshake where the thumb extends over the back of the hand with a respectful space between the participants. Instead Jed flipped their hands so that each hand clasped the counterpart's wrist at the base of the thumb, at the same time drawing Steve towards him, so that their faces were almost touching. 'We'll meet again. Let me know how your song ends.'

Steve searched for Jed's eyes, but all he could see was his own reflection in Jed's shades. He realised that he hadn't seen Jed's eyes the whole time they'd been together. After a moment during which it seemed that something flowed between them, Jed released him, turned and strode off into the night, raising a clenched fist in farewell.

On their way back down Mill Road, Steve said to Ginny, 'Well, I didn't expect to be spending the day with Jed Morgan.'

'No, it all turned out rather well.'

'He certainly took a shine to you.'

'Musicians on the road are like that.'

'It made me feel a bit uncomfortable.'

'I would say that's Jed's modus operandi. If it puts you off him, that's no bad thing. Don't confuse the artist and the person.'

But if I hadn't been there, would you have made it with him?'

'Steve, you've got some strange ideas about me. I'm not gagging for sex with all and sundry. You fulfil my sexual needs.'

'Is that all?'

'Isn't that enough to be going on with? What more do you want from me?'

Steve couldn't answer that question immediately. 'I don't know. I just don't want to lose you.'

'That's just possessiveness. I'm not a chattel. You have to earn the right to be in a relationship, day by day. We both do. We have to renew the relationship all the time or it will die.'

Snarky Bards

The Arts Theatre,
Monday, 29 July 1974

STEVE WOKE EARLY ON the Monday morning conscious that a new phase of his working life was about to begin. He felt oddly nervous, in a way that he hadn't when he'd begun the milk round. And yet, surely working in the theatre was more suitable for the kind of person he considered himself to be. But if the last few months had proved anything, it was that the image he had himself was not strongly rooted. The acid trip had only speeded up a process of psychological realignment that had been going on since he had arrived in Cambridge.

A job in the theatre, as Angie had shrewdly pointed out, was hardly something that he had set as a goal for himself. He had stumbled into it. Mightn't it just be another example of his tendency to temporize, to put off what he really ought to be doing? Perhaps. On the other hand, he was rather proud of his ability to improvise. No doubt what he ought to be doing and what he wanted to do were different things. And right at that moment, what he really wanted to do, apart from staying in bed with Ginny, was to get on with his poem in the light of the experiences of the last few days.

He was rescued from this train of thought by Ginny waking and rolling over to embrace him. He kissed her and said, 'You're incorrigible.' She moved her hand towards his groin and said, 'So are you.' As she moved closer to him, he said, 'I'm not sure we've got time.' But

Ginny was not to be deterred, and on reflection, Steve couldn't think of a better way to inaugurate this new phase in his life.

For his first day in the box office, Steve had been assigned to the late shift which meant starting at lunchtime and sharing the afternoon session with Seb and the evening session with Fiona, the manageress. He was a little alarmed at the prospect of Seb being in charge of his orientation programme, but he needn't have worried because there was none. Seb pointed to the seating charts, observing that it had been a slow morning and almost immediately went off for his lunch. Fortunately trade did not pick up in Seb's absence, much to Steve's relief and he found himself surreptitiously reading *The Guardian* from cover to cover to while away the time. It got busier in the early afternoon, but not much, and Steve and Seb spent the next couple of hours chatting. Seb might have had an idiosyncratic approach to inducting a new colleague, but Steve found him to be an amusing if somewhat voluble workmate.

He had soon provided Steve with an improbably detailed account of his life. He had grown up in Cambridge, dropped out of a course at the Tech to take up with Graham, a man twenty or so years his senior, much to the dismay of Seb's family. Graham, it transpired, was a successful graphic designer and had worked on Alan Aldridge's *The Butterfly Ball*. He and Seb lived in a 30s house on Milton Road, which they had furnished with classic items of mid-century furniture. Steve must come and have tea with them soon. He would certainly be impressed.

Seb was also a terrible gossip. By the time Fiona came in, Steve knew who was sleeping with whom at the theatre, the precise details of a particular individual's medical condition, the financial difficulties that the Arts found itself in, the tensions between front of house and backstage and much more. Steve quickly realised that no piece of information was safe with Seb. Once he knew something, so would everyone else at the theatre. Steve made sure to provide only the briefest of details about his own background, provoking Seb to say, 'Ooh, I do love a man with a bit of mystique. What terrible secret are you hiding? Do tell.'

Steve assured him that there was nothing to tell. Seb wasn't convinced.

Once Fiona arrived, Steve took his own break and, after consuming a toasted ham and cheese sandwich from the little snack bar between the stage door and Red House Records in St Edward's Passage, spent the rest of his break in the public library at the back of the Guildhall.

The second half of his shift was much busier especially in the hour before curtain up for that evening's performance. But Fiona had finished cashing up by nine o'clock and Steve thought that he might have a quick pint in the Eagle before heading back to Ainsworth Street.

He went into the little side bar which he preferred to the back bar with the ceiling graffitied by wartime bomber crews, ordered a pint of Abbot and found a table. He pulled out his notebook and jotted down a few impressions of his day. He was trying to capture something of Seb's conversational style when he heard a familiar voice saying, 'Well, hello. Didn't know this was one of your watering holes.'

It was Gary. Standing with him was a broad-shouldered, barrel-chested guy in his mid-thirties.

'Hi, Gary. Now I'm working at the Arts, I imagine I'll be in here quite a lot.'

'As a matter of fact this fine fellow I'm drinking with also works at the Arts, but on the stage crew. Butch, this is Steve.'

Steve nodded at Butch, who said with a big grin on his face, 'Nice to meet you, petal. How's your knob?'

That was a new one on Steve, who affirmed that, the last time he'd checked, his knob was fine.

Gary laughed. 'Butch is incorrigible. But I'm the one who's doing the tempting here. I'm afraid I can't say more than that at the moment.'

Steve wasn't sure why it was necessary to be so mysterious, but these thoughts were interrupted by Butch. 'Have you looked around backstage yet, petal? I'd be delighted to give you a guided tour. Just ask for me with the stage door keeper.'

Steve thanked Butch and said that he'd drop by in the next couple of days. Gary said that he and Butch would leave Steve to his beer, but suggested that if Steve took up Butch's offer, not to get stuck in the prop room with him. He was a notorious lech.

Butch winked at Steve as he and Gary took their drinks outside and said, 'Take's one to know one, petal.'

Steve chuckled to himself. He soon finished his drink and stepped out into the courtyard and headed for the gates of the old coaching inn, waving to Gary and Butch who were sitting at one of the outside tables deep in conversation.

* * *

The next day, Seb was once again in charge of Steve's induction. They were busier than they had been the previous day, no doubt due to a favourable review of *Kismet* that had appeared in the Cambridge Evening News.

Just before lunch the doors to the auditorium opened, revealing the mighty bulk of Butch. He strode up to the window box office and greeted Seb with his customary 'Hello, petal'.

Seb simpered. 'Not often we see you at the box office.'

Butch ignored whatever implication Seb was trying to convey. 'Is Steve in there with you?'

Seb uttered a conspiratorial *Ooh* and told Steve that Butch wanted a word with him. Steve frowned as he opened the door to the foyer. 'Hello, Butch. How's things?'

'I wondered when your break was. Thought I'd show you around backstage.'

'Not for an hour or so unfortunately,' Steve replied.

Seb had overheard the exchange. 'I don't mind holding the fort. You can take the early break. A backstage tour with Butch is an opportunity not to be missed. But watch out for those dark corners.'

Steve said that he'd already been warned, but thanked Seb, who said that he'd give some thought to how Steve could repay the favour.

Butch suggested they get a sandwich first from the sandwich bar in St Edward's Passage. A few moments later Butch pushed open the door to the little shop and squeezed inside, his huge bulk seeming to fill the entire space. 'Hello, Rita. This is Steve, he's just started working in the box office.'

'Hello, dear, you were in here yesterday, weren't you?'

Steve confirmed her supposition. Butch ordered two toasted cheese and ham sandwiches to carry out and refused Steve's offer to pay. 'We'll have them in the prop room,' he explained.

They walked the few paces from the sandwich bar and turned into the stage door set in the embrasure of the big doors to the scene dock. Butch introduced Steve to Howard, the stage doorkeeper. 'Howie. This is Steve. He's just started working in the box office.'

Steve poked his head through the little window and greeted Howard. He noticed that the stage door office also served as a little cloakroom for the restaurant upstairs and a reception desk for the administration offices.

Steve followed Butch through the inner door and found himself in the scene dock and the space that gave access to the backstage area, to one side of which was a small door through which Butch now disappeared. Steve followed him into what appeared to be part store and part kitchen. Most of the room was used to store tools and equipment but there were also chairs and a table at one end next to a sink and an area for making tea and coffee.

Butch asked Steve what he'd like to drink. Steve chose coffee and asked, 'So, what is this room?'

'This is the prop room, petal. but it's also where the stage crew hang out.'

They ate their sandwiches and sipped the tasteless coffee that Butch had made. Steve had done a small amount of student drama and was rather surprised at the location of the scene dock doors. Butch said, 'It's certainly not ideal. The closest you can park a truck is outside the shops in Peas Hill. So everything that comes through those doors has to be carried along St Edward's Passage. That means there's plenty of scope for things to get wet or for pedestrians to get in the way. Fortunately, most get-outs are late on a Saturday night, and most get-ins on a Sunday.'

When they had finished their lunch, Butch led the way back into the scene dock and turned left to bring them to the stage left wings. He pointed to a black and silver desk squeezed into the space just behind the base of one of the legs of the proscenium arch. It looked like a space age version of a Davenport desk, with a series of switches on a console above a sloped surface large enough to accommodate a sizeable prompt book. The desk was also equipped with an intercom headset and what looked like a microphone on a flexible metal stalk. The wall to the left of the desk sported more switches, a row of phones, a couple of large red buttons labelled STOP, a fire extinguisher and a grill marked SPRINKLER RELEASE. Butch gestured at the desk. 'This is where everything is run from. If you ever make it to deputy stage manager, this will be your station.'

They then walked onto the stage and looked out into the auditorium. It was a pretty little theatre with stalls, a circle, and two boxes. The seats were in red plush and the walls were surfaced in wood veneer with vestigial Art Deco detailing. Butch turned and looked upwards. 'That's the flying grid up there.'

Steve looked up. 'Phew, that's high.'

'Well, actually it's not really. This is a funny little theatre. The back wall of the stage is not even square, not parallel with the front of the stage in other words. Something to do with a dispute between King's

College, which was Keynes's college and Corpus Christi College, when the theatre was being built.'

They walked to the opposite prompt side. Butch pointed to the cable that operated the house curtains, or 'tabs' as he called them, and the fly gallery, which towered above them and stretched to the back wall of the stage. 'That's where I normally work. Have you got a head for heights?'

Steve nodded. They walked to the back of the stage and climbed a metal ladder to the fly gantry. Butch pointed out how each of the cables ran up to the grid, which was the metal structure that spanned the stage area, and down to a counterweight. Some of the cables were marked with a piece of white tape. 'So we know where to stop the cable when we're flying in a piece of scenery without having to look at the stage. Mortal sin to let anything hit the deck with a bang. Here, have a go. Don't pull hard, it's all nicely balanced.'

Butch released the brake on one of the cables and Steve gave it an experimental pull. It moved smoothly and silently. Butch took over, moved it back to its original position and re-engaged the brake. They clambered back down the ladder, re-crossed the stage, turned right past the prompt desk and descended some stairs. At the bottom, Butch said, 'This is the green room, where the actors sit, when they're not needed on stage. The dressing rooms are over there and the under stage space for when we use the trap door is over there. It also gives the band access to the orchestra pit, which we're using at the moment because *Kismet* is a musical. When we don't need a pit, we can put in two more rows of stalls seats. It's a bit of a bugger setting it up and taking it down, to be honest. The main thing we use it for is the annual pantomime.'

Steve poked his head into one of the dressing rooms, which struck him as being rather dingy and on the snug side for the six people it could accommodate to judge from the number of mirrors. Not much privacy in there, he imagined.

They went back up to the stage level and then stepped down into the auditorium through what Butch called the pass door. 'This door is fire proof and an important part of the theatre's fireproofing along with the safety curtain, so the audience can be isolated from any fire that breaks out on the stage. Fire is a big worry in theatres and the word should never be used when there are members of the public in the theatre. Instead we use the expression "Mr Sands is in the house".'

As they walked up the lefthand aisle to the back of the stalls, Butch pointed to the back of the circle and said, 'That's the lighting and sound control room up there. I'll take you up there another time.' He opened the doors at the back of the auditorium and ushered Steve into the foyer. 'So now you know your way around. And Howard knows you too. Drop by when the rest of the crew are here and I'll introduce you.'

Steve thanked Butch for his kindness and went back to the box office.

Seb was grinning mischievously. "What took you so long. How long does a blowjob take?'

'You've got a one track mind, Seb, nothing like that.'

'Well, why would Queen Butch show you around backstage then? Never happened to me.'

'Butch is a friend of a friend. I bumped into him in the Eagle last night after work. I think he's just doing it as a favour to this guy, Gary.'

'Likely story,' said Seb. 'Anyway, I'm starving.' With that he handed over to Steve and went out for his break.

Steve wasn't convinced either. It was almost as if he were literally being shown the ropes before starting a new job. Not that there had been any such talk. And in any case he doubted that Mike Wallace would be any too pleased if he lost his maternity cover staff member to the stage crew within a few days of Steve starting.

It was the day of Rob's party. On the assumption that this gathering was unlikely to be as sophisticated as Grace's, Ginny had decided to wear a deco-patterned maxi Biba dress with long sleeves and gathered shoulders and a plunging neckline, together with a pair of pale pink stacked high heels and, to finish off, a little beret and silk scarf. Privately, Steve thought that Ginny's idea of a more informal outfit was not what most people would consider as dressing down, but he had to admit that she looked amazing. As a concession to the importance of the evening for Steve, she had allowed him to revert to his normal get-up of jeans, tee shirt and plimsolls. But once again she was unable to resist putting some kohl around his eyes and styling his hair.

As they made their way to Rob's, they looked like a very ill-sorted couple, Ginny tottering on her platform shoes, dressed to the nines, and Steve affecting the careless teenager look. A casual observer might have supposed that a scruffy youth was escorting his older sister to a smart party before he went on to the ten pin bowling alley.

Steve rang the doorbell of the little house in Aylestone Road not far from the path that led to the Fort St George footbridge. After a few moments, the front door was opened by Robin. 'Steve, Ginny so glad you could make it. Come in.'

He waved them into the narrow hallway. 'Lots of people here already. Some you'll know. A lot of poets, I'm afraid. But really they're quite harmless, unless you get them talking about, Charles Olsen, or Louis Zukofsky.'

'I don't even know who those people are,' replied Ginny, 'so there's little chance that I'll be taking part in such conversations.'

Steve pushed the bottle of wine that they had brought at Robin. 'You're not making me feel more comfortable about this, Rob. Please don't put me in any kind of embarrassing situations.'

Rob ignored this plea. 'Well, I'm afraid there is a bit of a situation. Martin Lockwood is coming later and he wants to talk to you about *Event/Horizon*.'

'Rob, that's a low blow.'

Rob wasn't in a mood to accept Steve's absurd sensitivities. 'You gave me permission to talk to him. And he wanted to talk to you. You can't be completely invisible. You have to manifest yourself to a few disciples. Come through and stop being so pernickety.'

Ginny gave Steve a shove in the back and Robin led them into the back room. The house was bigger than the Ainsworth Street house, but not by much. The room was full of young men, many bearded, some wearing safari jackets, all engaged in intense conversation. There were few women, but those few were much in demand. Steve was surprised to see so many people from the Cambridge poetry scene considering that it was the middle of the summer vacation. When Robin had told him that there would be a lot of Cambridge poets and theorists at the party, he had only half believed him, reflecting that most of them would not be back in Cambridge for some weeks, but it seemed that Rob had spoken truthfully.

Robin asked Steve and Ginny what they wanted to drink and went through to the kitchen to fulfil their requests. When Rob was out of earshot Steve turned to Ginny and said, 'We don't have to stay long. We can have a drink and then go.'

Ginny shook her head. 'Stop being so childish, Steve. Rob's helping you out here. You're going to have to tough it out.'

'This isn't my natural habitat,' protested Steve.

Ginny was not convinced.

She gazed around the room. Their entrance had not gone unnoticed by the other guests. Steve had also been conscious of the synchronisation of the collective gaze as they entered the room. It had, of course little to do with with his own presence and everything to do with the dark and mysterious Aphrodite, who accompanied him. Eventually one youth plucked up the courage to approach them.

'Steve, great to see you. Back for the Words and Music Festival?'

'No, I've been here all summer.'

'Getting a head start on your research, then?'

'I'm not doing postgraduate work, actually. I've been working as a milkman.'

'Really?' The newcomer felt sure that Steve was winding him up, which to an extent he was. Not for the first time Steve was dimly aware that he seemed to prefer presenting himself to the world as milkman rather than the box office clerk that he now was. What on earth was that about? Turning his face to the impassive Ginny the newcomer continued, 'Anyway, Steve, aren't you going to introduce me?'

Reluctantly, Steve did the honours, 'Ginny, this is Nick. Nick, Ginny.'

As was her wont, Ginny's demeanour scarcely changed, but Nick, emboldened by the introduction, immediately asked, 'And what do you do, Ginny?'

Steve grimaced at Nick's gauche enquiry, but Ginny replied smoothly, 'I work in the fashion industry, I used to be a model.'

'Would I have seen you in Cosmo or the Sunday Times colour supplement? You do look familiar. Or do you do catalogue work?'

'No, mainly magazines like Vogue and Harper's.'

Nick was not quite sure how to take this. It didn't really make sense that Steve Percival, a famous slacker, would turn up at a Cambridge poetry scene party with a catwalk goddess on his arm and Nick was reduced to observing, 'We don't get many models at our gatherings.'

'So it would appear,' said Ginny, surveying the room.

Nick turned his attention back to Steve. 'I gather Martin's going to run a substantial piece of yours in *Outwrite*.'

'Yes, I believe so, but I've had no direct communication with Martin myself. Rob has acted as the go-between.'

'Well, congratulations, anyway. I heard that Martin might put in an appearance later on.'

The conversation faltered. Nick said, 'I could do with another drink. Can I get you two anything?'

Steve said, 'No thanks, Nick. Rob's getting us something.'

When Nick had disappeared into the kitchen, they caught each other's eye and Ginny said, 'Relax.'

Steve was going to suggest that Ginny take her own advice, but at that moment Rob reappeared with two glasses of wine in his hands.

'Sorry that took so long. Kept getting trapped in conversations. I hope you'll help yourselves after this.'

Steve immediately felt guilty about his panic on the doorstep. 'Rob, I'm sorry about earlier. I really am grateful to you. I'm just very nervous about having to talk about my poem to Martin Lockwood.'

'You'll be fine, Steve. He's a really nice guy and he wouldn't ask to meet you if he didn't like your stuff. Just be yourself.'

Ginny thought it was time to change the subject 'What I'd like to know is. Is there going to be any dancing?'

Rob laughed. 'I'm sure there could be, especially if you kicked things off, Ginny.'

'Then you'd better put something more danceable on the hifi.'

Rob did as he was commanded and a few seconds later 'Dancing in the Street' by Martha Reeves and the Vandellas started pumping out of the loudspeakers. Ginny grabbed Steve's hand, pulled him into the middle of the room and started cutting some neat shapes. Whatever expectations Steve had had of the party beforehand, it certainly had not included his performing an exhibition dance in front of a gathering of Cambridge poets, but to have shown reluctance would have put him in an even more uncomfortable position. There was nothing for it. He would have to look as though he was a fully paid up extrovert. In fact he was not a negligible dancer in the modern mode. He had perfected an effective way of mirroring and highlighting his partner's moves and threw himself into this approach now. Ginny caught his eye and gave him the tiniest smile of encouragement.

Next up was 'I Can't Help Myself' by the Four Tops. Soon other couples and number of solo dancers joined them on what passed for a dance floor. There was very little space to move, but the constraint called forth varying degrees of innovation, from the catatonic to the epileptic.

Having shaken things up, Ginny said, 'Let's get a drink.'

They threaded their way through to the kitchen and got a couple of glasses of wine. The backdoor that led to the garden was open and an evening breeze was wafting in. Ginny pulled Steve into the garden, pushed him up against the wall and kissed him hard.

'You're a sexy guy, Steve Percival. I've got the hots for you.'

Steve was certainly not averse to a smooch, but when Ginny reached for his fly he said, 'Ginny, not here, not with that lot in there.'

She threw her head back and laughed. 'I'm glad you thought I was serious.'

'Lady, my starting point is that you are serious about everything. I'll have to know you a darn sight better, before I know when you're not serious.'

Ginny removed her hand from his fly and kissed him tenderly this time, holding his head in both hands. As they were coming out of this clinch Rob appeared in the kitchen doorway.

'I wondered if I might find you two out here. Sorry to interrupt. I realise that this is a new relationship and you can't keep your hands off each other, but Martin and Marion have just arrived. They're in the kitchen. It's not as noisy as the other room. I'll introduce you.'

Steve wiped his mouth with the back of his hand to remove any lipstick traces and said, 'Yes, of course.'

Ginny smiled to herself and straightened out Steve's rumpled shirt. They followed Rob into the little kitchen where a middle aged couple were standing by the kitchen table trying to choose something they could bear to drink from the bottles of cheap wine arrayed before them. The man was dressed in Levi jeans, cowboy boots, a Brooks Brothers button down Oxford shirt and a leather jacket, the woman was wearing a long purple Indian print dress with contrasting short sleeves in red and an Indian silk scarf, with silver bangles at her wrists.

Rob said, 'Martin, Marion, this is Steve Percival, and this is Ginny his partner. Sorry, Ginny, I don't know your second name.'

'Stern,' said Ginny, raising her chin. 'Pleased to meet you.'

Rob continued with the introductions. 'As I'm sure you know, Steve, Martin and Marion run Silken Twine on Magdalene Street and Martin publishes a whole raft of poetry publications through the Intrinsic Spin imprint and of course *Outwrite*, which is the purpose of bringing you together this evening.'

Martin said, 'Steve, it's great to meet at last. Rob has spoken a lot about you. But you are clearly an elusive fellow.'

'Great to meet you too, Martin. Of course I've been into your shop, many times, mainly for the poetry readings, but I've never had the courage to read myself.'

'Well, maybe we can get you on the bill, when the next issue of *Outwrite* with your piece in it finally sees the light of day. It always seems a miracle to me that we ever manage to get an issue out. Of course, the poetry magazine scene is much healthier since Eric Mottram and Bob Cobbing mounted their coup at the National Poetry Society, but it doesn't make publishing a little magazine any easier. And it now means we have real competition from the mainstream in providing a platform for innovative writing.'

Steve confessed that he was not *au courant* with events at the National Poetry Society. Martin explained that Poetry Review had been a moribund journal for many years. Administered by the mandarins of the Arts Council, it had promoted poetry of an extraordinarily conservative and narrow range. But following the International Poetry Incarnation at the Albert Hall in 1965, starring and inspired by Allen Ginsberg, the radical poetry scene in Britain had taken off. By the summer of 1971 Eric Mottram had been appointed as the editor of Poetry Review. Immediately, a much wider range of poetry had become available in the journal, a not entirely welcome development to the panjandrums in the higher echelons of the Arts Council or to a vociferous section of the Poetry Society's membership.

As Martin was sketching out these developments, Steve was conscious that the two women were not being included in the conversation. He also noticed that Rob had slipped away to effect other introductions. Steve needn't have worried. Ginny and Marion had made an immediate connection based on the clothes they were wearing; Ginny praising the Indian print dress and silk scarf that Marion was wearing, Marion reciprocating in her appreciation of Ginny's classic Biba outfit. Once Ginny realised that the fabric that Marion's dress was made from was available in Martin and Marion's shop, she said she'd be there first thing on Monday morning to look through their stock.

Steve returned his attention to Martin, who was saying that despite the welcome developments at the National Poetry Society, the radical wing of the UK poetry scene was still way behind developments in the USA and still seriously fragmented, for the most part based on location or clustered around charismatic or energetic individuals, in the case of Cambridge very much centred around Jeremiah Flynn. Steve was, of course, aware of Flynn's influence. He admired what he had read of Flynn's work, but he was reluctant to be pulled into his orbit, and even more apprehensive about the effect that Flynn's style was having on his own work.

'I'm trying to stay away from Flynn. He's such a powerful voice and technically so assured.'

'Everyone has to learn, needs time to develop, even Flynn. He doesn't like to be reminded of his first collection *Half Nelson*.'

Steve had not been aware of the fact that there had been a collection before *Landslide*. He wondered whether it was still possible to get hold of a copy. If not, he ought to be able to find it in a library.

Martin took a sip of his cheap wine and grimaced. 'So, what is your own approach to composition? I notice that, rather like Flynn, you introduce all sorts of material into *Event/Horizon* that one doesn't often find in a poem. But whereas Flynn introduces geology and botany, you seem to have a lot of material derived from recent theoretical physics and cosmology. I presume you are not a theoretical physicist.'

'No, but I have a friend who is an astronomer, and was the first person to detect, in a manner of speaking, a black hole and I thought I could use the image of this new kind of constellation.'

'And so you incorporated these ideas into the poem?'

'It wasn't really part of any compositional strategy. In general I don't think first and then write, I think *through* writing. Or at least that's the way it seems. So, as I wrote, these images started to emerge, the idea that the self I created through writing, the event horizon, if you like, was at some remove from the real self, which in one sense is empty, but which in another is very dense and compacted, and, crucially, inaccessible to introspection. Hence a black hole.'

'Would I be doing violence to your image if I were to equate the self of the black hole with the Freudian unconscious?'

'No, that would also be a resonance and in fact an early working title was *Self/Contained*. The trouble with Freudian metapsychology is that it's a fertile hunting ground for cultural schismatics. Cosmology and astrophysics have not been colonised by liberal arts freebooters to quite the same extent.'

'Is that how you see yourself then, a freebooter? A pirate?'

'Even the lone voice crying in the wilderness shares a language.'

'Indeed. I presume you must have discussed these ideas with others whilst you were writing the piece?'

'Not really. I'm constantly disappointed, I suppose, both at my failure to engage in real dialogue with other writers and also at their failure to prompt that in me. Of course, there are exceptions. Rob is a mate and I owe him a lot. But we don't really talk theory or praxis. We're not having this ongoing debate about poetics. We're much more likely to be talking about the latest Dylan, or Joni Mitchell album. And to be quite honest, even though we're mates, we're also competitors or antagonists and always have been.'

'You don't feel part of a distinct generation of poets, then?'

'Not really. But I suppose there must be a group identity that is obvious to outsider observers. If I had to guess, I would say it was marked by the rejection of forms that are just a series of examples, the circular poem, the well-made poem. That's why so many of us have adopted the sequence.'

'So, let me try and sum up my understanding of your poetics. The idea of binary relationships gives you a very useful motor with which to generate the sequences of your poem: the binary pair of the unthinking self and the constructed self, the binary pair of a visible star rapidly orbiting a black hole, and the binary pair of an image and its referent.

'But it seems to me that perhaps there is another opposition which is not overt in your poem, but which gives it a lot of its energy and that is your relationship with Flynn, which I read as a negative one. In the poetic constellation, to use your term, in which you operate, Flynn equates to the black hole that holds other bodies in its gravitational grip, a grip which will ultimately destroy them. It may be that the deconstruction that takes place under this intense pressure, or centripetal force we might say, creates a force field in which those bodies can locate their own poetic selves. But ultimately the process is cannibalistic. The structure is not at all stable and certainly not a constellation of equals. In your case, however, the polarity is reversed, so that a centrifugal force is moving you away from the centre.'

As Steve was reflecting on this very succinct encapsulation and extension of his own rambling explanation, he noticed from the corner of his eye that Marion was hovering nearby. Taking advantage of Steve's silence, she mentioned quietly to Martin, that he was neglecting other people.

Martin moved smoothly to her side.'Of course, my dear. I'm sorry. I was fascinated by Steve's account of the genesis of *Event/Horizon*.' Then, addressing Steve, 'I'll try and get some proofs to you soon, and I'd like you to put some of what you've just been saying into a preface or introduction.'

BLACK DOG

STEVE WOKE THE NEXT morning feeling pleased with life. The gamble he had taken at the end of May when he had finished his Finals seemed to be paying off. His poem had been granted an imprimatur by one of the most significant impresarios on the poetry circuit at a gathering of Cambridge poets. As a bonus his muse, who had caused a considerable stir at that same gathering, had anointed him in a rather more erotic way afterwards. He rolled over to share his sense of contentment with Ginny, but she pushed him away. Only mildly disappointed, he decided to go downstairs and make a cup of coffee. On his way down, he went into his writing room and picked up his notepad. Even if his current muse was exhausted by the exercise of her duties, his former muse might take some pleasure in hearing about his recent experiences.

A few minutes later seated at the kitchen table with a mug of coffee to hand he began a letter to Angie. There was a lot to tell her. He knew that she would be shocked to learn that he had taken acid, but he wanted to reassure her that he was not on the rocky road to dissolution. It had been one of the most profound experiences of his life. Chemically induced profundity was routinely mocked by those who had never had the experience. No doubt Eliot had had something

276

else in mind, but having had the experience, it was practically impossible to miss the meaning.

What the acid had done for Steve was to reveal that everyday life, ordinary perception was a construct, a projection. Most of the time we were automata, seldom examining our preconceptions, the mind trundling along in its well-worn ruts. The tiny pill disclosed how pre-programmed we actually were. At the same time, it didn't completely undermine those preconceptions. It just made the familiar strange, the *heimlich unheimlich*, as he'd suggested to Rob. Certainly, many people might find exposure to this kind of radical revaluation threatening, but on the strength of this first experience, Steve was prepared to assert that its effects were only beneficial.

He told Angie that a lot of the credit must go to Ginny. She couldn't have organised things better. He'd felt confident in her care. Steve admitted that the only moment he had doubted this was when they had walked down Mill Road to The Locomotive. That part of the trip had initially been a bit scary, but he had quickly adapted. He was glad that Ginny had persuaded him to go out, because it had been instructive to apprehend the negatives of contemporary life, as well as the positives. But The Locomotive had been a haven, and the jukebox, which he had always loved anyway, a different kind of revelation.

He also tried as best he could to describe the sense of ego loss and the feeling of giving birth to a new version of himself, although he thought it best not to go into the feeling of dissolving into another person during sex, nor to discuss how the relationship was developing.

He then told her about how positive Rob had been about *Event/ Horizon* and that he had passed it to Martin Lockwood, who owned Silken Twine in Magdalene Street and ran Intrinsic Spin. Lockwood liked the poem and was going to publish an extract in *Outwrite*. Steve knew that he hadn't always been very kind about Rob, and had been irritated by his persistence in asking to see the poem. But he really owed him a lot. And he was also grateful to Ginny because she had given him a portable typewriter, which had enabled him to type the poem up. He was pretty sure that Martin Lockwood would have been unlikely to have read a handwritten poem, especially one as long as *Event/Horizon*. He told her about Rob's leaving party and the meeting with Martin and he also said that he and Ginny had been to dinner with Grace Mitchell, his former supervisor, and her husband, Peter Newman, the boss of Inflexion Books.

Finally, he realised that Angie had no idea that he had quit his job at the dairy and started work at the Arts Theatre. He gave a brief idea of what his days were now like and described his new colleagues. He hadn't meant to write so much and realised with a shock that a couple of hours had passed. And there was still no sign of Ginny.

He went out into the kitchen, made some tea and took it up to her. Putting the mug of tea on the bedside table, he sat on the edge of the bed. 'Ginny,' he called gently.

Ginny's muffled voice came from under the blankets, 'Go away. I don't want to talk.'

'Why? What have I done?'

'You haven't done anything. Go away. I don't want to talk about it.'

Steve hesitated.

She reached out her hand towards him. 'I'm all right. We'll talk later.'

Steve picked up his own mug of tea and went back downstairs. He wondered what it was that triggered her bouts of depression and how long they usually lasted. There was not much he could do right now other than keep her supplied with drinks and make sure that there was food in the house. He would go for a walk and pick up a few things for supper on his way back. It was lovely day and he could do with some fresh air. He scribbled a note for Ginny and put it at the bottom of the stairs, then went out.

He headed towards Parker's Piece. On the way he put the letter to Angie in a pillar box. As he was crossing the huge expanse of grass, he heard someone calling his name. He looked around to see Grace Mitchell, dressed in running gear, jogging towards him. She reached him, puffing slightly and attractively flushed, and said, 'Thought it was you.'

'I didn't know you ran.' This wasn't exactly true. Not only had she told him that she had just come back from a run the day that he had taken his reader's report around to Glisson Road, but he had also seen her running across Parker's Piece some time before that.

'I don't think I could live without it. Mostly, I go out in the mornings. But the weather is so lovely today. And I was nodding off over my work.'

'I like running too. I used to do a bit myself, but I seem to have got out of the habit. I settled for a stroll instead.'

'No Ginny?'

'She's having a bit of a mood crash, a black dog. She told me she gets them. But this is the first one I've observed in the time we've been together. She said that I should just let her sleep and pull herself together.'

'Oh, Steve, I'm sorry. Depression is a terrible thing. Has anything happened to trigger it?'

'I don't think so. We had a great time when we came to yours for dinner. And then we've just been hanging out, enjoying being together. And that was all good too. Apart from that I have just been working on my poem. When I made you that copy, I also made one for a friend who's active in Cambridge poetry circles. He liked it. He's just had his first collection published by Intrinsic Spin and he asked me whether he could pass the poem to Martin Lockwood. He thought he could persuade him to publish an extract in *Outwrite*.'

Grace was delighted. 'So you no longer need my view of your work.'

'No, no, I'd like to hear what you have to say.'

'Well, why don't you come around one day next week?'

'I've started a new job at the Arts Theatre and so my timetable, while not as unsocial as the milk round, is a bit complex.'

'I see. What about if you joined me on one of my runs? We could talk about it then.'

Steve thought this was a crazy idea. 'But you said you normally run in the morning.'

'Yes. What's wrong with that? You're the guy who was a milkman. I'm not suggesting you get up at four-thirty. We could meet at seven-thirty and run for an hour or so.'

Steve was doubtful.

But Grace was adamant. 'What time do you start work?'

Steve admitted that the earliest he started was ten-thirty.

'Steve, that gives you plenty of time. I'm not asking you to start training for the Olympics. I'm sure a guy like you could run three miles in flip-flops. I'll be running on Tuesday. Why don't you join me?'

Steve was his usual indecisive self and mumbled that he'd try to make it, but Grace shouldn't count on him. Satisfied with her latest attempt to organise Steve's life, Grace said she'd better get along, but she hoped to see him outside her place in Glisson Road at seven-thirty on Tuesday morning. With that, she resumed her jogging and set off across Parker's Piece in the direction of Gresham Road. Steve watched her velour-clad bottom appreciatively and wondered, not for the first time, what on earth Grace Mitchell was up to.

When he got back to Ainsworth Street later, Ginny was still in bed. He went up to see how she was and found her still buried under the blankets. He sat on the edge of the bed and took her hand.

'Ginny, I'm really worried. Is there anything I can do or get you?'

Ginny shook her head 'Don't be worried. It'll pass. I warned you about this.'

'Yes, yes, but I'll be back at work tomorrow and so I'll be out for most of the day.'

'That's fine. I'll be okay. It's probably better if you're not around. You can get me a cup of tea though. Otherwise just leave me alone. I think it might be better if you slept in your own room tonight.'

When Steve got home from work the following day, she was still in bed, but at least she was sitting up. And also, after he had brought her a cup of tea, she permitted him to run a bath for her.

While she was in the bath, Steve tidied up the room, remade the bed and found a clean nightdress from the chest of drawers. Ginny returned wrapped in towels and thanked Steve for his efforts. She put on the clean nightdress and dried her hair. Steve sat on the edge of the bed and watched her, hoping that the resumption of care for her appearance was evidence of the fit of depression abating. When her hair was dry, she said she thought she'd get back into bed. Steve pulled back the bed clothes and said that he'd go downstairs and make something to eat. Back in the kitchen he realised the cupboard was notably bare. He had forgotten to pick up supplies on the way home. Cursing himself for being so thoughtless, he went across to the Empire Stores.

As he pushed open the door of the little shop, the tinkle of the bell brought old Bert from the back room. Over the weeks that Steve had been living in Ainsworth Street, he had become rather fond of Bert. Sadly, Bert had lost his wife a few years previously, but was determined to keep the shop going for as long as he could, even though he must now be in his seventies. Steve conjectured that it was unlikely that Bert made much of a profit. In fact he wouldn't have been surprised if Bert was actually subsiding the shop from his meagre pension or savings. It was hard to see anyone taking over the business once Bert had passed on.

Whatever meal Steve might be able to assemble from the Empire Stores' limited stock, he was pretty sure that it would be nowhere near the standard routinely achieved by Ginny. He scanned the shelves and decided that it was a toss up between the pork sausages and the fish fingers, plumping eventually for the sausages. Did Bert have any potatoes? He did, though once Steve saw the shrivelled tubers that Bert produced from behind the counter, he wasn't so sure. Unfortunately Bert had already put some into the pan of the scales and Steve didn't have the heart to change his mind. Bert bagged up the potatoes and asked Steve if he wanted anything else. Steve needed a vegetable to go with the manky spuds and the greasy bangers. His gaze lighted on a tin of Batchelor's peas, which he added to his order, suspecting that this was likely to be the only part of the meal that would be at all palatable.

Later when he had finished eating his own meal, Steve went up to see how Ginny was getting on. He was surprised to find that she had cleared her plate. Steve reflected that she had eaten very little over the previous couple of days and must be starving, even so he was rather proud that he had been able to produce a reasonably tasty meal from such unpromising materials. As he took her plate, she thanked him meekly for the meal, but said that she had still not completely re-covered her equilibrium and would keep to her bed.

On his way to bed, he realised that the following day was the day Grace had suggested he went running with her. Steve had started to warm to the idea, but had not yet been able to talk to Ginny about it. It was possible that she might take a dim view of this expansion of his relationship with Grace. But surely there was no harm in it. She certainly wouldn't thank him for waking her up to have that conversation now. Nor would she be better disposed to have the conversation at the seven o'clock the following morning. Maybe he should just do the run with Grace, get her feedback on *Event/Horizon* and only mention that Grace was involved, if it started to become a regular feature of his morning routine. He located his running shoes, shorts and tee shirt, set the alarm clock and fell into bed. He was soon asleep.

Steve arrived at Glisson Road just before seven-thirty the next morning. Grace emerged from her house a couple of minutes later and waved to him cheerfully. He was heartened to see that despite the early hour Grace was once again in brief shorts and a close-fitting tee shirt. She joined him on the pavement and said 'I'm glad you could make it. You won't regret it.'

Steve hoped that that would be the case, but confined his response to saying, 'Rather cold this morning.'

Grace laughed and said, 'Don't worry, we'll soon warm up.'

Steve had been a keen runner in his teenage years. He hadn't done much running in recent years, but he hadn't totally lost his fitness, thanks in large part to his weeks on the milk round. Grace was clearly a good runner and Steve let her set the pace. As they ran side by side, she suggested they head for Midsummer Common and see how they were doing for time, before deciding whether to go on as far as the river or to swing around and head back to Glisson Road.

Once they had got into their stride, Grace said, 'Do you want me to give you the good news or the bad news?'

'I prefer bad news first.'

'Well, you've got to deal with your phallocentrism, if you want to develop further as a poet.'

Steve was mystified not just by the nature of her diagnosis, but also by its specificity.

'But I thought you liked my stuff. You were positive about it when we came around to you for dinner.'

'You chose the bad news. The good news is that your work is promising. In the context of the dinner party, it was inappropriate to adopt a critical tone. But very few artists emerge fully formed. It's not helpful to any artist to have people going around saying, "Oh, wow! You're so great!". You know yourself that this poem in its current state is not the finished thing. The question is, are you prepared to try and make it better?'

Steve paced along in silence for a while. 'Of course, I want to make it better, but I'm not sure how to go about it. Angie thought it was a serious piece of work but that the language was not conventionally poetic. She said that one of the risks of being too avant-garde was the lack of an established audience. I would have to find a way to develop that audience. Ginny liked it, but said it lacked heart and that I needed to be braver and reveal more of myself. And you're saying that I've got to deal with my phallocentrism, which sounds as if I'm revealing too much. I'm not sure any of that helps me improve *Event/Horizon*. I was hoping that you at least could give me some practical advice.'

'Steve, things aren't that easy. You have every right to be proud of what you've done, but you can't treat it as your testament.'

Steve fell silent again enjoying the rhythm of their running, but irritated by the turn the conversation had taken.

After a little he said, 'What did you mean by dealing with my phallocentrism? It's not as if I'm the Don Juan of the biro.'

'Aren't you? You seem to have three attractive, not unintelligent women vying for your attention.'

'Three?' Steve was puzzled. 'There's only Ginny. Angie made it clear in her letter that things are over between us.'

'And there's been no further communication between you?'

'Well, yes, I did write to Angie a couple of days ago,' Steve admitted.

'I don't know her, of course, but I do know something about women and the way they respond to men. I would say that that particular relationship is far from over. At least not yet.'

'Okay. But there isn't anyone else. Who is the third?'

'Me, you idiot.'

'You? You're my teacher. Well, you were my teacher. I wouldn't presume . . .'

'You don't think I get into my running kit for all my students, do you?'

Steve was consumed with embarrassment.'You're married . . .'

'What's that got to do with anything? I may be too old for you, but you're not too young for me.'

'Of course you're not too old for me, if you know what I mean, not that I think of you like that.'

'Don't you? How do you think of me, Steve?'

'I think of you as a really intelligent, wise, erudite person. And also, I now realise, a good runner.'

'But you don't think I'm attractive?'

'Of course I do. You look fantastic.'

'But not fantastic enough for you to wonder in a corner of your mind what, you know, it would be like.'

'Well, only abstractly . . .'

'Steve, it was obvious. How abstract it was is another matter.'

Steve blushed, 'I'm sorry.'

'There's no need to apologise. To some extent I was complicit. But you need to be honest about your sexuality, get a better understanding of how it works, how it informs the other things you do.'

This was ridiculous. Whatever he had thought might be involved in going for a run with Grace, it had not included anything like the conversation they were currently having. He accepted that he was probably in denial about the way he looked at women, although it pained him to think that it was so obvious. He did not see himself as someone who ogled women. But when he thought about it, he had to admit there was always some kind of assessment of nubility at work in even the most fleeting glance. Perhaps that's what she meant by his phallocentrism. What really shocked him, however, was that it had never occurred to him that there must be a reciprocal mechanism at work by which women assessed men.

They both fell silent, running easily beside each other. After a couple of minutes Grace resumed, 'I'm sorry, Steve. This is not really fair on you. But I thought it might be easier for us to have this kind of talk in a neutral public space. What I wanted to get across to you is that writing poetry, specifically lyric poetry, involves more than the poet's intellect. It also involves unconscious aspects, sexual aspects. And if you don't recognise this, you're not in a good position to channel the material. So you have to ask yourself, why are you writing this material? And why are you presenting yourself in this way? And you may think it's simply spontaneous, improvisation or inspiration, whatever you like to call it. But, in fact, it comes from the deep structures of your personality.'

Steve acknowledged that Grace was a brilliant close reader. She had opened his eyes to all sorts of unexpected dimensions in a number of French poets they had worked on together for his degree. But he felt that the process of writing poetry was different. He didn't know in what way. It seemed like something that was almost impossible to analyse.

'The thing is, Grace, unless you're actually a practitioner, unless you have actually done some of this, it's all so theoretical.'

'So what you're saying is, because I'm just a reader, because I'm *not* a practitioner, I haven't got anything to say here.'

'No, I'm not saying that. But being a practitioner does give you an insight, which perhaps readers don't have.'

Well, what would you say if I told you I was a practitioner.'

Steve was momentarily lost for words, but he recovered himself and said, 'Well, I wouldn't be surprised. But I didn't know that.'

'I wonder why you thought that I might not write poetry too. Is it because only people like Steve Percival write poetry, people with a full set of male genitalia in other words?'

Steve didn't reply. He got the point.

'Would you be interested in reading what I've written?'

'Yes of course I would. I mean I'd be delighted to. It's just that you never mentioned it before.'

'But your presupposition was that I didn't. Might that not reflect the fact that your world view doesn't seem to include the idea that women write poetry? As a matter of fact I happen to have had work published and for all you know Ginny and Angie might write too.'

Putting to one side the improbability that Ginny was a secret poet, Steve said, 'Yes, of course I would love to read your stuff, and I would be very grateful for you to advise me on how I should proceed in my own writing. How to incorporate the things that you have just pointed out, and some of the things that Ginny noticed and even some of the things that Angie has said about how I produce my work. I admit it. I seem to know less than any of you. But I am open to being instructed in these matters.'

Grace turned to him as she loped along and gave him a beautiful smile. 'Well, that kind of attitude is all that a teacher could hope for. So let me ask you a question. You haven't read my work, because you didn't know it existed until just now. But how many women poets have you read? Have you read Emily Dickinson? Have you read Marianne Moore? Have you read Elizabeth Bishop? Have you read Sylvia Plath? Have you read Veronica Forrest-Thompson? My bet would be that you haven't read any of them. Not even Emily Dickinson.'

Steve was ashamed to acknowledge that he had indeed read none of the poets Grace had listed. He resolved to put that right as soon as he could.

They had now reached Midsummer Common and Grace stopped running.

'So what do we do? Do we go on or shall we swing back?'

He was feeling fine, but he thought he needed some time to gather his thoughts and to get ready for work.

'Let's go back,' he said.

They retraced their steps, more or less, cutting through to King Street, crossing Christ's Pieces and New Square and finally reaching Parker's Piece. After this they ran along in silence for five minutes, both lost in their own thoughts. Soon they came to the bottom of Glisson Road and Grace said, 'Oh, I nearly forgot. Maybe you could pass on to Ginny, that I'm having one of my semi-regular life classes this Saturday. She would be very welcome to join us. It will be a small group. Just women. There will be nibbles and drinks, and it will be very relaxed.'

Steve said, 'I'll let her know, but I don't know if she'll have recovered by then.'

Grace understood. 'Of course.'

As they reached her front gate, she said, 'I'm running again on Friday morning. Why don't you join me then? Same time, same place.'

Steve said he'd think about it. Just before he turned to set off for Ainsworth Street, he said, 'Is there a male equivalent for nubile?'

Grace laughed. 'Good point. If there's not an obvious term, then there probably isn't a mental category. *Stripling* sounds too immature but *mature* sounds too old. *Marriageable* is gender neutral. I'll give it some thought and let you know what I come up with next time we meet.'

When he got back home, the first thing he saw on opening the front door was Ginny sitting at the bottom of the stairs in her nightdress. They looked at each other in silence for a few moments. Steve was first the first to break the silence.

'How are you feeling?'

'I'm not sure. I just came down to get myself a drink. I thought you'd gone to work, even though it seemed rather early.'

Then, taking in the fact that he was in running kit, 'You've been running.'

Steve took a deep breath. 'Yeah, I've been for a three mile run down to Midsummer Common and back with Grace.'

He waited for her response, hoping that she wouldn't complain that he hadn't discussed it with her. But Ginny merely shrugged. Steve thought she was still so out of it that perhaps she'd not taken in what he was saying. By way of clarification, he added, 'I bumped into Grace on Sunday when I was out for a walk. She was running across Parker's Piece. Apparently she runs a couple of times a week and suggested I join her this morning, because that seemed the only time that she had to talk to me about my poem.'

Even Steve was unconvinced by the explanation, but Ginny merely continued to gaze vacantly at the floor, scarcely reacting to the additional information. Steve who had been hovering on the threshold, closed the front door behind him and moved towards her, reaching for her hand and kissing her tenderly on the cheek.

'Let me get you back up to bed. Then I'll get you some breakfast.'

He helped her stand up and they went upstairs to her room. Steve straightened the bed clothes and then helped her back into bed. He covered her up and sat on the edge of the bed.

He noticed the time and said, 'I've got to get ready for work. I'll just have a quick bath, and then I'll bring you some breakfast.'

When he returned fifteen minutes later, with a mug of coffee and a couple of slices of toast, she was asleep again. He put the rudimentary breakfast on the bedside table bent down to kiss on the forehead and then set off for work.

On the way home he stopped off at a little supermarket on Mill Road and picked up some courgettes, a pot of fresh cream, a packet of fusilli, a hunk of Parmesan, and some bird's eye chilies, in short the kind of things that Bert did not stock. He also picked up a bottle of white wine from the off licence next door to the supermarket. When he got back to the house, he went upstairs to see Ginny and found her sitting up in bed. She seemed to have more colour in her cheeks and gave him a sad smile.

'How are you feeling? You look a little better.'

She nodded and stretched out her arms. He embraced her, burying his head in the crook of her neck and breathing in the tantalizing scent of her body. This was the first substantial bodily contact they had had for what seemed like a long time, but was in fact, only three days. After a little, he attempted to prise himself from her embrace, but she held on to him for a moment before releasing him. He told her what he was planning for supper and said that he'd bring it up to her in bed.

Steve went downstairs, put the radio on, unpacked the shopping, put the wine in the fridge and started slicing the courgettes. He worked happily at the task of preparing the meal. It was a simple recipe and before long the dish was assembled. He was about to get the bottle of wine out of the fridge when the door to the little kitchen opened and Ginny entered wearing a loose robe.

'I thought I'd join you,' she said softly.

Steve pulled out a chair for her and said, 'You're just in time for a glass of wine.'

He poured them each a glass of wine and they clinked glasses. She took a sip and said, 'Mm, that smells delicious. I'm starving.'

He laughed. 'With luck it'll be better than last night's Empire Stores bangers and mash.'

He served her first and then himself and they ate in silence for a few minutes. Eventually, Ginny broke the silence. 'I didn't know you ran.'

So she hadn't completely failed to take in what he'd said when he got back from the run.

'I haven't run for several years, but I used to do a lot at school. I wasn't sure if I'd be able to keep up with Grace. It seems she does quite a lot.'

'That's one way to keep a trim figure.'

Steve felt it was best not to amplify that comment in any way at all and remained silent filling the awkward moment by taking a sip of wine. He then remembered the invitation to join the life class that Grace had extended to Ginny and seizing on it as a way of diverting attention from the conversational contemplation of Grace's figure said, 'By the way, Grace said that she was having one of her life classes on Saturday and asked me to tell you that you are very welcome to join the group.'

'What about you?'

'It's women only apparently. Anyway, as you know, I can't draw. It's just a few people, drinks and nibbles. I told her you weren't feeling well and so probably wouldn't be able to make it. She said there was no need to reply formally, just turn up if you felt okay.'

Ginny pushed her empty plate away. 'I don't think I'll be up to socialising by the weekend. And even if I were, I'm not sure I'm feeling stable enough to do any life drawing in public.'

Steve was sympathetic. 'Of course, but I promised her that I'd tell you.'

Ginny swirled the wine around in her glass. 'So what did she say about *Event/Horizon*?'

'Well, if you recall, when we were around at her place she was pretty positive about it.'

'Are you sure about that? I thought she said things that were equivocal, things like "quite remarkable" and "extremely ambitious".'

'You know, you're right. It just shows you how narcissistic I am. I heard those comments as distinctly positive. This morning she was far from equivocal. I think I suggested at some point that it's one thing to be a reader or a critic and quite another to be a practitioner. And she said what made me think she wasn't a practitioner. I said that she'd never mentioned it. And she said that I'd never asked. I was too self-obsessed. She said for all I knew you might write poetry too. She saw it as evidence of what she called my inveterate phallocentrism.'

'What a woman! I think I might have underestimated her. My poor little poet, she really sliced you up. So we have the diagnosis, did she recommend any particular cure or therapy?'

'She said there was no way to fix *Event/Horizon* in the short term. But in the longer term I need to read more poetry by women. I need to get in touch with my feminine side.'

'Do you think that's something you can do?'

'Well, I can certainly read some Emily Dickinson.'

'Are you upset?'

'Well now you mention it, I think I am. I think she contrived the whole thing. It was slightly weird to be running through Cambridge, in the early morning, and to have someone who up until a couple of months ago was my teacher, taking my work to pieces, not just my work but my personality too.'

'Well, they're one and the same thing really.'

'Yes, she said that too. It's almost as if you two had exchanged notes.'

Ginny laughed and covered the back of Steve's hand with hers. 'We've had no communication on the subject, but perhaps we both have your best interests at heart.'

Steve studiously ignored whatever meaning was packed into this bland statement and said, 'I mentioned what you said about *Event/Horizon* lacking heart. She didn't disagree with your take.'

'Oh dear. You poor guy, what are you going to do?'

'I don't know. I'm fed up with the whole thing. At least Rob hasn't tried to rebuild my psyche, or try to get me to change the way I write.'

'I don't really know Rob, but sometimes those who are most obliging are only helping us into further difficulties or furthering their own ambitions in some oblique way. So how did you leave things with Grace?'

'We didn't really get to any conclusion. She suggested that I join her on another run on Friday morning, but I don't feel like another therapy session quite so soon, so I've wriggled out of it.'

'You should do it.'

'Really? I thought you would be pissed off at my going on one run with her, let alone, making it a regular thing.'

'Oh yeah, I think she's got her eye on you. But I don't think she's ready to make a move. Yet.'

This was not the kind of answer that Steve was expecting.

'I don't know, I'll think about it. It doesn't feel right to be leaving you on your own, when you're feeling like this.'

'You've been great. When I go into these things, I just have to ride it out. So stick to your routine. Anyway, I'm starting to feel a lot better.'

'That's good to hear. And thanks for being so understanding. I didn't realise how upset I felt.'

'I think that's part of what Grace is saying. You need to recognise the role your emotions play in what you do.'

Ginny and Grace were reading from the same script again. Steve got up from the table and cleared the supper things away. Ginny watched him fondly.

Galley Proof

WHEN STEVE GOT BACK from the theatre the following day, he found Ginny in the kitchen. She was back in domestic goddess mode with her hair up and wearing a pinafore. A delicious aroma of baking was emanating from the oven. Steve gave her a kiss, and pushed a strand of hair out of her eyes.

'My goodness. You seem to have made a good recovery. It just shows you the benefit of allowing me back into your bed.'

Ginny gave him a playful slap in the face with her floury hand, saying, 'I think Grace's remarks about your–what was the term? Phallocentrism?–was just about right.'

She allowed him to wrap her in his arms, but when he began to caress her bottom, she pushed him away and said, 'Steve, this is the kitchen and I'm cooking.'

Steve laughed, reflecting that, in the short time they had been together, making love in unlikely situations seemed to be Ginny's fundamental modus amandi and let her go. She pushed another strand of hair out of her eyes daubing her forehead with flour and said, 'If you want to make yourself useful, put the kettle on.'

While Steve was getting the tea things together, Ginny said, 'Oh, by the way, a package came in the post for you today. It's in the sitting room.'

Steve went next door and returned with the package. He took a knife from the cutlery drawer and slit it open, withdrawing several sheets of paper. Lost in thought, he sat down on one of the kitchen chairs and commenced reading the contents of the package. The kettle came to the boil, activating the little whistle on the spout. Steve remained oblivious to the piercing noise, prompting Ginny to say, 'Steve, for goodness sake, turn the kettle off.'

Steve lifted his head from his reading. 'Oh, sorry.' He reached over to the stove and turned the gas off but did not attempt to make a pot of tea.

'Steve, what is it you're reading? You seem to have gone into a trance.'

'It's the proof of the extract that Rob and Martin selected for *Outwrite.*'

'That's good.'

'I'm not sure that it is,' Steve muttered.

Ginny was mystified. 'But you wanted it published.'

'Yes, I did. I was happy to have the poem or a section of it published, but this isn't my poem any more.'

'What do you mean? They surely haven't got it mixed up with another one.'

'No, but they've edited it, edited it substantially.'

'That's what editors do.'

'This is a poem, not a piece of journalism.'

'But you gave Rob permission to edit it.'

'I thought that would be a light dusting. This is a completely different poem.'

'Maybe it wasn't Rob's doing. Maybe Martin had a hand in it.'

At that moment Steve realised there was that there was a handwritten note paper-clipped to one of the sheets. It was from Martin.

Dear Steve,

Please find a proof of the extract from *Event/Horizon* enclosed. You will see that Rob has done a very good job of shaping your text. I made one or two small amendments myself. Read the whole thing carefully, just in case between us, Robin and I have missed something. Please get back to me as quickly as you can because this issue is already running late.

Best regards,

Martin Lockwood, Intrinsic Spin

Steve threw the letter on the table and went back to the proof pages, shaking his head in disbelief as he read back over them. Ginny washed her hands at the sink and dried them on her pinafore.

'I'll make the tea and then we'll talk.'

By the time Ginny poured the tea, Steve had finished his second read-through. Ginny put a mug in front of him and sat down on one of the other kitchen chairs. She picked up the sheets of paper and said, 'Can I read it?'

Steve took a sip of his tea and said, 'Of course.'

Ginny read carefully through the pages and then put them back down on the kitchen table.

'Obviously I don't know the poem as well as you. But apart from the layout, this seems very much like what you gave me to read a couple of weeks ago.' Ginny knew she was treading on thin ice, but she thought Steve was overreacting.

'If I'd wanted it laid out like that, that's how I would have typed it up. But those are not the only changes. There are quite a few additions of unnecessary punctuation. And the lineation has been changed in a number of places. Most annoyingly, there are two important sections that are completely missing from the sequence.'

'That was probably for reasons of space.'

'But it breaks the sequence and therefore the effect of the ideas and images.'

'Those missing sections can be replaced when the book of the poem is published. In fact, everything can be returned to the way you want it. But if you want to make any progress in this world, you're going to have to get used to this kind of thing.'

'I bet no one changes a single comma of Flynn's stuff.'

'Apart from the fact that he is already an established poet, didn't you tell me that Flynn repudiated his first book?'

Steve agreed reluctantly that this was so. Ginny continued trying to coax him into a more positive frame of mind. 'My suggestion would be, if there are no actual spelling mistakes or clearly unacceptable substitutions, put it to one side and give yourself 24 hours or so to come to terms with the situation. If you still can't bear to let it appear like this, then pull it from the magazine or make a fuss about the edits, but in the full knowledge that this could affect your chances of getting published.'

Steve's irritation at the way his poem had been edited had abated a little by the following day, but had by no means evaporated. Fortunately, it was a busy session in the box office and that and the banter with Seb drove the matter from his mind for the best part of his shift.

Back at the house in the evening, he noticed, as he closed the front door, that there was a letter from Angie lying on the doormat. It was odd that Ginny hadn't seen it. She normally put mail addressed to him on the shelf in the kitchen. A few moments later he discovered that the reason she hadn't done so was because she wasn't at home. His initial reaction was one of relief. It meant that she wouldn't be aware that Angie had written to him, but he was also a little concerned. At breakfast she had seemed distracted and he had feared that she was not quite over her attack of nerves.

He made a pot of tea and carried both mug and letter through into the sitting room. He tore the envelope open and read.

Dear Steve,

It was great to receive your letter with all your news. Thank you for having the courage to write.

First of all, what a lot has been going on in your life! I hope things work out for you. And, as you know, I came to the conclusion before I left Cambridge that there was more to Ginny than met the eye, even though what meets the eye is certainly very lovely. No doubt you consider her something of a muse, although, I'm bound to say, that I'm not sure that she's exactly what you need at this stage in your development as a writer. Would it be inappropriate of me to say that she might be somewhat high maintenance? But there, I've said it! Perhaps it will do you good to have to put another person first. Of course, I may be wrong about Ginny. She may bolster your sense of yourself as a writer and encourage you to do the work. It was certainly noble of her to get you a typewriter. I could do with one myself!

I'm sorry if this all sounds rather bitchy. The fact is, even though things have come to an end between us, I still care about you. In saying that, I am not expressing any desire or hope for us to get back together. But I think that last year, for both of us, was intense. And probably formative, whatever else happens in our lives. What worries me, though, is that, whilst you undoubtedly have talent, you also have a terrible tendency not to take things seriously, to undercut or depreciate your own projects. You're a strange mixture of grandiosity and timidity.

I am also concerned that you are now taking acid. I accept that the experience seems to have been amazing and you write very well about it. But I am not sure this is an altogether positive development in your life. Once again, Ginny does seem to have looked after you very well, but I worry about where you now set the boundaries when it comes to drug experimentation. You and I both know that it is only a small step to getting involved with much harder drugs. I'm sure you think that you are merely following in the footsteps of Aldous Huxley, but, if I may say so, he was a more mature individual when he embarked on these investigations. In addition I think there are now rather more unsavoury characters involved in the drug scene, whose only interest is pecuniary. Nor is it for me to say, not having had the experience, but I am doubtful that these experiences are likely to make you a better poet. They might make you *feel* like a better poet, but that is a different matter.

I'm sorry to sound so negative. That was not my intention when I started this letter. I was truly glad to hear from you. And I hope that we might maintain a correspondence, though I suspect that this is less likely once you read the foregoing. In an attempt to redress the tone of this letter, let me say at once, how delighted I am at recent developments with *Event/Horizon*. Even if it is a Work in Progress, it is a substantial *and* substantive piece of work and deserves publication. What a good friend Rob has been in this respect! I have always liked him, and not just for having interceded with Martin Lockwood on your behalf. I have a feeling that without his encouragement *Event/ Horizon* might never have been written. His party sounded fun. You know how I love a party. Your account of your conversation with Martin Lockwood was fascinating. (By the way, you mentioned that it was Rob's leaving party. I thought he was staying in Cambridge to start a PhD.)

And then a swanky dinner with Grace Mitchell, who it turns out is married to the mighty Peter Newman. Did you not know that when she was supervising you? My, my! Your social network has certainly changed from our days as undergraduates. It looks as if you will soon be leaping nimbly from publication in little magazines to publication in a tastefully designed volume under the imprint of one of our leading publishing houses, assuming of course that Newman likes your stuff. I'm sure you will have a powerful advocate in Grace in that respect. I always thought she had a bit of a soft spot for you and was a more likely rival for your affections than Ginny, but that of course was before we got to know that dark beauty better. In any case, that's all water under the bridge now.

No wonder you decided to give up the milk round. The Arts Theatre sounds a much more appropriate environment for you to operate in. I look forward to getting to know some of your colleagues in your inimitable pen portraits in future letters, if I have not deterred you from writing to me again by the tone of the earlier part of this letter. I'm sorry. It has not been easy getting used to the prospect of a life without you. I hope I do not sound too sorry for myself. I'm really looking forward to Edinburgh and wish you well in what you do. And in that regard, I suppose I might as well confess that I have been spending a lot of time in Oxford and that Declan and I have been seeing a lot more of each other. Whether it is one for the long haul remains to be seen, but it certainly has its compensations at the moment. The only fly in the ointment is that Declan has landed a research fellowship at St John's, just as I'm on my way to Edinburgh. Oh well, *que será* and all that.

I'd better finish now. Take care of yourself,

With affection, Angie.

Steve put the letter down with mixed emotions. As with anything written by Angie, not only were the sentiments subtle and perceptive, but the very handwriting was wonderfully expressive too. In the year they had been lovers, a strong bond had developed between them, which recent events had not entirely broken. Not surprisingly, Angie was hurt and had decided not to disguise the fact. It was clear that she thought that Steve had been seduced by a beautiful siren, not necessarily to his longer term advantage. She was also undoubtedly correct about his tendency to undermine his own projects. But he was irritated by her admonitory tones in relation to the acid trip. Had she not detected in their time together, that he was fundamentally a level-headed person with a well-developed sense of self-preservation. Or was he kidding himself? Wasn't that what everyone thought about themselves even as they plunged the smack laden spike into a vein.

And paradoxically, the acid hadn't made him *feel* like a better poet. It had made him feel that poetry, being a poet, was meaningless.

But even as he tallied up these irritations, he was aware that he would have liked Angie to have been at Rob's party and around Grace's dinner table. Her observations of the different personalities and her amazing memory for the conversational exchanges would have been priceless. Her comment about Grace having a soft spot for him chimed not only with Ginny's observations, but also with Grace's own intimations on their run together earlier in the week. Maybe he wasn't as perceptive as he thought he was.

Clearly Angie still had warm feelings for him. He had hurt her. And if that reference to Declan was a calculated attempt to get back at him, it had worked. He too now felt the icy tendrils of jealousy clutching at his heart. And the guy had just landed a research fellowship at St John's. Thank God it was at the Oxford college of that name. With luck the relationship wouldn't survive Angie's move to Edinburgh.

This was an unworthy train of thought. It was starting to look as if he really was as perverse as Angie had suggested in her letter. He brooded for some time until he heard Ginny's key in the lock. He hurriedly folded Angie's letter and stuffed it in his pocket. Given the rather personal comments that it contained about Ginny, he could hardly let her see it. And in any case he was not at all sure that he wanted her to know that he had been in touch with Angie.

Ginny came into the sitting room. 'Are you still fretting about how Rob's edited your poem?'

Steve was glad that Ginny had interpreted his mood as being related to the issue of how *Event/Horizon* had been edited.

'Yes, I'm sorry. I know it's childish.'

Ginny came over and kissed him on the forehead. 'Look, why don't you do the run with Grace tomorrow and see what she thinks. After all, she is knowledgeable about that world and she's married to a successful publisher too. She will be able to tell you if it is appropriate behaviour, and hopefully reassure you.'

Steve was grateful to Ginny for her suggestion. Clearly any fears she had that Grace might be a rival for Steve's affections were not particularly deep-seated.

'Thank you, Ginny. That's an excellent idea.'

'And you can tell her at the same time that I will join her group on Saturday evening. I've just been out to buy some new art materials.'

Steve was a little shocked at the sudden volte-face, but read it as evidence that Ginny's mood had stabilised.

'Excellent. You really have made a good recovery. Hopefully it will be the start of a new phase in your artistic career too.'

'Let's not rush ahead of ourselves. I'm actually quite nervous about it. And I'd appreciate it if it were treated somewhat confidentially for now. Apart from Grace and the other members of the group, I'd rather not have it talked about.'

Early next morning as Steve watched Grace emerge from her front door, he was a little disappointed to note that she was wearing a tracksuit. He had been looking forward to admiring once again her long, smooth legs. But he had to admit that for someone about to set out on a three mile run she still looked remarkably attractive: carefully made up, hair brushed, and as she came close to him, a subtle but powerful scent of perfume. He felt distinctly shabby by comparison and reflected that if he were going to get back to running on a regular basis, he should acquire some proper kit and not run in his plimsolls and crumpled tee shirt. Fortunately Grace seemed oblivious to his shabbiness and said, 'Good man. Glad you could make it. Shall we see if we can get a bit further today?'

Steve nodded and they set off along Glisson Road. They ran in silence until they got to Parker's Piece. Steve was still lost in his thoughts, alternating between replaying the contents of Angie's letter and wrestling with the fact that he had to come to a decision about *Event/Horizon*. It was, however, not lost on Grace that Steve was brooding about something. Eventually she turned towards him and said, 'Are you okay?'

It was probably pointless to try and hide from her what was on his mind, and indeed Ginny had suggested that he talk to her about his reservations, but in a fit of petulance he bundled his querulousness into an oblique reproach to Grace herself.

'I've been turning over in my mind what you were saying the other day.'

'I'm sorry, Steve, if I went a bit hard on you.'

'No, that's okay. In fact I dismissed most of it immediately. But then I recounted to Ginny what you had said when I got home, thinking that she would take my part, but in fact she pretty much agreed with you. I was starting to think that you two must be in cahoots. But then I got a letter from Angie, my old girlfriend. And whilst not completely in line with your and Ginny's observations, her view of me was not entirely flattering either.'

For a minute or two Grace silently considered Steve's somewhat paranoid comments.

'You are clearly feeling a bit beaten up by the women in your life. But it's only because we care about you, in different ways and to different degrees of course, that we say these things. Speaking for myself, I'm sure you have talent, but I'm not sure you know how to channel it. I can assure you there has been no collusion. My suggestion that you read some women poets was to help you escape the powerfully subjectivising tendencies in your own poetry.'

'My own poetry! Ha! It's starting to feel as if it's not mine at all.'

'I don't know what you mean.'

'I got the proofs of the extract of *Event/Horizon* that Martin Lockwood wants to run in *Outwrite*. It's been changed beyond all recognition.'

'Really?'

'Ginny says I'm exaggerating and perhaps I am.'

'In what way has it changed?'

'Well, to begin with there are two sections missing from the extract that I think alter the meaning considerably.'

'Do you really mean the meaning? I thought you were very much of the school that rejects the solace of meaning. I thought you liked to encourage the reader to grapple with rival discourses in the poem, to resist facile naturalisation.'

'Yes, you're right. I don't mean meaning. But the sequence is important. It's not just that one section adds to another. Sometimes they're meant to undermine each other, rival discourses as you put it.'

'Okay, I can see that might be a problem. But perhaps there is also a problem of space on Martin's side. However, it will be clear, when the poem is published in full, how it's meant to work. This is merely an extract to alert readers to your work. You can't surely be saying that there's nothing of value or impact in the extract, even as edited, that wouldn't be conveyed to the reader.'

'No, I suppose not. And that's certainly what Ginny was saying too.'

'Well, my advice to you would be to let it go. Your poem has to make its own way in the world.'

Steve fell silent. He knew she was right, as Ginny had been right. But it didn't feel right. The poem wasn't ready. He wasn't ready.

Grace had definitely adopted a faster pace this time. She must have been going easy on him the first time. As a consequence, Steve had less breath for conversation. For a time he concentrated on doing his best to match Grace's pace. As if answering his unspoken thoughts, she said between deep breaths. 'I'm determined to get to the river today. Is that okay with you?'

Steve nodded. Soon they were running across Midsummer Common, but this time instead of turning back continued down to the towpath, at which point Grace without consultation turned right and headed in the direction of the Elizabeth Way bridge then swung right onto Walnut Tree Avenue and ran up to the little stile that led back onto the common. She was really bounding along now and Steve held up his hand to indicate that he needed to catch his breath. She stopped running but continue to jog on the spot.

'Sorry, Steve, I'm already quite far into my training schedule, the key to which is not to get into a training rut. So I try to mix up distance and pace from day to day.'

Steve had caught his breath and said, 'You're a really good runner and stupidly I thought I'd somehow kept the level of fitness I used to have.'

'It's obvious to me that you'll soon get it back. After all, this is only your second run.'

One good thing about the greater intensity of today's run was that it had pushed the negative thoughts about the fate of *Event/Horizon* from Steve's mind, leaving space for other matters, one of which was Ginny's decision to join Grace's life group.

'By the way, Ginny said that she will come to your life class on Saturday. She seems to have pulled herself out of the depressive state she was in rather rapidly.'

Grace was delighted. 'And Peter asked me to tell you that he will be in the Free Press on Saturday if you'd like to join him.'

Steve laughed. 'So you're creating a man-free zone for the evening.'

'I don't exclude men. There have been periods when one or two men have been regular attendees. Although it is also the case that the atmosphere is different when a man is present. But the real reason for getting Peter out of the house is that he is just too talented as an artist to participate.'

Reflecting that this would be his last free Saturday evening for a couple of weeks, Steve said that he'd be delighted to join Peter. Grace said she thought Peter would be pleased and resumed running, this time following the top edge of Midsummer Common, but in deference to Steve, at a slightly slower pace. In due course they made their way back to Glisson Road. As they got to Grace's gate, she said, 'I forgot to ask how you're getting on with reading some of those women poets I suggested.'

Steve admitted that he'd made no progress at all. But he promised to go to the library and borrow some of the books she had mentioned. He then ran on back to Ainsworth street and got himself ready for work.

THE FREE PRESS

The Free Press
Saturday, 10 August 1974

STEVE COULD SEE THAT Ginny was nervous about the life class at Grace's that evening. After art school, Ginny had constructed a life in which she was the passive object of gaze, not the beholder. Now for the first time in a number of years she was reverting to being a practitioner of the graphic arts but was no longer so sure of her own abilities in that regard.

Which was not to say that Steve wasn't a little nervous about his own evening encounter. He and Peter had got on well enough at Grace's dinner party, eventually. But it was an odd situation to find himself in, having a Saturday evening drink with his former supervisor's husband, even allowing for the Frankfurt connection. He was worried that once they had exchanged some platitudes about Frankfurt, there would be little more to talk about. He had little expectation that Peter would have any interest in his poem.

Ginny calmed her nerves by having a very long bath and doing complicated things with her hair and nails. Steve occupied himself by working through some Jed Morgan exercises on his guitar. Ginny then took an inordinate amount of time getting dressed, trying on several different outfits. Given that the evening was a woman only event, with one of the participants unclothed for most of the evening, Steve was at a loss to understand Ginny's reasons for taking so much trouble with her outfit. But then he supposed that women dressed for each other as much as for men, perhaps even more so. In fact he suspected that Ginny might have been much more comfortable, if she were the one without clothes on. In some sense she would have been in her natural element. Or was this line of thought more evidence of his phallocentrism?

For his part, Steve was going to make no sartorial effort. The cord trousers, tee shirt and plimsolls that he'd been wearing all day would do for the evening too. When Ginny finally came down the stairs, Steve was struck by the incongruity of the scene as she floated down the stairs of the little house glowing with a supernatural beauty, as if she were on a Paris catwalk. What on earth was she doing in a place like Ainsworth Street? For a moment he doubted that he actually knew her or anything about her.

He put his jean jacket on and said, 'Ready?'

By way of response Ginny said, 'You're not going out like that, are you?'

Steve gulped and said defiantly, 'Of course.'

Ten minutes later, they parted company at the Mawson Road turn off from Mill Road. They had both been wrapped up in their own thoughts for the best part of the walk and had exchanged few words. Steve gave Ginny a perfunctory kiss and watched her as she swished down Mawson Road. He waited until she had turned the corner into Mill Street, which she did without so much as a glance back, then resumed his way to the Free Press.

Peter was already ensconced in a corner when Steve arrived. He waved Steve into the seat that he had managed to keep free.

'No easy thing getting a table in here on a Saturday evening,' Peter said, by way of greeting.

Steve concurred. The Free Press was not a spacious pub and the back room or Snug was surely the smallest bar in Cambridge. Generations of students had vied with one other to see how many people the back bar could accommodate. Steve seemed to recall that it was a number large enough to require bodies to be laid on top of each other. To his mind that was not a legitimate solution. Surely, each person should be able to quaff from a regular beer glass. Peter slid a full pint across the table to Steve and said, 'I took the liberty of assuming that you drank bitter. I don't see you as a G and T drinker.'

Steve raised the pint of bitter and said, '*Prost*'.

They clinked glasses and drank deeply. Steve wiped the beer from his mouth with the back of his hand and said, 'Thanks for the beer and thanks for inviting me to join you. This is my last free Saturday night for a couple of weeks. Next week I get to run the box office at the Arts on my own.'

'Well, we'd better make it a good one, then. I'm sorry I can't supply you with any *Ebelwoi* here in Cambridge.'

Ebelwoi was the Hessian dialect word for *Apfelwein* or cider. Steve laughed. 'That's a thought for a new business venture in Cambridge, not forgetting the *Rippchen* and *Sauerkraut*, of course.'

Peter joined in the laughter and asked Steve about his time in Frankfurt. Steve explained that he had worked at Metallgesellschaft's head office in Frankfurt in the year between school and Cambridge. Steve had arrived in a snowy Frankfurt early in January 1971. Two weeks later the UK had been hit by a national postal strike, which had saved him the bother of having to write to his mother for the first couple of months of his stay, though she had managed to get letters through to him via friends who were travelling abroad.

Those first weeks had been rather difficult. Steve's spoken German was not as good as he thought it was, nor as good as his new employers had been led to believe. Furthermore he had no knowledge of the workings of the international metals trade or indeed of clerical work in a commercial concern. When Steve's boss realised that Steve was in effect a complete beginner and not the management trainee that he thought he was acquiring, he had set him to work producing invoices. Fortunately, Steve's spoken German and his understanding of the trade in scrapped American car radiators soon improved and as a result he was put to work on more interesting matters.

He had thoroughly enjoyed living and working in Frankfurt and had contemplated not returning to the UK to take up his place at Cambridge. He had requested an interview with his boss and asked whether it would be possible for him to extend his contract. His boss who had always been rather scary suddenly became avuncular and said that the firm would not countenance Steve neglecting his education, but that they would certainly employ him when he had completed his studies.

Peter listened carefully and when Steve paused to moisten his throat with a mouthful of beer asked, 'Have you been back since?'

Steve shook his head.

'There have been a lot of changes since you were last there. The U-bahn has been enormously extended and there are tall buildings going up all over the place.'

'The tallest building I can remember was the Binding brewery's Henninger Turm.'

Peter laughed. 'It figures that the only thing to rival banking in German life is brewing.'

'And book publishing, of course.'

'Indeed, which is my only reason for returning now.'

Steve knew from their conversation on the evening of the dinner party that Peter's parents had returned to Germany after the war.

'How soon after the war did your parents return?'

'In 1950. I was doing national service here in Britain. I couldn't believe that they wanted to go back. We had lost many family members in the Holocaust, including both my grandmothers. But my parents were pillars of the pre-Nazi establishment and, not untypically, had become Lutherans. My father was a First World War hero and had been awarded the Iron Cross. After the war he went into the law and became a judge. In 1935 when the Nazis started to force Jews out of the professions, something I knew nothing about at the time, my father decided to train to be a pastor. Ironically it was only then that he learned Hebrew. We moved to a little place called Lörrach near the Swiss border, so that he could study with Karl Barth in Basel. That's how we managed to escape. We literally walked across the border. Contact had been made with an English bishop who was making arrangements for Lutheran clergy of Jewish descent who were under threat from the Nazis' race laws to move to Britain. In early 1939 we flew from Basel to Croydon in funny little Imperial Airways plane.'

'Were you afraid?'

'Of the flight? No, I was rather excited.'

'No, I meant with the threat to your safety, especially after Kristallnacht.'

'No, I didn't understand what was going on. I had had no trouble at school, because my father was seen as a war hero and a Lutheran pastor, but around about that time he had to submit to having his passport stamped with a J, so it would only have been a matter of time before the Gestapo picked us up.'

'What a terrifying experience! If you don't mind me saying so, there isn't a trace of German accent in your English.'

'I was still young enough to integrate. And when I was older and learned what had happened to other members of my family, I had little desire to return. However, that was certainly not the case with my parents. They never really got to grips with the English language and despite everything were desperately homesick. So little more than ten years after they arrived, they decided to return. They didn't go back to Berlin, though, because of its status as a Western enclave within the DDR and because the family associations would make it too painful. As for Frankfurt, they had only been there a few years and had not really put down roots. So they decided to base themselves in Karlsruhe, where my father established himself as a theologian.

'Of course, it was completely the other way around for me. Even though I had been born in Berlin, I really had no memories of it. My earliest memories were of Frankfurt and Lörrach. But by now I considered myself British. I had a British passport. I was doing military service in the British Army. I was about to go to the Slade. I think my parents understood how it was for me. And even though they were disappointed, they didn't try to pressure me to return with them.'

Peter fell silent and Steve felt unable to say anything sensible. The two men stared at their nearly empty beer glasses. After a little Peter said, 'It all seems like a bad dream now.'

'I feel ashamed that I don't know as much about these terrible events as I should. One thing seems clear from your account is how fragile our democracies are. The trouble with any system that replaces plurality by an appeal to collectivities based on class or race runs the risk of descending into totalitarianism.'

'Quite. So you're not a member of the counter culture, one of these people who believes that voting doesn't change anything?'

'Certainly not. I got very involved in February's General Election. It was the first time I was able to vote.'

'And would you mind if I asked you which party you voted for?'

'Not at all. I voted Labour, although it's hard to see how they can keep going as a minority government.'

'Wilson is a wily operator. I'm sure he'll find a way.' Peter took a sip of his beer.

'You say you are a supporter of democracy,' he continued, 'but how do you justify a system in which the Liberals got nearly 20 per cent of the vote, but only 2 per cent of the seats? Doesn't that mean that 20 per cent of the electorate were disenfranchised?'

'Yes. And I think we should have a form of proportional representation, so that all substantial bodies of opinion can be represented in Parliament.'

'Then why didn't you vote Liberal?'

'I didn't think they had any chance of forming a government.'

'So how will things ever change?'

'The Labour Party should make proportional representation a manifesto commitment.'

'And do you think that's likely?'

'Not at present. The policy will have to be argued for in local Labour parties and gain enough momentum to be debated at the party conference.'

'Do you see yourself being involved in that process?'

'Not really.'

'So that's a rather sad state of affairs. Why, then, did you vote Labour?'

'Not everyone who votes for a political party needs to be a member of that party. Would you mind if I asked you who you voted for and whether you were a member of that party or indeed have ever been a member of a political party?'

Peter laughed. '*Touché*. No, I don't mind telling you. I voted Conservative at the recent election and I've never been a member of a political party. I'm sorry. I was being a little heavy-handed, although the underlying issue of electoral fairness is an important one. I like Heath, because he has taken us into the EEC. And I think that will ultimately be good for Britain and to be frank also a way of containing Germany. I'm not sure that Labour is quite so pro-European. I assume that you consider yourself a europhile.'

'I do. And I'm concerned that Labour decided to commit to a referendum on remaining in the EEC in their manifesto, but I can't see many people voting to leave.'

'I wouldn't be so sure. The left of the Labour Party is vehemently opposed to Europe. Wedgwood Benn and Foot will go all out to campaign to leave.'

'In which case I will vote to remain. But I was more concerned in the General Election to elect a government that could sort out things with the miners. I spent two of my three winters as an undergraduate reading or writing essays by candlelight. To be fair to Wilson, he seems to have solved that particular problem.'

'By increasing the miners' wages by 35 per cent. If I had to give everyone who worked for me that kind of pay rise, I'd go out of business. And if you give one sector of the workforce that kind of deal, other sectors will be looking to get the same kind of deal. Inflation is already around 15% and rising fast. It doesn't bode well for the economy.'

Steve didn't feel on secure ground when it came to economics. He knew that the price of oil had increased dramatically following the Yom Kippur war the previous autumn, but he was not clear to what extent that was the main driver of inflation. Nor did he enjoy this kind of loggerheads political debate and was starting to feel that there was a considerable gulf between their views, one that the shared point of interest in Frankfurt was not strong enough to bridge. But it seemed too early to bring the evening to a close. Clearly another round of drinks was called for. Peter agreed that this was a good idea and asked Steve to get some crisps as well.

Steve stood at the bar waiting to be served and reflecting on the conversation thus far. Things had been okay when he had been listening respectfully to Peter's lecture on pre-war Germany. But as soon as he had ventured to advance his own thoughts, particularly on the current political situation, the tone of the conversation had deteriorated. Maybe he should just allow Peter to continue pontificating, not that a submissive conversational posture came easily to Steve. Indeed, he had previous form himself, when it came to pontification.

His train of thought was interrupted by the barmaid who asked him for his order. Steve pointed at the Greene King IPA and asked for two pints in straight glasses. As she started to pull the pints, Steve noticed that that the way she leaned forward to exert pressure on the handle of the beer engine provided him with with a clear view of her cleavage. For a few moments Steve allowed his gaze to linger at the vanishing point of her soft curves. Suddenly aware, despite all Grace's efforts, that he had slipped into ogling mode, Steve raised his gaze to find that he was now looking into the bright blue eyes of the barmaid who flashed him a conspiratorial smile. Steve smiled back and gestured helplessly, to which the girl's response was an surreptitious wink.

Steve passed a pound note across the bar to the girl, taking a sip from one of the glasses while he waited for his change and brooded. Suddenly she was back in front of him again, proffering the change. Steve snapped out of his reverie and took the coins.

'Something on your mind, love?' she asked sweetly.

'Sorry, I was just trying to decide whether to pull the plug on the evening now or tough it out till closing time.'

The barmaid was all twinkling sympathy.

'Oh dear. Date not working out?'

Steve nodded. 'That might be one way of describing it, although it's not that kind of date, unfortunately.'

'Ooh, sounds a bit kinky.'

Steve laughed, 'Sadly not. I'm babysitting the husband of my old teacher. There's a bit of a gap in our ages. The conversation isn't exactly flowing. I'd probably have a better Saturday night out with the vicar.'

There was a grain of truth in what he said, but you'd have to squint carefully to see it that way. The barmaid lowered her voice and leaned forward, offering Steve another glimpse of her charms, 'Well, if you're still here at closing time and need cheering up, . . . My name is Mandy.'

Steve allowed himself to run a quick feasibility study on the un-voiced conclusion of the proposition, but decided that the logistics of anything other than a quick fumble in the alley at the back of the pub were unrealistic. Not that a quick fumble with one so amply endowed was to be lightly dismissed.

'Mandy, you've cheered me up already, but things are a bit complic-ated.'

Steve picked up the glasses.

'Maybe another time,' Mandy replied brightly, undeterred.

She moved down the bar to take another customer's order. Steve carried the beers back to Peter's table, who looked at him archly and said, 'You were getting on well with the pretty barmaid with the flashing eyes.'

Steve had come to no conclusion in his ruminations at the bar as to the best way to deal with Peter and so reverted instinctively to his earlier truculence.

'Yeah, she was suggesting we hook up when she gets off work.'

'Are you going to?'

'It's not really a practical proposition.'

'But if it were a practical proposition, would you be up for it?'

Steve sensed that he was being lured into a trap, but couldn't resist upping the ante. 'I'm not short of action at the moment, but yeah, probably . . .'

Peter seized on Steve's braggadocio. 'Of course you would. Wouldn't any of us?'

Steve immediately regretted his posturing. He had no wish to be signed up as a member of the guild of philanderers. 'Whatever you may think, Peter, I am far from experienced in these matters.'

'But I can see you have an innate talent.'

Steve laughed bitterly. 'Well, it's a relief to have my talent recognised, even if it wasn't the one I was expecting.'

'Says someone who's just about to have a substantial piece of work published in *Outwrite.*'

'Well, that's petty weird too. I mean, honestly, I don't think *Event/ Horizon* is actually any good.'

'Is that so? Would it surprise you to know that I agree with your own assessment of your poem. I can see that it's right up Intrinsic's street, but it's not the sort of thing my firm would be publishing.'

Steve winced. It was one thing to be nobly self-deprecating, quite another for one's work to get the thumbs down from a leading publisher. Steve was momentarily lost for words. Mastering his anger, he said, as evenly as he could, 'I thought you weren't going to read it. But since you have and now have such a decided view about it, perhaps you'd be prepared to flesh out your opinion.'

'Are you sure?'

'Yes, I'm ready to hear your professional opinion about my poem, now that we've established my supposed irresistibility to women.'

'Okay, but you're going to hate me.'

'You know what . . .?'

Peter laughed mirthlessly. 'To begin with, your poem's pretentious, astronomically pretentious, literally so. If it's set anywhere, it's set in a black hole, which is essentially a non-place. Or more accurately, just outside a black hole, but within its gravitational field, which is presumably somewhere like Hemel Hempstead. This is an arid space in which nothing happens and which only those of a nihilistic disposition would recognise. There appears to be no redemption possible or solace to be found in this space. The vision is bleak and unremitting, but at the same time, the writing feels artificial and contrived, not lived or experienced.'

Steve had already had enough of the line that Peter was taking and fought back. 'Innovative poetry or what people often call free verse is attacked on one side from people who say it is little more than oddly arranged prose and on the other side from people who say that Bob

Dylan is a better poet than Seamus Heaney. For me, metrical verse, free verse and song are three different genres. It's as absurd to compare them as it is to compare sculpture, painting and architecture. Nor does it make sense to rank one above the other. The whole debate is futile. Individual practitioners in any of these modes can be excellent.'

An uncomfortable silence interposed itself. They both concentrated on their beer for a few moments. Eventually Peter broke the silence.

'Okay, not a bad defence. Let me try and put it this way. I prefer Auden to Pound, formal constraint to parataxis.'

Steve leaned forward. 'So do I. I write the way I do because I'm writing *now*. I find the *Cantos* indigestible and not just because of their anti-semitism, but I quite like the early Pound, the Imagist stuff. And I love the formal ingenuity of Auden.'

'Well, that does surprise me. What you seem to be saying is that you like formally constrained poetry, but you don't feel that you can write it. And for some reason, which may require further elucidation, when writing in this free mode, you feel the need to write in an extremely abstract register.'

'That's actually pretty much the case. I'd much rather write in a more realist mode, but every time I sit down to write, *Event/Horizon* is the kind of thing that seems to emerge.'

'Maybe you're not suited to poetry. What about another genre? Fiction perhaps?'

'It has occurred to me, but a novel is a huge commitment. And to be honest I'm not interested in action or plot. I think more in terms of conversations conducted in public spaces.'

'One of the greatest modernist novels, Thomas Mann's *Zauberberg*, is really nothing other than a whole series of conversations.'

'*Der Zauberberg* is probably my favourite novel, but it exemplifies everything that I feel is beyond me, the size of it, the range of knowledge, the ironic poise, the realist sheen hiding the symbolist depths.'

'But of course Mann didn't start there.'

'Yes, I know that. He started with *Buddenbrooks*, which is almost as good. The odd thing about this bloody poem is that it's like something that I was working on in the laboratory, but now it's escaped and taken on a life of its own.'

'Well, that suggests it's got something about it. No doubt I am in entirely the wrong age group to be able to respond to this kind of material. And I have to admit that my intention this evening was to put you under pressure and make you defend your work, to see what you're made of.'

Steve was puzzled. 'So, you actually like the poem?'

'Oh, no. I really don't.'

When Steve got back home, he discovered that Ginny was not yet back from her own social event. He was relieved not to have to give an on the spot summary of how his own evening had gone because he still hadn't come to any conclusion about what had transpired. He made himself some tea and a cheese sandwich and sat down pensively at the kitchen table. Apart from the bag of crisps, Peter hadn't seemed in the least interested in getting something to eat in the pub and by the time that he had suggested that they find a late night eatery Steve was ready to head home.

To an extent, Steve felt that the whole thing had been a bit of a performance. The assault on his poem had been vigorous rather than surgical. Any single one of Rob's mates, deploying the jargon of contemporary poetics, could have done a better job of demolishing his poem. To be fair, Peter had made it clear that innovative poetry was not the sort of material that was routinely discussed over the Inflexion Books boardroom table. On the other hand Inflexion was widely considered a nimble-footed operator in the trendy area of popular culture. Peter had built up a highly successful company and clearly had a firm grasp of what was commercially viable. He had no need to apologise for his firm's editorial approach.

The more Steve thought about it, the more convinced he was that Peter's unconvincing monstering of his poem had not been the real reason for the meeting. Nor the shared reminiscences of Frankfurt, which had been formulaic on both sides. Even the political difference of opinion had felt like a bit of byplay. Yet despite the alpha male posturing, Peter had trusted Steve enough to share what must still be painful and ambivalent memories. No, something else was going on. But Steve was unable to put his finger on what that might be.

As he sat there suspended in this thought process, he heard the sound of a key in the lock and a few seconds later Ginny joined him in the kitchen. She dropped her bag on the table, embraced Steve warmly and then went over to the stove and put the kettle on. 'So, how was the evening with Peter?'

'Pretty weird actually. He told me a lot about his early life in pre-war Germany. He and his parents managed to get out in early 1939, but much of his family, including both grandmothers perished in the camps. I can't even begin to imagine the sense of guilt you must bear in such cases. I just listened and felt grateful that he trusted me enough to tell me about it. There's not much you can say to someone whose life has been touched by that kind of tragedy.'

Ginny looked thoughtful and said, 'I wondered . . .'

Steve waited for her to complete the sentence, but she thought better of it and turned to finish making the tea. He sensed he should change the subject. 'But then we moved on to my fucking poem, which he made very clear he didn't like. To be honest, that didn't really surprise me. I don't like it myself. But let's not talk about my evening. What about yours?'

'It was great. I'm really grateful to Grace for suggesting I join the session. It was an interesting group of women, very supportive. You might have noticed that I was nervous about drawing in public again, but it seemed to come back to me. And the most important thing is that I didn't feel that it was a competitive environment. Actually, Grace is not a particularly good draughtswoman. She's too careful, too cramped in her gestures. But there was one woman who is really very talented, her style is a little academic, but she had a good eye. And the model was a delight to draw, lovely curves, not all skin and bone and scraggy tits like me.'

That wasn't how Steve would have described Ginny. Undoubtedly she was slim and had a somewhat androgynous body, but she was not without curves. He had, however, wondered from time to time, whether she suffered from an eating disorder or had an unhealthy physical self image. Furthermore, he knew Ginny well enough by now to know that she positively thrived in a competitive environment, as long as it was one in which she could express her superiority. Ginny brought her tea over and sat at the table. 'Would you like to see the work I did?'

Of course Steve wanted to see what she had produced, but, aware of her earlier diffidence, he had stifled the impulse to request a viewing. Ginny pulled her sketch pad out of her bag and put it on the table. 'Go ahead, take a look.'

Steve opened the cover and an image of a buxom, middle-aged woman presented itself. She had drooping breasts and fleshy thighs, not at all Steve's idea of feminine beauty. But he had to admit that Ginny had managed to capture, with her vigorous, yet assured marks, a real sense of lazy feminine gracefulness. He turned over the pages. Ginny explained that at the start of the evening they had done a series of five minute sketches to get everyone warmed up. Only when she had got her eye in did she start to build up her images with shading. The final piece of the evening was a challenging pose with the model lying on her back, her head furthest from Ginny's point of view. Ginny had executed the foreshortening flawlessly. Steve closed the album.

'Ginny, these are amazing. They're really lovely.'

Steve didn't think he'd ever seen her so unselfconsciously elated. She was clearly still high on the experience and said, 'Grace wants to do these sessions monthly and asked us all whether we'd commit to that. I said I would. Crazy, I know, I'll probably pull out and she'll never speak to me again. But it felt so great to be back with a piece of charcoal in my hand.'

'That's fantastic, Ginny. I'm sure the skills and techniques will come back to you. From the point of view of an artistic duffer, it looks as if they already have. Did you work all the time or did you take a break and have a glass of wine?'

'Several. Glasses of wine, that is. It was a very nice vibe. So much better without men.'

Nursing Dr Stern

On the following Monday morning, as Steve and Ginny were having breakfast together before Steve set off for his shift at the Arts, there was the sound of mail dropping through the letterbox. Ginny went out to the hall and returned with a small bundle of letters. Most were for Beth or Sandra and Ginny put these in the drawer that she had cleared out to accommodate such items. She then passed a letter to Steve and retained one for herself, which she proceeded to open. As far as Steve could see it contained two sheets of paper, which Ginny scanned quickly, sighing heavily. She folded the sheets and slipped them back into the envelope with a troubled look on her face.

Steve was concerned. 'Are you okay?'

Ginny sighed again. 'It's my father. He's ill. I'll have to go and see him.'

'Where does he live?'

'Hampstead.'

'When will you go?'

'I think I better go down today. It's his heart. He's a doctor himself, so I think his assessment of his condition is probably quite realistic.'

'Oh, Ginny, I'm sorry.'

'He's been ill for years. And to be honest, we don't get on, as I think I've mentioned. But he is my father.'

'Of course.'

While Ginny was getting herself together to go to London, Steve looked at the letter that he had received. He didn't immediately recognise the handwriting. He opened the letter to find that it was from Beth. She had been awarded a travel grant to study at Harvard for a term. So she would be out of the UK until just before Christmas. In addition, Sandra had decided to move in with her boyfriend. The upshot of all this was that they were planning to visit Ainsworth Street the following week, if it was convenient for Steve; in Sandra's case to clear her possessions out completely, and in Beth's case to pick up the things she would need for her stay in the US. The other consequence was that the house would be available until the end of the year and Steve was welcome to stay on in the house on the same terms, although he was under no obligation to do so. She finished the letter by asking if Steve could write back and suggest a date and time convenient to him the following week.

Steve put the letter down, vaguely troubled. He had been apprehensive about moving Beth's and Sandra's things from the bedrooms, but had been swept along by Ginny's dynamism, telling himself that they would probably have decamped from the house before Beth and Sandra had repossessed it. But now he would have to be present when they discovered that all their things had been removed from the bedrooms and stored in the conservatory. On the other hand, everything had been carefully packed and labelled and it would surely be convenient to Beth not to have to find another tenant at short notice. In addition, from Steve and Ginny's point of view, it meant they could put off the hunt for somewhere else to live for several more months, which, considering the effort that Ginny had put into fixing up the house and garden, was a decided bonus. When he got to work, he would check on his schedule for the following week and suggest in his letter to Beth, that she come on one of the days on which he had a late start.

When Ginny came downstairs, he decided to keep the information to himself for now. She had enough on her plate with her father's news. She had packed a small overnight bag and was dressed in smart clothes, almost as if she were a junior executive.

'I'll stay at my father's tonight and come back tomorrow evening, but it might be longer, depending on his condition.'

'Let me have his telephone number and I'll phone you from work or from a telephone box.'

'I'd rather not have him being disturbed by the phone ringing. If I can't come back tomorrow, I'll ring you at the theatre. Or leave a message if you're not there.'

Steve didn't think that was the best way of handling things, but thought it better not to make an issue of it. She picked up her bag, gave him a somewhat distracted kiss and set off for the railway station.

It was odd waking the next morning without Ginny beside him. This was the first night they'd been apart since Jon's departure and he missed her already. Fortunately, it was another running day. He jumped out of bed, pulled his running kit on, had a quick cup of tea and headed in the direction of Glisson Road which he reached just before seven-thirty. A few minutes later, he saw Grace emerge from the front door of her house, delighted to see him again and they set off towards Parker's Piece on the now familiar route. Once they had settled down to an even pace, Steve said, 'Ginny really enjoyed the life class. It's reawakened her enthusiasm for doing art. Thank you for inviting her.'

Grace laughed. 'I'm not sure I would have, if I'd realised how good she is. Way better than the rest of us. She left one of her sketches behind by accident and Peter found it. He was impressed too. He didn't know it was Ginny's, though he sure as hell knew it wasn't mine, and asked since when I'd started inviting talented artists to my evenings. And Pete doesn't offer praise purely out of politeness.'

'I noticed,' said Steve ruefully. 'He really went to town on my poem.'

'Oh, dear. I'm sorry. He didn't mention that he had been critical. He actually said that it had been a good evening and that you were an interesting person.'

'I wish people would stop saying that about me. I can't think what he meant by interesting. He didn't like the poem. Suggested I ought to give up and write a novel. He didn't like my politics. He was okay while we were talking about his childhood, which I have to admit was a remarkable story.'

'Well, I can tell you, you are in a privileged group in that respect. He generally doesn't talk about that stuff. What he actually said about you was that you had bags of potential and the you probably just had to find the right direction to go in. He said it was like when he finished at the Slade, he didn't really click until he gave up all thoughts of being an artist. He also said you seem to be irresistible to women and that you were having quite a lot of success with the bar maid.'

Steve scoffed. 'It was just a bit of banter, initiated by the girl. It wasn't going to lead to anything.'

'He was envious of the way you could be so cool about it, that you are so ephebic.'

'Grace, I'm afraid that I don't know what that means.'

'It's the word we were looking for a while back, the male equivalent of nubile. From *ephebe* ancient Greek for a youth about to enter man's estate.'

Steve didn't think he'd be adding that particular term to his word-hoard in the near future. He also found it bizarre to be envied by someone as successful as Peter. 'Well, I'm glad he thinks I've got something going for me, even if it isn't my poetry.'

'His taste in poetry *is* rather conservative. But he likes to understand what makes people tick, and on that score he was genuinely impressed. Even more than he was with Ginny's sketch. So how is she today?'

'I'm not sure. I hope she's okay, but I haven't seen her since yesterday morning. Her father's been taken ill and she's gone down to London to be with him.'

'Oh dear, poor Ginny. When we were having our wine after the life class had finished, she was telling us something about her family. I didn't realise that her father had been in a concentration camp.'

Steve was shocked. She hadn't mentioned it to him. 'Oh, I didn't know that.'

'Oh, Steve, have I put my foot in it again?'

'No,' Steve said gallantly. 'I did know he was an older man and that Ginny's relationship with him was difficult, so I hadn't pushed to find out more.'

'Well, I can tell you what I know. He survived the Nazi concentration camp, but his wife and daughter were not so lucky. He came to Britain after the war and resumed practising as a doctor. He married a younger English woman and they had a daughter. Then tragically his second wife, Ginny's mother, died when Ginny was still a teenager. That's as much as I know.'

They ran in silence. It seemed to Steve that this probably explained a lot about Ginny. But he too had lost a parent, in fact he'd never really known his father. He'd been killed in the Korean War when Steve was just a baby. All he had were a few tiny black and white photographs showing his father cradling Steve in his arms before he went out to Korea, never to come back. Maybe that was a link that he and Ginny had. Of course the deaths of her father's first family in a concentration camp was a trauma beyond any kind of comparison. And in fact Steve didn't consider himself traumatised. He'd always thought of it as his mother's tragedy, but perhaps he had just been kidding himself all this time and the circumstances of his childhood had indelibly marked him.

Grace could sense that he was having some difficulty processing the information and apologised again. Steve assured her he wasn't upset. 'I was just thinking that it's something Ginny and I have in common, not members of one's family being murdered in a concentration camp, but the loss of a parent. My father died when I was an infant. My mother never remarried and brought me up on her own. She's an amazing woman. Strong, intelligent, uncomplaining. I've never thought that it had any effect on me, but I suppose it must have.'

'I'm sure it has, but I'm also sure you have transcended any disadvantage, thanks to your mother. In my experience people don't talk about these things, but sometimes something happens which opens the dam. I get the impression that although Ginny was a model for a while and no doubt led a glamorous life, she has also been in some dark places. I don't know any details and you may know more than me in that respect, but I think she has been badly hurt and she's still in recovery. You need to be gentle with her, Steve. I'm sure you are, but you have perhaps taken on a grave responsibility.'

Steve knew that Grace was right and he would have liked to have shared more information with her. In a moment of clear-sightedness he saw that he was hardly strong enough to take care of himself, let alone care for someone as screwed up as Ginny. He had wriggled out of commitment to Angie, a person who needed very little support and had landed up with someone who needed a lot, or at least support of a different kind.

They had reached the river now and stopped for a couple of minutes. As they set off again, Steve said, 'The truth is that my mother devoted herself to me and I just accepted that as the way things were. I helped around the house and I don't think I was much of a problem, but I didn't actually support her or care about how she felt. I just acted as if you could have a relationship without having to put anything into it, or give up other things for the sake of the relationship. And I went on doing that with Angie. And now I am in a relationship with a person who demands a lot. I do feel out of my depth and I do feel that I have screwed things up.'

319

'Don't be too hard on yourself up, Steve. It may work out. You mustn't allow yourself to think that everything is predetermined. It is possible to change things. I can assure you that you and Ginny look as though you are high on each other. I don't see why that shouldn't go on for a while, but you do need to anticipate some kind of come down.'

They ran the rest of the way back to Glisson Road in silence. When they reached her gate Grace said, 'See you Friday, if you're up for it.'

Steve said he'd be there.

Grace smiled, 'That's better. Take the positive approach.'

Later at work, Vicky, one of the secretaries from the office upstairs, came by. She had a message for Steve. Ginny had phoned and said she wouldn't be back that night, but hoped to be back the following day. Steve thanked Vicky for bringing the message and spent some time pondering what to do with another evening on his own. But soon things got busy with the pre-performance rush and and thoughts about his evening were pushed to one side. When the rush had subsided, Steve helped Fiona cash up.

So it was only as he was turning into Ainsworth Street later, that he realised that there was no food in the house and that the only things he had eaten all day were a bowl of cereal for breakfast and the toasted sandwich at lunchtime. It was late enough that not even the Empire Stores was open, but not so late that the pubs were closed. He thought he'd go along to the Geldart at the end of Ainsworth Street and hope that they had a stale sandwich or a scotch egg left. Failing that, he'd have to make do with a bag of crisps or peanuts.

He pushed the door of the Geldart open and found himself face to face with familiar faces, Sid, the gaffer from the dairy and Bert from the Empire Stores.

'Well, well, what have we got here?' said Sid.

'Hello, Steve. Nice to see you,' said Bert.

The only thing more surprising than seeing Sid in the Geldart was the fact that he was in conversation with Bert.

'So you know Bert?' This was Sid. Clearly being on good terms with Bert counted with Sid and went some way to cancelling the black mark that Steve had probably acquired by leaving the dairy in the lurch.

'I live right opposite the Empire Stores. Drop in most days.'

'Haven't seen you in here before,' Sid continued, not entirely convinced.

'First time. I just got back from my new job and I realised there's no food in the house. Girlfriend's away. I'm hoping they might have something left here. Haven't had much to eat today.'

'You'd better hurry then,' Bert suggested. 'Young chap like you needs your grub.'

Steve asked what they'd like to drink. Bert's tipple was mild and Sid's IPA. Steve wasn't particularly keen on Tolly Cobbold beer and decided to have a bottle of Guinness instead. Most of the food had gone but there was a slice of pork pie left, which would have to do. Steve carried the drinks back to Sid and Bert's table and asked if he could join them. Sid gestured towards the empty seat.

As Sid took a sip of his beer, he said, 'So you've given up early starts for late finishes?'

Steve laughed. 'Yeah, I quite miss the old round really, but it was playing havoc with the love life.'

Bert joined in here. 'Your girl's a bit of a looker, if you don't mind me saying. But she always has time for a chat, when she comes into the shop.'

'Yeah, she's had to go to London. Her dad's ill. That's why I've come in here,' said Steve through a mouthful of pork pie.

'But talking of the ladies, Beth and Sandra are coming by next week. Beth has got a bursary or something to study in the United States, and Sandra is moving in with her boyfriend. So Ginny and I will be staying in Ainsworth Street, at least until the end of the year.'

'Well, I hope they pop in to see me,' Bert said. 'I've got a bit of a soft spot for Beth.'

Steve said he'd do his best to remind them.

He took a swig of the Guinness and addressing Sid said, 'Do you live in Ainsworth Street too, Sid?'

'No, I live in York Street. Same thing really.'

'I wondered why you were always at the dairy whatever time I got there.'

'Well, since Doris passed away, I don't like spending more time in the house on my own than I really need to. In the evening, I come in here and have a pint with old Bert here or one of the other blokes.'

Steve had soon finished the pork pie, but still felt hungry.

'You two go back a long way?' he asked.

'I hope you don't think I'm as old as Bert, but yeah, quite a few years.'

They chatted on. Steve liked the idea that he was being accepted in the local by a couple of regulars, even if the pub was in other respects not much cop. He finished his beer up and said that he'd be tootling along. Bert said he'd join him. When they reached the shop Bert said, 'That piece of pork pie wasn't enough to keep a young bloke like you going. Wait here, and I'll get you a pack of bacon, half dozen eggs and some bread.'

Steve said that would be amazing but he didn't want to put Bert out. A few minutes later Bert reappeared with the comestibles.

Steve asked, 'How much do I owe you?'

'We'll sort it out another time. I've got the takings locked up in the strongbox.'

Steve said that he'd be in the next day to clear the debt, but Bert gave an airy wave of the hand and said there was no rush.

As he disappeared back into the shop and locked up, Steve crossed the road and let himself into the empty house. He soon had a decent fry-up on his plate and went to bed well fed.

The next day, Steve was on the early shift, which, he was beginning to appreciate, was the least busy shift of the day, one reason no doubt why Seb favoured it. It also meant that he could be home by late afternoon, as long as he didn't drop into a pub on the way. In the hope that Ginny would be back that evening, he thought he'd better to get in some supplies, so that he could make her a meal. On the way home he stopped off at a supermarket and filled two large carrier bags with supplies. But when he got home, Ginny was back and already cooking up something delicious, to judge by the wonderful aromas wafting from the kitchen.

She greeted Steve with a bright smile as he put his shopping down. 'Did you miss me, lover?'

'I did as a matter of fact.'

'Absence and all that?'

'Yeah, I suppose so. I hope there was a reciprocal feeling on your side.'

Ginny laughed. 'That would be telling.'

'In that case you can *show* me later,' Steve shot back.

Over supper, Steve told Ginny about the letter from Beth. Ginny looked quietly satisfied, 'See, things work out sometimes.'

'They certainly seem to be doing so at the moment, but I'm still slightly concerned that Beth and Sandra might object to the fact that we moved all their stuff.'

'Don't be. Which day are they coming?

'I've suggested next Wednesday.'

'Okay, leave it to me.'

Steve wasn't exactly sure what he was leaving to Ginny, but decided not to pursue the point. Any anxiety was almost certainly down to his own guilty conscience. In any case he was more interested in whether Ginny was prepared to tell him more about her father and his circumstances than the brief details she had already confided. With a certain trepidation, Steve asked Ginny how her father was.

'He's okay but he's not going to get better.'

Steve was wondering whether to mention what Grace had said about Ginny's father based on the conversation at the life class, but Ginny seemed to infer what was on his mind and gave him a brief account of her father's history.

'So you see he's really quite old and also doesn't have a great desire to go on living. My mother was a nurse and they met when he was finally permitted to practice as a doctor in Britain. She was a lot younger than him and had lost her fiancé during the war. There was a shared experience of tragedy and they fell into each other's arms.

I don't think that either of them saw it as permanent relationship. It seems never to have occurred to him that a sexual relationship with a younger woman might result in a child. Odd for a doctor, really. Maybe he thought that the abuse he had been subject to in the camps had made that unlikely. So, initially my mother was his nurse, wife and, in a way, also his daughter, or at least a woman who was not much older than his first daughter would have been. And then I came along and confused this neat superimposition of roles. So far as he was concerned, I was a nuisance and once I perceived that that was how they saw me, I made sure to be as difficult as possible. I'm pretty sure that's why I got packed off to boarding school.

'And then just after I'd left school, my mother died of cancer. He was inconsolable. The one he wanted was dead, and the one he didn't want was still there. Or at least that's how it felt to me. He didn't seem to consider that it was *my* mother who had died, not just his wife. You might have thought he'd be delighted to have a daughter to share the grief with, but, of course, I couldn't replace the daughter who had been murdered by the Nazis, nor the daughter surrogate, who had shared his bed and died before her time or, more strictly, his time.'

'But now he expects you to look after him?'

'No, he can afford carers. I think he wants to punish me for not having taken my mother's place.'

Steve could scarcely comprehend the reverberations of pain and grief and the darker implications contained in Ginny's carefully worded conclusion. It was like something from a Greek tragedy.

'So, what are you going to do?'

'I will visit him every week or so. With luck, he'll be dead before the end of the summer. He might even apologise before he dies.'

Steve was shocked by the casual bitterness.

'If there's anything I can do to help . . .'

'There's nothing you can do.'

STRIKING POSES

In the altogether
Friday, 16 August 1974

GINNY'S FATHER'S ILLNESS NOTWITHSTANDING, Steve and Ginny now
entered a more settled phase in their relationship, in which the earlier
urgent physicality gave way to a spirit of easy-going tenderness. They
had become altogether more comfortable with each other. Despite the
evident bitterness that she felt towards her father, it was clear that
Ginny fully intended to care for him to the best of her ability. In turn,
Steve resolved to support her in this endeavour to the extent that she
would allow him.

Fortunately, there were few other external demands on Steve's
energies. His job was hardly onerous. Seb could be irritating, but no
more than that. Fiona was a delight and Mike Wallace ran things with
a very light touch. Butch would pop in from time to time and, despair-
ing of Steve ever introducing himself to the rest of the stage crew
under his own steam, had dragged him around one day when everyone was there and introduced him to Spike Palmer, the stage manager,
Colin, his deputy, Terry, the lighting technician and Jeremy, his assistant.

Another evening, Butch arranged for Steve to observe a performance from the wings, during which Terry asked Steve if he'd like to
spend an evening in the control room and observe how the lighting
and audio aspects of the show worked. Steve felt a little embarrassed
at the attention he was getting, but found the experience fascinating

and was beginning to wish he was working backstage rather than front of house. There was a real esprit de corps between the members of the stage crew which spilled over into long sessions in the Eagle, whereas there was absolutely no out of office socialising between the box office staff.

When Steve got back late after that particular evening, Ginny had already gone to bed, but she had left some supper out for him. He finished the meal, washed up his plate and cutlery and went through to the sitting room to read for a while before going up to bed. As he entered the room, he was puzzled to see that the full length mirror from their bedroom was standing in the middle of the room. He looked around to see if there was anything else that might explain its presence in the room and noticed that there was a wooden easel, with a drawing board attached, standing in the corner of the room and beneath it a portfolio with a number of loose sheets lying on top. Steve picked up several of the topmost sheets and found that he was looking at a number of expressive self-portraits. It was clear that Ginny had been putting in some practice by using herself as a model. Steve was once again impressed by Ginny's skill as an artist. It couldn't be that easy to be both artist and model.

He leafed through more of the pages of sketches. Having assured herself that she could capture a likeness, Ginny had clearly decided that she needed to practise her figure drawing. For the next series of images she had removed her blouse and bra and had done several studies of herself with a naked upper torso. Finally she must have repositioned the easel and the mirror, removed all her clothes and done three full length nudes of herself. The images were not what he would have called flattering. Ginny had portrayed herself as more gaunt and angular than she was in the flesh, or so it seemed to Steve. He slipped the sheets back into the portfolio and went up to bed. As he climbed the stairs, he wondered if Ginny was still awake.

The next morning, Steve was on the early shift again. Of course, early was not early in the way that starts at the dairy had been. But even so, Ginny was still sleeping peacefully, when he slipped out of their bed and went downstairs to get himself some breakfast. He was eating a bowl muesli with his thoughts drifting ahead to the day's activities, when the door to the kitchen opened and a bleary-eyed Ginny entered as naked as she had been in the final sketches she had made the previous day.

'Sorry, I was busting for a pee.'

She went into the bathroom and Steve heard the tinkling sibilance of her urination, followed by the sound of a sheet of toilet paper being torn off the roll to pat herself dry. She re-entered the kitchen and used the hot water that was left in the kettle to make herself a cup of coffee. She then sat down beside Steve and leaning over gave him a kiss.

'You were back late last night.'

'Yeah, sorry. I went with the guys from the stage crew for a quick pint after the show. It was a fascinating evening. I'd much rather be doing that than working in the box office.'

'Maybe you should see if they'd let you change jobs.'

'I don't think my boss would be very happy if I did. He'd have to look for another person to cover the maternity leave.'

'Still, might be worth asking.'

'But it wouldn't be very fair on you. I'd be working every night. It'd be even worse than the dairy job.'

'But much more like the kind of thing you need to do. Don't worry about me. You need to work out what is best for you.'

Steve tucked that thought away for further consideration.

'Aren't you cold sitting there with no clothes on?'

'A bit. I thought you might have time to come back to bed.'

Steve looked at his watch. He thought he probably did.

When he got home from work, shortly after five o'clock, he found Ginny in the sitting room, still naked, working furiously at her drawing. He wondered whether she had spent the whole day unclothed, but was sensitive enough not to enquire in this regard, because he could see that she was extremely frustrated with her work. He said he'd make them both a cup of tea.

He returned a few minutes later with the teas. Ginny was sitting on the sofa, chin cupped glumly in hands, elbows on her knees.

'What's the problem?' he asked carefully.

'I'm not making any progress. I can only set up the mirror and easel in a limited number of ways, which means that the only poses I can model are forward-facing and, for the most part, standing poses. They're not really interesting or challenging. I need practice with a model lying down or crouching. I need to work with more difficult perspectives.'

'Could we ask someone to pose for you?'

'Who do you suggest?'

'I don't know. It's not the easiest thing to ask a woman.'

'It doesn't have to be a woman.'

'Do you know any men who would pose?'

'You.'

'Me?' Steve was taken aback.

'You said you would, when we were at the Fitz.'

It was true, he had said something of the sort, but not in the expectation that the offer was likely to be called in. He had seen it more as a part of their foreplay.

'Well, I'm not sure I'd make a good model. I'm not that confident in my body. I'm not a particularly manly guy and haven't really kept myself in shape.'

'Don't be ridiculous. Even if all that were true, it would be better than trying to draw myself. I know being a life model is not an easy thing to do. So, why don't you pose for me clothed, and we'll see how we get on.'

On the basis that it was a trial and he would be fully clothed, Steve thought he could hardly decline. He asked Ginny how she wanted him. She suggested he stand with his weight on one leg, with the other leg slightly crooked, so that his arms and shoulders were twisted off axis from his hips and legs, and to look away. It took him a while to get into a comfortable position. Soon he became aware that Ginny was sketching rapidly, but because he was looking away from her, he only caught glimpses from the corner of his eye. After a while, she asked him to strike a new pose. This time because he was looking at her more directly, he was aware of the absurdity of the situation, the artist was naked, while the model was fully clothed.

At the next change of pose, he took a deep breath and said that he felt he was now ready to remove his clothes. Ginny said nothing but went out to the kitchen to get a glass of water for each them. When she came back with the water, Steve was unclothed and feeling very self-conscious, even though this was hardly the first time that they had been naked together. Paradoxically he thought that he might feel a bit more comfortable if Ginny were to get dressed, but she seemed oblivious to the fact that she too was naked. She was, however, not unaware of his discomfort and said, 'We'll take it very easy. You can stop anytime you want. To begin with, I won't need you to hold any pose for longer than five minutes.'

Steve felt that should be manageable.

'Let's start with something where you don't feel so exposed. Let's have you sitting on that small table with your back to me and with your hands linked behind your head. That will enable me to make a study of the contours of your back, shoulders, and buttocks. Ginny did three quick sketches of his back, asking him to change his angle relative to her between each pose. After that series she suggested he stretch his limbs before they tried something a little more challenging.

'Let's have you sitting on the floor, side on to me, with your ankles crossed, your arms resting on the outside of your knees and your head turned towards me.'

Steve tried to do what she said, but he didn't understand the instructions. In the end, she was forced to demonstrate the pose herself so that he could copy it. Once again she said she wouldn't make him hold the pose for too long. As he sat there trying to empty his mind, he became aware of the fact, which was hardly news to him, but which was not much of an issue when one was clothed, that the male genitalia were in constant motion. He tried to focus his thoughts elsewhere, but they kept circling back to the way his genitals were exposed, which in turn seemed to provoke further flexion and movement. He seemed to find it impossible to banish awareness of his own cock. If this was the phallocentrism that Grace had referred to, it was absurdly literal. Eventually, Ginny said he could drop the pose. He stretched out, amazed at how tense he had become.

When he had relaxed a bit, she suggested that he face her kneeling and sitting on his heels, with the backs of his hands pressed to his forehead. In itself the pose was quite easy to hold but it made him even more apprehensive, not just because his genitals were on direct view, but also because there was something abject about the pose, almost as if he were a prisoner. Ginny could see that he was having difficulty and asked him whether he'd like to stop now. He shook his head and said he'd be alright. At least this time, his thoughts were not focused on his anatomy, but what the pose suggested or expressed. Was he finally entering into the spirit of what being a model entailed? If so, it was abundantly clear that being a life model was a far from passive activity. At the end of that pose, he said he could do with a drink.

He drained the glass of water Ginny fetched for him and recomposed himself. 'Okay, what now?'

'Right. Face me standing, with legs apart, hands on hips, chin up, looking straight at me. Be brave.'

As Steve got himself into position, he thought that this was probably the easiest pose she had asked him to adopt. He didn't see why he needed to be brave. But after a while, he realised that she was intending to make him hold the pose for considerably longer than the previous poses. In addition, now that he was looking directly at her, he had the odd feeling that she was deconstructing him and reassembling him as someone else. Not for the first time, he wondered if he had been bewitched. What on earth was he doing here in the front room of a little house in Ainsworth Street without a stitch on whilst a woman, whom, in truth, he didn't really know very well, and who was as naked as he was, sketched him in charcoal? What was going on? He started to tremble. His muscles were shrieking. Beads of sweat ran down his temples. Ginny could see he was finding it tough. 'Just another few seconds, I promise.'

He blinked to communicate his assent. It wasn't just the physical strain involved in holding a pose for that long, it was the mental concentration too. The usual stream of loosely associated thoughts seemed to have ceased and his mind was filled with a kind of hologram of his body, lit up by meridians of pain. Eventually Ginny released him and Steve squatted down for a few moments, holding his balance with one hand on the ground, while the knots and cramps in his body unlocked. 'My God, I was spacing out.'

'Yeah, it can be a kind of meditation. You might have found it a bit easier, if you'd ever done some yoga. Take a break and we'll do one last pose.'

Steve took another sip of water and stretched his arms and legs. He was feeling very weird.

'Right. Let's try a recumbent pose. Lie on one side, head propped on your hand, elbow crooked, foot of top leg sole down on the inner knee of the lower leg, hand of top arm on the upright knee. Try not to think about your cock, just let it fall naturally. Try and enjoy the pose. This one shouldn't be so hard to hold, but I want you to try and hold it for 15 minutes. Do your best, but if it gets too much you can stop whenever you want.'

The pose was, as Ginny had predicted, more comfortable and he soon felt relaxed enough to watch her at work. She sketched quickly, making bold gestures, stopping to look at him and, from time to time, stretching out her right arm to estimate proportions with her thumb or piece of charcoal. She seemed deadly serious, almost in a trance, whispering quietly to herself, at no point catching his eye. He wanted to talk to her, but she seemed in no mood to talk while she was sketching and, in any case, he wasn't at all sure that he had the energy to think, let alone talk. His mind seemed to be empty, defocused.

At the start of the session he had worried about, and also, if he were honest, looked forward to, an erotic dimension to the experience, but now the fact that they were both naked didn't seem to signify in that way at all. They had both been engaged in some kind of joint enterprise, in which his role as a model, far from being passive required a good deal of hard work. Finally she put her charcoal down and came over to him. She took him by the hand and pulled him up. 'Brave boy. You did really well for a first time. You've helped me immensely. I think this calls for a celebration.'

Steve couldn't imagine what she might have in mind by way of celebration, but he hoped it didn't involve sex, or at least not for an hour or so. What he could actually do with right at that moment was a strong drink, but it became clear that Ginny had decided to mark the occasion with a joint. She dug out Jon's stash box and declared that there was plenty of hash left. While she attended to the construction of the joint, Steve went in search of a bottle of wine and returned a few minutes later with two glasses of cold, white wine, by which time she had finished rolling the joint. She patted the place on the sofa beside her. Steve sat down and took a mouthful of the cold wine. Ginny lit the joint, dragged deeply on it and then passed it to Steve.

'Would you like to see yourself?'

In fact, right at that moment, Steve wasn't at all sure that he did want to see himself, or more accurately, what she'd made of him. He had a feeling that whatever he saw now was not what he was, but what he was becoming. He wished now that he hadn't had the joint, it made him so suggestible. But it was too late. Ginny had gathered up the sheets of paper and brought them back to the where Steve was sitting on the sofa.

There was no denying Ginny's talent. The images were bold and vigorous, but he just didn't recognise himself in them. He knew she was doing a study of a male body, rather than a portrait, but in the images that she had produced he looked more elemental, more heroic than he thought he looked in reality. It was probably a consequence of the kind of poses that she had asked him to adopt. None of them were postures that, in his opinion, reflected his personality. He hoped he did not routinely stand with his arms akimbo and his head cocked at an imperious angle, nor lounge on his side, as if he were a Roman emperor. But if those images seemed to portray someone more decisive than he felt he really was, the image of him kneeling looked a good deal more abject that he could ever imagine being. The only thing that pleased him was the fact that she had given his cock more girth and length than he thought it possessed. But now was not the time for quibbles.

'Ginny, they're fantastic. I feel privileged to have modelled for you. I can't say I found it easy. And I doubt that I could do it for anyone else, but it has been an amazing experience.'

'You're a natural. You're a great model. And you'd soon get used to it. I think it would be good for your development, if you were to model for people you don't already know or have an intimate relationship with.'

'I don't know what you have in mind, but I'm not entirely comfortable with the direction the discussion is taking.'

But Ginny was not paying attention. 'And we should spend more time unclothed. Clothes are inhibiting. We are both sitting here naked and it feels absolutely normal. In our so-called civilised society nudity is generally seen as a prelude to sex, but it doesn't have to be. It should be an aesthetic choice too.'

'If you're trying to persuade me to be a naturist, you're wasting your time. I really don't fancy going to holiday camps, or recondite beaches, where everyone walks around starkers and tanned blokes play volleyball. Too much flopping around for my liking.'

'What about if it was young women playing volleyball? I don't suppose you'd object to several pairs of bouncing breasts.'

'No objections at all. You're the one who's suggesting separating nudity and the sexual impulse. In reality I'd be far too embarrassed to be a participant. And I'd be just as embarrassed to be a spectator, a naked spectator that is. I have enough trouble as it is controlling a certain part of my anatomy.'

Ginny laughed. 'I noticed, my little Priapus. We'll save the full Monty for another time.'

If she meant by that sketching him with a full erection, she could forget it. But Ginny had returned to her general point. 'Without clothes, people move, behave and interact differently.'

'No doubt. And, right at this moment, I am very happy to interact with you. It is after all the middle of August and so far as I know neither of us has further plans for the evening.'

'Steve, I don't think you're taking my comments seriously.'

'I'm just trying to live up to the way you've portrayed me in those sketches, or most of them.'

'You will only gain the strength you think you see in those images, if you are also prepared to submit to me. I can only free you, if I possess you.'

Steve didn't particularly like it when Ginny adopted her dominatrix mode. No doubt she had a lot to teach him, but if the price of her tutelage was submission, she could think again. He had no desire to be in a sadomasochistic relationship, whichever way they configured it. He might be prepared to indulge in the occasional bit of light spanking, but that was as far as he was prepared to go. The trouble was he doubted that Ginny did anything playfully. He could do without this kind of conversation. It was time to wimp out.

'Ginny, I've done something today I never thought I'd do. I've already overcome some of my barriers. I can't go all the way in one day.'

'No, of course not.' Her mood softened. 'Come here, lover boy, give me a hug.'

'Gladly. Hugs I can do.'

Fences & Failing Hearts

Ainsworth Street
Saturday, 17 August 1974

As IT TURNED OUT, Steve was not required to submit to anything more humiliating than having to eat a delicious meal and the only slaving that was required of him was to help Ginny in the garden when he got back from his shift on Saturday afternoon. The garden was now starting to look almost like something one might see in a weekend colour supplement. The geraniums, echinacea and dahlias that she had planted were now well-established. The patch of grass, that she had uncovered, was never going to be a bowling lawn, but she had edged it neatly and removed some of the more aggressive weeds, while retaining a sprinkling of daisies and buttercups.

What she wanted to do now was to fix the fences, which were in a sad state of repair on both sides. Fortunately the posts were concrete and still reasonably upright. She persuaded Steve that there was time to drive to the garden centre in the VW to pick up enough larch lap fence panels to re-fence the garden. Good fences made good neighbours apparently, not that they'd had any problems with the neighbours yet. Steve was mystified why they were going to this expense and trouble to improve something that they neither owned nor were likely to be able to enjoy for more than a few months, even if they did stay until the end of the year, but as so often he deferred to Ginny's focus and energy.

Once at the garden centre she also persuaded him that they could do with a couple of garden chairs and a garden table so that they could have their evening glass of wine in their own patch of verdant heaven. Steve protested that he wasn't sure if they could afford it, but she brushed aside his objections and pointed out that they had Jon's money, didn't they? It was true that Ginny had transferred the money from Jon to his account, rather more in fact than he had been expecting. He suddenly felt ashamed of his parsimony and wrote out the cheque for the panels and the garden furniture without more ado.

Back at the house he set to work on dismantling the rotten panels and piling them in a corner for later burning or disposal. Neither of them had actually measured the old panels before they set off for the garden centre, but by some miracle they fitted perfectly, which puzzled Steve, because in his experience the inanimate world normally conspired against him, doing its best to thwart him at every turn.

In the meantime Ginny set up the new table and chairs under the old rose that she had cut back when she had first started work on the garden and which was now covered in a profusion of fragrant white blooms. Before long Steve had fitted all the new panels and stood back to admire his handiwork, not quite believing what he saw. At that moment Ginny, who a few minutes previously had gone into the kitchen to go to the loo, re-emerged bearing two cold beers.

'Fantastic. What a brilliant job. I like a man who understands boundaries.'

Steve accepted the plaudit, even though, as with many of Ginny's utterances, he really didn't understand what she meant.

She kissed him and they sat down at the new table by the rose bush.

'Here's to us,' she said raising her glass as they toasted each other in the evening sunshine of their restored garden.

Steve sipped his beer thoughtfully and surveyed the beautiful little garden they were sitting in. How had this happened? It had been a wasteland a few short weeks ago.

After all their hard work in the garden on the Saturday, it rained for a good part of Sunday, confining them indoors. But that had its compensations too, apart from also being good for the new planting. He and Ginny spent the whole morning in bed, quietly chatting. When they eventually got up and had their baths, it was well after midday. Ginny fixed them a brunch. After the meal, Steve said that he thought he'd go and do some work on his poem. Ginny approved and said that she was going to take one of the sketches she had done of Steve and work it up into something more finished, adding some highlights and so on. They finished the day by listening to records and further depleting Jon's stash. As they embraced before falling asleep, Steve said, 'It has been the most marvellous weekend. Thank you. I am sorry I was being curmudgeonly about spending money on the garden. It really is worth it.'

She squeezed his hand and turned over in the bed and soon they were both sound asleep.

When Steve got back from work on the Monday, Ginny was out, but had left a note saying she wouldn't be back until late. He should go ahead and eat. She would grab something later. He went into the sitting room and saw, propped on the mantelpiece, a letter addressed to him, in a hand he didn't immediately recognise. He opened the envelope and saw that it was a short letter from Rob. He had some sad news. Martin Lockwood had been taken ill. Some kind of problem with his heart. He was not in immediate danger, but he might need an operation. Unfortunately, this meant that the next issue of *Outwrite* was on hold until Martin was back on his feet. It wasn't yet clear how long that would be, but it would certainly be several weeks. Rob would keep Steve posted. He hoped he was well and would bring him up to date with his own news in a future letter.

Steve was sorry to hear that Martin was ill, but he was not too dismayed in so far as it affected his poem. It gave him more time to consider whether he was happy with the way that Rob and Martin had edited it. But what was troubling was the fact of another dicky heart. He stuffed the letter back in its envelope and went out to the kitchen to get himself something to eat.

When they were going to bed on the Tuesday night, Steve reminded Ginny, that Beth and Sandra were coming the next day, Sandra to move all her stuff out and Beth to pick up the things she needed for her trip to the USA. The plan was for them to arrive mid-morning and with luck to have finished doing what they needed to do by early afternoon. To accommodate the uncertainty about how long the process might take Steve had asked Fiona if he could do the late shift in the box office. It would be his first time cashing up on his own.

He was however much less apprehensive about that than accounting to Beth for the wholesale changes that had been made to the arrangements in the Ainsworth Street house. In particular, the fact that their clothes and effects had been moved lock, stock and underwear drawer, to the storage area that Ginny had created in the conservatory. As was her wont, Ginny remained unperturbed by the prospect of the encounter and told him not to worry. He should leave everything to her.

First thing next morning. Ginny embarked on an energetic bout of cake baking. She suggested that Steve vacuum the rooms. Steve was puzzled. 'But we don't have a vacuum cleaner.'

Ginny looked up from her bowl of pastry. 'There's one in the cupboard under the stairs. We forgot to return it to the other house.'

Steve felt sure that there had been a substantial element of deliberation in the oversight, but now was not the time to quibble about whether the vacuum cleaner was booty or not. He zoomed around the rooms, making sure that his and Ginny's clothes were put away and the beds were made. When he got back downstairs, Ginny had got the cake in the oven and had a pot of freshly ground coffee brewing. She asked Steve to make sure the bathroom was spick and span, while she cleaned up the crockery and utensils that she had been using to make the cakes.

With that stage completed, she suggested that they compose themselves by listening to something serene on the record player in the sitting room. They took their coffees through. Steve flipped through the LPs and placed a recording of Bach's *Art of Fugue* on the Dansette. Ginny settled on the sofa and leafed through a glossy magazine. Steve took one of the armchairs and concentrated on the music as he sipped his coffee. It seemed they had become a placid middle-aged couple, content with themselves and each other. He looked around the room approvingly, impressed once again by the domestic magic Ginny had wrought. Suddenly his gaze fell upon Ginny's easel, standing in the corner of the room behind the door. For some reason he had not noticed it when he had been hoovering. He was alarmed to see that the sketch of him that Ginny had been working on a couple of nights previously was still clipped to the drawing board.

'Don't you think we should take the image down?'

'Why?'

'Well, it's a picture of a naked man. And that man happens to be me.'

'Don't be ridiculous. It's a piece of serious art. Since it's not a portrait and the facial features are not developed, the sitter can't be identified.'

Steve was not convinced, but any qualms in that regard were immediately dispelled by the sound of the little front gate creaking open, followed by a sharp double knock on the front door. Ginny looked up from her magazine and said gently, 'Showtime. You'd better answer the door.'

Steve went into the hall, opening the door to find, not surprisingly, Beth and, he assumed, Sandra on the doorstep with a tubby man in his early 30s standing behind them.

Beth smiled at him. 'Hi, Steve. Thanks for being in. This is Sandra and this is Gavin, Sandra's boyfriend.'

Steve greeted all three and invited them in. He took them through to the sitting room and introduced them to Ginny, who was sitting demurely on the sofa. She got up and kissed the women on both cheeks and shook hands with Gavin. 'What can I offer you? Tea? Coffee?'

There was no immediate response to this question because Beth and Sandra were looking around the room in amazement. Beth was the first to break the silence. 'The place looks so lovely, so tidy.'

Ginny simpered. 'Thank you. We are really grateful to be here and we've done our best to look after your home in your absence. It really is a lovely little house. As a gesture of our appreciation and to save you extra work, we've packed all your things safely in boxes, all marked with your names and which room of the house they came from.'

Steve held his breath as the astonishment grew on Beth's face, but Ginny was already in full flow. 'I'll show you.'

She opened the french windows to the conservatory and, pointing as she spoke, said, 'Beth's things are in these boxes and Sandra's in these. We got a rail for things that needed to be hung up, Beth's this end and Sandra's the other end.'

Beth and Sandra peered into the conservatory, unsure how to react. The awkward silence was broken by Gavin who said, "Well, that's going to make things a lot easier. I thought we were going to have to pack Sandy's things before we could start loading.'

Sandra brightened, realising that the job she had been bracing herself for, was now practically half done. She returned to Ginny's original offer of refreshments. 'I don't think we'll have any coffee now. I'd like to get on with loading the van. But we'll probably need it later.'

Ginny gave her a piercing smile. 'Well, when you're ready, I've baked some coconut macaroons and some ginger nuts. And of course, please feel free to check upstairs and to make sure we haven't over-looked anything.'

Beth, who didn't seem quite as pleased as Sandra at the arrange-ments that Steve and Ginny had made, asked if she could look around first, before she picked out the clothes and things she would need for her trip to the States. Ginny was the soul of benevolence. 'Of course, let me show you around while Steve gives Gavin a hand to take Sandra's boxes out to the van.'

Steve, who had been rooted to the spot, observing these exchanges said, 'Yes, yes. Consider me a willing porter.'

Beth and Ginny disappeared upstairs and soon Steve and Gavin were going back and forth with boxes from the conservatory to the small van, which Gavin had parked beside Jon's camper van, while Sandra folded her coats and dresses and packed them into several large checked nylon laundry bags. On one of his trips back into the house to pick up another box, Steve noticed that Ginny and Beth were now in the garden and Ginny was pointing out various features of the transformation she had effected.

On his next return trip, Steve found Beth in the conservatory putting things, mainly clothes, into a grip she had brought with her. Steve couldn't help noticing that the box that she was rummaging in at that moment was the one that contained her underwear. She had a distinct frown on her face and appeared to be looking for something in particu-lar. This reminded Steve of his attempt to work out the appropriate owner of the items of underwear that had been left on the rack in the bathroom when he had first moved in. He now realised as he looked at Beth bent over the box in her tight summer tee shirt that it was she who had the fuller figure, not Sandra, and that he had misattributed the garments. How had he not noticed her attractive figure on the previous occasions that they had met? He was normally quite attentive to those aspects of the women he came into contact with. Beth must have subliminally felt his eyes scanning her chest because she looked up and caught his appraising gaze. Much to Steve's relief she gave him a friendly smile and pushed back her hair with the hand nearest him. As he picked up another of Sandra's boxes he registered that Beth had in effect given him the eye. That was certainly not what he had been expecting. Still glowing from the eye contact, he carried the box out and stowed it neatly in the van.

Just as he was about to go back into the house, Gavin appeared with the final box, puffing with the effort involved. When it too was stowed in the back of the van, Gavin said that he needed to catch his breath, which for him meant pulling a packet of Marlboro from his pocket, waving it in Steve's direction and having received a shake of the head, lighting up and dragging deeply on the slim tube of tobacco. The two men stood chatting while Gavin smoked. He asked Steve whether the camper van was his. Steve said it was, in a manner of speaking. Gavin was an enthusiast. He'd driven one all around Europe when he was younger.

By the time Steve and Gavin returned to the conservatory to check if there was anything else to load into the van, Beth was no longer in evidence, but Steve noted that her grip was packed and zipped up. He went in search of her to see if she wanted him to put it in Gavin's van. He found her deep in discussion with Ginny in what had been her bedroom and was now Steve's writing room. As he entered the room, Beth said, 'Ginny tells me that Martin Lockwood is publishing a long piece of yours in *Outwrite*. Congratulations. That is quite an endorsement. He is a judicious editor.'

Steve thanked her. 'No one is more surprised than me. The only fly in the ointment now is that I heard a couple of days ago that Martin is ill with a heart problem and so the next issue is going to be somewhat delayed.'

Beth promised to keep an eye out for the next issue when she was in the States and Steve asked her if he should put her bag in the back of the van, to which she assented. Steve took the grip out to the van and found Gavin having another cigarette. Steve said he thought they'd got everything now. Gavin locked the rear doors of the van and they went back into the sitting room, where they found Sandra slumped on the sofa. Gavin sat down beside her, mopping his brow with a handkerchief. At that moment Ginny and Beth re-entered that room. Ginny, with a beaming smile on her face, declared that it was time for some refreshment. They all went into the kitchen where Ginny had laid out cakes and biscuits and a fresh pot of coffee on the table. Beth looked around the kitchen admiringly. She had finally succumbed to Ginny's magic. 'I don't know what to say. The house is spotless. But what really takes my breath away is the garden. It looks lovely. You guys have put so much effort into it. I feel ashamed of the way we left it.'

Ginny pooh-poohed her protestations. 'We haven't had anything else to do. And we were very grateful that you let us have the place. It's meant that Steve hasn't had to rush into hasty decisions about what he's going to do now he's no longer a student.'

Gavin, who was helping himself to to two or three more macaroons, said, 'Well, I'm eternally grateful to you both. I've been dreading packing up Sandra's stuff. I thought we were going to be here all day. As it is, I feel shattered.'

Before they left, the visitors went into the sitting room to check they hadn't overlooked anything. Everyone was more relaxed now. Beth admitted that she had been a little shocked when she arrived to find that all her things had been moved, but she now agreed that it had been a good idea and that she felt ashamed that she had not really given much thought as to how another couple were meant to live in the house when she was away. If she had had any doubts before, she certainly had none now. Steve and Ginny were excellent tenants and she had no hesitation in leaving the house and her possessions in their hands while she was in the United States. She had in fact been unable to find one or two items of clothing that she had hoped to pick up, but they were probably in one of the other boxes. She wasn't blaming Steve and Ginny. She shouldn't have left things in such a state.

As she was making this awkward apology, which still contained a small payload of complaint, she spotted Ginny's figure study of Steve on the easel in the corner of the room. 'Who's the artist?'

Steve inclined his head in Ginny's direction and said, 'Another of Ginny's many talents.'

Beth looked more closely. 'It's very good. I draw a bit myself, but nowhere near as well as that.'

Ginny acknowledged the approbation with an almost imperceptible flutter of her eyelashes. Gavin, who was peering over Beth's shoulder, chortled, 'Your model was well endowed. No wonder he didn't mind flaunting his body.'

A wicked grin now played around Ginny's lips. 'It's not easy finding men who are uninhibited enough to expose themselves like that. Not many men are prepared to submit to the female gaze.'

Steve caught Ginny's eye and realised as he did so that Beth had noticed the look that passed between them. He sensed that she realised that he was the model. Steve tried to ignore the blush he felt colouring his cheeks and asked whether there was anything else they needed to talk about in relation to their tenancy. Not that Beth could think of. She had scanned the pile of mail addressed to her when they were having the coffee and cakes and she and Steve had made arrangements for the payment of the bills over the next few months. No, they should be off.

Good wishes were expressed on all sides and the visitors squeezed into the van and set off.

Once they had said farewell to their visitors, Steve said he needed to be getting to work. He reminded Ginny that he wouldn't be back until late. She said she'd probably be in bed when he got back, but that she'd leave him something to eat.

When he crept into their bedroom later that night, he found her still awake, sitting up in bed reading, Steve undressed and joined her in bed. He leant across and kissed her. 'Thank you. You handled everything beautifully. I think Beth was really impressed with what you'd done to the house and garden.'

'That's not all she was impressed by.'

'I don't follow you.'

'She realised that you were the model for the figure study. She suddenly saw you in a completely new light.'

'Ginny, you did that on purpose.'

'Come on, Steve, don't tell me it didn't give you a little thrill when she glanced down at your crotch.'

'Well, it just seems a bit blatant.'

'But it was okay for you to make a close study of her chest.'

'What do you mean?'

'I saw how you were looking at her when she was packing her bag in the conservatory.'

'Ginny, are you jealous?'

'No, but maybe it gives you some idea of what women have to put up with on a regular basis.'

Steve realised that it was not a good idea to pursue this matter too far or to try to explain about the repatriation (if that was the right word) of the underwear. 'Okay, point taken. You understand these things much better than me.'

'Relax, Steve. You're getting there.'

Later when they were in bed, Ginny announced that she would be going to her father's again the following day and staying overnight.

Steve drew her towards him. 'Ginny, I'm starting to feel rather jealous of your father.'

'He's dying, Steve. I need to be with him.'

'Yes, I know. I'm sorry. I just miss you.'

'I would have thought the attention I have been paying to your nether regions recently might have tided you over for a couple of days.'

'I'm not complaining on that score.'

'I should hope not. Anyway it means that you'll now be able to spend some time with your other woman.'

'I don't know what you mean.'

'Isn't Friday one of Grace's running days?'

'Yes, but she's not my other woman.'

'Sorry, Steve, I'm teasing you. I'm pleased you're getting into the running. I can't be doing with a flabby model. I need those abdominal muscles nicely delineated. Pelvic thrust on its own is not enough, however pleasurable it is for me in other respects.'

'Ginny, I'm starting to feel a little uncomfortable with all this objectification.'

Ginny laughed and snuggled up against him.

On the Friday morning once they'd settled into their run, Grace asked Steve how Ginny's father was.

'I'm not sure. I think it's just a matter of time. Ginny went down yesterday and I haven't had the latest bulletin yet.'

Grace sighed sympathetically. 'It must be very worrying for her.'

'She seems okay. As you know it's not an easy relationship, but she's prepared to do what she has to do. I think rediscovering her interest in drawing had been a useful distraction for her.'

'Do you think she'll come to the next class?'

'To judge from the amount of time she's putting in with the sketch pad and charcoal I'd say it's pretty certain.'

'It's not so easy to practise life drawing skill without a model unfortunately.'

Without thinking Steve said, 'She does have a model. I sit for her.'

As soon as he said it, he knew that he shouldn't have.

'That's very brave and helpful of you.'

Steve tried to explain. 'She was trying to use a mirror to do studies of herself, but she was getting frustrated with the complexity of the process, so I volunteered. Obviously, I'm not as interesting as a female model.'

'Oh, I don't know. I'm sure you provide a different kind of challenge. Didn't you feel nervous? Or have you done it before?'

'Never. And I was petrified. I also found it physically and mentally demanding.'

Grace was thoughtful. 'I don't suppose you'd consider modelling for my group?'

'I simply wouldn't have the bottle to get my kit off for a group of women.'

"Well, you've been doing it for Ginny . . .'

'She's my girlfriend.'

'I'm not sure that makes things any easier.'

'That's true, but you're my teacher. Or were.'

'Steve. We're running together on a fairly regular basis now.'

'Even that still seems slightly odd, but it's not the same as half a dozen women peering at my cock.'

'Careful, Steve, it's not all about your cock. When you're trying to get the foreshortening on a tricky pose the last thing you're thinking about is the model's genitals. They're just not important.'

Steve felt ridiculous. He shrugged as best he could while running. 'Anyway. It'd just be weird for me to be naked with both you and Ginny looking at me.'

Grace could see that he was uncomfortable with the idea. 'Oh, well. It's not that we need a model. Jackie is very good, although she occasionally lets us down at short notice.'

'Grace, I'm not going to volunteer to be backup for Jackie.'

Later as he was getting ready for work and unsettled by what he now saw as a deliberate campaign by Grace to get him to sit for her life group, Steve decided to take a break from the early morning runs with her for a while. He would have to hope that Ginny's comments about his abdominal muscles were just a reflection of the teasing mood she had been in after Beth and Sandra's visit.

SOLAR WIND SHUTTLE

A FEW DAYS LATER Steve received a letter from Angie. She would be in Cambridge for the weekend, arriving on the Friday evening. Declan was taking up his research fellowship at St John's and Angie was going to help him settle into his new accommodation. Was there any chance of their meeting up? All four of them perhaps. She'd understand if Steve didn't think it appropriate, though it would be odd to be in Cambridge and not see him. She herself would be heading up to Edinburgh in a week or two. So there was unlikely to be another chance to meet until the end of the year. She realised it was short notice and she would understand if it wasn't possible. Steve could leave a note at St John's, care of Declan, to let her know his decision.

Steve was perturbed and confused by the letter. He had been assuming that Declan's fellowship was at St John's College, Oxford. But it was now clear from Angie's letter that the St John's in question was the Cambridge one. As so often Steve had added two and two and got five. There was no doubt that he would have liked to see Angie, but, given the unpredictability of the interpersonal dynamics, he was less certain that it was a good idea for all four of them to meet up. Back in June there had definitely been some chemistry between Angie and Ginny, although even at the time it had felt somewhat contrived. Declan, on the other hand, was a unknown quantity, but Steve already hated him.

Declan would have to be unassuming in the extreme not to provide grist to Steve's mill of resentment.

He also didn't trust himself not to fall into old ways with Angie, a little endearment here, inadvertent physical contact there. It was undeniable that she was still in his bloodstream and perhaps he was still in hers. The fact was he would prefer to meet Angie alone, without Ginny or Declan in attendance. But the mechanics of contriving that were simply too difficult and could easily backfire. The best thing would probably be to send a note saying that they were committed that weekend, which to an extent they were, and that, sadly, they wouldn't be able to meet. He would talk it over with Ginny when she was back from London, without going into too much detail about his apprehensions.

Over a cup of tea the next day, having first asked after her father's health, Steve said, 'I've had a letter from Angie.'

Ginny looked up. 'What did she say?'

'She's coming to Cambridge, with her new boyfriend, this weekend.'

He hoped Ginny had noted the stress he applied to the word *boy-friend*.

'Apparently he's taking up a new fellowship at St John's, and she's going to help him move in. She wondered if we'd like to meet up with them. This Friday or Saturday.'

He looked at Ginny circumspectly.

She trained her gaze on Steve. 'I thought he was at Oxford.'

'So did I. I must have misinterpreted something. There's also a St John's at Oxford.'

Ginny laughed. 'I must say I like her style. She doesn't believe in pussyfooting.'

'No, that's my preserve.'

'Quite. Well, do you want to?'

'I don't know.'

'Come on, Steve. Surely you'd like to see her. I know I would.'

'Well, yes, but it could be somewhat awkward.'

'Steve. I'm assuming here, that you're being sensitive towards me. If you are, let me tell you, you don't have to be. I'd be happy to meet them on Friday. Saturday is out, of course, because of Grace's class.'

He thought he might as well be honest, or what with Steve passed for honesty. 'I *am* sensitive to your feelings, but I'm also not sure if I can handle it.'

'If you can deal with Jed Morgan, I'm sure you can handle Angie's new beau.'

Jed Morgan might be one tough *hombre*, but he was just a man. What Steve was having to deal with here was something much more difficult, contrasting instantiations of the eternal feminine.

'I can't say that I'm looking forward to meeting this guy, but it's not him that I'm worried about. It's Angie.'

'Are you afraid she's come to prise you out of my grasp?'

'No, but I hurt her and it's not impossible that she'd like to deliver a few home truths. But, putting that to one side, if we were to agree to the encounter, would it be better to meet in a pub or restaurant? With a pub, we could make a quick escape, if things weren't going well, whereas, in a restaurant, we'd have to finish the meal and sort out the bill.'

'Steve, you see problems where I see none.'

'You see more clearly than me.'

'We've been through this before. You need to be yourself.'

'That's the point about the fucking poem. I don't know what my *self* is.'

Ginny simply ignored this obfuscation.

'I don't anticipate any difficulties. It would be nice to catch up with Angie and meet Declan. I think we should invite them here. We can make a nice supper. There'll be on our ground and our guests. They'll be constrained by the etiquette of the situation.'

He was far from certain that what Ginny was suggesting was a good idea. But she had already moved on from considering the advisability of the encounter to planning the details of the evening. He should have known by now that when Ginny set her mind to something, she went right ahead and did it. Why wasn't he like that?

'Which shift are you working on Friday?'

'Late, but I can probably change it.'

'Okay, let's invite them around on Friday evening. I'll do the meal. You can tidy the place up and get the wine.'

Ginny was already moving into whirlwind mode.

'Reply to her letter, asking them to come around here at seven-thirty on Friday, and drop it off at Declan's college tomorrow.'

On the Friday, for the second time in less than ten days, Steve found himself wielding the purloined vacuum cleaner. When he had completed the task, he went into the kitchen, where Ginny had multiple pots and pans bubbling on the little stove. The aromas were delicious. Steve asked what else he could do. Ginny wanted candles in the sitting room, which could be lit later, and the back garden path swept and fresh towels put in the bathroom and a quick clean of the lavatory bowl and check that the beds were made and that there were no clothes left lying around. Everything should go back in wardrobe, chest of drawers or the laundry basket as appropriate.

Shortly before seven-thirty, Steve and Ginny arranged themselves in the living room with Miles Davis's *Kind of Blue* on the Dansette. Steve had poured them each a glass of wine. He needed something to steady his nerves and felt like knocking the glass back in a oner, but resisted, confining himself to frequent sips. They didn't have long to wait. Two sharp knocks on the front door reminded Steve that Angie was notoriously punctual. He had been listening out for the creak of the front gate, but registered that it was another thing that Ginny had fettled in her relentless programme of improving their temporary accommodation. Brushing out the wrinkles in her skirt, Ginny looked at Steve and indicated with a small nod of her head that he should be the one to answer the door.

Steve went into the hall, taking a couple of deep breaths to prepare himself, and opened the front door to reveal a smiling Angie on the doorstep, her long blonde hair replaced by a stylishly angular bob. She looked much more grown-up and sophisticated than the image of her that Steve had been carrying in his mind. Behind her stood a tall, well-built, man, with wavy light brown hair, who looked as if he might be a handy rugby player or rower.

'Steve, it's lovely to see you. Thank you for inviting us over. This is Declan.'

Steve and Declan exchanged pleasantries and Steve showed the visitors into the living room, whereupon Ginny rose gracefully from the sofa, embraced Angie, and then, on being introduced to him, shook Declan's hand. Angie looked around admiringly. 'What a lovely place! I'm sure I got the impression from Steve, that it was a bit of a dive.'

'It was, but it was no match for Ginny powers of transformation.'

Ginny ignored Steve's explanation and said, 'Let's get some drinks organised, and then I'll show you around.'

Steve asked Angie and Declan what they'd like to drink. White wine was fine for them too. Steve went out to the kitchen to fix the drinks and top his own glass up. When he got back with the drinks he found the trio admiring Ginny's life studies, which also meant that this was yet another group of people studying representations of his naked body. Steve had considered moving the easel upstairs when he had been hoovering, but he suspected that, had he asked Ginny, she would have rejected any such suggestion. Feigning nonchalance, he handed the drinks around. Angie was responding positively to Ginny's evident talent. Taking a glass from Steve, she said, 'Steve, I'm impressed that Ginny was able to encourage you to overcome your natural reserve. It always seemed to me that you were uncomfortable with being analysed and preferred to think of yourself as the observer.'

Steve said, in a desperate attempt at indirection, 'I'm surprised you think it's me.'

Angie laughed. 'Of course it's you. Ginny has captured you perfectly.'

Ginny was pleased with the plaudit, but felt impelled to adjust Angie's take on Steve. 'Steve is actually a great model. He is amazingly confident with his clothes off. Any diffidence is only skin deep.'

Everyone laughed at Ginny's neat turn of phrase, even if it was nonsense as far as Steve was concerned. But he stayed silent and resisted siding with either view.

Ginny led them through the little conservatory, easier to negotiate now that Sandra's stuff had gone and the hanging rail had been reduced by half its length, and stepped into the remodelled garden. Angie was delighted by it.

'What a beautiful little garden. Steve didn't mention that there was a garden.'

Ginny explained the situation with unconcealed pride. 'This was a complete jungle when we moved in. We've done what we can, given that we've started late in the season. If we'd been able to move in earlier in the year, we could have planted it properly. We'd been looking for somewhere for ages. Steve's been a great help. He's not much of a gardener, but it's been useful to have someone to drive me to the garden centre and to take the garden waste to the dump.'

Steve had already started to accept that Ginny's reality distortion effect sought to influence future events, but the distortions now seemed to be affecting the past as well. She and Steve hadn't been looking for somewhere 'for ages'. In the spring and indeed until three months ago, Steve had been with Angie. Ginny was conflating Jon and Steve.

Angie was puzzled. 'But don't you have to move out in a few weeks?'

Steve explained the situation with Beth and Sandra. 'So we've got the place until the end of the year now.'

Ginny felt that even that simple statement needed some oracular burnishing.

'You can tell that Beth has a first class academic brain. I wouldn't be surprised if her placement is extended, and then we'd be able to stay here for a good deal longer.'

Steve was alarmed by this statement. There had been no suggestion from Beth or from any other source that such a thing might be likely.

Ginny led them back inside into the kitchen via the backdoor. The aromatic homeliness of the kitchen elicited appreciative noises from Angie. Steve was aware that, so far, Declan had said almost nothing. Home-making was probably not a top priority with him. Ginny said she wouldn't keep them from their supper much longer. She just wanted to show them the upper floor of the house. She led them upstairs and indicated the door of Steve's room.

'This is Steve's writing room.'

She threw open the door and Steve noticed that the Olivetti was out of its case and a sheet of the *Event/Horizon* typescript was in the machine. He had not left it like that. In fact he had not worked on the typewriter for some time, preferring to compose in longhand in a notebook. But Angie was impressed.

'What a lovely room to work in. And what a stylish machine.'

Steve tried to disguise the fact that he was getting flustered. 'Yes, it was very generous of Ginny to get it for me. It's meant that I have been able to submit my work to a publisher.'

This prompted Declan to finally break his silence. 'So is this a page from the long poem you're working on that Angie has told me about.'

'Yes, I believe it is,' Steve replied hesitantly.

'You believe it is?' Declan didn't understand Steve's uncertainty.

'I mean I don't remember leaving it out.'

Ginny could help with this. 'Steve says that quite often he doesn't recognise something he wrote the previous day. He says it's as if it were written by another person. I've noticed that he seems to go through a process of self-forgetting when he's writing. But he needn't worry, he's so expressive that he can't help revealing himself in everything he does. That's the quality in him that I was trying to capture in those sketches.'

Steve wished Ginny would stop trying to encapsulate his character.

Declan was oblivious to Steve's discomfort, but he was interested in the poem. He was in fact something of an expert on modern poetry, and was keen to read Steve's work.

'Angie told me that an extract from the poem will be appearing in the next edition of *Outwrite*. That's quite a mark of recognition.'

'I can't quite believe it myself. It all seems a bit unlikely, especially now that Martin Lockwood is ill.'

Declan hadn't heard this news. 'Oh dear, I hope it's not serious.'

'Apparently not, but it is to do with his heart.'

'Does that mean that the next issue is going to be delayed?'

'That's what my friend Rob, who is close to Martin, is saying.'

'Would it be possible, in that case, for me to see the extract in typescript, or if it wasn't being too cheeky, the whole thing, or what exists of it? It's my subject, from an academic point of view, of course. I studied with Heaney at Queen's before I went to Oxford. I don't think I've got my bearings yet in the Cambridge school.'

Steve laughed. 'I don't think my work would be much of a guide to the Cambridge poetry scene. In fact I've been trying to distance myself from it. You need to talk to Rob. Unfortunately, he's on his way to Edinburgh.'

Steve only now realised that when he had made the typescript of copies of *Event/Horizon* for Robin and Grace, he had omitted to make one for Angie. That had been inconsiderate of him, even allowing for the difficulties in their relationship at the time. He consoled himself with the thought that the original poem had been expanded to the point that it was now virtually a new poem. That meant that any impression that Declan had of the poem was based on Angie's reading of it at the beginning of June. She would no doubt have given a faithful account, but the poem had changed since then, almost beyond recognition.

'I don't have a copy of the current state of the poem, but I can certainly type one up and get it to you. I presume you're now in Cambridge for the duration.'

'Yes. Thanks, Steve. I look forward to seeing it.'

Ginny, who had decided that there had been enough discussion of Steve's poem, now ushered them through to the bedroom she and Steve shared. Steve had promised himself that he wouldn't be involved in this aspect of the visit, but found himself trailing behind the other three in ghastly fascination.

Ginny was describing the state of the bedrooms, when they moved in. 'There were clothes everywhere. Hardly anything put away. The girl, whose room this was, had a ridiculous number of shoes. And I speak as someone who was in the fashion business. We had to take all their clothes downstairs and put them in packing cases before we could even sleep in here.'

This wasn't strictly true. Steve had slept for several nights in Beth's bed without even changing the sheets. Ginny was confusing Steve with Jon again.

She was warming to her theme. 'Steve was knee deep in women's underwear. He was having a whale of a time carrying them downstairs.'

Steve choked softly. 'I'm not sure why they thought it was okay to leave the house in the state it was in when I arrived. It was as if Beth only decided to find a tenant at the very last moment. Anyway, to be quite honest, I was more amazed at the shoes than the underwear.'

Angie laughed. 'Women's shoes and underwear, a fetishist's delight.'

Ginny joined in the laughter. 'Quite.'

Steve writhed in embarrassment while Declan's face wore an expression of restrained amazement. Peering at the bedroom arrangements of people one scarcely knew and talking about the fetishistic properties of female undergarments and footwear was a hitherto unsuspected social activity. Steve caught his eye and tipped his head slightly to one side in a subliminal flicker of apology.

They descended the narrow staircase and Ginny took them out to the little kitchen. 'It's a bit snug in here, but it is possible to fit four people around the table, if we put the serving dishes on the side.'

Steve refilled glasses and Ginny pointed out that, as in many of the unmodernised cottages in Cambridge, the lavatory was on the ground floor. Angie decided that she would avail herself of the facilities. When she returned, Ginny commenced serving a starter of Serrano ham and melon with rocket. A toast was proposed to new ventures and glasses were raised. They started eating, but Ginny had not quite finished with her crusade to redefine Steve's personality. Through a mouthful of rocket, she credited him with encouraging her to get back to drawing. She had joined a life class, something she thought she'd never do, run by a woman called Grace, who had been Steve's supervisor. Steve wondered where Ginny was going with this apparently innocuous intro. He didn't have long to wait.

'Steve and Grace go on early morning runs together. I'm not sure whether to be jealous or to encourage it. It seems to be good for Steve's state of mind, although I do worry that Grace has designs on Steve's body. But then I suppose we all do.'

Declan excluded himself from this select group to the general merriment of the gathering. Steve presumed that all Ginny's comments were designed to demonstrate to Angie that if she had the slightest thought of rekindling things with Steve, she could forget it.

But Ginny had not finished with calling Grace in aid as a second line of defence. 'I suppose I could tolerate a little cupboard love. Grace's impulses are largely maternal, I think. And I'm pretty sure that Steve would keep a weather eye out for Grace's husband, who seems to be a bit of a brute.'

Angie was puzzled. 'But isn't she married to Peter Newman, the boss of Inflexion Books?'

Ginny confirmed that that was the case. 'I don't think there's any rule excluding brutes from the ranks of the publishing confraternity. In fact, I should think being a bit of a hard man would be a distinct advantage in that world.'

Ginny cleared the starter plates and produced the main course, chilli con carne and rice with a side salad. Steve replenished the glasses.

So far the evening had been every bit as terrible as Steve had feared. Ginny had been provocative in the extreme. Angie was sticking up for herself, but was constrained, as Ginny had anticipated by the code of politesse that she subscribed to. Declan seemed totally bemused by the encounter and Steve was in a state of shock. Fortunately, Ginny seemed to have decided that she had now done enough to establish that Steve's affections were not in play and let the conversation develop in other directions.

Angie recounted some of her experiences of teaching English to European teenagers. In the end she had quite enjoyed her weeks in a seedy seaside resort. She was not so sure, however, that enduring a bleak English winter there would be quite as pleasurable. Declan laughed and said that she might well revise her views after a first winter in Edinburgh.

The meal was a culinary success and, after the initial opening salvoes between the two women, the conversation settled down to exchanges less freighted with subtext and innuendo. When they had finished the desert of tarte au citron, Ginny suggested they have their coffee in the garden, since it was still light. This suited Declan because he was ashamed to admit that he was a smoker and there was nothing he liked better than a post-prandial ciggy. They carried the coffees outside, but, in fact, there was a chill in the air and the women decided it would be more comfortable inside. Declan said that he'd stay out for a few minutes to finish his cigarette. Steve volunteered to keep him company.

Declan sat and puffed on his cigarette, while Steve stared into the gathering dusk. Finally, Declan broke the silence.

'It was kind of you to invite us. But I would have preferred to have met in a pub.'

'Me too.'

'I guess Ginny prefers her own ground?'

'Yes.'

'I assumed that all the tension would be between you and me, but it seems to be entirely between Ginny and Angie.'

'I believe so.'

'To be honest, I would have preferred not to have had this meeting at all. I've only just moved here and Angie is heading up to Edinburgh shortly. I didn't really fancy being interviewed by her ex and his moll. Little did I realise that instead I would be witnessing a psychodrama between Angie and her rival.'

'Do you see them as rivals?'

'Definitely.'

'Yes, I suppose that's right.'

'Are you doing some kind of Robert Graves thing here?'

'Maybe. Recklessly, I got myself embroiled in the composition of a long piece of writing that I had the temerity to call a poem at the cost of a good degree, a job in the city and my relationship with Angie. I didn't think of it like that at the time, I just felt I needed to do it. But in the meantime I seem to have fallen into an alternative reality, which was perhaps there all along, and which somehow I had failed to notice.'

'That is often the way with these things.'

'Do you write? I imagine you do.'

'Only academic work. In the sense in which you're asking, I am a resolute reader.'

'Very wise.'

'Very cowardly.'

'So that must have been interesting, to have been in Heaney's orbit.'

'It was. And, of course, Seamus wasn't the only Seamus in town, as it were. There was Seamus Deane, with whom Heaney had been at school and then as an undergraduate at Queen's, and the Longleys and in my generation Muldoon and McGuckian. And there was a lot of interaction between the generations. When Heaney had been an undergraduate, he'd been spotted by Philip Hobsbaum who ran The Group, and was instrumental in bringing him to Karl Miller's attention at the *New Statesman*. But Seamus seemed to have arrived as a poet fully-formed, so somewhat intimidating if he was your teacher.'

'Yes, I know someone like that. Not yet, an established figure, but he will be. It can be very annoying. But surely, in that environment, you were tempted to show your own work?'

'Not at all. I can hear the music, I get the shivers, my aerial picks up the message, but my voice can't reproduce it. No talent. And no courage. I can't stand up in a group of sardonic poets and nail my own stuff.'

'Nor can I.'

'You must have. How did Lockwood get to hear about *Event/Horizon*?'

'Through my mate Rob, one of the fully-formed ones.'

'What a great friend!'

'Yeah, but I sometimes feel I should have kept it to myself.'

Declan was thoughtful. 'From what Angie's told me, I don't think I'm going to like your stuff.'

'That's fine. I don't like it myself. It is what it is. Normally I don't work at things. They come freely, they are given. With *Event/Horizon*, it's very different. It's something that has to be sustained. But that means it's fairly rickety. There are all kinds of factors at work in the process of composition, some rational, some irrational. One's loyalty to a personal superstition can sometimes overwhelm one's artistic better judgement. The trick is to match the subconscious and the semantic energies of words. I imagine this is an approach you have little truck with. It will be hard having been exposed to Heaney not to feel that a poem ought to be rooted in homely vocabulary and the nub of experience.'

'Well, no, I don't think you should consider all Ulstermen as wedded to the bog. If you take the other Seamus, Seamus Deane, what you get is a high style of utterance. It might be difficult at times to untangle the sense. Occasionally the reader is left bewildered, but it is undoubtedly exhilarating.'

'I don't know his work. I must take a look. As you describe it, it seems more like my own praxis, at least the bewilderment and the fleeting sense.'

'Maybe it is. Where I might have reservations, is that I object to subject matter just being dumped in a poem, rather than transformed.'

'I couldn't agree more. I don't say that I succeed in that regard, but that is what I aspire to. Doesn't Eliot say somewhere that the subject matter is simply a device to keep the reader distracted while the poem performs its real work subliminally? Or something like that.'

'Nice.'

'Perhaps we agree on more than we think we do, or thought we might. Perhaps I should destroy all trace of the poem and just leave it that we agree in this one respect.'

Declan threw down the butt of his cigarette and stubbed it out beneath the sole of his shoe. 'But that would never do. We might end up being friends, and I came here determined not to like you.'

'The anticipatory dislike was mutual.'

At that moment Ginny appeared through the conservatory door.

'How many poets does it take to smoke a single cigarette?'

The two men jumped to their feet and went into the living room where Angie and Ginny were listening to *Court and Spark* and finishing the bottle of wine.

When their guests had gone, Ginny and Steve unwound with a small joint and a cup of tea. Steve had decided not to make an issue of Ginny's curious behaviour. Nothing would be gained by it.

'That went well,' said Ginny with undisguised satisfaction. 'Angie seemed to like the house and what we'd done to the garden.'

Steve nodded, 'And I liked Declan more than I thought I was going to. I'm relieved. He'll be a good partner for Angie.'

'I thought he was a bit of a pudding, lacking any kind of creative spark.'

'It's hard to imagine that that's how Angie sees him. Why would she enter a relationship with someone like that?'

'There are plenty of people who just want to be in a relationship with someone predictable, the more boring the better. But I don't think that's Angie's motive. I think she sees having a relationship with a quiet Cambridge academic as an excuse to visit Cambridge frequently so she can get to see you without saying that's what she's doing.'

'Ginny, I think you ascribing levels of manipulative scheming to Angie that are simply not part of her character. Why would anyone stay in a relationship with another person just so they could gain access to a third party?'

'What's so incredible about that? It happens more often than you might think.'

'But it would require the third party to be complicit . . .'

'Maybe he is . . .'

Steve felt uncomfortable talking about Angie in this way, but at the same time felt he needed to defend their friendship. 'There's no reason for us not to be in touch from time to time. We have a lot in common, many friends for instance.'

'I think you'll find that that will all change. Of course, when you're student, you think those relationships are going to last for ever. But they seldom do.'

'But I see no reason to hasten the process.'

'I'm not saying that it's something you have to do. It's just what's likely to happen. Of course, I'd rather you didn't communicate with her behind my back. Otherwise I really might start to feel that my suspicions about her relationship with Declan were well founded. And then it would feel a bit like betrayal. I'm sure you'd feel the same about me and Jon, if we were seeing a lot of each other.'

Steve was momentarily lost for words. 'Ginny, that sounds incredibly possessive and controlling.'

'It applies to me as well.'

'You may be right and the relationship probably will wither, but I don't think we should be putting restrictions on each other's relationships.'

'I'm not imposing restrictions. I don't mind your going on your runs with Grace. I don't mind you seeing anyone from your past. I just think that in the cases of Angie and Jon, it'd be better if we both kept them at arms length while we're establishing our own relationship. I'm not making a big deal of it.'

Steve thought that just talking about it like this was making a very big deal of it. They needed to change the subject very rapidly, if they weren't soon to be at each other's throats.

'So, I'm working tomorrow night, but that's okay because you've got the life class.'

'Yes, thanks for changing your shift. I appreciate it.'

'Are you looking forward to it?'

'Not really, to be honest. I was surprised that I enjoyed it so much last time. We'll see. Now that I'm getting my eye and hand in a bit, I'm not sure if it's challenging enough.'

Steve realised that whatever the topic the conversation was, it was going to have an edge. He got up from his chair. 'I'll go and start clearing up.'

Contrary to everything he thought he'd come to know about Ginny, she said, 'No, leave it. We can sort it out in the morning. Let's go to bed.'

Steve's late shift on Saturday passed without incident. Afterwards, he went around to the Eagle to get something to eat and drink. He had just finished his poacher's pie and coleslaw, when he spotted Angie put her head through the door of the bar. There was no sign of Declan. Steve attracted her attention. She came over to his table. 'I hoped I might find you here. I went to the stage door and the man in the little office said this is where you'd be.'

'Angie. What a lovely surprise. Isn't Declan with you?'

'No, once we knew we were meeting you last night, he was able to accept an invitation to high table from the master. He feels he needs to put himself on the map at St John's. Unfortunately, there was no room for me.'

Steve asked her what she'd like to drink. When he returned with her gin and tonic, with plenty of ice, he said, 'Thanks for coming, yesterday. It was lovely to see you. I was expecting not to like Declan, but he seems like a nice guy.'

'He said much the same about you. He said that even though you seem to be firmly in the innovative poetry camp, your instincts seemed quite different.'

'Well, it is odd. I seem to be working on a poem that I heartily dislike. When I'm writing it, it all seems to make sense, but when I look at it later, it seems like nonsense, yet somehow I can't stop working on it. It's as if I were enchanted.'

'I think perhaps you are in a manner of speaking and I don't think it's good for you.'

'Well, I should finish it soon and then I can reconsider matters.'

'Wasn't it you who told me that poems are never finished, only abandoned.'

'I was quoting Valéry.'

'It's pretty clear he knew what he was talking about. I think you should take his words to heart. Finishing things is not you, Steve. This poem is not you.'

'That's not very supportive.'

'Steve, I've tracked you down tonight, because I care about you, a lot. I want to help you.'

'I know my behaviour must seem strange and I'm sorry about the way I treated you.'

'That's not what this is about. There's no need to apologise. I don't bear a grudge. I just want the best for you. And I don't think you're in a good place at the moment.'

'Didn't you like the house and the garden?'

'I didn't mean place quite that literally. Yes, the house is lovely, but it's not you. What happened?'

Steve still seemed to be wilfully misinterpreting her words. 'When she sets her mind on something, Ginny has this intense energy. She just seemed to transform it from a shit heap to an ideal home in a single weekend.'

'You must have helped.'

'I was still on the milk round. But I did a lot of carrying and hoovering when I got back from work.'

'What about Jon?'

'He had to do a gig.'

'Why am I not surprised? And he's out of the picture now?'

'Apparently.'

'To be frank, it didn't look like he'd ever been there. There was absolutely no sign of his presence.'

'There's the camper van.'

'Do you know for a fact that it's his?'

'Well no, but he did say that he'll pick it up when he gets back from the States.'

'The USA seems to have been very helpful in bringing you and Ginny together and keeping you together.

'Ginny is a formidable person, but I don't think even she can cause bursaries from American universities to be awarded. Anyway, why would she be so desperate to keep hold of *me*? She can have whoever she wants.'

'I don't know. But she's not doing you any good. You need to get away from her.'

'Well that's easier said than done.'

'Sounds like you don't entirely disagree with what I'm saying.'

'I don't want to be disloyal and it's kind of weird talking to you about this. All sorts of things are great, but there are some tricky areas. I wouldn't say that I was in control of the situation.'

'What can we do about it?'

'I don't know. Once the poem is finished. Or at least once the extract has appeared in *Outwrite*, then perhaps I can reconsider things.'

'You might get the poem written, Steve, but it'll hurt you. Stop making it a pretext for your behaviour.'

He was shocked. 'I'm just trying to find myself, my *self*.'

'It seems to me that you're confusing the quest to understand yourself in the sense of what motivates you with what emerges when you write, but I think that is to misunderstand the central image of your own poem. If the self is the singularity, the black hole, then by definition you can't see it. You can only infer it, see its effect on other matter, the limit case of which is the event horizon.'

Steve was devastated. It was true, he didn't understand his own poem.

Angie hadn't finished her deconstruction. 'You keep talking about the poem, but that is a quite different thing to your writing. The *poem* is an illusion, a will o'the wisp. You don't need me to tell you that this is what happened to Mallarmé. I remember when you were working on *un coup de dés* with Grace that you told me about the book that he was engaged on which would be the culmination of his life's work. *Le Livre, the* book.'

'Ah, yes. " . . . *que tout, au monde, existe pour aboutir à un livre . . .".*'

'But, I seem to recall that you said that what he meant by that was literally *one* book and that was what he was working on, the book to end all books.'

'I don't see where you're going with this.'

'*Event/Horizon* is your *Le Livre*.'

'And?'

'*Le Livre* never materialised. Fortunately we have the exquisite poems that he produced before this madness engulfed him.'

'I see. Well, it's not entirely true that it didn't materialise. He left notes and plans. Oddly he envisaged the book as a kind of theatrical performance and spent a lot of time working out the seating in the auditorium and the price of the tickets.'

'I hope you're not implying that *Krapp's Last Tape* is merely a working title for a theatrical performance of *Event/Horizon* at the Fringe.'

Steve laughed mirthlessly. 'That's not a bad idea.'

'Steve, stop it. Stop it now. Drop *Event/Horizon* and get back to writing poetry.'

They both fell silent staring at their drinks. Finally Steve found the courage to speak, from a part of his mind that he felt had been submerged in icy water for a long time. He managed, under his breath as though someone else might hear, to say. 'Angie, I miss you terribly.'

He hung his head in shame. When he raised his gaze again, she was looking directly at him. 'I miss you too.'

'This is a fuck-up, isn't it?'

'The thing is, Steve, actions have consequences.'

'So do inactions.'

'Can that word be used in the plural?'

Steve laughed at Angie's poise, but almost immediately relapsed into misery.

'What are we going to do?'

'Steve, I've told you what I think you should do. I can't do it for you. I am just going to stick to my course, not out of pig-headedness, but so you know where I am.'

Steve took a mouthful of beer, unsure if he should broach what he was going to say next. 'Ginny says you and I should no longer stay in touch and she doesn't like the idea of my contacting you behind her back as she put it.'

'What did you say to that?'

'I said I thought she was being possessive and that you and I had a lot in common including friends. She said that's what you feel like at the end of your student career, but that in practice most college relationships don't last very long. I asked why it didn't apply to her and Jon and she said it did.'

'Don't you think that sounds a bit extreme?'

'Yes, but she also said positive things about you, that Declan was a good partner for you and said that you would realise that I was in safe hands.'

'Oh, you poor love, she really is doing a number on you.'

'Do you think so?'

'I do.'

'What am I going to do?'

'Are you going to observe her strictures?'

'I don't know, but it sounds like you won't be able to write to me confidentially.'

'I'm not going to stop writing to you, but from now on I'll make sure that any letters sent to Ainsworth Street are as anodyne as possible and suitable for both of you to read. There's no reason, though, for you not to write to me as frankly as you wish.'

'But you won't be able to reply in the same tenor.'

'Yes, that is a problem. Who could we use as an intermediary? Is Grace trustworthy?'

'Yes, I think she is, even though at this very moment, Ginny is at Grace's.'

'Can you give me her address now?'

Steve scribbled Grace's address on a sheet of paper torn from his notebook. Angie took another sheet and wrote down her address in Edinburgh.

'Keep this safe. And you'll have to warn Grace that she might receive letters from me that will include a sealed envelope for you. How often do you see her?'

'I've been going running with her twice a week recently. But I decided last week to take a break for a bit.'

'Could you resume? Or is Ginny against that too?'

'No, I think you heard her say that she has no objection to my running with Grace.'

'Yes. Why is that?'

'I don't know. I suppose it's because Grace is much older than me.'

'As if that would make any difference.'

Steve managed a small laugh. 'That's what Grace says.'

'Oh really? Should I be worrying about her too?'

'No, she's a good person.'

'I'm not sure I trust your judgement when it comes to women. And yes, I know that can apply to me too.'

Steve couldn't even laugh this time.

'But Angie, this all sounds a bit paranoid. Maybe I've been doing the drugs too much.'

'Maybe you have, but I haven't and I'm worried by what you've told me.'

'When are you leaving Cambridge?'

'Tomorrow afternoon. I'm going back to my parents and then I'm going up to Edinburgh at the end of the week. Let me know when you've set up the arrangement with Grace and I will reply thereafter via her address. And of course you can cancel the arrangement with Grace at any time. But if you ever do want to change the address I should write to you at, put a reference in the letter to something that only the two of us would know.'

'Like what?'

'I don't know. Come on, think. What were we talking about when we were last having fun together?'

'I can't remember.'

'Steve, don't be so hopeless. What was that song we were listening to, when you bought the Django LP?'

'"Limehouse Blues"?'

'Yes, that's it. Blues from East London. If you ever need to change arrangements, make sure to include a reference to "Limehouse Blues" or I won't be able to trust the contents of the letter.'

'You'd recognise my handwriting surely.'

'You might type a letter on that lovely machine that Ginny gave you.'

Steve nodded disconsolately. 'Okay.'

Angie said that she needed to be getting back. Declan would probably have had enough fellows' port by now. They stepped out into the courtyard of The Eagle. Steve was feeling more miserable than he could ever remember. Before they parted on St Bene't Street outside the gates of the old coaching inn, they embraced. Steve didn't want to let go. He was apprehensive at the prospect of the conversation with Ginny when he got home. He felt that she would sense that he had been with Angie, less than twenty-four hours after she had attempted to ban any such encounter.

In the event, Steve was relieved to find that Ginny wasn't in when he got home. It gave him a chance to ponder what Angie had been saying, and to prepare himself to deal with a suspicious or depressed Ginny. He didn't have long to wait. At the sound of the key in the front door, he put the kettle on the gas and put some ground coffee in the jug. When Ginny walked through the door into the kitchen, he couldn't tell immediately what mood she was in, but he greeted her brightly and embraced her warmly.

'I'm just making some coffee. Would you like one?'

Ginny nodded, dropped her bag and sat down on one of the kitchen chairs. She looked tired. Tentatively, Steve enquired. 'How did it go?'

Ginny leaned back in her chair and pushed her hair out of her eyes. Steve held his breath.

'Pretty well, actually.'

Until he knew more, Steve decided to keep anything he said as neutral as possible.

'That's good. The same group?'

'More or less.'

'A range of abilities?'

'Quite.'

'I hope there was at least one person whose technique you could respect.'

'There was as a matter of fact. It was good to have a real challenge.'

Steve had never thought of drawing as a competitive sport, but perhaps all artistic endeavour was competitive.

'Can I see what you've done?'

'Yes, of course, but could we leave it until tomorrow. I'm really tired and could do with going to bed.'

Steve was happy to comply. He had only asked to see her work to preclude the accusation that he wasn't interested. As they were getting into bed, Ginny turned to him and said, 'How was your evening?'

'Not too bad. I've got doing the box office books down to a fine art, which meant I had time to get some food and a pint around at the Eagle.'

Ginny seemed satisfied by this account, rolled over on her side and was soon asleep.

Dead Letters

ON THE RUN

AUGUST TURNED INTO SEPTEMBER. The days were getting noticeably shorter and the colours in the garden were changing, but the weather remained fine. Ginny's father's health continued to deteriorate with the result that she was now spending two nights a week with him. This inevitably had an impact on Steve and Ginny's sex life, but relations between them remained loving and supportive. In the meantime Steve continued to work on his poem and Ginny spent more time in front of the easel, occasionally with Steve as her model. But Steve had not returned to running with Grace, partly as a way of avoiding any further talk of him modelling for her life class and partly because he had still not yet decided whether to ask her to be the intermediary for letters between him and Angie. In the intervening weeks since Angie's visit, there had been little in his relations with Ginny to substantiate Angie's fears for him, which now seemed baseless and alarmist. Perhaps her motives were not quite as altruistic as she claimed.

Towards the middle of the month, Ginny reminded Steve, that the coming Saturday was the date of the next meeting of Grace's life class. On his way to the kitchen on the morning of the day in question, Steve spotted several letters on the doormat one of which was an envelope addressed in Angie's distinctive hand and another that looked as though it was from Rob. Steve was slightly disturbed by the synchronicity, but more worried about what Ginny's reaction might be to a letter

367

from Angie. His first instinct was to conceal it, but that approach had gone wrong before. And, to be fair to Ginny, there had been no more talk recently about communication with Angie being abrogated.

Ginny had not yet come downstairs, so Steve decided to read it quickly to ensure that it was the kind of letter he could mention to Ginny, maybe even let her see. He opened the envelope to find that the letter comprised a meagre two sheets of Basildon Bond note paper written on one side only, and not the usual multiple pages densely covered on both sides. There was no address, just the word *Edinburgh* and the date. The salutation was addressed to both Steve and Ginny and it was followed by a neutral account of Angie's first days in Edinburgh. She trusted that Steve and Ginny were well and signed off with best wishes. Steve was initially shocked at the formality and lack of any real engagement, but then he remembered that Angie had said that she would send the occasional bland missive to allay any suspicions. And he did after all have her Edinburgh address safely stowed in a folder in his room. He then opened the other letter, which was indeed from Rob and in substance very similar to Angie's, but in his case giving his address in Edinburgh.

A few minutes later, Ginny appeared in her nightdress, her hair deliciously mussed, on her way to the loo. She yawned, bending down to give Steve a kiss, but stiffened as she saw the letters. Steve affected nonchalance. 'We've had a note from Angie letting us know she's now in Edinburgh. And I've had one from Rob too. The new academic year is getting into gear.'

Ginny sniffed and went into the bathroom without comment. While she attended to her ablutions, Steve went next door to the living room, as if to look for something, purposely leaving the letters on the table. When he returned a little later with a book in his hand, Ginny was sitting at the table sipping from a mug of coffee. She seemed more relaxed. He guessed she had cast her eye over Angie's letter, as he had indeed intended, and had noted that it was not only devoid of emotional content, but didn't even have a return address.

She smiled quizzically at him. 'Aren't you late for work?'

'No, I'm on a late shift today. It's better than spending a Saturday evening on my own.'

'Oh, Steve, I'm sorry. Would you rather I didn't go to these things? I don't mind stopping.'

'No, no, that's not what I'm saying. I'm really pleased you're getting back to the art. It's just since I have to do a certain number of late shifts, I might as well do them on the evenings you're not here.'

'Steve, you're such a sweet boy.'

'It's enlightened self interest.'

He caught her eye. She smiled again, this time more brazenly.

When Steve got home from work, Ginny was still not back from the life class. He made himself a cup of tea and went up to his work room intent on replying to Rob. Before he sat down to start writing he thought he'd cast his eye over Rob's letter. He opened the folder in which he kept his correspondence. The most recent one from Angie was lying on the top of the pile, but he was unable to find the one from Rob that had arrived on the same day. It wasn't like Steve to mislay things. Occasionally he propped correspondence that he needed to deal with on the little mantelpiece. But it was not there either. He checked in the drawers of the desk and on the bedside table, to no avail. Irritated at himself for being so disorganized, he scribbled a rough draft and resolved to have a thorough search for the missing letter the next day. He would need it for Rob's new address. He then went next door to their bedroom and read until he heard Ginny's key in the door.

A few moments later she entered the room and dropped her bag. Steve put his book down.

'That was a long one.'

Ginny nodded. She was busting for a pee. 'I'll tell you about it in a minute.'

She went down to the bathroom and returned a little later, makeup removed, moisturiser applied, teeth cleaned, hair brushed and gleaming. She slipped off her clothes and folded them before pulling her nightdress over her head and climbed in beside him. Steve found the gracefulness and the poise, with which she undressed extremely arousing. And it was Saturday night. But he felt that as a matter of sensitivity, he should let her unpack the details of how the evening had gone before they got down to more routine nonverbal matters.

'So, how was it? Were you pleased with your work?'

Ginny lay there, staring dejectedly at the ceiling. 'I didn't produce any work.'

'You mean work that satisfied you?'

'No, I didn't do any drawing. Jackie, the model, didn't turn up. Grace was going to abandon the evening. So I volunteered to be the model. It's not as if I haven't done it before.'

'Oh, Ginny, that was very public spirited of you, but it must have been very frustrating too.'

'Yes it was. I was thinking of coming back here to persuade you to come and model, but then I remembered that you were at work. Anyway, I rather enjoyed it. I told Grace that she could consider me Jackie's stand-in.'

Steve sucked on his teeth but resisted saying anything, thankful that he had volunteered for the late shift and that the chances of his being asked to model for Grace's group had now diminished.

Just as he was about to turn over and close his eyes, he said, 'You haven't seen the letter from Rob lying around, have you? I wanted to reply to it, but I seem to have mislaid it.'

Ginny shook her head. 'Steve, I'm happy to cook your meals and provide you with other services, but I can't keep track of your correspondence as well. I'm sure it will turn up. It's probably got mixed up with Beth's mail.'

Steve thought that was unlikely, but said, 'Yes, that's probably it.'

Steve loved Sundays. He and Ginny had got into the habit of staying in bed late and then having a bacon sandwich brunch with copious cups of tea as they read the *Observer* and listened to the radio or to records.

At one point, Ginny looked up from her reading and said, 'There's a piece here about Inflexion Books and a profile of Peter.'

Steve looked up from his own reading. 'Really? What does it say?'

'It's just a publicity piece, really, about how many prizes their authors have won and the new books they've got coming out in the autumn. And there's a photo of Peter holding up one of their books. What do you think that Grace sees in him?'

'I'm surprised you ask. It can't be too bad being married to a successful publisher. Some people might even think he's rather good looking.'

'But he's just a businessman. Really, Grace is much more interesting.'

'I'm not Peter's biggest fan, especially after that evening I spent with him in the Free Press, but I don't think you can call him uninteresting. His background is tragic and fascinating. And I'm sure being a successful businessman has its compensations if you're his wife.'

'But the downside of that is that he has to spend more and more time in London, according to Grace. They've got a flat in the Barbican, but she can't get down there much during term time.'

Steve laughed. 'Ginny, your concern for their marital relations is very touching. I didn't have you down as a marriage guidance counsellor.'

Ginny grinned. 'No, I just feel sorry for Grace. Even when the woman in a couple is empowered, the man still seems to get the better deal.'

'You may well be privy to information that is unavailable to me.' Steve said. 'The life class conversations you've been having recently are probably very different from those she and I had when she was taking my essay on Proust apart.'

'Well, you must talk about something on those early morning runs.'

'There's not a lot of talking gets done and in any case I haven't been on one for at least two weeks.'

'Why have you given up?'

'I haven't given up really. I've been concentrating on the poem.'

'Come on, Steve, surely you can do both. When's the next session?'

'Tuesday, I suppose.'

'You should go.'

After breakfast, Steve went up to his room to do some work on his poem. As he walked past the end of the bed he glanced at the mantelpiece and noticed a letter propped against the wall. He picked it up and studied it closely. It was the letter from Rob. That was odd. He was sure that it hadn't been there the previous evening. He took it over to his desk and slipped it into the folder. He would write to Rob later.

Encouraged by Ginny and reassured by her willingness to be the stand-in model for Grace's life class, Steve joined Grace on her Tuesday run.

Grace greeted him warmly. 'Hello stranger. Where have you been?'

'I don't know, the time has just flown by.'

'Well, it's good to see you, but could I suggest you get yourself proper running kit, or at least a decent pair of running shoes. It's not good to run in plimsolls.'

'Yes, ma'am.'

They set off on their usual route. Once they'd got into their stride, Grace said, 'Do you mind if we go a bit further this morning? I've decided to sign up for the Cambridge 10k, and I need to start getting comfortable with a longer distance.'

It wasn't quite what Steve had been expecting on the first day of his return to running, but said, 'That's fine. If I get into difficulties, I'll drop out.'

After a while, Grace said, 'How's Ginny?'

'She's having to spend a lot of time at her father's in London. He's not well, sounds like he's dying. To begin with, she was staying over just one night a week, but it's starting to be a couple of nights a week now.'

'Oh, that must be a worry for her.'

'Yeah, it takes her some time to recover when she gets back.'

'I can imagine. When does she next have to go?'

'She's there at the moment. She went yesterday and will be back tomorrow, all being well.'

'So you're fending for yourself at the moment.'

'That's okay. I'm not totally out of my depth in the kitchen.'

'I'm sure you're not. But how about coming to my place for supper this evening? Pete's away too. So, we could have a light supper, not too much to drink, and I will try and persuade you to enter the 10k as well.'

Supper at Grace's appealed, even if being talked into a 10k did not. Could he make seven-thirty? There was no need to bring a bottle.

In the event the longer distance presented Steve with no real difficulties. He felt good and was grateful to Ginny for having encouraged him to get back to running.

On the return leg, Grace returned to the subject of Ginny. 'I wonder if Ginny explained what happened the other night at my life class?'

'Yes, she said the regular model was unwell and that she volunteered to pose.'

'I'm glad she told you. It was very brave of her.'

'Well, it is something she has done before, on a professional basis.'

'Yes, she didn't appear in the least daunted. But she was clearly disappointed that she didn't get to draw.'

'I can assure you that Ginny only does what she wants to do.'

'I'm sure that is so. Unfortunately it seems that Jackie is going to be indisposed for a while and so unless I can find another model, Ginny will have to pose at the next session too. It seems cruel to impose on her again, when her enthusiasm for drawing has only just been re-kindled.'

Steve didn't like the turn the conversation had taken. 'If Ginny doesn't want to model for the group, I am sure she will make it abundantly clear.'

'Of course.' Grace paused for a moment, choosing her words carefully. 'I've asked you this once before, and you weren't keen, but I don't suppose you'd reconsider being the model at the next session.'

'Honestly, Grace, the prospect fills me with dread.'

'Come on, Steve. Ginny says you're a very good model.'

'It's one thing posing for her, quite another for a group of people I don't know.'

'Of course, I understand that. But these things are all in the head.'

'No doubt.'

'Okay. I'm sorry, Steve. I didn't mean to put you under pressure. I got the impression from Ginny that you'd become comfortable with the idea recently. Don't worry about it. I will be the model for the next session. Put it out of your mind.'

'I'm sorry, Grace. You must think me very childish.'

'Not at all. I'm sorry I brought the subject up again.'

They reached Grace's gate.

'After all that, are you still up for supper this evening?'

Steve felt that it would just seem like petulance, if he now changed his mind. 'No, no. I'd love to come to supper.'

Grace smiled at him gratefully and disappeared through her front door. Steve jogged back to Ainsworth Street.

This life class business was getting out of hand. He was pleased that Ginny had rediscovered her enthusiasm for art, but he was far from delighted that she and Grace seemed to be united in trying to persuade him to be a life model for sundry spinsters of the parish. Back at the house, he had a quick bath, got dressed for work and headed out to the Arts Theatre.

Grace had said not to bring a bottle, but he didn't want to arrive empty handed. He also wanted to make up for his intransigence over the issue of modelling for the life class. He had noticed the flicker of disappointment that had crossed Grace's face and felt that his manner had verged on the truculent. He remembered the advice that the gaffer had given him on his last day at the dairy about the usefulness of flowers when having a spot of bother with a member of the opposite sex or 'her indoors' as the gaffer had put it. Grace could hardly be considered to stand in that relationship to Steve, but she was most definitely a member of the opposite sex. Acting on this advice, although not entirely convinced by it, he bought a large bunch of chrysanthemums from a stall in the Market Square during his lunch break in the hope of restoring good relations.

As he was walking back to the theatre with the flowers, he noticed that one of the stalls nearby was selling shoes and had several pairs of running shoes on display. On an impulse he asked to try on a pair of Adidas TRX running shoes. The first pair he tried were a little too snug. But the next pair fitted perfectly, so he bought them. Grace had also said that he should get clothes that were better suited to running than the rather basic tee shirt and shorts that he had been wearing on their runs. Unfortunately the trainers had cost more than he anticipated. He would therefore have to defer getting the rest of the kit to the following week. He went back for the afternoon session in the box office pleased with his purchases.

Later that evening, not without a trace of unease, Steve presented himself at Glisson Road. He was wearing his new trainers, ostensibly to break them in, but actually to demonstrate to Grace that he was prepared to follow her wishes in most respects, and carrying in his arms the big bunch of chrysanthemums as a peace offering. As Grace opened the front door, Steve thrust the flowers at her.

'Steve, they're lovely. Thank you. Come in.'

She led him into the big kitchen at the back of the house.

'You can open a bottle of wine, while I put these in some water.'

Steve uncorked the bottle of Médoc that was standing on the table and poured two glasses. Grace stirred something in a pan on the hob, then sat down at the table and took an appreciative sip of the wine.

'So how's the job going?'

'Oh, the job's okay, if a little boring. But it pays the rent. And the people I work with are a nice bunch, but to be honest I prefer the stage crew. There's this guy Butch who has been showing me around backstage and explaining how things work. My stint in the box office comes to an end just before Christmas. I'm rather hoping I might get a job as a casual on the stage crew in the new year.'

'I gather you are now a regular in The Eagle.'

'Yes, that's where the stage crew hang out.'

'And the Scaramouche too, I believe. I didn't have you down as a frequenter of gay clubs.'

'I wouldn't say frequenter. Who's been telling on me?'

'Matt and Gary, of course. I have my spies everywhere.'

'I must have missed them when I was there.'

'Does Ginny know about this aspect of your life?'

'No, I don't think she does. My purposes for being there are entirely post-hours alcohol related.'

Grace winked at him. 'That's what they all say. Your secret is safe with me. And how's the poem going?'

'It's not really. I was looking at it yesterday, and it just seems to have become nonsense. Angie thinks I should abandon it, in the spirit of Paul Valéry.'

'Well, Valéry certainly knew a thing or two about writing poems. And your former girlfriend may well have a privileged view. So, you two are still in touch?

'Yes. She and her new boyfriend came to dinner a few weeks ago. And then the following day, I bumped into her in The Eagle.'

'It's that kind of place. I presume this was in the absence of your current partners.'

Steve looked down in embarrassment. 'Yes, as a matter of fact, but it wasn't contrived, not on my part, at any rate.'

'But possibly on Angie's part?'

'Well, I'm not saying that either.'

'But during this chance encounter, she suggested you abandon the poem you've been working on for months?'

Steve wasn't sure how to proceed. Grace could see that she had put him on the spot.

'Don't answer that right away. I need to concentrate on the meal for a few minutes. Would you mind laying the table, the cutlery is in the right hand drawer of the dresser. There's a baguette in the bread bag, and a breadboard and knife nearby. And a jug of water, and some tumblers over there.'

Steve jumped up, happy for the opportunity to consider his response to Grace's question while he laid the table. Soon the supper table was laid and Grace served spaghetti with a carbonara sauce and a green salad. She asked Steve to grate some Parmesan, while she served the pasta.

They started to eat. Grace loaded a fork with some pasta and before conveying it to her mouth fixed Steve with a questioning look.

'I'm sorry, Steve, it's not my business really. You are, of course, old friends. And there's absolutely no reason why you shouldn't meet up, although I am a little surprised that she should seek to deter you from finishing the poem.'

Steve took a sip of his wine. 'No, actually I wanted to talk to you about the situation. It's just that I didn't know where to start. Maybe it's better if I do it backwards, but I've got to ask you to be very discreet about what I'm going to say.'

Grace made it clear that she could keep a confidence.

'It was Ginny's idea to invite Angie and Declan around to our place. Ginny has worked wonders, making the place nice. I think she wanted to show Angie that we had a great place to live and that I was in safe hands. The evening went well. But after they'd gone, Ginny said that she'd rather I didn't stay in touch with Angie. I said that she was an old friend and we had friends in common. It's not as if we were likely to bump into each other much. She was going up to Edinburgh a few days later.'

'But you did bump into her the very next day.'

'Yes, by chance on my part, but Angie admitted that she had tracked me down because she was worried about me. She didn't think I was in a good place. The thing that really hit home is that she said that I didn't understand the central image of my own poem. And for good measure she said that finishing things wasn't my style.'

'Well, she has a point.'

Grace topped up their glasses, while Steve resumed his account.

'She said that the poem had become an endless task that kept me attached to Ginny.'

'But you started the poem before you hooked up with Ginny.'

'That's true. But as far as I could make out, Angie was saying that Ginny had somehow made herself the subject of the poem. She was the dark star and I was caught in her gravitational field.'

'Wouldn't it be easier to interpret Angie's reactions as simple, old-fashioned jealousy?'

'Yes, but if you knew Angie, I think you'd see that she's not like that. And in any case, there was no talk of us getting back together. She and Declan seem to be getting on fine.'

'But it does sound like you miss her.'

'I do. And I'm actually a little afraid of where things are going with Ginny.'

Steve had said more than he had intended. But Grace realised there was still more to come. 'So, where do I come into this?'

'Angie said that I could write to her confidentially, but she wouldn't be able to be quite so candid in her responses, unless she could get a letter to me through an intermediary.'

'Because Ginny might intercept or read a letter sent to you at Ainsworth Street?'

'Yes. And I thought of you. I know it sounds melodramatic and I'm sorry to ask.'

Grace was silent for some time. Steve was afraid that he'd mis-judged the whole situation.

'I don't know, Steve, I'm not sure I want to be dragged into this. It does seem melodramatic. I've come to like Ginny. And all I know about Angie is what you've told me. On the other hand, I know you quite well and I don't have you down as a drama queen. But it doesn't bode well for a relationship when one of the the partners starts to hide things from the other.'

Steve felt ashamed. 'I'm sorry, Grace, I've abused your friendship.'

'Don't be absurd. I'm glad you trust me enough to talk to me about it. I am sure you have friends in Cambridge who would be prepared to act as your dead letterbox without any questions asked, so I imagine that in asking me you anticipated or wanted a bit of push-back. You know I care about you. I'm just not sure about the best way to help you. And I'm even less sure I should be abetting you in this escapade.'

'And I'm not even sure that it's a mechanism I want to activate. I needed some help to think it through.'

'Well, okay, but I do feel a little awkward *vis-à-vis* Ginny.'

'Honestly, so do I.'

They finished their meal and Grace suggested that they go into the living room, play some records and avail themselves of Peter's single malts. Steve was happy to change subject and location. They went through to the front room. Steve glanced admiringly once again at Peter's modernist take on the Rokeby Venus that hung in that room, while Grace went over to the shelf of LPs.

'Don't worry, I'm not going to subject you to more Serge Gainsbourg. I'll find something less dated. You pour the whiskies. You know where they are. You choose and I'll see if I can guess which malt it is.'

Steve opened the drinks cabinet and found a large collection of whiskies. He remembered that when he and Ginny had previously come to dinner they had both drunk Lagavulin, so he passed over that one. Since he had no idea what any of the others tasted like, he picked one at random and poured two generous shots of Oban, adding a splash of water to each, as he had seen Peter do. Meanwhile the room filled with the sound of cool jazz. Once the otherworldly muted trumpet came in, Steve guessed it was Miles. Grace occupied the chesterfield, directly beneath Peter's canvas, curling her legs up beneath her. Steve handed her a tumbler of whisky and sat in one of the armchairs. Grace took a sip of whisky and said, 'Nice try, but you can't catch me like that. Slightly peaty, so you immediately think Islay, but I'm pretty sure this is Oban.'

Steve was impressed. 'Spot on.'

He took a sip from his own glass, appreciating that it was considerably less smoky than the Lagavulin. He was certainly no connoisseur but felt that the flavours were better balanced. After a few moments of meditative silence, as they savoured their drinks, Grace said, 'So, what are we going to do with you, Mr. Percival?'

Steve shrugged and said nothing. Grace tried a different approach. 'Ginny is an intense person. I don't imagine that life with her would ever be plain sailing, but I'm sure there are compensations. What was her previous partner like?'

Steve gave her a brief portrait of Jon.

'I see. Someone older than you, with an air of danger about him, but unreliable.'

Steve concurred.

'So that was an explosive situation, with two such intense people living together. And Ginny probably values you for all the ways in which you're not like Jon. How long had they been together?'

'Several years. Ginny called it a marriage of convenience. Not that they're married. Jon saw off unwelcome male attention directed at Ginny and she enhanced his rock star image.'

'Sounds plausible. Then you came along.'

'And that's the point at which ideas of plausibility break down.'

'I don't know. There's certainly something intriguing about you. Helping a young man evolve away from inherited models of masculinity is the kind of project that might appeal to a certain kind of woman and if that happens to involve long nights of passion, that's just one of those things that has to be endured.'

Steve blushed. Grace knocked back her whisky and said, 'Would you mind pouring me another and help yourself too. You were a bit conservative with the measures.'

Steve downed his own, took Grace's glass and went over to the drinks cabinet. As he passed the coffee table that stood in front of the sofa that occupied the bay window, he noticed that Grace's sketchpad was lying on it, open at a highly accomplished and expertly shaded life study of Ginny observed from a challenging, if somewhat intimate, point of view. It must have been done at Saturday's life group.

'Grace, what an amazing piece of work! I didn't realise that you were such an accomplished artist.'

Grace was puzzled. Steve pointed to the sketch.

'Oh, that's not mine. That's Peter's work.'

Steve was shocked. 'Peter?'

'Yes, I can't do anything as brilliant as that.'

'But I thought it was a woman only group.'

'Well, de facto really, there was no particular rule. Ginny left one of her sketches here after her first session. Pete found it and was impressed, he decided that he'd like to compete with her. That's the kind of person he is. So he joined us for the end of August session. He and Ginny were trying to outdo each other. I think that's why she was disappointed that she had to model the other day.'

Grace noticed the look of confusion on Steve's face. 'You didn't know about this, did you?'

Steve shook his head slowly. Grace could see that, in the context of the conversation that they had just been having, this piece of information was not particularly helpful.

'Steve, I can assure you, it was all very proper.'

Steve didn't reply. He refilled the glasses, handed Grace hers and sat down.

'I'm sorry, Steve. You're upset, not because she modelled for us. You knew that. It's that she didn't tell you that Pete had joined the group and you're reading something into that. You're the one feeling a sense of betrayal.'

Steve didn't know what he felt.

'I have no doubt that Pete finds Ginny attractive. What man wouldn't? But his motivation here is purely competitive. He realised from the sketch that Ginny left here, after the first session that she came to, that she too is both classically trained and talented. He saw it as a challenge. As did she, I imagine. The fact that she volunteered to pose the other day was a matter of frustration to both of them I would say. In any case, he's working around the clock at the moment, getting ready for the Frankfurt Book Fair.'

Steve wasn't convinced. 'I just don't know why she didn't tell me.'

'Just like you didn't tell her about meeting Angie? It works both ways, you know.'

Steve could hardly deny the parallel and sipped his whisky morosely.

Grace realised that Steve had had enough of home truths. 'You are in a state, aren't you? I'm sorry. This evening was a bad idea. I think we'd better bring things to a close.'

Steve agreed. He finished his whisky and thanked Grace for the meal. Grace drained her own glass. 'Maybe we should confine this kind of conversation to our runs. I notice you're wearing new trainers. I hope that means you're taking the idea of the 10k seriously. Did you get some running togs too?'

Steve said that he hadn't. Grace jumped up from the sofa. 'Wait there. I'll be back in a moment.'

While she was out of the room, Steve went back to the coffee table and studied Peter's study of Ginny. Hearing Grace's step on the stair, he returned the sheet to the approximate position it had been in and regained his chair. Gace re-entered the room with a bundle of sports clothes in her arms and a large carrier bag.

'There's some running vests her and a couple of pairs of shorts. They're Peter's, but he hasn't worn them for ages. He's put on too much weight recently.'

Seeing the expression of doubt on Steve's face, she added. 'They've been washed and aired.'

Without waiting for a reply she put the clothes in the bag and pushed it in Steve's direction. 'They were about to be put out. If you don't want them, drop them off at Tiger Lily. I'm sure they'll take them. They're already design classics.'

Steve took the bag not wishing to seem ungrateful, but feeling that this was a very strange way to rectify the situation that had arisen. He moved towards the door. Grace stood in his way and put her hands on his shoulders.

'Put this out of your mind. You'll see, there's nothing in it. Cut her a bit of slack.'

She pulled him towards her and gave him a hug, holding him for a moment. He was aware of her scent and the strands of auburn hair that brushed his face, but resisted her embrace, maintaining a respectful distance between their bodies. She released him and said, 'And yes, I'll act as your dead letterbox. But please don't use it too much.'

He thanked her again and made his way to the front door. She followed him to the threshold.

'Steve, there are two other conditions. The first is that you don't dismiss entirely the idea of being our model at the next life class session and the other is that you enter the 10k, to which end I'd like you to join me on the Friday runs too. It will do us both good. And it will give me another chance to try and convince you that there's nothing to worry about.'

Steve attempted a smile, accepting the additional conditions wordlessly and went out into the night, deep in thought.

Peter might be a trained artist, but his participation in Grace's life class smacked of *droit de seigneur*, motivated more by voyeuristic than aesthetic impulses. He was angry with Ginny too. Why hadn't she mentioned that Peter had been at the class? He found it hard to believe that it was just an oversight.

Ginny was already home, bustling around in the kitchen, when Steve got back from work the next day. She seemed to be in a good mood. She gave him a friendly kiss on the cheek and said, 'Cup of tea?'

He nodded and sat down at the table. Ginny put the kettle on and then sat opposite him. She instantly saw that something was wrong.

'Steve, are you okay?'

'I'm fine.'

'You don't look fine. What's on your mind?'

The brave thing would have been for him to express his unhappiness about Peter having participated in the life class, even if it meant coming across as unsophisticated. But he was reluctant to raise the matter.

That was surely the problem with their relationship. Increasingly, Steve was avoiding the difficult conversations in the quest for a quiet life, a policy diametrically opposite to that followed by Ginny herself. Exchanges could be light-hearted with Ginny. She had a nice line in joshing. But, if Steve joined in the mood too wholeheartedly, she could just as quickly flip back to her default sullenness and shut him down. This made conversations, even the simple ones, a minefield. Joshing with Ginny was a one way street.

And this wasn't a simple matter. It could easily get out of hand. He pulled himself together and resolved to keep the mood as light as possible.

'I'm sorry. It was a busy day at work. The tea will perk me up. More importantly, how was your father?'

'Much the same.'

'But not worse?'

'Hard to say. What about you? What did you get up to, while I was away?'

'I followed your suggestion and went on a run with Grace. She tried to talk me into entering a 10k race. I'm only running about half that distance at the moment, so I would need to do quite a few more training runs. She said that if I was serious about doing it, I would need to get a proper pair of running shoes. Running that distance in plimsolls is not a good idea.'

'I would say that she knows what she's talking about. Did you get some?'

'I did, but I haven't run in them yet. She also invited me to supper.'

Steve wasn't sure how this last piece of information would go down, but Ginny seemed completely unperturbed. 'I'm glad there's someone else to look after you when I'm not here.'

'She also said how grateful she was to you for helping her out of a jam with the life model.'

Ginny shrugged. 'It was the least I could do.'

'She said you'd mentioned that I posed for you and wondered whether I would be prepared to do so for the class so that you wouldn't have to stand in for Jackie.'

'Did you succumb?'

'Not exactly. I said I'd give it some thought.'

'That sounds like a yes to me.'

'Maybe I've been getting this prevarication thing all wrong. I thought it was code for no.'

'You *are* getting it wrong.'

'Well, I was just trying to convey my reluctance, but not very effectively by the sound of it. Anyway she's in the picture now.'

'As indeed she is. I hadn't realised that the big canvas in their front room is one of Peter's pieces for which she posed.'

Suddenly, Steve found himself straying into the very territory he had planned to avoid.

'Peter is clearly a talented artist. I saw an image that he made of you at the last session.'

Ginny drew in a sharp breath and steadied herself. 'What did you think of it?'

'I'm not a competent judge. His work seems very accomplished. The vulvocentric point of view must have been quite a challenge, though.'

'Steve, I'm sorry I didn't tell you. I thought you might be angry, in a protective way. But the whole thing was very proper.'

That was exactly the phrase that Grace had used.

Ginny pressed on. 'I daresay I will feel much the same, when you're revealing your taut, young body to that bunch of middle-aged women.'

Steve wanted to say that clearly the group wasn't only women now, but settled for an almost inaudible, 'I suppose so.'

So much for his resolve to keep the mood light.

Ginny studied his face closely. 'Steve, I do believe you're jealous. What an old fashioned chap you are! Please don't worry. I can look after myself.'

Steve finished his tea. 'I know you can. I just don't trust *him*.'

He stood up. 'I think I'll go upstairs and do a bit of work before supper.'

Ginny came over to him and put her arms around him, pressing her body against his. Initially he resisted her embrace, but almost immediately found himself reacting to her proximity. Reassured that she could still work her magic, Ginny kissed his neck and whispered 'Later, then.'

He went up to his room where more brooding than writing was done until he was roused from his melancholic lucubrations by Ginny calling him for supper. The food and a glass of crisp white wine put him in a better mood. By the time they got to bed, he was in a more responsive frame of mind.

Ginny and Steve didn't return to the subject of Peter and his infiltration of the life class and over the next few days Ginny paid Steve more attention than of late. Reassured by her pampering, he started to think that he might have got the whole thing out of proportion. Perhaps it had been a mistake to have expressed his fears so explicitly to Angie. And maybe Grace had been right to query the dead letterbox arrangement. He would join her for the Friday run and tell her that he had decided to cancel the arrangement. It was unnecessary and not really fair to Ginny. And it would be an opportunity to sport his new kit.

On the Friday morning he presented himself in Glisson Road in his new trainers, singlet and shorts. Grace was delighted and said, 'I hope you're not in a rush this morning. We need to increase our distance.

And by the way, I have now put you down for the race. It's on Sunday the 17th of November.'

Steve accepted the commitment with equanimity. It was six weeks off, so beyond the normal range of his anxiety radar. As usual, he let Grace make the running.

Once they had settled into a comfortable pace, Grace said, 'How was Ginny when she got back?'

'She seemed fine. Her father's condition is stable at the moment. So she didn't seem quite as stressed as when this all started. We've actually had a really nice time since she got back.'

'That's good to hear.'

'We talked a lot. She apologised for not having mentioned that Peter had joined the life class. She hadn't thought it merited any special mention. And she was amused and touched that I was being so jealous. She asked me to consider how she might feel with me in the buff, flaunting my manhood in front of a bunch of women at your next class.'

'She has a point, Steve. I'd better make sure to have some smelling salts to hand.'

Steve continued. 'So things have been fine between us. I feel a fool.'

But Grace wasn't going to let him beat himself up this fine morning. 'I blame myself. My handling of various aspects of this sorry saga could have been better. For a start, I could have been more sympathetic to your concerns. And we both probably drank more than was good for us that evening, especially for two people who were about to get into training for a 10k.'

Steve said, 'Quite. Anyway, now that I've calmed down, the dead letterbox arrangement seems ridiculous. I'm going to write to Angie and suggest we abandon it. But in the meantime, I'm afraid that you'll probably get one or more letters from her.'

On the homeward leg of of the run the following Tuesday, Grace said, 'Your first letter arrived yesterday. I'll nip in and get it for you when we get back to my place.'

Back at Ainsworth Street, Steve sat down at the kitchen table and looked at the envelope, experiencing a little surge of pleasure at the site of Angie's bold, expressive handwriting. He tore the envelope open and began to read.

Dear Steve,

Well, what a place Edinburgh is! I had no idea how beautiful it was. I've spent the last few days criss-crossing the city. And what a city of contrasts! The Gothic of the Old Town and the Georgian elegance of the New Town, pinnacles and monuments everywhere, and, towering over the lot, the gaunt hulk of the Castle. Most of the buildings are made of stone and built on very generous lines. I'm staying for now with some friends in New Town. They have a flat in a very grand but rather gloomy Georgian house.

The university is much grander than I was expecting. In fact, the whole place makes Cambridge seem a little parochial.

It was good being able to talk frankly when we "bumped into" each other in the Eagle. The performance that Ginny put on the previous day was quite extraordinary. She must think I am gullible in the extreme if she expected me to be taken in by it. To be quite honest I have not changed my mind about what I suggested to you that night. You are not in a good place and you should be making strenuous efforts to disentangle yourself and to do that you need to assert yourself.

I do feel sad that we are not exploring this marvellous city together and I do think that you have behaved in a childish and petulant way. At least you had the good manners to send your poem to Declan. I think he has enough experience of the poetry world to know whether a young poet has what it takes. I just hope that you have done enough in the work in progress to correct his initial misgivings.

I am sorry to write in such negative terms, but the reality of being in this beautiful city without you makes me sad and angry.

With love, Angie

When he had given Angie his approval for the dead letterbox scheme, Steve had not had any very clear idea of the nature of the communications he might be receiving from her. He had imagined they might be consoling, encouraging, maybe even slightly flirtatious, leaving him a way back. But that did not seem to be what Angie had had in mind. She was using it as a opportunity to speak her mind, as a way of shaking Steve out the hypnotic trance that she believed he was in.

Steve realised that if he had been more sensible, he too might now be getting to know what sounded like an amazing city. He felt a sharp stab of regret. But then, he supposed, that was exactly Angie's intention. He also felt that the brief interaction with Declan had been positive despite the initial misgivings on both sides. Perhaps Declan had not been sincere with him and had subsequently shared more critical thoughts with Angie. But what really puzzled Steve was why Angie should write such a hurtful letter..

The more he tried to make sense of the letter, the angrier he became. He had dealt honourably with Angie. How he lived his life with Ginny, or with anyone else for that matter, was really none of her business. She said he should assert himself, but was it only self-assertion when the other person approved of the behaviour, and solipsism otherwise? He was fed up with asking for permission to write his poem, to live his life the way he wanted to live it.

He wasn't the hapless youth she and others seemed to take him for. There was more to him than winsome charm and a vague air of being interesting. He could be tough and decisive when it was appropriate. And he considered himself resourceful and self-reliant. Angie had got him all wrong. And so for that matter had Ginny. She treated his writing as if it was a harmless hobby. To an extent he expected that from Ginny, but not from Angie. There were only a handful of people who actually valued what he wrote. Well, two in fact, Rob and Martin. And actually, now he came to think of it, there was one other - Grace.

MICHAELMAS GLOOM

Cambridge/Edinburgh
Sunday, 22 September 1974

THE MICHAELMAS TERM HAD started and lectures and supervisions were in full swing. Steve felt sad not to be involved. It was the first time since he was a small boy that the start of the academic year had not marked a new beginning. Even though he was still smarting from Angie's letter, it was not lost on him that had he stayed with her, he might now be experiencing a new beginning in Edinburgh. And by contrast not only did life with Ginny no longer feel new, but the good relations that he had reported to Grace at the end of September had evaporated. Her trips to London to look after her father seemed to exhaust her more than ever and it often took her a day or two to recover. Any intimacy between them was now almost non-existent. When Steve did manage to prevail upon her to accommodate his needs, the verve and imagination she had shown previously in the summer had been replaced by a grudgingly dutiful approach to the matter.

It didn't help that the national mood was gloomy too. The Labour administration under Harold Wilson had brought the dispute with the miners to an end, but the economy was still struggling. Nor had there been any let up in the IRA bombing campaign. Following the outrage of the M62 coach bombing at the start of the year which had cost 12 lives, the sporadic attacks had continued, most recently with the bombing of two pubs in Guildford, no doubt in response to Wilson's announcement on 18 September of a General Election. This campaign, the second one that year, had been distinctly lacklustre and Labour had won with a majority of three seats. Steve had cast his vote for Labour again, but Ginny had shown absolutely no interest in the matter and he did not think she had voted. In Cambridge there had been a tiny swing to Labour, but most of the votes had come from the Liberals and David Lane was returned for the Conservatives with a healthy majority. It seemed unlikely that the new Labour government would be able to achieve much with such a slim majority, especially when there were substantial internal divisions over Europe.

On the second Monday of the month Steve was down for the late shift and consequently was in no particular hurry that morning, unlike Ginny, whose preparations for visits to her father were becoming ever more elaborate. Steve kept out of her way as she rushed around, ironing a couple of blouses and packing her overnight bag. Eventually when she had her things together, she came into Steve's room where he was once again trying to make some sense of the most recent draft of his poem and gave him a peck on the cheek.

'I'll see you on Wednesday. Be good.'

Steve walked downstairs with her and stood on the front doorstep as she set off for the station. He watched her sashay to the end of the road, admiring how chic she looked in her tailored skirt and jacket, topped with a scarlet beret and carrying her small overnight bag, totally out of keeping with the dusty marginality of Ainsworth Street. He hoped her father at least appreciated what a smart, good looking young woman his daughter was. Steve waited until she turned the corner and then went back inside to get himself ready for work.

Since he had resumed running in mid-September, Steve had not missed a single one of Grace's training runs. She was beginning to notice that his speed and stamina had improved considerably. On more than one occasion she had had to ask him to slow down. Now in mid-October he felt he was ready to stretch himself a bit. He therefore decided to warm up with a fast three or four miles on his own before joining her for a few miles at a pace that suited her better.

The only problem was that it was difficult to time his arrival in Glisson Road and when he got there she had obviously assumed that he wasn't going to show and had set off on her own. Spotting her already a couple of hundred yards down the road, he sprinted to catch up with her and came abreast of her, puffing hard. Grace laughed when she saw how hard he was breathing and said, 'I thought you were getting fitter, but if that's what a jog from Ainsworth Street does to you, I don't rate your chances of finishing a 10k.'

Steve grinned and said between breaths, 'I've done more than jog from Ainsworth Street. I've just done three or four miles at quite a lick.'

Grace was impressed.' Well, I hope you don't mind doing another five or six at my pace.'

Steve shook his head. 'I'll treat it as a warm down.

Grace laughed. 'Get you, Dave Bedford.'

Soon, as in previous weeks, they were running along in companionable silence. Later back at Glisson Road, Grace said, 'I nearly forgot. There's another letter for you.'

Steve was embarrassed. 'I'm sorry, Grace. I still haven't got around to cancelling the arrangement with Angie.'

'Not to worry, she's clearly not overusing the facility. This is only the second letter in three weeks or so.'

He took the letter and jogged back to Ainsworth Street with a degree of apprehension. If this letter was anything like the previous one, he wasn't sure how keen he was to see its contents. He let himself into the house, went through to the kitchen, put the kettle on for a cup of tea and tore the letter open.

Dear Steve,

I'm writing to apologise for my previous letter. I had no right to be so critical. It was written in a fit of petulance at the realisation that I did not have you here to discover Edinburgh with me. I am not surprised that you did not reply to it and I am now feeling remorseful. It's hard to imagine that you weren't hurt by my comments, especially when, as I know, you have been doing your best to steer an honourable course through the hazards of relationships and, at the same time, produce a significant piece of work. And I particularly regret my comments about your poem and those that I made when we met in The Eagle. I really don't think you should give it up.

You may wonder what has prompted this act of contrition. And you may not be entirely surprised to learn that I bumped into Rob the other day at a faculty event. Over a drink later, he told me how much he admires you and your work. I immediately felt ashamed that I hadn't taken your work as seriously as he does. What a good friend he is! He thinks you should be given every encouragement to finish

Event/Horizon. If he does have a criticism, it is that you don't take your own work seriously enough, but he also appreciates that the path of the artist is not always a direct one. We can all be blown off course by the storms and encounters of life, but it may be that these are all grist to the poetic mill.

Please allow me to withdraw my earlier comments and accept my apologies. I only want what's good for you.

With love, Angie

PS Declan and I have decided not to continue our relationship. This is not the place to go into the reasons for our decision, but we remain friends.

Steve put the letter down and sipped his tea thoughtfully. He was glad that he had not dashed off a reply to Angie in the retaliatory spirit that her previous letter had provoked in him. He now had the opportunity to reply in more measured tones. He was was grateful to Angie for her bravery. It can't have been an easy letter to write. In the context of her reiterated promise to hold to her course, last week's letter had seemed completely out of character. He was a little surprised that Angie and Declan had called it a day, but not excessively so.

Right at the moment, though, the person to whom Steve was most grateful was Rob. Once again, Rob had shown himself to be the best friend any writer could wish for, especially one so lacking in self-confidence. Rob routinely went out of his way to help others, an approach that was distinctly absent from Steve's own social skill set. For instance, he still hadn't even acknowledged Rob's letter of two months previously informing him of Martin Lockwood's illness or the more recent one, which he had briefly mislaid giving his address in Edinburgh. In fact, he couldn't remember the last time he had actually written to Rob. For a moment, he saw himself as he supposed others saw him, a self-centred brat. There wasn't a spark of altruism in him.

He finished his tea, stripped off his running kit and climbed into the bath. He made a solemn promise to himself not to go to The Eagle that evening. He would write to both Angie and Rob when he got back from work. Once dressed, he popped across to the Empire Stores to pick up a packet of frozen fish fingers, a tin of peas and some potatoes, so that he had something to eat when he got home.

Bert was his usual chatty self. "Saw you going off early this morning in your sports gear. What do they call it? Jogging?'

Steve laughed. 'Yeah, I prefer to call it running. Jogging is just a bit of a fad.'

'Supposed to be good for you.'

'I suppose so.' Steve was reluctant to admit that he was motivated by anything as mundane as concern for his health.

To Bert's way of thinking running, or jogging, as a way of keeping fit didn't make any sense. 'Why don't you play football? There's plenty of running involved. There's also a point to it. Score more goals than the other side. And then there's the camaraderie with your teammates.'

Steve acknowledged the cogency of Bert's view, but claimed to have no ball skills, when, in actual fact, what he lacked was the team player mentality. His own mother had pointed out as much, when he had tried to convince her that he was capable of taking a production of *The Importance of Being Earnest* to Edinburgh. She had doubted his story on the basis that she knew him to be a lone wolf.

In an attempt to rise above his inveterate self-absorption, Steve said, 'You know, Bert. I think you might be right.'

As Steve pushed open the shop door, Bert called after him, 'What's 10k in old money anyway?'

Steve, laughing, shouted back over his shoulder, 'Six and a quarter miles.'

That evening, after his fish finger supper, Steve got out his notepad and dealt with the reply to Angie first. He apologised for not having replied to her first letter. It was not because he was irritated with what she had written, it was that Ginny's father was dying and she needed a lot of emotional support at the moment. He knew that none of this was exactly true, but he convinced himself that it was the best way to put Angie's mind at rest.

He then moved on to the poem. So far as that was concerned, his own thoughts were not so different from Angie's. It seemed to have become some kind of Sisyphean task, one which he would dearly love to relinquish. Nor was it impossible that Ginny had indeed become its centre of gravity. He couldn't work out whether she represented the feminine side of his nature, or the dark side, or perhaps both. He felt that if he abandoned the project now, it was not only the poem that would be left broken. So he just had to battle on.

Aware that he had spent a considerable part of his reply on an elaborate justification for the failings of his poem, he now turned to the subject of Rob. He was glad that Angie had caught up with Rob, who, as Angie said, was indeed a thoroughly good bloke. He was also feeling guilty that he hadn't written to him for ages, but he was now planning to put that right as soon as he had finished this letter to Angie.

And finally, there was the matter of Declan. He was sorry that he and Angie were no longer an item. He was sure that Angie would soon meet a suitable replacement in Edinburgh. Despite the strained circumstances in which Declan and Steve had met, Steve had actually warmed to him. He would still be interested his take on the poem, even if it was critical.

Steve signed off affectionately and stuffed the letter into an envelope. He realised that the missive he had just penned was a prime example of what Angie had once called an exercise in the art of digression. He told himself that she would be reassured by this. He then hurriedly scribbled a note to Rob, apologised for not having acknowledged Martin's illness, thanked him for his contact details, promised to write to him at greater length in due course and hoped that he was enjoying Auld Reekie. He would post both letters the next morning.

The letter from Angie had stabilised Steve's mood with the paradoxical result that he was now very much looking forward to Ginny's return. On previous Wednesdays by the time he got home, Ginny had generally got something already on the go for supper. He didn't want her to feel that he took her cooking and housekeeping for granted and wanted to do something to show his appreciation. During his lunch break, he picked up a good bottle of wine and a large bunch of flowers.

His delight in the anticipation of their reunion was shattered midway through the afternoon session, when one of the secretaries came down from the administration offices with a note for him from Ginny. Her father's condition had deteriorated. She was going to have to stay in London for another day or two. She hoped to be back on Saturday, but she couldn't guarantee it. She would keep him posted. Steve thanked the girl for bringing down the message and went back to his work. He knew it was an uncharitable thought, but he just wished the old man would hurry up and die.

The news left him in a bad temper for the rest of his shift. He trudged home with the bunch of flowers tucked under his arm and the bottle of wine in his shoulder bag. On Mill Road he picked up some fish and chips from the chippy. Back at the house, he plonked the flowers in a vase, uncorked the bottle and proceeded unceremoniously to eat the fish and chips out of the paper, not something that Ginny would have approved of. When he had finished the food, he took the bottle of wine through to the sitting room and spent the rest of the evening playing Led Zeppelin records very loudly. An hour or so later, having drained the bottle, he stumbled upstairs and threw himself down on the bed, fully clothed, and went to sleep.

The following evening, Steve decided to forego the pleasures of fish and chips scoffed from the wrapping paper. Instead he went to The Eagle after work. It was late by the time he got home. He pushed the front door open to find a letter addressed to him on the doormat. He took the letter through to the kitchen and, squinting at the handwriting, identified it as being from Rob. He threw the envelope on the table and put the kettle on. It seemed unlikely that it was a reply to his own letter. He had only put that letter in the post the previous day. Their letters must have crossed in the post. Mug of tea in hand, he sat down at the table and opened the letter.

First of all, Rob was delighted to be able to tell Steve that Martin was much better and was back at work. So production of the next issue of *Outwrite* could resume. Rob had volunteered to do the copy-chasing for Martin. Was Steve happy with the extract from *Event/Horizon* Martin had chosen and the few edits he had made? Unless Rob heard from Steve by the end of the month, he would assume that he was happy for Martin to go ahead.

Still on the subject of poetry, Rob announced that he had made inroads into the Edinburgh poetry scene. He was pleasantly surprised at its diversity. He had already been invited to perform at a number of readings. He was looking forward to unfurling the banner of Cambridge obscurantism north of Hadrian's Wall and letting the Jocks have both barrels, if that wasn't an inappropriate image for flyting. *Just like Rob*, Steve thought, *he doesn't let the grass grow under his feet.*

Rob apologised for the brevity of the letter, but he did have one more thing to tell Steve. He had bumped into Angie at a faculty get-to-know-you drinks party. He had taken Steve's advice in the typewritten letter that he had received from him in mid-September, for which he thanked him, and had plucked up the courage to ask her if she'd like to come to his next reading. He was delighted to say she had agreed. But suddenly he was much more nervous about what Angie would think of his work than the reaction of the Celtic bards. He was worried that she might find his stuff a bit tame compared to Steve's own work. Rob also mentioned that he was surprised at the clarity of Steve's insight into the female mind. Clearly access to a typewriter had revealed a hitherto unexpected sensitivity in Steve.

Short though the letter was, it packed a considerable payload, some of which Steve found incomprehensible. He already knew from Angie's letter that she and Rob had encountered each other. It was always nice to see a familiar face in an unfamiliar environment, he supposed. But she had said nothing about supporting Rob at a poetry reading. Steve reflected that this was not something that she'd ever offered to do for him. Admittedly she could hardly be faulted, since he'd resolutely refused to do readings. But in a way, he still resented this small act of kindness. He knew that he had a lot to be grateful to Rob for, as he had in fact admitted in his letter to Angie and as he even admitted to himself from time to time, but he did hate the way that Rob made Steve out to be some kind of anointed bard when the exact opposite was the case and it was Rob who was the coming man in the poetry world.

Steve read the letter over again. What was this business about Rob being grateful for Steve's advice? So far as Steve could remember he had not given him any advice recently, or indeed ever. It was not in Steve's nature to hand out advice. He had enough difficulty plotting his own course through life. And even if he had been minded to, he would have been hard pushed to name a single competence in which his expertise was demonstrably superior to Rob's. The flow of advice was routinely in the opposite direction.

And what was this nonsense about the Olivetti revealing another side of Steve? As if a dumb machine was some kind of crystal ball or scrying cup. Perhaps he was talking about Steve's poem, because apart from the one letter he had put in the post the previous day, Steve hadn't written to Rob for some time and in any case he didn't use the typewriter for personal letters. In fact the only thing he had used the typewriter for so far was the poem. But if the sections of the poem that Rob had already seen revealed another side of Steve Percival, then Rob was reading the poem in a way that wasn't obvious to Steve himself.

Pleasant anticipation at Ginny's return now turned into truculent impatience. He was too unsettled to join Grace on her run on the Friday morning. On his lunch break he bought a new bottle of wine and the components for a beef casserole which he cooked later that evening so that he would have something already prepared for when Ginny got back the following day.

The early shift on Saturday seemed interminable. Midway through the afternoon he asked Fiona if he could leave a little early. He explained that his girlfriend had been away for a few days caring for her ailing father and was coming back that evening. Fiona was happy to accommodate him and he finished his shift an hour early. With luck he'd be back before Ginny. When he got home, he was relieved to find that she was not back yet, which gave him enough time to tidy up the house. He rushed around, making the bed, doing the washing up, putting some gentle music on the hifi and lighting some candles and finally putting the casserole on a very low heat in the oven.

By seven o'clock the casserole was starting to smell delicious, but there was still no sign of Ginny. He could really do with a drink. Maybe he could just have one glass of wine. He opened the bottle and poured himself a very meagre glass. Half past seven came and went. He was starting to get anxious. Well, irritated more than anxious, but anxious too. If Ginny was staying in London another night, she would surely have left a message at his work. Unless there had been some kind of emergency. He poured himself another glass, this time a full one, and checked the casserole, turning it down even lower.

Then just after eight o'clock he heard a key in the door. A few seconds later Ginny appeared in the kitchen. She looked strained. Steve was alarmed, 'Ginny, are you okay?'

She slumped in the chair. 'I'm exhausted. It was a terrible journey, the train broke down.'

Steve poured her a glass of wine. 'At least it wasn't something awful with your father. I thought there might have been an emergency.'

'Not an emergency, but he's not well. I'm afraid I've got to go back to be with him tomorrow. I've come home to get a change of clothes. I'm not sure how long I'll be away. I hope to be back on Monday, but I'll keep you posted.'

It looked like the crisis had arrived. The old man must be close to the end. Steve didn't really know what to say. Maybe it would be a good idea if she had something to eat. 'I've made a casserole.'

'Thank you, love, but I'm too tired to eat. I'm going to drink this glass of wine and then go to bed. Thank you for making something. You go ahead and eat on your own.'

Steve commiserated and stroked the back of her hand, which she withdrew after a moment and said, 'Would you mind sleeping in the other room tonight? I just need to crash out.'

Steve could hardly object, she looked terrible, but it was not what he had been anticipating. 'Can I run you a bath?'

She shook her head. 'I'll just use the lavatory and clean my teeth and then I'll go up.'

She went into the bathroom, closing the door behind her. When she emerged a few minutes later, she pecked Steve on the cheek, picked up her bag and went upstairs.

DISENCHANTMENT

GINNY DIDN'T RETURN ON the Monday and nor did Steve get a message from her. He didn't understand why she was so secretive about the telephone number at her father's house. Getting messages to him through the theatre's administrative office was cumbersome to say the least, nor did he like the idea that his colleagues must be starting to wonder about his relationship, no doubt fuelled by unfounded insinuations from Seb. He was beginning to wonder about it himself. He couldn't understand why she wouldn't let him support her through this difficult time.

After work, he moped around, too distracted to do any work on the poem. At least the next morning was a running day. He wondered whether he could confide in Grace about these latest developments. But when he got to Grace's door the next morning, he was disappointed to find a note pinned to the front door bearing the enigmatic legend, 'Something rather unexpected has occurred'. Frustrated, he set off on the run on his own. Taking advantage of the absence of his usual running partner, he upped the pace considerably and was pleased to find that he was able to maintain it for nearly an hour. He arrived back at Ainsworth Street puffing hard but feeling more positive than he had for several days. Why didn't he go out on his own more often?

On his way home from work later that day, he picked up some more provisions, even though there was still plenty of casserole left. Back at the house, he was delighted to find Ginny sitting in the kitchen, waiting for him. His delight soon subsided when he saw how pale she was and the strained look on her face. She accepted his welcoming kiss without enthusiasm and blankly watched him unpack the shopping. When he'd put everything away, she said she'd make a cup of tea. Steve would have preferred something stronger, but Ginny said. 'I think we should stick to tea.'

Steve took this mean that she had bad news to impart, about her father presumably, and sat down without demur. The act of making two mugs of tea seemed to take an inordinately long time. Steve, who could bear the tension no longer, said, 'Ginny, speak to me. What's happened? Is it your father.'

Ginny sat opposite him and passed him a mug of tea. 'No, it's not my father,' and after a pause, 'I don't actually know how to put this . . .'

Steve couldn't remember a single moment in the time that they'd been together when Ginny had been lost for words. She took a deep breath and then said, 'Steve. I'm leaving you.'

Her words didn't make any sense. 'What do you mean you're leaving me?'

'I'm moving out. Our relationship is over.'

Steve still didn't get it. 'Over? Why? What have I done?'

'It's not what you've done. It's what I've done, what I'm doing.'

'Ginny, for God's sake, stop talking in riddles.'

'I'm leaving you. For someone else.'

'Who?'

'Peter Newman.'

The additional information didn't make things any clearer.

'Ginny, are you okay? Have you been taking something?'

Ginny had now gathered enough momentum to explain things properly.

'I've been seeing Peter for some time. I was with him in Frankfurt, last week. He's leaving Grace. We're going to live together in his flat in the Barbican. I'm sorry, Steve, I didn't expect it to turn out like this.'

'Do you mean that all this business with your father has just been a ruse and that he's not ill at all?'

'No, he's ill and he really is dying. But I haven't been with him all the time that I've been in London. I've been with Peter.'

'But you don't even like Peter.'

'No, I love him.'

'I don't believe you, Ginny. There's something else going on here. Where's Peter now? Does Grace know this?'

'Yes, Grace knows.'

'Why didn't she tell me then when I last saw her? She didn't behave like a woman whose husband had just left her.'

'That's because she only really found out yesterday.'

'How?'

'I don't know all the details, but someone saw Pete and me together in Frankfurt and told her. She then searched Pete's things and found a note to him from me in a jacket pocket. He shouldn't have been so careless, but I shouldn't have written it. She decided to have it out with him and went down to the Barbican flat yesterday. Unfortunately, I was there with Pete. The situation got rather ugly.'

Steve didn't know what to say. He still couldn't take it in. But Ginny hadn't finished. 'We meant to manage things better, prepare you and Grace, but we lost control of the situation. Grace wants a divorce, which is fine, because that's what Pete wants too.'

Steve wished she would stop calling him *Pete*.

'And she doesn't want him back in the house, other than to pick up his things. Despite the brave face she and Pete put on things, the relationship was over a long time ago. But in our case, I'd hoped that I'd be able to let you down gently. Maybe gone our separate ways when we had to move out of this place, but Grace has rather raised the ante.'

'So, what? You were going to continue having a relationship with me, while you were shagging Peter on your Florence Nightingale trips to London?'

Ginny was unrepentant. 'Something like that.'

'Don't you think I might have started to suspect something?'

'Perhaps, but the realisation might have developed gradually, giving us both time to adjust and to make arrangements.'

'Ginny, this all sounds heartlessly calculating.'

'Steve, you knew we were only temporary lovers.'

'I knew no such thing. I've given up a lot for you.'

'And you got a lot too. We've had a wonderful time together. You're a lovely guy. You deserve someone better than me.'

'Ginny there isn't anyone else like you. I admit that you're not always easy to live with, but you're beautiful, sexy, intelligent and talented . . .'

'Steve, I'm truly sorry, but you can't persuade me to change my mind.'

They wrangled with each other for another half an hour until Ginny called a halt. She would be going back to London the next morning and would return in a few days to move her stuff out. She didn't want any supper. She was going to bed now. Steve should sleep in his own room. On no account should he come into her room. There was nothing more to be said. She went into the bathroom, emerging a few minutes later, face washed and hair brushed into a gleaming knot. She made no attempt to kiss Steve, moving swiftly towards the door. Her one concession to the fact of their proximity was a murmured 'Good night'.

Steve stared blankly into space. He didn't feel angry, so much as foolish. Right from the start, Ginny had advised him not to invest too heavily in the future. He just hadn't understood that she meant their future together. She'd recommended taking things as they came, enjoying being with each other while they could. Everything had turned to ashes. Suddenly he felt very sorry for himself. Angie had been right. He'd assumed her attitude had been driven by jealousy, but he now saw that she had anticipated some kind of disaster. What a fool he'd been! Waves of misery swept over him. He didn't know what to do.

He was only able to escape from this vortex of self-pity, by turning his thoughts to Grace. What must she be feeling? Had she had any inkling of this? Would she blame Steve? After all, he was the one who had introduced Ginny into their lives. And if he felt guilt in relation to Grace, he felt visceral anger towards Peter.

Steve was still sitting at the kitchen table an hour later. He'd gone over every detail of their conversation in his mind. He had tried to work out at what point Ginny had started to deceive him. He imagined it was probably after the life class when she had modelled and Peter had joined the group. Or was it possible that she had identified Peter as her next lover the very first time that she and Steve had gone to Glisson Road for supper. He realised this was crazy thinking and was somewhat letting Peter off the hook. It was just as likely that it had been Peter, who had been the one doing the manoeuvring.

He knew it wasn't particularly helpful to indulge in such speculations. The sensible thing to do would be to have some supper and go to bed, but he had no appetite now. What he really wanted was a drink. Fortunately he had enough sense to realise that getting drunk was not going to solve anything and might in fact make things a great deal worse. So in the end he settled for making himself a cup of tea and having an early night.

A short while later he lowered himself onto the bed in his writing room, only a few feet from where Ginny herself lay in the bed which until recently they had shared. The two doors that separated them may have been made of cheap deal, but at that moment they might as well have been forged steel. He wondered if Ginny was still awake. He had no desire to resume the bitter conversation of earlier, but he would have liked to hold her in his arms just one more time, make love to her, just one more time. Even as he framed the thought, he dismissed it. He switched the light out and sipped his tea in the dark, straining to pick up the slightest sound of her breathing. If she were crying, he could perhaps offer to comfort her. The reality was, of course, that he was the one who was on the edge of tears.

Eventually he drifted into a shallow sleep. In the fitful dreams that ensued he rose from his bed and went into the next room intent on joining Ginny in her bed. He could hear the gentle sound of her breathing. He stood for a moment and inhaled the indescribable scent of her body. He yearned to hold her. He pulled back the duvet and was shocked to find that the bed was empty. Suddenly he heard a noise of footsteps behind him and as he turned, caught sight of a figure in a nightdress slipping out of the room. He followed her out, but by the time he was on the landing she was already at the bottom of the stairs. He went downstairs and found himself at the end of a long corridor in an unfamiliar house. There was no sign of Ginny. He searched the house, which now had many more rooms than seemed possible. He soon realised he was lost and couldn't even find his way back to his own room to retrieve the manuscript of his poem. He woke with a start not sure whether he was more troubled by the loss of Ginny's love or the loss of his manuscript.

A little later, washed and dressed and ready for work, he sat at the kitchen table, morosely munching his way through a bowl of cereal. Maybe Ginny would resile from her hard line of the previous evening and join him for a cup of tea, offer some words of comfort perhaps or at least say goodbye. But no sound of movement came from the up-stairs room. He didn't want to breach her rules of conduct for these last hours and minutes together, but he did want to see her one last time.

Given the layout of the house it occurred to him that he could simply wait there in the kitchen until a call of nature brought her downstairs, even if it meant he was late for work. In the end he knew that her determination not to interact with him was stronger than her urge to empty her bladder.

Reluctantly he concluded than he would have to go to work without seeing her. Before he put his coat on, he went upstairs to his room and got his notepad out. He sat down at the little desk and wrote a short note.

> Dear Ginny.
>
> I'm so sorry that things have turned out like this. I have loved you. And I thought you loved me. Perhaps you did for a while. These last few months have been the most intense of my life. I am hurt and sad, but I'm also grateful for the time we have had together. I will never forget you, and I will always love you. Perhaps we can even remain friends. I know this is a cliché of romantic fiction, but I don't want to think of a future in which we don't see each other from time to time. I hope things work out well for you.
>
> With love, Steve.

He folded the sheet of paper in two and wrote Ginny's name on one side. He took it downstairs, propped it on the kitchen table and set off for work.

When he got back that evening, the note had gone. There was no sign of Ginny. He went upstairs and saw that the door of her room was open. He looked inside. The room looked as it always did. But as he turned to go out he noticed that the red suitcase that normally sat on top of the wardrobe was no longer there. He drank in the details of her room, the scarves, the clothes, the shoes.

Later he heated up the casserole and ate it disconsolately. He saw no reason not to drink this evening. There was no one to have a fight with, except himself. He opened the bottle of wine and poured a large glass. The house was already losing its magic. When he'd finished his supper, he took the bottle into the sitting room and put a record on. Ginny's easel was still in the corner, the image of him that she had been most pleased with still taped to the board.

On the Friday morning he put his running kit on with a feeling of trepidation. It wasn't beyond the bounds of possibility that things could turn nasty. He got to his usual position outside Grace's house and jogged on the spot. After a short while the front door opened to reveal Grace, standing on the doorstep in her dressing gown. She waved him over. 'Steve, there's too much to talk about to go on a run, and the subject matter is too upsetting. Come inside, and we'll have some breakfast and talk. That is, if you don't mind.'

She could see the hesitation on his face. 'I understand if you don't want to talk, but I need to explain a few things.'

Steve thought he'd better hear what she had to say and followed her inside. Grace put the kettle on. 'Coffee?'

Steve nodded again. Neither of them spoke, as she made the coffee. She passed him a mug of coffee and sat down on the other side of the big table.

'I assume you've spoken with Ginny.'

'She did most of the talking.'

'I can imagine. So you know the basic situation. First of all I'd like to say that I'm so sorry. I feel that I've exposed you, your relationship, to a person who just takes what he wants.'

Steve wasn't sure what to say. This wasn't how he had expected the conversation to go. He'd anticipated being the one doing the apologising.

'I should have warned you about Peter. I think I tried to persuade you that Peter's motives for joining my life group were to do with his artistic competitiveness. But I am afraid that I was glossing over his record as a philanderer. This is not the first time. We had couples counselling the last time he strayed. I honestly thought he'd got control of himself, but clearly I was mistaken. Maybe I was deceiving myself. And I failed to warn you. I shouldn't have let him attend the class. I shouldn't have let Ginny pose. The whole mess is my fault.'

It did seem remiss to have been so blasé about Peter's propensities.

'If they'd just stuck to screwing at the London flat, it might have all passed over in due course with no one else any the wiser, or hurt. Unfortunately, they thought they'd be safe in Frankfurt to act like a couple. The trouble is Peter is a well-known figure in the publishing world and Ginny is not someone you fail to notice. A friend who is also in publishing phoned to tell me that she had seen Peter at the Frankfurter Hof with a beautiful girl on his arm, who was vaguely familiar.

She probably thought she was doing me a good turn, but no one wants to have their nose rubbed in their partner's infidelity.'

'I'd remove that friend from your Christmas card list if I were you.'

Steve immediately regretted the tone of his remark. But Grace simply ignored his comment and continued with her reconstruction of Peter and Ginny's dastardly doings.

'At first I assumed it must be one of the girls from the office. So at that stage I decided that I'd just give him a hard time when he got back on the Sunday evening. We'd have an almighty row. He would be repentant, having had his fill of adoring totty in Frankfurt. But then he phoned late on Sunday saying that his flight had got in late and so he was going to stay at the flat. He wouldn't be home until Wednesday. I immediately smelt a rat. I didn't buy his explanation that he had a series of post-Frankfurt meetings. I sensed that he had the girl with him.'

'So, you immediately thought this was more serious than one of his routine infidelities?'

'Yes. The jealousy was gnawing at me by now. I couldn't really go down to London at that time at night, but I figured I might find proof of his infidelity in the house. He is notoriously careless. I searched through the folders on his desk and found nothing incriminating. As a last resort, I went through the pockets of his suits and found what I was looking for, a love letter. But the thing that was particularly wounding wasn't that the letter was from one of the office bimbos. It suddenly became clear that the woman he'd been with in Frankfurt was Ginny. And that meant that things had been planned in advance, which in turn meant that they'd been having an affair for some time.'

Ginny's behaviour over the last two months suddenly made much more sense to Steve. 'They must have been meeting when Ginny went to London ostensibly to look after her father. What a gullible idiot I am!'

'You had no reason to suspect Ginny, but I had plenty of reason not to trust Peter. I was furious, of course, but mainly with myself. I went to bed determined to go down to London the next day and have it out with him. Unfortunately, I had lectures so I couldn't get away until late afternoon. In any case, he would have been in the office. I thought I'd probably get to the flat before him and that would give me a chance to look for other proof. But I needn't have bothered. When I got to the flat, I found both of them there *in flagrante*.'

'Please don't go into details.'

'I blew my top and screamed obscenities at them. If it had just been me and Peter, we might have calmed down a bit, but having the sphinx-like Ginny observing us screaming at each other, just made us both take up more entrenched positions. I ended up saying it was over between us. I didn't want him back. He could stay with his floozy. I would be seeking a divorce and citing Ginny. That was the only time that she looked anxious, the rest of the time she seemed to be quite enjoying it.'

'Yes, for some reason, Ginny is desperate to preserve her incognito.'

'Obviously, I couldn't stay. I said I was going back to Cambridge and that Peter should not return to the house. He could arrange to get his things through my solicitor. As I was leaving, I said to Ginny that I hoped she wasn't going to leave it to me to speak to you. She said that she would speak to you the following day.'

'Which is exactly what she did. She was pretty brutal about it, no beating about the bush. She was leaving me. Peter was leaving you. She and Peter were going to live in the Barbican flat. She said she had hoped to let me down gently, but that your arrival had rather precipitated matters. She said we'd had a good time together, while it lasted. I deserved someone better than her.'

'She doesn't do sentimentality, does she?'

'The problem was that I couldn't get a sense of what you were feeling I wanted to come around sooner to talk to you. I realised you'd be upset, but I thought you might be angry with me too, so I decided to wait for the regular Friday run.'

'I was more angry that you *didn't* come around. I convinced myself that Ginny hadn't told you, or had persuaded you that it was a mistake and it would all blow over or that I'd gone crazy.'

'So what happens next?'

'Who knows? The unravelling?'

'Grace, I'm sorry to be so prosaic, but I've got to get ready for work.'

'And so have I. I'm glad we've had this talk, I guess it's going to be rather unpleasant for a while. Let's try and stay friends. At least we've got the 10k.'

For the first time that morning, they both almost laughed.

Over the previous weeks, Steve had coped reasonably well with Ginny's increasing absences, because the assumption had been that she would be back a day or two later. But now that she had left, Steve felt unmoored. It wasn't the first Friday evening that he'd been alone in the house, but now he didn't know what to do with himself. He seemed to have forgotten how to structure his time without her.

Life with Ginny had been very inward-looking. As a couple they had been intensely wrapped up with each other. Steve was hardly an extrovert but he'd had a reasonably wide circle of friends before he and Ginny had started living together. It wasn't as if he didn't know people in Cambridge, even if most of his immediate friends had left town, but somehow he hadn't got around to searching them out. Apart from his growing friendship with Butch at The Arts, none of his work relationships amounted to much. He saw Grace once or twice a week, but usually in the context of training for the 10k. But apart from that, he and Ginny had kept themselves to themselves. It was almost as if they had been confined to an island, of which they were the sole inhabitants. But now suddenly he had been freed, or more precisely perhaps, abandoned.

Other guys of his age would be in a pub. And there was nothing to stop him having a session himself at The Loco, or almost any other pub in Cambridge, but he simply couldn't muster the enthusiasm. In truth, he felt bereft. Ginny may have gone, but her presence pervaded the whole house. The scent she used still hung in the air and most of her things remained where they had been placed when she had transformed the interior of the house that first weekend. No doubt, at some point, she would make arrangements to collect them, but even before that her aura would begin to fade. He needed to drink it all in now before it went completely.

After a basic supper, Steve decided to try and record his impressions of life in the Ainsworth Street house with Ginny. In the absence of a camera or any ability with charcoal and sketchpad, he was reduced to trying to capture those rooms and spaces in writing, supposedly his core competence. But his writing skills now seemed entirely inadequate for the task in hand. At the very least, he supposed, he could make an inventory of what she had left. He looked around the kitchen, but was unable to identify any personal items of hers in that room. He had already noted the previous day that Ginny had removed her toiletries from the bathroom. Everything had gone, even the box of tampons and the small bar of her favourite soap that normally sat on the glass shelf above the sink. Not that such items would have been the kind of evocative object that he was looking for.

What he really wanted to find was an example of Ginny's handwriting. The routine exchange of handwritten notes and letters was an important part of Steve's life and relationships. A week without at least one letter would be drab indeed. A person's handwriting was effectively as unique as his or her fingerprint. He prided himself on being able to tell who a letter was from just by looking at the envelope. Even now, every time he recognized Angie's handwriting on an envelope, his heart beat a little faster. In contrast the note that he had left Ginny the previous day had been the first written communication between them.

For Steve, for whom writing was evidence of existence, even more than it was the life blood of correspondence, the absence of anything in Ginny's own handwriting gave him the eerie feeling that she had never really been there, that the relationship had been a fantasy. And now that he thought about it, he was not sure that he had ever seen Ginny writing. Drawing, yes. She had filled several sketchbooks in their time together, but so far as he was aware she had not used her sketchbooks for to do lists or notes. But surely she must have made the occasional shopping list? He hunted through the kitchen cabinet and the drawer in which they kept Beth's mail, but could find nothing. Perhaps there was something in another part of the house.

He went next door into the sitting room. Most of the books and records in this room were Beth's. The easel with the study of Steve taped to the drawing board in the corner of the room was by Ginny, but that was not what he was after at that moment. The only other thing that was not Beth's, apart from candles on the mantelpiece, was Jon's stash box, which was, of course, really Ginny's stash box. No, if there was going to be any written material in Ginny's hand, it was most likely going to be in her bedroom.

He climbed the stairs and pushed the door of her room open carefully as if somehow she might still be there. For a moment he was taken aback at the thought of how much time he had spent in that room, never thinking that sleeping with Ginny would be so short-lived. He also felt that in some way he was intruding, which, given that it had been his bedroom too for the last six months, was absurd. It was true, however, that there was little sign in the room of his own occupancy. At Ginny's request, he had kept his clothes next door in his own room. If it weren't for the copy of Nietzsche's *Human, All Too Human* on the bedside unit on his side of the bed, he might have doubted that he had ever slept there.

He went over to the identical unit on Ginny's side of the bed. The bottom drawer contained underwear, the top one a miscellany of objects intrinsic to female life: a blister pack of contraceptive pills, a small plastic tub of aspirins, hair clips, lipsticks, tweezers, bangles and a pot of face cream, but not so much as a scrap of paper, with or without her handwriting. The objects in the drawers might have been personal, even intimate, but none of them evoked Ginny in the way that a sample of her handwriting might have. He sat down on the bed in despair. A line from a Hardy poem came to mind; 'Not a line of her writing have I, not a thread of her hair'.

When Steve got home from work on the Monday, he found a letter on the mat. For a moment he thought it might be from Ginny, or maybe even Angie, immediately rejecting both thoughts; Ginny on the basis that she didn't write and Angie on the basis that she didn't yet know that it was safe to write to him at the Ainsworth Street address. On examining the envelope, it became clear that it was in fact from Rob. Steve carried it into the kitchen, put the kettle on and sat down to read the letter. He trusted that it wasn't another paean to his insight into the female mind.

A few minutes later, he found himself regretting his levity. The letter was brutally brief. Martin Lockwood had died suddenly a few days earlier. He had had a massive heart attack. Everyone knew that he'd been unwell, but the prognosis had been favourable. The funeral was in Cambridge at eleven o'clock on 5th November at St Giles, with the interment immediately thereafter at the Ascension Parish Burial Ground. Rob was coming down to Cambridge for the funeral. Steve was, of course, welcome to attend the service. But if he couldn't make it, Rob hoped that they could meet up in the evening. He was staying with a friend and would be returning to Edinburgh early the following morning.

Steve put the letter down and stared into space. He was roused from his reverie by the realisation that the kettle had been boiling furiously for several minutes. He turned the gas off and sat down again without making any tea. He had only met Martin once, but at the time it had seemed like a life-changing moment. He was the only other person, apart from Rob, who had engaged with his poem in a positive spirit. He had allowed himself to imagine Martin's response to the new material he had produced since that meeting, incoherent though it might be and which had cost him so much grief. There was, of course, no guarantee that Martin would have liked it, but Steve felt sure that he would have read it with an open mind. Steve imagined that Rob would now take over full editorial duties on *Outwrite*.

He went up to his room, feeling more deflated than ever. Steve wasn't sure if he could bear attending the funeral. It wasn't really the issue of his work schedule. He could probably find somebody to swap shifts with him. It was just that he felt that he already had enough grief to deal with. Of course, Rob would be disappointed in him, but he would explain his reasons later over a pint. They would then drink deeply to the memory of Martin. Wracked with guilt and irresolution, a typical combination for Steve, he deferred replying to Rob until the following day, telling himself that it would be better to sleep on it.

He was still undecided the next morning, when he joined Grace on her Tuesday morning run, although he was almost sorry that he had made the effort. She was tight-lipped, her face drawn, with dark bags under her eyes. She had clearly not been sleeping well. Almost as soon as they set off, she complained that Steve was going too fast. He apologised and shortened his stride.

He wondered whether Grace had heard the sad news. 'I had a letter from my friend Rob saying that Martin Lockwood has died.'

'Yes, I heard that too. It's a big loss to the contemporary poetry scene. Are you going to the funeral? There's bound to be a big turnout.'

'I'm not sure. I'm on the early shift that day. But I hope to meet Rob later that evening. I imagine he'll be one of the chief mourners. I'll try and pay my respects another time.'

After that they ran along in silence. Neither of them referred to Peter or Ginny. Steve realised that Grace's mood the previous Friday had been a combination of anger and hysteria. Clearly she had now been engulfed by the inevitable wave of depression.

By the time Steve got back to Ainsworth Street, he had decided that he wouldn't go to the funeral. He had no wish to rub shoulders with the great and the good of the poetry world. He hastily scribbled a note to Rob saying that he wouldn't be able to attend Martin's funeral, but he looked forward to seeing him later in The Six Bells. He then penned a brief note of condolence to Marion Lockwood and dropped both letters in the post box on his way to work.

Signed and Sealed

As THE WEEK WORE on, Steve found that he too was slipping into a state of depression. He gave the Friday run a miss. He had stopped trying to keep the place tidy. The kitchen sink was piled high with dirty dishes. He was beginning to feel uncomfortable just being in the Ainsworth Street house and spent an increasing amount of time in the pub.

One evening after work, he dropped into The Locomotive. He found a corner table and over the course of a couple of pints tried to lose himself in *The White Goddess*. He was on the point of leaving, when the door of the pub opened to admit a personage he was far from pleased to see. He shrank down behind his book, hoping that he might be able to slip out before he was noticed, but it was too late. Jon had spotted him and was striding across the room.

'Cool, man, I was hoping I'd bump into you. I didn't fancy coming around to your gaff. I thought there might be a few sticky moments with Ginny.'

Steve rapidly calculated what Jon did and didn't know. He almost certainly didn't know that Steve and Ginny had split up, but only because he probably didn't know that they had been in a relationship in the first place. So Jon's reservation about encountering Ginny must be to do with the manner of his walking out on her. Steve decided to tread carefully.

But Jon was not one to pussyfoot. 'Has she found somebody else?'

Steve could answer this truthfully. 'Yeah, an older guy. He's loaded.'

Jon wasn't surprised. 'That'll be the two of them, then.'

It took Steve a moment or two to work out that he was saying that Ginny was loaded too. Now that he came to think about it, he supposed she must be. She didn't sign on like other people he knew who had no work. She had beautiful clothes and travelled up and down to London regularly. And after all her father was a Hampstead doctor on the point of death and she the only heir. He felt stupid for not having asked her about it and why, if she had money, she lived as she did. But Steve thought it better, so far as possible, to stay off the subject of Ginny with Jon.

'How was the tour with The Syndrome?'

'Fab. I'll tell you more about it later, but first I'll get some drinks in. You're sitting there with an empty glass.'

Steve protested, that he'd already had plenty and was about to head home. Jon was having none of it, went across to the bar and came back with three drinks, the third of which was a gin and tonic.

Puzzled, Steve said, 'Who's the third drink for?'

Jon took a deep draught of his beer and wiping his mouth with the back of his hand said, 'Tamsin, my chick.'

The answer didn't make sense. 'But you're gay . . .'

Jon roared with laughter. 'Who told you that? Let me guess. Ginny?'

Steve cursed himself for having spoken without thinking

Jon narrowed his gaze. 'So, I'm also guessing that that was the line she spun you when she dragged you into her bed. *Jon was a bit fey, couldn't get it up.*'

Steve was reluctant to confirm the substance of this surmise, but Jon was not going to wait for an answer. 'When, in fact, she knew that I'd been seeing Tamsin for some time. The tour with The Syndrome was just a good moment for us to formalise the split.'

Steve was feeling dizzy. 'Do you mean that you two were already splitting up when you moved into Ainsworth Street?'

'Of course.'

Steve was angry now. 'But you didn't tell me.'

'Well, at that point, we were operating on a need to know basis with you, because we didn't know how long it might be before I had enough dosh to move out. I'm sorry I didn't tell you and I'm sorry I stiffed you for the rent.'

Steve still hadn't learned to keep his mouth shut. 'But you didn't. You sent all the rent to Ginny and she paid it into my account.'

Jon shook his head. 'I don't think you get Ginny's situation. She's the only child of a wealthy man. He keeps her on a tight leash financially because he's afraid she'll squander it on drugs. The truth is she'd be much more likely to blue it on clothes. From what I could make out, her allowance is considerably better than what you were picking up on the milk round or even what I've been getting on The Syndrome gig. And when the old boy pops his clogs, she'll get the lot.'

'But why would she tell me that you sent it?'

'That's the way she works. She doesn't like people to know she's an heiress who collects waifs and strays, puts them back on their feet, brushes them down, and puts a bit of fire back in their loins. So she flies under the radar.'

Steve's head was spinning. It didn't make any sense. Except it did. 'But you rescued her from a life of hard drugs and prostitution.'

Jon laughed again. 'Other way around, mate. Well, the hard drugs, at least. She helped me get cleaned up, made me believe in my guitar playing, sorted the money hassles out.'

Jon was winding him up surely, doing a number on him?

At that moment a curvy, blonde girl entered the pub, looked around and then came over to their table. Jon jumped up, took the blonde in his arms and proceeded to give her an unnecessarily passionate kiss. Steve found the sight unnerving. Removing his tongue from the girl's receptive mouth, Jon seated her in front of the third drink and said, 'Tamsin, this is Steve. He's a crazy dude, into weird plays. He was a milkman for a while.'

Tamsin didn't seem fazed by the incongruity of the capsule portrait attached to Steve, merely simpered charmingly. From time to time, strange gurgling sounds issued from her mouth, but, as far as Steve could tell, they bore no semantic content. Steve found it hard to believe that Jon had forsaken Ginny for this giggling nonentity, even if she did have rather fuller figure. It had never occurred to Steve that Jon might be a tit man.

The presence of the new girlfriend didn't seem to deter Jon from continuing with his mission to disillusion Steve. 'So, I'm guessing that Ginny insisted you fuck her brains out. Then she persuaded you to trip, during the course of which she reprogrammed you. And when she felt you could stand on your two feet, she moved on to the next deserving case.'

Steve was horrified at this reading of his life with Ginny during the last few months. But he had to admit it made a kind of sense, apart from the idea that Peter was a deserving case. Anyway, Steve was too stunned to resist Jon's interpretation and nodded weakly.

Jon beamed back. 'Cool. You must be a quick learner. If she's already moving on. You can get back to your blonde chick. Angie, right?'

Steve nodded again. His brain had frozen, he couldn't think what to say. The girl looked at him with goo-goo eyes. When he had seen Jon enter the pub, Steve had been worried that if Jon discovered that Ginny was no longer at Ainsworth Street, he might ask about moving back in, but it looked as if Jon's needs, at least for now, were being met by Tamsin.

In the end, Steve got home much later than he had been intending and much the worse for wear. Fortunately, he was on the late shift the following day, so he was able to sleep off the alcohol. As he was slowly regaining some semblance of sobriety, Steve's thoughts returned to Jon's explanation of Ginny's behaviour.

He had dismissed most of what Jon had said as pure fantasy, but, in the cold light of a hangover, it seemed to make more sense. He'd always found the idea that Ginny was an ex-junkie hard to believe. He'd accepted the information at first, because it had been transmitted to him at the peak of his infatuation with her. But as the weeks went by, there was precious little evidence of an addictive personality in Ginny's behaviour patterns.

In truth, the account that Jon had given the previous night was much closer to Steve's presuppositions of the man. Jon took things to the limit and was a person of large appetites. By contrast, apart from the odd joint and penchant for vigorous sex, Ginny was the soul of sobriety. The business concerning the rent also suggested that Jon's account was truthful. If he had come clean about the fact that he had not honoured his debt for the rent, it was not so much out of a sense of guilt, but from a perverse pride in his own bad behaviour.

But the clincher was Jon's supposed homosexuality. Steve was wary of being swayed by his own biases, but Jon simply did not come across as gay. In fact, if his descriptions of what he'd got up to on the road with The Syndrome were anything to go by, he was very old-school macho; love them a lot, knock them about a little, move on.

He had shown no shame in describing in unnecessarily graphic detail how many, and in what ways, he had fucked a series of groupies and had made no attempt to spare Tamsin's blushes, although in point of fact she had displayed none. Jon's prowess with young American women only seemed to increase his attraction in her eyes and provoke her to enthusiastic gurgles of admiration. The only person blushing was Steve. He was, of course, aware that there was an element of the rock god protesting too much in Jon's lurid catalogue aria. But the degree of unseemliness involved suggested that this was the unpleasant truth of the matter.

But if so, why had Ginny made him out to be gay? Presumably so that Jon's departure could be seen as a positive development for both men. Unlike the situation that Steve now found himself in, losing out to a rival. And indeed Ginny had been clear that the accelerated trajectory of their breakup had not been intended and had been precipitated by Grace's 'helpful' friend.

But that then made a nonsense of Ginny's explanation for the sound of crying early on in their tenancy. She had said that it was Jon sobbing because he couldn't get it up and had gone out to have sex, it was implied, with a man. But if it wasn't Jon sobbing, it had to be Ginny. So might Jon have in fact hurt her? Physical violence, however, was not the only way to hurt someone, as indeed Steve was starting to find out. The simple explanation was that Ginny had tried to initiate sex and Jon had made it clear that he was keeping his powder dry for another woman. He had then sped off in the van to give the other woman, Tamsin, no doubt, a good seeing to.

This was also a plausible explanation for why Ginny had come back to Ainsworth Street after Jon's gig on that weekend at the start of the summer when they had cleaned up the house before Jon and Ginny moved in. Nor did Steve buy into Jon's idea of Ginny as a rescuer of fallen men. She had simply enjoyed sex with Steve on that first occasion and had installed him as her lover until a more suitable partner came along.

Jon had also brought Steve up to date with current developments. It seemed he was only on a flying visit to Cambridge. There was still a series of UK gigs with The Syndrome to complete, but he'd be back in Cambridge shortly before Christmas. He looked forward to hanging out then, particularly since neither of them would be embroiled with Ginny. Much to Steve's relief, there had been no discussion about Jon moving back in.

But that reminded Steve, that it was a little more than a month until he needed to return the house to Beth. So he'd better start looking for somewhere else to live. Not only that, but he needed to find a new job, because the maternity cover job at The Arts was also coming to an end just before Christmas. The timing was not ideal. And right now, Steve had no idea what to do. With the rocketing levels of unemployment, jobs were not exactly thick on the ground. He wondered half seriously, whether Sid might take him back on at the dairy, but almost immediately dismissed the idea.

Things weren't looking great. His girlfriend had left him. He was going to have to find a new place to live in the next few weeks and at the same time his job was coming to an end. All in all, not good.

On the other hand, he'd finished *Event/Horizon*, or thought he had, although he had a suspicion that the new material might not sit well with the earlier work. Not enough time had yet passed to render the finished poem strange to him and enable him to make a proper judgement. Leaving that minor but fundamental point to one side, however, and once the obsequies for Martin had been completed, Rob would be able to press ahead with the next issue of *Outwrite*.

So maybe things weren't actually as bad as they seemed. Perhaps it was time for him to leave Cambridge. His liaison with Ginny had led him to neglect his mother and Angie, the two women in his life, who really cared for him. He could go back to his mother's for Christmas. She would be delighted. He could also write to Angie and suggest that now that she was no longer with Declan and he was no longer with Ginny, they could get back together. He would go up to Edinburgh and move in with her. Two could live as cheaply as one, as his mother had said, and work would probably be easier to find in Edinburgh.

The only problem was that he would need to find somewhere to live for the three weeks from the date that Beth was planning to resume occupation of the house until his job finished. Two possibilities suggested themselves. He could ask Grace if her could stay at her place for those three weeks. She was only too well aware of the upheaval in his life and would probably be sympathetic to his plight. Admittedly the situation was complex and she might not be ready to have a lodger, even if only for three weeks. Or he could write to Beth and see if she might be prepared to let him stay in Ainsworth Street for an extra three weeks. Because Sandra was not returning, there would be a spare room and thanks to Ginny's efforts, it would be straightforward to return Beth's things to her room. She might also welcome a little more rent.

And the bonus of moving the site of his activities to Edinburgh was that Rob was up there too. It would be just like their last year at Cambridge for the three of them, only north of the border. Steve would have a drinking partner who also doubled as his publisher and impresario, a reliable girlfriend with accommodation and he'd be on the doorstep of the Fringe which would simplify his plans to mount his production of *Krapp's Last Tape*.

The more he thought about it, the more he liked the idea. After all, the reason he had been staying in Cambridge was to finish the poem. And one way or another, it was now finished. It worried him only slightly that any plan that involved *Krapp's Last Tape* was further evidence of his besetting impossibilism.

On Sunday, Steve went out for a long run, conscious that it was only a fortnight until the 10k and that he needed to get some more runs in. For the rest of the day, he mooched around, reading and playing his guitar. At one point, he worked through 'Stormy Monday', trying to play the dominant sevenths and the minor sevenths in as many different places on the fretboard as possible. The chords reminded him that it was the song that he had played in response to Jed Morgan's challenge to perform something in Tom's flat above Solstice bookshop. That in turn reminded him of the song that Jed had improvised that night. At the time Steve had assumed that the song was dedicated to Ginny and that Jed was putting the moves on her. In hindsight he saw that Jed had contrived the whole scene to help Steve overcome his fear of playing in public and Ginny had been complicit.

He wondered how Ginny was and where she was staying. Still at her father's or had she already moved in with Peter? Steve had half expected her to be in touch by now. He still harboured a forlorn hope that she would admit that she had made a terrible mistake, beg his forgiveness and ask him to take her back. He knew that this was beyond any likelihood. They were not characters in a Mills and Boon novel, and in any case Peter fitted the stereotype of a bodice-ripper hero rather more closely than Steve himself. At the very least, she could have dropped him a line to let him know when she planned to pick her things up. It was more likely that Grace had a better idea about how things were unfolding between Peter and Ginny and would pass on what she knew on the Tuesday morning run.

After work on the Monday evening, unequal to the task of fixing his own supper, Steve decided to eat out. The problem was that if he went to The Eagle he would end up hobnobbing with one or other of the stage crew, normally an agreeable experience, but in the present circumstances not something he felt he could face. This meant choosing a pub which was not one of his regular haunts. He walked up Trinity Street towards Bridge Street and decided to go into the Baron of Beef on the basis that it was a Greene King pub and he could do with a pint of Abbot.

Having ordered a pint and some food and found a table at the back, he opened his copy of *Eros And Civilisation* and settled in for the evening. Gradually he relaxed and was reminded of how much he enjoyed sitting in a pub on his own reading something absorbing, the murmur of voices, the understated conviviality, the relaxed sense of community.

He was half way through his second pint when he became aware of a tall guy at the bar waving in his direction. Initially he assumed the guy must be waving at someone else, because he certainly didn't recognize him. But this assumption was soon overturned, when the guy pointed straight at Steve and then pointed to the beer pumps. Suddenly with a sinking feeling he realised that it was Declan and he was planning to buy him a drink. Steve mimed the outline of a mitre above his head and readied himself for an encounter he could do without.

A few minutes later Declan appeared at the other side of the table and greeted Steve warmly.

'Have I guessed your charade correctly?'

'Abbot?'

'Indeed.'

'Thank you.'

'Have you done mime training?'

'No, but I've drunk a lot of Abbot.'

Declan, who was still standing the other side of the table, passed the pint across to Steve and said, 'May I join you?'

How could he object? Delighted at the idea that he had potential as a mime, Steve gestured elaborately with both arms to signify that Declan was welcome to take a seat.

When Declan had settled himself and taken a mouthful of beer, he said, 'Haven't seen you in here before.'

'Haven't been here for ages, but I assume, given the proximity to St John's, you're in here a fair bit.'

'That would be one way of putting it.'

Declan took a mouthful of beer. 'I believe that Angie let you know that we are no longer together.'

'Yes, I'm sorry.'

'Thank you, though I'll take your commiserations with a pinch of salt. I'd rather not go into the details. Let's just say that no sentient beings were harmed during the process.'

'I'm glad to hear it. I will enquire no further.'

They both laughed uncomfortably. Steve felt this was not the time to go into his own relationship woes. In any case having cleared the air in relation to Angie, Declan still didn't look entirely comfortable. Steve assumed that he must be calculating how frank to be about *Event/ Horizon*. It was ridiculous how that fucking poem interposed itself in every relationship. Grateful for Declan's tact, he was happy to help him out.

'I only sent you the poem because Angie kept on at me about it. I have this reputation as someone who is not reliable and doesn't deliver on promises.'

Declan looked startled at Steve's self-deprecation. 'That sounds like a response to a statement I haven't made,' he said defensively.

'I'm sorry, but I'm getting rather used to conversations that have my poem as their invisible gravitational centre and I just want to point out that there's no need to pussyfoot. I agree completely with the bulk of the criticism which has come my way. I have no idea what induced me to declare myself a poet. I have come to realise rather late in the day that not only is it a surefire way to call down obloquy on one's own head, but that it is also a fast track to fucking up one's life.'

Declan drew in a breath through the corners of his mouth. 'Ouch! Surely you were aware that that comes with the territory?'

'Yes, I suppose I was.'

'I was, of course, going to thank you for sending me your poem. To be quite honest, it's not an easy read, but I have read every last word. Several times actually. You have a way with words, but not one I'm particularly drawn to. That is perhaps a failing in me. But perhaps it also suggests that you are unaware of the challenge you set the reader.'

'I do have some sense of that. The problem is that I'm an inveterate reviser. I rewrite innumerable times so that the finished lines scarcely resemble the original phrases and ideas.'

'One does get the feeling that you're trying to repress the material that has welled up from your unconscious. I'm not suggesting that you don't tidy things up, remove redundancies, keep an ear on the beat. But I get the impression of a lyric voice weighed down by program-matic disavowal. Why not trust your first thoughts?'

'It's a good question and I don't have an answer.'

Steve was thoughtful. He had been expecting derision, pity perhaps, incomprehension certainly, but he had got none of that. Whilst it was true that Declan had stopped some way short of praise, he had clearly read the poem carefully and had zeroed in on the way that Steve's intrinsic reticence undermined it. Steve recognized in Declan's critique an affiliation with Angie's approach, which in itself was not very surprising.

Steve wondered what it was that had led to Angie and Declan ending their relationship. It seemed unlikely that they had been together long enough to tire of each other. Was it simply the realisation that the distance between Cambridge and Edinburgh would make it difficult to conduct a relationship that had not yet put down strong roots? It would be an exaggeration to imagine that Steve was disappointed, particularly in the light of developments in his own life, but Declan seemed a nice bloke and very much on Angie's wavelength. Still, as Declan had surmised, Steve was unable to feel too upset that they were no longer together.

When Steve had finished his pint, he apologised that he couldn't stay longer. It was not normally his style not to buy his round, but he was in training for the Cambridge 10k and he needed to be up early on the morrow. Declan accepted Steve's excuse without adverse comment and said that he was in the Baron most evenings around this time, if Steve ever felt like continuing the conversation.

But when Steve woke the next morning, he had come to the view that he was still not ready to exchange further notes with Grace about their respective feelings of hurt and betrayal and decided not to join her on the run. It also seemed somehow inappropriate to be taking part in athletic activities on the day of Martin's funeral. It was not lost on Steve, as he lay in bed brooding, that this was a wholly inadequate rationalisation of the guilt he felt at not attending the obsequies and paying his respects.

Later at work he found it hard to concentrate and made several stupid mistakes, which caused Fiona to take him to task. He was not normally so slapdash. What was the problem? Steve apologised and said he wasn't feeling well. She said that he could go home. Steve thanked her and said that he could make it through to the end of his shift. He half believed his own excuse and was only too relieved when finally the clock on the wall of the box office showed that it was six o'clock. Steve put his coat on and stepped out into the dark and chilly fenland evening, Guy Fawkes fireworks already lighting up the sky. He trudged up to The Six Bells and was not surprised to find Rob already there.

Rob looked up from his book and smiled, 'Steve, good man. I was beginning to think you might not make it.'

Steve apologised and asked Rob what he was drinking. When he got back to the table with the drinks, he noticed that Rob seemed preoccupied. He must have been badly affected by the funeral. After all, Martin had been his mentor. Steve wasn't sure if talking about the funeral was the best way to start the conversation, but what else was there to talk about really? Tentatively, he asked Rob if there had been many mourners.

'*Tout le Parnasse*, apart from you.'

Steve shifted uncomfortably in his chair. 'I'm sorry, Rob. I've had too much time off recently.' It was a lie, but a plausible one.

Rob wasn't convinced. 'Well, it was an historic occasion. There was a great gathering. You will come to regret that you didn't make more of an effort to be there.'

Steve was surprised. Rob was normally indulgent towards his foibles and made allowances for his patheticisms.

'Rob I'm sorry. You know me.'

Rob nodded and, as if to underline his earlier assertion, proceeded to name the great and the good, who had been in attendance and a number of those who were neither great nor good. The service had been held in St Giles in Castle Street. Despite the Christian setting, the mood of the readings was more secular or pagan, depending on your ideology. There were readings from Martin's own work. After the service the mourners processed to the Ascension Parish Burial Ground, a very suitable place for the last resting place of a Cambridge worthy, rubbing shoulders with Wittgenstein and assorted Darwins. Rob painted a picture of a hieratic gathering in which Steve would have been accepted as a peer despite his meagre qualifications. Why had he excluded himself?

As Rob continued with his account Steve had a premonition that, with the passing of the years, Martin's funeral would come to be marked, in the histories and memoirs of the British poetry scene in the 1970s as a watershed moment and no doubt immortalised in poems of variable quality. With each new addition to the corpus Steve would be reminded, well into his dotage, of his jejune response to the event. Rob had every right to be annoyed with him. Maybe if he explained that the reason for this particular delinquency was that Ginny had left him, Rob would cut him some slack.

He was wondering about the best way to broach the matter, when Rob said, 'I'm sorry to be so critical, Steve, I'm feeling a bit tense. The funeral was really rather magnificent, but I'm letting my account be affected by another matter, a rather sensitive subject, that I need to talk to you about.'

Steve blinked. It wasn't like Rob to be so enigmatic or so tetchy. He couldn't imagine what it was Rob needed to talk to him about which was so shocking. Glad to be let off the hook of his own backsliding, Steve said, 'C'mon, Rob, get it off your chest. Whatever you've got to say is hardly going to shock me.'

Rob swallowed hard. 'I hope you're right. The fact is Angie and I are now in a relationship.'

He held Steve's gaze and let the news sink in. Steve blinked again and struggled to respond to the statement, but no words came.

Emboldened, Rob pressed on. 'It was your suggestion, of course, and I thank you for that. I'm sure we would have got together eventually, being in the same city and in the same faculty, but your words gave me the courage to take the initiative. Angie is everything I want in a woman. She is sexy, beautiful and clever. We have so much in common.'

Steve was spluttering. Unable to deal with the momentousness of the wider point, he was reduced to trying to find a form of words with which to disabuse Rob of the idea that he and Angie had a lot in common. That he was an adequate judge of sexiness or the the right person to respond to that quality in Angie didn't make any sense. Oblivious to Steve's silent apoplexy, Rob pressed on.

'But even though it was your suggestion and you are in another relationship, it's not hard to see that there's still a strong emotional bond between you and Angie. She admits as much herself and wanted to tell you face to face, but I said I'd be seeing you today and since we are old friends and since you had raised the matter with me in the first place . . .'

Steve had had enough of this madness, 'Rob. I don't know what you're talking about. I have never made any such suggestion. I had no idea that there was any spark between you and Angie. If you're telling me that it's more than that and you're getting together, then, of course, I accept what you're saying, but it certainly is a bit of a surprise.'

Rob looked crestfallen. A flash of anger coloured his face. 'I must say, I find that a bit insulting. We're not all as successful with women as you.'

He glared at Steve.

Steve winced. 'That's nonsense. I am not particularly successful. But putting that to one side, it was not my idea and I never suggested you try it on with Angie. When was that?'

'You did, you wrote to me a couple of months ago.'

'I've written to you a number of times, but I don't remember writing any such thing. I don't know what would have prompted me to do that. It's not my style to intervene in other people's lives like that. Perhaps you're putting an extreme interpretation on one of my convoluted jokes.'

'No, you were explicit. Anyway, that's beside the point. I really don't know why I should be seeking your approval. I suppose I thought you'd be happy to see Angie and me together. I wanted you to share in our good news. We both did.'

Steve felt shabby. Rob was a decent bloke and Steve was making things very unpleasant. But why on earth should he feel any pleasure at this development? Deep down Angie was his girl. Okay, they hadn't been a couple for the last few months and had both had other partners, but now that Ginny and Declan were exes, there was no reason why he and Angie shouldn't get back together again. Rob was not and never would be a suitable partner for her. And Steve couldn't stand this nonsense that Rob had cooked up about it all being Steve's idea. He would have respected Rob a bit more if he'd just gloated a bit, instead of being so passive aggressive about it. *I stole your girl, mate*, rather than *I only did it, because you suggested it*. They were angry with each other. This was not going well.

Steve knew he was being boorish and was behaving as if both Rob and Angie had betrayed him, a grievance to which he had absolutely no right, but his reading was that Rob didn't seem entirely sure of Angie's affections. He'd be even less sure of them once he found out that Steve was no longer with Ginny and was a rival for those same affections. It was time for Steve to put his cards on the table.

But before he could do so, Rob took an envelope from his pocket and said, 'Angie asked me to give you this. She said that getting letters through to you is complex. She didn't explain why. She suggested I only give it to you, if our conversation wasn't going smoothly. I said that was unlikely, but she clearly knows you better than I do. She said it would be better if you read it while we were still together and on speaking terms. I'll go and get some more drinks and allow you to read it in privacy. I have no idea what it contains.'

He handed the envelope to Steve and then went to the bar.

Steve examined the envelope. It bore his name and the instruction *Please read this before you and Rob take leave of one another*.

This was a curious turn of events. He wasn't sure he wanted to read the letter, but after a moment's hesitation he tore the envelope open.

Dear Steve,

I am sorry that you have had to find out about Rob and me this way. I would have preferred to tell you face to face. It did occur to me to come down to Cambridge with Rob, but I was conscious that the last time I saw you I said a number of things that were inappropriate. I am sorry. You have the right to manage your relationship as you see fit. It is not the business of a former lover to tell you how to do it.

But that also applies to you. Rob and I have fallen in love and that is our business. It is not for you to approve or disapprove of our relationship.

Rob is a lovely, generous man. He is very fond of you and values your friendship. Just as I should have been more positive about your relationship with Ginny, I beg you to be happy for Rob and me. Even as I write this letter, I can sense your anger. Please master it. I just want us all to be friends. And I genuinely include Ginny in that wish.

Steve, I will always care about you, and I hope you will continue to care about me. Let us be happy for each other.

With love, Angie.

Steve folded the letter, put it back in the envelope and slipped it into his inside pocket. He wanted to cry.

At that moment, Rob returned with the drinks and sat down. He pushed the pint across the table toward Steve and looked at him silently. Steve, took a slug of his beer and then said, 'Rob. I'm sorry I've been so curmudgeonly. There are reasons, which will become clear in due course, but not tonight. I'm delighted for you and Angie. You make a great couple and you will be good for each other. You do have a lot in common and I know you will be very happy together. I appreciate your telling me face to face, especially on this day, when we are mourning the passing of Martin Lockwood. Let's drink a toast to his memory.'

Even as they raised their glasses, Steve was aware that he had somehow turned what should have been a toast to Rob and Angie into one to the memory of Martin. But Rob was happy to join in the toast, pleased that Steve had regained his composure. Putting his glass down, he said, 'There must have been some powerful prose in that letter.'

Steve said. 'She is a great writer. I don't think I should really show it to you, but I can assure you that it doesn't contain anything you would disagree with.'

Rob shook his head. 'No, no, I wouldn't dream of wishing to see your private correspondence. I trust Angie completely.'

'And so you should. I am happy to tell you, however, that she was apologising for being critical of Ginny. She thought it might lead me to think she carried a torch for me. She made it clear that she didn't and that she is in love with you, but she'd like us all to stay friends.'

Rob seemed relieved. 'And that's what I want too. When Angie and I have got a flat together, you and Ginny should come up and stay with us for a few days. Edinburgh is an amazing city.'

'Yes, so I gather,' Steve said dryly and then with more enthusiasm, 'I'd like that very much.'

Rob seemed satisfied. 'Good. I'm glad we got that out of the way. I didn't want it to affect our friendship.'

Steve forced himself to sound light-hearted. 'No chance of that on my side. I consider you Martin's anointed successor and I am prepared to submit to your editorial judgement. I know I have been slow in getting back to you about the extract from *Event/Horizon*. I assumed things were on hold, pending Martin taking up the reins again. I wanted to take the opportunity during that pause to finish the poem and to make sure the extract was representative of the whole. I'm delighted to be able to say that the poem is now finished and I'd like to have your opinion of it. I will send you a typescript of the whole thing in a day or two. And I presume responsibility for the long-delayed issue of *Outwrite* in which the extract is to appear is now in your hands and you'll press on with publication.'

Rob looked uncomfortable. 'Steve, I'm happy to be your editor, but I don't think that *Outwrite* will be appearing again. It is actually Marion's decision. It seems Martin has left things in a mess, financially. It

looks like she will have to close Silk Route and the publishing operation too. She's talking about moving abroad.'

'But couldn't someone else take on the publishing side of things?'

'Well, it all takes money and basically it seems that nearly
everything that Martin published made a loss. In the present economic
climate, it just doesn't make sense.'

'So what you're saying is that the extract from *Event/Horizon* is not
going to appear.'

'I'm afraid so. I only found out about all this today. I certainly don't
want to put any pressure on Marion. She's already very upset. But I'm
happy to help find another outlet for your work. I'm already making
good contacts in Edinburgh.'

Steve knew that everything that Rob was saying was true. It all
made sense. What else was likely to be the fate of a poem about a black
hole? He could hardly blame Rob for the economic state of the world.
He forced himself to sound optimistic. 'Of course, Rob, plenty of other
fish in the poetry publishing sea.'

He was aware that his attempt at levity was almost as ponderous as
inaccurate. He drained his beer glass and said, 'I'd better be getting
back.'

They both stood. Steve gave Rob an embarrassed hug. 'Honestly,
mate, I'm very happy for you both. Send Angie my love. I look forward
to being shown around Edinburgh.'

As Steve pushed the door of the pub open, Rob said, 'Well, Angie
and I very much look forward to seeing you in Edinburgh. And Ginny,
of course.'

Steve flinched and said, 'Of course,' before heading in the direction
of Mill Road.

Steve didn't know how he got through the next few days. He could no
longer escape the realisation that he had fucked everything up and that
his prospects were not bright. Fiona became seriously worried about
him and suggested that he take a few days off, but the last thing he
wanted to do was to sit at home and brood. At least being at work took
his mind off contemplation of the dark place he was in, even if his
work was suffering as a consequence.

There was no point in complaining that it wasn't fair. He had
brought it upon himself through a combination of arrogance and
naïveté. While his friends had made sure to secure their futures, as far
as one could in these strange times, Steve had acted as if everything

would fall into his lap. Actually, he could take that. What he couldn't take was the fact that he had squandered Angie's love and had now lost her, to his best friend. It was no more than he deserved.

As he writhed in squalls of self-recrimination, he knew that sooner or later he was going to have to write to Angie and congratulate her on getting together with Rob. If he didn't, Angie might not entirely believe Rob's assurance that Steve had blessed their union. It would be petty to withhold that blessing from her, although Rob's insistence that it had been Steve who had suggested the union still irked.

The problem, well, one of the problems, was whether he should tell Angie, and by extension, Rob, about the the breakup with Ginny. But it seemed wrong to freight a letter of congratulations to the partners in a new relationship with the news of the demise of one's own. And maybe, just maybe, it wasn't over yet. It was at least possible that Ginny might bethink herself and return to him. Her things were still in the house. He had had no further communication from her. Perhaps she was having second thoughts.

Eventually, he forced himself to sit at his desk and pen some approbative lines. But when he read back over what he had written, the whole tone of the letter seemed wrong. It was devoid of what he considered his hallmark verve. The phraseology was leadenly formulaic, lending credence to the inevitable reading that his sentiments were not sincere. Steve redrafted the letter, but his second attempt was no better. He seemed incapable of simulating approval. Angie would have to settle for this second version. Even if she doubted the sincerity of the sentiments expressed in the letter, the fact that it was handwritten would attest to its authenticity in a way that the same letter if typewritten might not.

Suddenly, as Steve struggled with these notions, it became clear to him what was behind Rob's repeated assertion that it was Steve, in a typewritten letter, who had encouraged him to declare his suit to Angie, and the oblique rider that in that letter Steve had also displayed a hitherto unsuspected power of insight into the feminine mind. Rob had indeed received a typed letter from 'Steve', complete with a convincing handwritten signature. But it had not been written by Steve, nor signed by him. And Steve now had a good idea of the identity of the author with profound insight into the feminine mind.

Finally, he made it to the weekend. It was now only a week until the Cambridge 10k. The ambitions that he'd had for his training schedule had been completely upended and he'd done virtually no running since Ginny's bombshell. He consoled himself with the received wisdom that it was a good idea to reduce one's training schedule a week or two before an event. But reduction didn't mean complete abstinence. It meant tapering the programme.

For the past several days the weather had been as gloomy as his mood, Now at last the clouds cleared and a weak sun shone from a clear blue sky. Responding to the changed meteorological conditions Steve felt that it would do him good to go for a long gentle run on his own. He pulled on his running kit and set off. He got back an hour and a half later, feeling as well as he'd felt for at least two weeks. The surge of well-being that suffused his body after a run was not unexpected, something to do with endorphins, he'd read. On this occasion, however, it was so pronounced that he wondered why he didn't run every day.

After a leisurely bath, he made himself a huge fried breakfast, and then spent much of the day reading and playing his guitar. Pleased to find that the endorphin rush had also improved his playing, he opened the Jed Morgan book and worked through a number of his riffs, transposing them to successive keys in the the cycle of fourths and fifths. He spent the rest of the day reading and in the evening rolled a joint from the stash box and listened to records. He went to bed that night in an altogether more positive frame of mind and woke the next morning in much the same mood. Perhaps living on his own wouldn't be so bad after all.

LOAD OUT

BY THE TUESDAY MORNING, Steve had regained his composure somewhat, though not enough to join Grace on her run. He felt guilty, of course, as he always did. He was sure she could do with some moral support. But he was also anxious to preserve what little equanimity he had managed to cobble together and reluctant to allow Grace's speculations or observations to hypostatize the situation.

Taking advantage of the fact that he was on the late shift, he spent the morning sprawled on his bed reading *Love's Body*. He was soon immersed in his book. It was only when he needed to use the loo that he realised that he had lost track of time and was now running late. He pulled on his work clothes and took the stairs two at a time. His urgent rush for the bathroom was brought to a sudden halt by the sight of a letter lying on the doormat. He knew instantly, that it was from Ginny. He picked it up gingerly as if it was an unexploded hand grenade and sat down on the bottom of the stairs, turning it over in his hands. None the wiser about its payload as a result of this procedure, he slit the envelope open with his thumbnail to reveal a single sheet of notepaper, which bore a short message on one side of the paper.

Apart from the customary salutation, there was nothing personal in the few lines, nor any expressions of regret or sadness. There was simply an announcement to the effect that she would be collecting her stuff on Saturday. There was no need for Steve to be there, she still had

428

her key, which she would leave once she had packed everything into the car. The valediction was without flourish or endearment. She was not asking for permission or checking whether the date was convenient. Nor did she ask how Steve was or report on her own state of health or mind.

Steve felt winded. It was nothing that he couldn't have anticipated, but somehow he had convinced himself that the rupture was all a terrible mistake. For two days the clouds had lifted but now he was plunged back into an even deeper gloom.

At work Fiona decided that in this mood he would be a liability dealing with members of the public and put him on a series of administrative tasks. At lunchtime she even expressed her concern to Mike Wallace. Mike, knowing that Butch had taken Steve under his wing, said that he'd ask Butch to have a drink with Steve and see if he could get to the bottom of it. Butch needed no second bidding. He dropped by the box office the same afternoon and suggested that Steve join him for a drink in The Eagle after the show that night. Steve tried to wriggle out of the invitation, but Butch was not to be gainsaid.

Later that evening Steve found himself nursing a pint of Abbot while he waited for Butch to join him. He didn't have long to wait. Soon Butch's bulky frame was visible in the doorway. Butch waved and indicated by gesture that he'd get some drinks in before he came over to join Steve at his table. A couple of minutes later Butch was doing his best not to cause too much of a seismic disturbance at the neighbouring table as he levered himself into the narrow space opposite Steve. He grinned broadly at Steve, 'Hello, petal. Looks like Uncle Butch needs to lose a bit of weight.'

Steve shrugged, lacking the emotional energy to deal wittily or gracefully with Butch's pantomime self-deprecation.

'Oh dear, you are down in the dumps, aren't you? Why don't you tell me all about it? And we'll see if there's anything we can do.'

Steve was irritated with Fiona. He assumed it was she who had alerted Bush to Steve's state of mind. He stared into his beer.

Butch took a swig of his own beer and said, 'I'm no psychic. But I'd lay good money that things are not going well in the old love life.'

Steve shrugged again, which Butch read as assent. 'What's happened? Has she found someone else?'

Steve looked up. Had the news reached Butch from Grace, courtesy of Matt and Gary or was Butch just guessing?

Butch inferred from Steve's reaction, even though he had yet to utter a single word, that he was on the right track. 'Thought so.'

Steve was dreading some well-intentioned homily, but that was not Butch's style. 'Fuck her, Steve, she's a cunt.'

His vehemence took Steve's breath away. Without thinking what he was doing, he leapt to Ginny's defence. 'No, no, she's amazing. I'm the one who's let her down.'

'How did you do that, petal?'

Steve wasn't sure.

'I'm just so fucking half-hearted. She was trying to help me, but I'm a slow learner. I guess she realised that I was never really going to change.'

'I'm not having that, Steve. Relationships shouldn't be about changing the other person. You're not Eliza Doolittle and she's not Henry Higgins, if you get my drift. We should love a person for what they are, not what we can make them.'

'No, no, she had good intentions. It's what she does. So it was bound to come to an end.'

'Well, how is that different from people who discard one lover after another?'

'Because she was doing it *for* me.'

'Are you sure? If her aim was to mould you, then on your own admission, she's failed, and you're being discarded as a factory second or reject. What's altruistic about that? Do you know her new man? Is he a more suitable case for treatment?'

'I do know him as a matter of fact. I would say that he is someone who doesn't need any help.'

'Bastard.'

'Yeah.'

Suddenly they were in agreement.

'Look, petal, I know it's easy for me to say it, but you're well out of this one. I think I saw you in here with a lovely blonde girl a while ago. Any chance there?'

'That was my ex. The one I stupidly left for the girl who's leaving me.'

'Oh dear. That does seem to have been a bit of a mistake.'

'Yeah, I'm a fucking dick.'

'Very few of us get these things right. I'm not going to tell you that there are plenty of other fish in the sea. That is never a consolation.

You're going to have to pick yourself up and dust yourself down and start all over again, as Fred said.'

'Fred?'

'Astaire.'

Butch ignore the puzzled look on Steve's face. 'Stop beating yourself up. You're not the one who's failed here. You've been let down. Stop being so bloody generous. You have a right to be angry, but equally you have a duty to get over it. Don't wallow in it.'

'But everything seems to have gone wrong at once.'

'Of course it has, petal. That's the way things work. Why should everything work out just because you're Steve Percival? None of us can have everything we want, or things just as we want them. And if we could, it'd be a fucking disaster. You've got to figure out what is realistically achievable and work for it.'

Steve nodded morosely.

'So what else has gone wrong?'

'Well, apart from Ginny leaving me and my ex getting together with my best friend, I've got to get out of my pad in a few weeks. And at the same time the job in the box office is coming to an end.'

'I see. A full house. I can't do much about a girlfriend. Of course, I know a couple of nice boys, if you fancied swinging the other way. And I can't promise anything in the way of accommodation, but I'll keep my ear to the ground about a job. Now, drink up and let Butch get you another pint.'

Steve did as he was bidden and thought what a great bloke Butch was, as he watched him shoulder his way to the bar. He wondered why such a nice sensitive guy didn't have a regular boyfriend. He wasn't sure that he bought into the totality of Butch's analysis, but he was surely right that he needed to pull himself together and get on with his life. And perhaps he was also right that he was better off out of a relationship with someone who wanted him to be, in effect, another person. However much he changed he would never be that other person. By the time Steve left the pub, thanks to the Abbot and to Butch's encouragement, he was already feeling more positive, even if he still had to get through Ginny's visit on Saturday to retrieve her possessions. He had considered taking the day off, so he could be at the house when she arrived. But what good would that do? No, better to keep out of the way and let it happen.

* * *

Before leaving for work on the Saturday, Steve gave the house a thorough tidy. He didn't want to give her more reasons for why she had been right to drop him. He blitzed the sinks and the toilet bowl with bleach, put all the crockery and pans away, and made the beds. The sight of his running gear piled on the floor in his own room reminded him that it was the Cambridge 10k the following day. He hadn't been in touch with Grace for some days. It was she who had taken care of the race application for both of them and, therefore, was in possession of the identification number that he would have to pin to his running vest. He wasn't even sure what time the race started. It occurred to him that Grace might be working on the assumption that he had now given up any idea of taking part in the race. And perhaps that would be the best thing.

He bundled his running kit into the wardrobe and pushed the door shut, not that there was any reason for Ginny to come into his room. He then went into her room to check that everything was in good order. Having reassured himself that the room was pretty much as she had left it, he went downstairs and made himself a cup of coffee. As he was sitting there, mentally preparing himself for the day ahead, he heard the noise of the gate to the little front garden being opened. Now that Ginny was no longer around to ensure the smooth running of the household, the gate had started to creak again. A moment later, the morning post was pushed through the letterbox. Steve went through to the little hall and picked up the single letter that was lying on the mat. It was addressed to him in a hand that he didn't immediately recognise.

He opened it. It was from Grace. She hoped that Steve was going to join her for the race the following day. The race started from Midsummer Common at ten o'clock. She suggested that he got to Glisson Road by eight-thirty. They could have a light breakfast before setting off for the start. If he wasn't there by nine-fifteen, she would assume he wasn't coming. Steve was touched that Grace had bothered to chase him up despite his non-attendance on her training runs. She really was a kind person. Steve slipped the letter back into its envelope and finished his coffee.

Later at the box office, Steve threw himself into his work to the delight of Fiona who assumed that Butch must have got to the bottom of what was eating Steve when they had talked in The Eagle. In fact, Steve was doing his best to keep his mind busy with workaday matters in order prevent himself from imagining what was happening at that very moment at the little house in Ainsworth Street. He even worked through his lunch break to avoid time for reflection. This resulted in Fiona saying he should finish at five o'clock, rather than six. Steve said he was happy to work on, but she insisted.

He toyed with the idea of going to The Eagle again to ensure that he didn't arrive back at the house while Ginny was still there. But downing several pints the evening before the event was not the best preparation for a 10k race. In any case, Ginny must surely have finished clearing her things out much earlier in the day, especially since it was now already dark. But, just to be on the safe side, Steve stopped off at the shops on Mill Road to pick up something for supper and supplies for the next few days.

So it was something of a surprise, when he rounded the corner of Ainsworth Street, to see a large Volvo estate parked outside the house, the front door of the house wide open, and all the house lights blazing. Even worse, at that moment, he saw Peter emerge from the house with a large box in his arms, which he slid with some difficulty into the back of the Volvo. Steve stopped in his tracks. Peter had not seen him. What should he do? He could slip past on the other side of the road and hang out in the Geldart until Ginny and Peter had left.

But suddenly his former determination to avoid a scene evaporated. He now relished the thought of a confrontation and, resuming his progress towards the house, strode through the open front door to find Ginny and Peter in the kitchen, finishing a cup of tea. Neither of them seemed surprised to see him. They both looked at him expectantly, without saying anything. He put his shopping bags down and said, 'I'm sorry, I thought you'd be finished by now.'

Why on earth was he the one doing the apologising?

By way of explanation, Peter said, evenly, 'The traffic on the way down here was terrible, but we're nearly done. In fact, perhaps you wouldn't mind giving me a hand with Ginny's trunk?'

Steve felt he could hardly decline. Speechless with rage, he bent down and grabbed the strap at the end of the trunk nearest him. As he did so he noticed Ginny watching him with what he took to be a faint smile playing around her lips. Were they doing this on purpose? Were they taunting him?

Steve and Peter manoeuvred the trunk out through the narrow hallway to the rear of the Volvo. Peter raised the tailgate and between them they slid the trunk into the Volvo's capacious luggage bay. Peter brushed his hands together and turned to look at Steve.

'How's the writing going?'

Steve had not been expecting an apology, even less chit-chat about his writing, but he was at a loss to understand Peter's refusal even to acknowledge the fact that he had stolen Steve's girlfriend. It was as if those months that he had Ginny had spent together were of no significance. But Steve was unable to find the words to fit the situation. It was as if he were under some kind of spell, which was inducing in him a selective aphasia.

'Yeah. I finished it, even if it's not complete. Time to do something else.'

Peter nodded. 'I'd like to see a copy, when it's published, Steve.'

Steve offered a noncommittal grunt.

It was not difficult for Peter to decode Steve's thoughts. 'I'm sure I'm the last person you want to show your work to at the moment. But I've found over the years that it's best not to bear grudges, especially when the person involved might be able to help you.'

Once again, what Steve wanted to say was that he'd rather perish in obscurity as a writer than accept the blandishments offered by Peter, but what came out was a mumbled thanks. Peter's entire attitude seemed to be that he was doing Steve a favour and it infuriated Steve. He felt like taking a swing at Peter, but he managed to keep his cool, although, in truth, he felt that he was letting himself down.

Peter slammed the tailgate shut. 'I think that's it. At least I hope so. I wasn't expecting to pick up the entire stock of the Cambridge branch of Biba'

Steve didn't feel able to share Peter's mirth. He for one would be missing the private fashion shows.

As they turned to go back inside, Peter said, 'Grace tells me you're doing the Cambridge 10k with her tomorrow. I appreciate that.'

This was finally too much for Steve.

'Just fuck off, Peter. Or should I call you Pete? It's none of your fucking business. You've got an infernal cheek patronising me like this. I don't believe you got caught up in traffic. I gave you plenty of time to clear the place, but you couldn't pass up a chance to gloat. I was prepared to be civil about this, but I've had enough. I want you out of my place now.'

At the sound of raised voices, Ginny appeared on the doorstep and said, 'Will you two stop locking horns in public. Peter, you promised me you'd behave properly. It's time for us to go. Get your coat and then we'll leave.'

Peter smirked gleefully, as if he was looking forward to being chastised in private later. He pushed past Ginny, and went through to the bathroom to wash his hands, before retrieving his jacket. Steve hovered on the doorstep, he was still furious and now vented his anger at Ginny.

'I know you typed that letter to Rob.'

'Ah, yes. Not very subtle, I admit.'

'And that's the limit of your regret?'

'It seemed the right thing to do at the time.'

'Right for whom?'

'I'm sorry, Steve. In time, you'll see this is better.'

He was about to protest, but she put her finger to his lips and said, 'Don't say anything. Don't say anything now. It may not seem like it, but I do care for you.'

She took a step towards him, kissing him on the cheek, then turned and went back into the kitchen to get her own coat. Steve leant against the wall and sobbed quietly. After a moment he gathered himself, went into the sitting room and sat on the sofa. Soon Ginny and Peter appeared in the doorway of the room with their coats on, each carrying a case.

Peter said, 'Right, we'll be going, I'm sorry if you thought I was being patronising. I wasn't. I was being sincere. Please stay in touch, Steve.'

When Peter had finished speaking, Ginny simply said, 'Thank you, Steve.' She gave him one of her rare smiles and then slipped her shades on. If Steve hadn't been so upset, he would have laughed. What a ridiculous gesture! It was pitch black outside. But oddly, almost as soon as he was shielded from the incandescence of her gaze, he began to feel better. He followed them to the threshold and watched them climb into the Volvo. They drove off without waving, or looking back.

Steve went back into the house and shut the front door, leaning against it, overcome with the finality of Ginny's departure. After a few moments, he pulled himself together, went into the kitchen and mechanically put the food shopping away. He thought he might lie down for a while before preparing his evening meal.

He went upstairs, noticing that the light was still on in Ginny's room. He pushed the door open in order to switch the light off and was struck by how bare and empty it looked. She had removed everything. Somehow she had managed to fit her extensive wardrobe, her bibelots and hangings into the back of the Volvo. The entire *mise en scène* of their relationship had been dismantled. It was as if a company of players had packed up their set and costumes and had moved on to the next venue, leaving an empty stage, an impression emphasised by the harsh light from the bare light bulb hanging from a wire in the centre of the room. Ginny had had an aversion to overhead light. She had preferred to light her personal spaces with silk-draped table lamps and artfully placed anglepoise lamps, creating pools of soft, accentual lighting. It was hard now to visualise the room when it had been her boudoir and her lair.

He switched the light off and closed the door. He went next door to his own room and threw his jacket on the bed. He did not share Ginny's aversion to overhead light, but he was irritated to find the light to his own room had been left on too. There had been no need for either of them to come into his room. She knew very well that none of her things were ever kept in his room. But then he noticed that there was a large manila envelope propped on the keyboard of his typewriter. He picked up the envelope and opened it slowly. Inside was what looked like a notebook bound in black hardcover with a smaller white envelope tucked into the book. Steve withdrew the smaller envelope to find that it was addressed to him and contained a handwritten note from Ginny. He sat down on the edge of the bed to read it.

> Dear Steve,
>
> So that's it, then. There's no point in rehearsing the things we said, when I told you I was leaving. But I want to make it clear that I am not leaving you because of any fault or lack in you. You are a lovely man. These last few months have been great. But for reasons that I don't want to go into here, I have to move on. You will be fine, I know, but you will hurt. And you will be angry with me for some time. Believe me, though, you will emerge stronger and more resolute. It may sound preposterous to you right now, but Peter and I would like you to stay in touch. I don't expect you to want to act on this suggestion in the near future, but please believe it is sincerely meant.
>
> The book, which accompanies this letter is for you. It is a memento of our time together.

You will also find tucked into the pocket at the back of the book something else that I hope will help you through the next couple of months.

Look after yourself, Ginny.

Steve read the letter over a second time, with a tear in his eye. He opened the book and saw that what he had taken for a notebook was in fact one of Ginny's sketchbooks. He leafed through it slowly. The images were not entirely lifelike. There was something exaggerated about them, somewhat in the manner of French *bande dessiné*, or Japanese *manga* comics, but the identity of the figures was quite apparent. As he leafed through the book, a cavalcade of scenes from the past few months passed before his eyes; Jon in leather jacket, playing his Strat, with shirt off proudly displaying a Parachute Regiment tattoo on his well-developed bicep, Steve sitting reading, jamming with Jon, playing guitar, naked, sleeping on the bed.

It also contained sketches of the Ainsworth Street house in all its chaos, as it had been when they had first moved in, then after Ginny's lightning makeover. There were similar before and after views of the garden, a rather lovely study of the camper van. There was also a rather good portrait of Jed Morgan glowering from behind a pair of shades, a cruel caricature of Beth and Sandra as a couple of sluts. There were also a number of images of Grace. Ginny had given her a much more rounded figure than the image that Steve had of her, derived in his case from from seeing her in her running kit. But clearly, Ginny was responding to something else she saw in Grace and accented her curves. And finally there were even a couple of beautiful portraits of Angie, that took his breath away with the care with which they had been executed.

The book was a marvellous thing, but there were far too many images for Steve to take in all at once. He had certainly not studied every page but he realised that there were two figures missing from the pictorial record; Peter and Ginny herself. Steve was not at all disappointed at the absence of Peter, but he was distraught that Ginny had not portrayed herself. There were also a number of more fantastical images that did not seem to be drawn from life. Steve wasn't sure how or if they were related to the documentary material.

One that caught his eye could have been an image to illustrate Queen Mab or Titania in a *manga* edition of Shakespeare. Clad in a diaphanous robe, long hair flowing over her shoulders and crowned with a spray of tiny flowers above which hovered a bee, a seductress figure was rising from the corolla of a flower as if she were some humanoid pistil. She was shown advancing towards the viewer, offering her dancer's body, but what disturbed Steve was that she appeared to be weeping tears of blood.

Another series of images showed a figure that Steve took to be Marlene Dietrich, resplendent in fishnet stockings and a figure-hugging dress, a clutch purse gripped tightly in her left hand, smoke from a smouldering cigarette, held between forefinger and middle finger of her right hand, drifting up, so that the lines representing the spirals of smoke merged into those of her chevelure, while the tips of her middle finger and thumb of the same hand deftly held a martini glass by the rim at an angle which threatened to spill the contents.

But most perplexing of all was a rear view of a male ballet dancer, clad only in knee-high leg warmers, feet in fourth position as if about to execute a pirouette, arms and torso entangled in the tendril of a sweet briar which might have been a strand of barbed wire had it not been for the rose that rested in the palm of the dancer's hand.

Steve didn't know what to make of these images and in what way, if at all, they belonged in his story.

He realised that if he didn't get his supper soon, he would probably go to bed hungry. He could return to the book later. As he was closing it, he remembered to look in the pocket glued to the inside back cover of the book, and pulled out a cheque for £100, made out to him and drawn on a Coutt's account in the name of Miss Virginia Stern. The note attached to it hoped that it would cover the rent and bills to the end of the tenancy. Steve thought it would probably be more than enough and would enable him to put down a deposit on a new place too.

He went downstairs and started to prepare the meal; eggs, beans and bacon again. He'd also bought a bottle of wine, but he knew that if he opened it now, he was quite likely to polish off the entire bottle, which would have been an even worse way to prepare for the race on the morrow than spending the evening in the Eagle with Butch. So he settled for a cup of tea and promised himself that he'd make up for it the following day.

Before he fell asleep, it occurred to Steve that even if he didn't have any images of Ginny, he did now have a few lines of her handwriting.

CROSSING LINES

STEVE WOKE EARLY THE next morning, dismayed to discover that it was pouring with rain, a far from rare occurrence in Cambridge in November, but not ideal conditions in which to do a 10k. On the other hand, once he'd warmed up, it wouldn't make that much difference. It was just a matter of being careful with one's footing. He rolled out of bed and pulled his kit on, including the tracksuit that Grace had given him. If he was going to get to Grace's by eight-thirty, as she had suggested, he'd better get a move on. A few minutes later, he was jogging through the pouring rain to Glisson Road.

By the time he arrived at Grace's he was soaking. He rang the doorbell. A few moments later, Grace opened the door to him, already in her running kit. She laughed to see his bedraggled appearance. Steve stepped inside and took his trainers off and said, 'I don't know what you're laughing about. You're going to be just as wet shortly.'

Grace led him into the kitchen and said, 'Right, what's it to be? A fry-up? Boiled eggs? Or porridge?'

Steve plumped for two boiled eggs and a couple of slices of toast. Grace approved and said she'd have the same. She put a pan of water on to boil and handed Steve a mug of coffee. 'So, are you ready for this? Your tapering was rather steep, unless you've been running on your own.'

439

'I have been out a couple of times on my own. I'm sorry I didn't contact you. It's been a weird week.'

'You can say that again.'

Steve sipped his coffee thoughtfully. He wasn't sure if this was the right moment, but it seemed absurd not to make some reference to the events of the last few days.

'Peter and Ginny came around yesterday to pick up her stuff.'

Grace put four slices of bread into the toaster and said, 'I know.'

'I was at work all day, and I expected them to be gone by the time I got home. I gave them plenty of time to clear Ginny's stuff. I got the feeling that they intended to engineer an encounter. Peter and I exchanged some harsh words.'

'I don't blame you.'

'I had words with Ginny too.'

Grace brought the eggs and the toast to the table and sat down. She buttered a slice of toast and said, 'Pete was here the previous day for the same reason. But sensibly he came on his own. In any case, there wouldn't have been any room in the car for Ginny. He filled every cubic inch apart from the driver's seat. But let's not talk about that now. We can do that after the race. I hope you'll join me for some lunch. I prepared a boeuf bourguignon yesterday.'

Steve said he'd be delighted. He would have brought a bottle of wine, if he'd known. Grace said she had plenty. They weren't going to run dry.

Grace said, 'Let's talk tactics. There's no point us sticking together. You go as fast as you like, and we can meet up at the finish.'

Steve nodded. 'I'll probably go off too fast and pull something and you'll zoom past me as I'm hobbling to the finish line.'

'Well, let's both be careful. It's going to be slippery out there today.'

They finished their breakfast. Grace cleared the things away, and then said she was going upstairs to settle her stomach, as she put it. She reminded Steve that there was a downstairs lavatory if he felt a similar need. After he had completed his own ablutions, he retrieved his trainers from the hall. When Grace rejoined him she had put on her tracksuit and was sporting a natty headband to hold back her hair. Steve thought she looked great.

'What are we going to do with our tracksuits and keys during the race?'

'I'd suggest you leave your own keys and wallet here. I'm going to leave my house keys in a hiding place in the front garden. It's better than stuffing it in my bra. We can put our trackies into my backpack and leave it with the race marshals when we get to Midsummer Common. They have a trailer or something where runners can leave their stuff.'

Steve could see that she had everything worked out. Grace gave Steve his race number and helped him pin it to his vest with four small safety pins. She then asked him to do the same for her. She unzipped the jacket of her tracksuit. Steve was too embarrassed to pin the sign over the curve of her chest and proceeded to position it at midriff height. Grace laughed, 'Steve. This is no time to be bashful. Don't worry. I'm wearing a sports bra under my vest and it's practically armour-plated, so please pin it a little higher.'

Steve did as he was asked, blushing furiously as he attempted to push the pins through the fabric of her vest and snap them into the clasp without touching her body with the result that he dropped three of the four safety-pins, prolonging the embarrassment. When he'd eventually completed what should have been a simple process, Grace said, 'Well, I enjoyed that, even if you didn't. Sorry, Steve, I should have done it myself before I came down, but you managed it with appropriate decorum, if I may say so.'

It wasn't clear to Steve which aspect of the process she'd found enjoyable and he confined himself to muttering something about the pins being a bit fiddly, when in reality his embarrassment was the effect of a misplaced diffidence about the appropriate level of contact with the convexity of her bosom. He turned away, still blushing. Grace zipped up her tracksuit, not unaware of the effect that she had had on him and said, 'Well, we might as well get on with it.'

They stepped out onto the front garden path and Grace put the key under a flowerpot. She looked at her watch. 'We'd better get down to Midsummer Common smartish.'

She set off, with Steve following. He knew that time was getting on, but he was concerned that Grace had set off too fast, a not uncommon effect of adrenaline. It was one thing to get warmed up for the race, quite another to exhaust oneself or pull something before getting to the starting line. Grace turned into Gresham Road. There were puddles everywhere. Steve had decided on his jog over from Ainsworth Street that it was a waste of energy trying to avoid them. He had simply kept his line and splashed through them. But Grace had not yet adjusted to the conditions, and was trying to dance around the puddles. If she kept that up, she'd be even more exhausted by the time they got to the starting line, and no drier.

Looking ahead, Steve could see that there was a particularly big puddle coming up. Grace had seen it too, and was starting to take evasive action by stepping into the road. But she hadn't looked behind her, and the toot of an oncoming car made her veer rapidly back towards the pavement. Trying to avoid the puddle on the pavement, she misjudged her footing and tripped on the kerb. She let out a yelp and fell headlong into the puddle. Steve rushed forward to help her up. The driver of the car pulled up, and walked back towards them. 'I say, I'm sorry. Are you okay? I was just letting you know I was coming along.'

Grace waved him away and said she was fine, that it was all her fault.

Steve was concerned. 'Are you okay? Do you think you'll be able to run?'

Grace was rubbing her left calf experimentally. 'Yes, I think so.'

'Okay, but stop, if it starts to hurt.'

Despite the appalling weather, there was almost a carnival atmosphere among the competitors gathered in the 10k starting pen. There were, in fact, so many that when the race klaxon went off, all but those at the front of the pack were restricted to a very sedate pace. Steve and Grace jogged along side by side enjoying the occasion, relaxed in each other's company. But after a while the field started to thin out and Steve felt it was time to lengthen his stride. He turned to look apologetically at Grace, but she waved him on, blowing him a kiss. He was soon working his way up through the field. but, mindful of Grace's spill, he ran well within himself and was consequently disappointed when he crossed the line 48 minutes later with plenty left in the tank. If he'd pushed himself a bit more, he could have probably put in a good time.

Having got his breath back, he positioned himself near the finish line so that he could spot Grace among the throng of finishers. He was beginning to think that she must have dropped out, when he caught sight of her hobbling bravely down the final straight. Once the race marshal had logged her race number, he went over to congratulate her, giving her big hug. She collapsed into his arms, resting her head on his shoulder.

'Oh, that was tough.'

She was breathing heavily. Steve held her as her heart rate came down and said, 'There's a stall where they're handing out doughnuts and bottles of water to runners. You could probably do with some water and a hit of sugar. It looks like you were having difficulty with your leg.'

'It was okay until about the eight kilometre mark, but I wasn't going to give up at that stage. It is very tight now. You might have to help me back to the house.'

'Why don't we try and get a taxi?'

'We'll never get a taxi with this crowd. If we take it easy and you let me lean on you, it should be okay.'

It had rained for the duration of the race and they were both soaking, but elated. They retrieved their tracksuits, picked up some water and a doughnut each and walked slowly back to Glisson Road, Grace with her arm looped over Steve's shoulder to help her take the weight off the hurt leg.

The first thing that she did when they got back to the house was to open a bottle of champagne. They toasted their achievement. After a couple of glasses, Grace said that she would take a shower. Steve noticed that she was still moving with some discomfort. She came back some time later in a bath robe and and suggested Steve take a shower too.

'I'd love to, but unfortunately I didn't bring a change of clothes. I don't know why I was so stupid. My mind was full of other things.'

Grace said, 'There's another bath robe on the back of the bathroom door. Use that. I don't want a damp and sweaty lunch companion. There may be something in Peter's closet that you could wear.'

Steve wasn't delighted by the prospect of wearing anything of Peter's. 'I'd rather stay in a bath robe, if you don't mind me eating lunch dressed like that and then I'll put the tracksuit on to go home.'

'I have no objections at all. I'll do the same.'

Steve took a shower and returned a little later wrapped in the other bath robe. Grace poured them some more champagne and said, 'I'd better get on with the lunch. There's not much to do. Just needs heating up. I prepared it yesterday.'

As she stood up to go to the stove, she left out a squeal of pain. 'Ooh, my legs really are seizing up. The one I twisted when I fell in the puddle is particularly tight.'

'Maybe you should take some painkillers. They can help with the inflammation. And maybe some physio. I could try and loosen the tightness for you, massage it a bit.'

'I have no objection to your trying to free the knot in my calf, but I'll stick to alcohol for pain control at the moment. There's a sofa in the front room. You can treat me there.'

They went through to the front room, Grace leaning on Steve's shoulder.

She stretched out on the sofa on her front. Steve touched her left calf muscle gently with his fingertips and, having identified the knot, started to apply pressure. Grace flinched slightly, but soon relaxed.

'Mm, that's nice. You're good at it.'

Steve switched his attention to the other leg.

'Let's see if walking's any easier now.'

Grace swung her legs around, stood up carefully and took a few paces.

'It's still rather tight,' she said, affecting a doleful mien. 'What do you suggest?'

'We could try and take a more holistic approach.'

'What does that involve?'

'It means focusing on the whole patient, not just the point at which the pain is felt.'

'Okay. I'm happy to cross that line and put myself in your hands.'

Steve caught her eye, hoping that he'd got her drift. He moved towards her, reached out his hand and touched the side of her neck with his fingertips.

'This is an important meridian.'

He leaned in towards her and kissed her neck where he had touched her. She breathed out deeply and shivered slightly, but did not resist him. He untied her robe and kissed her breast. She parted her lips and uttered a small sound of pleasure. Loosening his own robe, he pressed his body against hers. She reached down said, 'I wondered when I was going to get to meet this gentleman. Do you think we could continue the treatment upstairs? Or do you prefer to operate *in situ?*'

Steve laughed. 'I think going upstairs would be much better from a therapeutic point of view.'

Several hours later, Grace and Steve were lying in her bed. Grace's head was resting on Steve's chest and she was drawing her fingernail down his torso towards his navel. He covered the exploratory hand with his own.

'Grace. I think we've exhausted the healing forces for now.'

Grace laughed. 'I'm sure I could think of something to help.'

Steve joined in the laughter. 'You've already tried that.'

'Young man, if you think I've exhausted my repertoire, you are very much mistaken.'

'I don't doubt it. All I'm suggesting is that we take a break, have a cup of tea, regroup. I'm sorry if I haven't attended properly to your needs.'

'Steve, I'm teasing. I haven't had such a thorough massage for a very long time.'

Steve pretended to push her away. 'I'd rather not know when the last time was and with whom.'

She pulled him back towards her. 'Let's not go down that path, but it wasn't with the person you think that it was. I'm sorry, that was a stupid joke. You're a very sensitive lover.'

These words brought a sob to his throat.

Grace looked at him carefully. 'Are you okay? If you're uncomfortable with this, we can stop now.'

Steve crushed her to his chest. 'No, I've wanted to be with you like this, since I walked into your college rooms, more than two years ago.'

'I have to admit that I was not entirely oblivious to the effect I was having on you. It's not as if I'm not used to horny young men glancing at my breasts. But it would have been inappropriate for me to have given you any encouragement.'

Steve felt abashed, 'I'm sorry. I didn't mean to make you feel uncomfortable.'

'You didn't. You always acted properly. And in any case by the end of our first year, you had taken up with Angie and it seemed that your libidinal needs were being taken care of in a more appropriate way.'

At the mention of Angie's name Steve groaned.

'It does seem that you have been a little reckless, Steve, but perhaps it's not impossible that you two will get back together.'

Steve told her about Rob.

Grace kissed him gently. 'I'm sorry, Steve, but at least that means I feel a little less guilty about this second line we've crossed today.'

Steve kissed her fiercely. 'This is lovely. I don't want to talk about other people.'

'But we both know this is not going to last.'

He looked at her sharply. Was she already calling time on something that had only just begun?

'Steve, you know this can't possibly work.'

'It hasn't felt like that over the last few hours.'

'True, but when you consider the circumstances, what might be propitious for a quick roll in the hay, is not the best basis for a long term relationship.'

'We don't have to think in those terms. We can just take each day as it comes.'

'But you haven't even begun grieving for your relationship with Ginny, let alone the feelings you still have for Angie. And Pete and I had been together for twelve years. That's a big chunk of my life. You're a piece of flotsam I have grabbed hold of in the shipwreck of my marriage.'

Steve bridled at the image. 'I object to being thought a piece of flotsam.'

'But that's what I am for you too, if you're honest with yourself.'

After the elation of the previous few hours, Steve now felt decidedly downcast.

Grace could see that she had capsized Steve's mood. 'Steve, I'm not going to kick you out of my bed. I hope we can resume these delightful investigations, when we've had something to eat and recharged our batteries. But let's be clear, what's going on here is a form of mutual first aid. It's probably not the cure either of us needs.'

Not only did Grace not kick him out of her bed, she invited him back into it after their supper and asked him to stay the night. But as a consequence of their sporting and erotic exertions, they fell asleep at an early hour, which was as well, since they both had work the following day.

So for the second time in 24 hours Steve found himself sharing a breakfast with Grace. Fortunately, Steve was on the late shift, giving him enough time to go back to Ainsworth Street and put on clothes that were more suitable for work. But Grace had reverted to the serious academic she really was and was studying her schedule for the day. Even though she was once again in her bath robe, there was little sign of the sex kitten of the previous day.

Steve realised that it would be better if he didn't linger. He went through to the utility room and retrieved his running kit and track suit, which Grace had put in the tumble drier the previous evening before they had returned to the haven of her bed. He took them to the cloak-room tucked into the space under the stairs and dressed himself. He had contemplated changing in the big kitchen, but such behaviour might have struck her as unseemly in the drab reality of an early Monday morning.

Decently attired, he returned to the kitchen and said, 'Right, I'll be going.'

Grace looked up at him. 'I hope you have a nice day.'

Steve hovered. 'When will I see you again?'

'Soon, but I don't want to fix a date right now. Don't worry this isn't the end, but let me get in touch with you.'

Steve walked around the table and kissed her on the side of the neck. She stood up and, pressing her body against his, kissed him on the lips tenderly and then returned to her work. Steve let himself out and walked pensively back to Ainsworth Street. He had a horrible feeling that it was indeed the end.

DECOMMODIFICATION

STEVE WAS PLEASED THAT he had pulled himself together enough to do the 10k, not only had he finished in a creditable time, he had also got to sleep with Grace. But neither achievement was any kind of compensation for the fact that Ginny had left him. Once he had accepted her departure, he had briefly entertained the thought of getting back together with Angie and joining her in Edinburgh. But the news that she was now in a relationship with Rob had closed off that possibility and at the same time completely floored him. To make matters worse Rob had been the main champion, indeed virtually the only champion, of Steve's work, but after the grudging manner in which Steve had offered his congratulations, he would be lucky to have much support from that quarter in the future. On top of which, Martin Lockwood's death had effectively put the kibosh on the immediate prospects of *Event/Horizon* reaching a wider audience. In any case, he was now heartily sick of the poem. It struck him as vacuous and pretentious. He now saw it as having had a malign influence on his life.

In planning to move up to Edinburgh, he had, of course, been clutching at straws. Even if Angie weren't now in a relationship with Rob, it was far from certain that she would have agreed to the proposal. And the idea of moving in with Grace or staying on at Ainsworth Street was almost as fanciful. So finding himself somewhere to live was a matter of urgency and if he was going to take on a rental, he would need a job. Although he had little less than a fortnight to find a new place to live, at least he had enough money to put down as a deposit on a new place, thanks to Ginny's parting gift.

Nor were things getting better in the wider world. After the brief euphoria of Labour's General Election win at the start of October, the IRA bombing campaign had resumed with the worst atrocity yet just a few days after the 10k. Two pubs in Birmingham were bombed, killing 21 people and injuring many more. Steve didn't feel directly threatened, but he was disgusted by the campaign and felt that it must surely be counterproductive.

During his lunch break he bought a copy of the *Cambridge Evening News,* and looked through the small ads. It soon became clear that there'd be precious little money left from Ginny's gift, if he were to take on the lease of a small house or flat. And it looked as if any formal tenancy would involve him in a commitment for a year or more. It had been a mistake to take on the Ainsworth Street house back in June and he had no wish to jump out of the frying pan into the fire. He rescanned the paper. The alternative seemed to be to rent a bed-sitter, the rents were much cheaper, and the period of notice less onerous. There were several not too far from the rail station catering to the clientele of the language schools that clustered around Station Road. He jotted down a selection of telephone numbers. He would ask Fiona if he could use the box office telephone.

By the end of the afternoon he'd set up viewings for three places over the next few days. One in Devonshire Road, another in St. Barnabas Road and the final one in Tenison Road. It didn't take him long to reject the Devonshire Road and St. Barnabas Road options. The room in the former was at the top of the house. It was tiny, and on his way up to look at it, he passed a primitive bathroom and a smelly separate WC.

The room in the St. Barnabas Road house was more spacious, but reeked of stale tobacco smoke and the bed was either a health hazard, or fire hazard, or both. By the time he viewed the Tenison Road option, he was starting to appreciate that his living arrangements for the previous six months, particularly once they had been taken in hand by Ginny, had been really rather good.

During his lunch break on the Friday he met a letting agent outside the house which stood on the junction of Tenison road and Tenison Avenue. It was certainly a more substantial property, and in better exterior condition than the previous two viewings. The agent was sorry to say that the room that had been advertised had already been taken, but another room in the house had just become available. The snag was that it was more expensive because it was a bigger room. On the plus side, the agent said grandly, it was the ground floor front room with 'impressive ceiling height and window bay'. To Steve's way of thinking, having survived three Cambridge winters, the supposed advantages looked very much like another snag. But it seemed a pity to have rushed up to there in his lunch break, and not to take a look at the room. The agent opened the front door and ushered Steve inside.

The hallway was distinctly spartan, but reasonably clean. The agent found the room key on his bundle of keys and opened the first door on the left of the passage. It was much as the agent had described it. There was a single bed ranged along the party wall with the hallway, a gas fire, two battered but stylish Ercol wooden armchairs, a table and two kitchen chairs, a combined wardrobe tallboy in the alcove to the left of the chimney breast and in the other alcove a sink and draining board with a cupboard underneath, and an Ascot water heater over the sink. Steve asked to see the bathroom and toilet facilities. Encouragingly, there was a separate bathroom and WC on the ground floor and also on the first floor. As in the other houses he'd seen, there was a basic scullery in the ground floor extension which gave on to a small garden, containing a number of dustbins. There was nothing particularly homely about the arrangements, but the house was close to the station and even closer to Grace's place, even though Steve was far from confident of further intimacies in that direction.

Despite the fact that the rent was more than he had been budgeting for, he decided to take the room and handed over the deposit. The agent said that he would also need the first week's rent. Steve would have preferred the rental period to run from the beginning of December, but the agent was adamant. If he wanted the room, he would need to start paying the rent immediately. Reluctantly, Steve handed over the extra cash, whereupon the agent provided him with two keys, one to the front door of the house, and the other to his room, and departed, leaving Steve standing in the empty room.

Steve was initially angry that he'd allowed himself to be hustled into a decision. After all, Beth wasn't back until the weekend of 30 November. But really there was nothing to detain him in Ainsworth Street. All it was now was the discarded wrapping of his time with Ginny. He resolved to move to Tenison Road the coming weekend and put Ainsworth Street behind him.

On the Sunday, he loaded the VW camper van with his possessions. Before locking the house up he cleaned it from top to bottom. He might not be in Ginny's league when he when it came to cleanliness, but he was determined to leave it in a better state than it had been in when he'd taken it over from Beth. He scribbled Beth a note, giving his new address and saying that he'd come over, when it was convenient, to sort out any outstanding issues. Before getting into the van, he went over to the Empire Stores and told Bert that he was moving out. Could he give Bert a set of keys to the house just in case Beth didn't have hers to hand when she got back? Bert was happy to be of service, but he was disappointed that Steve was forsaking Ainsworth Street.

'I'm sure Beth wouldn't mind if you stayed, with Sandra not coming back. And now that that other girl has gone too.'

Steve laughed. 'You don't miss much, do you, Bert?'

'Yes, I saw her father picking her things up. They skedaddled pretty quickly when you turned up.'

Steve shook his head ruefully and was about to point out Peter wasn't her father, but thought better of it. Instead, he said, 'Does Beth know you've got plans for me and her?'

'Not yet, but she will soon.'

'I appreciate your efforts, Bert, but the truth is I'm not very good at relationships.'

'That's exactly my point. You just need to find the right girl and I have a feeling that Beth is the right girl for you. You're both brain boxes.'

Steve laughed again. 'She most definitely is. She's doing a PhD and she's just been doing something at Harvard, whereas I'm working in the box office at the Arts Theatre.'

'Yes, but you're just biding your time.'

'I wish I believed that. I'm going to miss you, Bert.'

'Well, I hope you'll come back and see me. Or pop into the Geldart and have a pint with me and Sid.'

'I will, Bert, I promise.'

Suddenly Steve was overwhelmed with sadness, in a way that he hadn't been with Ginny's departure. There was something elegiac in the exchange with Bert. He handed Bert the keys and left the shop with a tear in his eye. He climbed into the VW and drove the short distance to Tenison Road parking the van in Tenison Avenue.

* * *

He let himself into the house and propped the front door open with a box of books while he was ferrying his things from the van. In his time at Ainsworth Street, he hadn't significantly added to his possessions apart from the typewriter and a handful of new books, so it didn't take very long.

He had nearly completed the task, when he heard footsteps on the stair and looked up to see a young, redheaded woman coming down the stairs. Steve apologised for blocking the hallway and introduced himself.

'Hi I'm Steve. I'm moving into the front room. I'll have this stuff out of the way in a trice.'

The girl stepped over one of the boxes. 'Hi, I'm Jude. I've got a room on the first floor at the back. Are you new to Cambridge?'

'No, I've been living the other side of Mill Road. But the tenancy was coming to an end.'

The girl, a veteran of Cambridge bedsitter land, nodded. 'This is more convenient for the station, if you have to go to London.'

'I don't really. Only to see my mother.'

She seemed to be in no hurry to get going. Or her curiosity had got the better of her. 'Well, it's nice to have someone in the front room again, someone to keep an eye on the front door. Having an obviously empty room at street level and not even a bit of front garden to shield it from prying eyes always seemed a bit of a security issue.'

Steve was starting to think that he should have given the choice of accommodation a bit more thought. 'But it hasn't been empty long, has it?'

'Oh yes. About six months. I think the agents found it difficult to let a room in which someone had od'ed.'

She could see from the look on Steve's face that this was news to him. 'Oh, you didn't know, did you? I'm sorry.'

Steve realised that the agent had lied to him. He was angry with the agent, even angrier with himself, but he no intention of admitting as much. 'No, I'd heard about it. It enabled me to haggle with the agent.'

'So it doesn't bother you living in a space in which someone has died?'

Steve thought he might as well go full braggadocio. 'In my experience if they don't get any action early on, ghosts just, well, give up the ghost, you might say.'

Jude chuckled. She wasn't entirely convinced by Steve's pose, but gave him marks for his improvisation.

Doing his best to stay in character, he said, 'Apart from the front room being ideal for guys who want to top themselves, what's it like living here?'

'I can't wait to find somewhere else.'

'That good, eh?'

'This place is full of weirdos. It's a total freak show.'

Steve wondered whether Jude was the exception or included herself in the cast list.

'That's a relief. My previous gaff was so boring.'

Jude could tell when she was being mocked.

'Anyway, I'm late for work. Better get on.'

It was not so long ago that Steve himself had been obliged to work Sundays, but it was still relatively unusual and, he felt, it justified an attempt at keeping the rally going.

'On a Sunday? What do you do?'

'I work for a small publishing company, Vanguard. We do political and social policy books. We've got a bit of a work crisis on at the moment. All hands to the pumps. I said I'd go in for a few hours.'

Steve have never heard of Vanguard. 'Interesting.'

'Yeah, it is. But it doesn't pay well. Still, I'm learning the trade and applying for other publishing jobs left, right and centre in the meantime.'

'Politically?'

'Ha ha! What about you?'

'I work at The Arts Theatre.'

'Oh, so you're a thespian?'

'No, a humble assistant in the box office. I'm covering for a maternity leave and my job comes to an end soon.'

'What then?'

'I don't know. Might have to sign on.'

'You'll be in good company. I think I'm the only person in the house who doesn't sign on.'

Steve considered this piece of information. 'Is it a sociable house, much interaction between the residents?'

'Not really. This is probably the longest conversation I've had with a co-tenant for three months.'

He didn't know whether to be reassured by this observation or dismayed. It occurred to him that moving into a new place where no one knew you gave you the opportunity to adopt a new persona. What did he want to be? An introspective loner or a sociable extrovert? It looked like he'd already plumped for the latter.

On an impulse he said, 'What time do you finish work?'

Jude looked at him in amazement. 'Are you asking me out?'

'Yeah, I thought we could have a drink in the Great Northern.'

'You're a quick worker.'

'No time to lose. I'll probably have od'ed by Christmas.'

She performed an elaborate mine of consulting her mental diary. 'Tuesday evening?'

Steve performed a similar mime. 'I'm working that evening. What about tonight? You can fill me in on the other people in the house.'

'Blimey, you're a bit of an operator!' Jude was beginning to think that Steve's account of haggling the rent down might be true after all.

'Okay, then. I'll knock on your door at seven-thirty.'

'Great.' It wasn't like him to be so direct. Was that all it took to feign self confidence?

Intrigued, but conscious that she was running late, Jude stepped past Steve and, turning on the threshold, said, 'But don't start thinking that means I'm going to sleep with you tonight.'

Steve felt that if he were being consistent with this new approach, he ought to say something like *Well, tomorrow night then*, but, aware that he was already out of his comfort zone, confined himself to an embarrassed shake of the head. Jude stepped out onto the pavement and gave him a quizzical look as she set off to her place of work. Steve leaned against the wall of the hallway. What on earth was he playing at?

A while later with everything stowed, he made himself a cup of greasy coffee and and sat down in one of the armchairs. He wondered how Angie was. He would have to let her know his new address. And Grace, too. He was a little perturbed that he hadn't heard from her in the last few days. He even wondered how Ginny was and couldn't help trying to imagine how different her circumstances were now, not that he had any idea what a flat in the Barbican was like.

He was also feeling disoriented by the change of accommodation. It seemed strange to be confined to one room. Ainsworth Street hadn't been particularly spacious, but at least it had rooms for the separate activities of sleeping, relaxing, cooking and eating, and a garden. Even more importantly, it had a bathroom and toilet he didn't have to share with others outside his own household. He suspected that he would be unlikely to be taking quite as many baths as he had become accustomed to in his time with Ginny. He was beginning to regret not having tried to make other arrangements. He could have just hung on in the Ainsworth Street house. Beth might well have welcomed someone with whom to share the rent. And Bert would have put in a good word for him. Why hadn't he checked with her before he had moved into the draughty room of a drug casualty?

Suddenly, he didn't know what to do with himself. Maybe he could go down to Glisson Road and see if Grace was in. He could say that he was just dropping by to give her his new address. It was a Sunday, so she was unlikely to be involved in any college or university work. And indeed it was only a week since they had completed the 10k and ended up in bed together. But she had made it clear that he should let her get in touch with him. Intuitively, it seemed to him, she was just trying to let him down gently. Better to settle for a drink with the redhead from upstairs perhaps. And the fact that she had categorically stated that she was not going to sleep with him tonight, had actually sounded more promising than it was probably meant to. Not that he had anything of the sort in mind. He had just been trying on a new persona.

But how to occupy himself until seven-thirty? Normally at such times he could find consolation in his guitar. But he had hardly touched it for the last few weeks. The fact was he was just kidding himself that he would ever be any kind of jazz guitarist. The Jed Morgan jazz chord system was just another aspect of the clouds of delusion that had engulfed him in recent months. That and the damned poem, which he now saw had been nothing more than a cover for an impulsive series of changes in his life. Whatever he had thought might be the consequence of those changes, it hadn't involved his being holed up in a horrible bedsitter in a house full of freaks, with no job, not much money left and no prospects. Clouds of delusion, indeed.

He now saw the poem as Angie must have seen it that time they talked in The Eagle, a transcript of an enchantment, the foetid effusion of a latter day *poète maudit*. She had advised him to abandon it; he had not heeded her words. But now that he had come to his senses, he would be done with it. And the only way to ensure that it didn't continue to extend its tentacles and drag him back into to its essential vacancy was to destroy it.

He went over to the box that contained his notebooks, pulled out his work in progress folder and withdrew the typescript of the poem.

There was too much paper to burn in his room. In any case he had no open chimney. Better to tear the pages up and dump the fragments in one of the smelly dustbins at the back of the house. He started to tear the first pages, but found it almost impossible not to read some of the lines. He realised that it would only be a matter of time before his eye would light upon a sentence that would ignite the train of thought that had given rise to it and immediately he would be caught in the poem's gravitational field again. If he was going to go through with his plan, he was going to have to dispose of the manuscript without further chance of reflection.

He needed to get it into a dustbin forthwith. He gathered up the sheets of paper and flung open the door of his room and rushed out to the backyard. The stench of overflowing dustbins assailed his nose. Identifying one that could still accommodate a modicum of refuse, he thrust the manuscript into it, and did his best to replace the lid. Aghast at what he had done, he went back into the scullery and washed his hands in the grubby sink.

Opening the door to his room in a state of shock, he noticed a sheet of paper lying on the floor. He must have dropped a page in his haste to transfer the manuscript to the dustbin. He reached down to pick it off the floor, intent on crumpling it up, when he noticed that it was in fact *Solar Wind Shuttle*, the *poème concret* that he had made at Ginny's behest. He paused. How strange! This was the first time he'd seen it since the day he gave it to her. So how had it come back to him?

He supposed that Ginny, in clearing her stuff from Ainsworth Street, had slipped it into his work folder when she had put her sketch book in his room. Clearly she didn't want to be reminded of Steve in her new life. His first impulse was one of anger. He had made the piece for her. It was something that had no meaning for him otherwise. He certainly didn't see it as a kind of distillation of *Event/Horizon*, which is what she had been suggesting. She'd also said somewhat portentously that she would look after it until he needed it. And right at that moment the last thing that Steve needed was to be reminded of the substantial poem that he had just consigned to a smelly dustbin.

But as he scanned the sheet of paper, it seemed to him that *Solar Wind Shuttle* actually did stand as something in its own right. Yes, it was related to *Event/Horizon* , but it had an emergent quality that was quite different from its substrate. It wasn't that hard to extrapolate from the longer work to the *poème concret*, but one would be hard pressed to reverse the process. If that was the case, then there was no harm in keeping that one sheet of paper, indeed it would be a painful but useful reminder of his folly. He slipped the sheet back into the work in progress folder and on the spur of the moment picked up a black marker, scored through the words *Work in Progress* and wrote underneath *Clouds of Delusion*.

Clouds of delusion? Where had that phrase come from? Yes, of course, it was from the brief but enigmatic lyrics of the Grateful Dead's 'Dark Star'. He was trying to remember the rest of the stanza, but couldn't get much further than 'Dark star crashes . . .'. What a shame that he didn't have the *Live/Dead* LP and a record player to hand.

But if he didn't have a record player, he did at least have Jon's tape recorder and headphones and, more to the point, Jon's bootleg tapes of Grateful Dead performances. If ever there was a time to begin his engagement with decommodified music and broach the Dead's transitive nightfall of diamonds, it was now that he had escaped Ginny's attraction, or more accurately, been expelled from her illusory paradise.

Steve lugged the tape recorder over to the alcove to the left of the gas fire where there was a power point and plugged it in. He opened the cardboard box that contained Jon's trove of Dead bootlegs, wondering as he did so what had become of his recording of *Krapp's Last Tape* and leafed through the collection of tapes. Each slipcase was neatly hand printed with the venue and date of a gig. Since they were all unequally unknown to him, he took one at random, noting that it claimed to be a recording of a gig that had taken place at the Fillmore West in San Francisco on 27 February 1969. He placed the spool of tape on the empty spindle of the Akai and fed the leader through the tape head guides, giving it a couple of turns on the take up spool. He put the headphones on, plugged the headphone jack into the socket on the recorder and pressed play.

Printed in Great Britain
by Amazon

38775333R00260